GETTING ELECTED

GETTING ELECTED

From Radio and Roosevelt to Television and Reagan

J. LEONARD REINSCH

HIPPOCRENE BOOKS
New York

DEDICATION

To my wife, Phyllis; my daughter, Penny, and my son, Jim, whose understanding made possible my taking extensive family leave to actively participate in national politics
and
to the thousands of unrecognized and unpaid campaign volunteers, whose untiring work and eternal enthusiasm in all elections make our political system work.

For information, address:
Hippocrene Books, Inc.
171 Madison Ave.
New York, NY 10016

Library of Congress Cataloging-in Publication Data

Reinsch, J. Leonard.
   Getting elected : from radio and Roosevelt to television and
Reagan / J. Leonard Reinsch.
      p. 337.
   Includes index.
   ISBN 0-87052-500-X
   1. Presidents—United States—Election—History—20th century.
2. Television in politics—United States—History—20th century.
3. Radio in politics—United States—History—20th century.
4. United States—Politics and government—1933–1945. 5. United
States—Politics and government—1945– I. Title.
E176.1.R355   1988
324.973'09—dc19   87-28462
                                                                        CIP

Printed in the United States of America.

Contents

Scene III: Looking Ahead

Illustrations *following page 162.*

ACKNOWLEDGMENTS

Out of a luncheon with the late Sol Taishoff, publisher of *Broadcasting*, and General Ted Clifton, former military aide to Presidents Kennedy and Johnson, came the idea for this book. It was the continued urging of both Sol and Ted that put me to work reviewing my notes and refreshing my memory. From Frank Stanton, former president of CBS, came many helpful reminders.

My national political activity started in 1944 when I was working for Governor James M. Cox, the 1920 Democratic presidential candidate. He had chosen as his running mate Franklin Delano Roosevelt. It was President Roosevelt's request to his friend Jim Cox, in the spring of 1944, to borrow his "chief radio executive" Leonard Reinsch that started me in national politics.

Critical editing of the manuscript was provided by Jeff Prugh, former national correspondent of the *Los Angeles Times*, with suggestions by Harold Martin, former *Saturday Evening Post* writer.

Untiring in her work, Verne Ramsaur deciphered my handwriting and completed the typing. My wife, Phyllis, checked the manuscript with an eagle eye, happy and relieved that I might finally dispose of some of the files accumulated over many years of political activity.

This book, I hope, shows my appreciation of the opportunities I have had to meet some great men and women, who devote themselves to the world of politics and government in ways we can admire and for which we should be grateful.

My many years in the national political arena gave me an opportunity, too, to meet some of the finest and most dedicated journalists in both print and broadcasting. It is their untiring efforts that bring light and understanding to our political processes.

A word about campaigning in the future: Advances in technology have given television greater power than ever. Effective use of the satellite, cable and VCR may provide the winning edge in future elections. Properly used, television and radio will produce better officeholders and a stronger democratic government.

I hope you will find enjoyment in the stories about the great and not so great, of the events that seemed important at the time, and the events history has found important.

J. Leonard Reinsch
Marietta, Georgia
January 1988.

Preamble

THE SCENE: DYCHE STADIUM on the Northwestern University campus, near Chicago. It's an autumn Saturday afternoon. America lies flat on her back, battered by the Great Depression. And the Northwestern Wildcats are playing football against the University of Iowa.

That young fellow at the WLS microphone in Northwestern's play-by-play broadcasting booth is yours truly. Two booths away—in the press box high atop the stadium—is a contemporary I barely know. He's an articulate fellow with a shock of ruddy, brown hair, and he sits behind a microphone inscribed "WHO," calling the game for the fans back home in Des Moines, Iowa.

His name: "Dutch" Reagan. Who would have dreamed that half a century later, he would sit behind a radio mike on Saturdays, talking to millions of Americans as the 40th President of the United States?

For that matter, who would have guessed that I, too, was destined for a double life in broadcasting and politics? My extracurricular career, however, would carry me to the White House decades before Ronald Reagan would arrive there. I would have the ear of four Presidents when it came to communicating their ideas over the airwaves to the masses.

Along the way, I would become the radio—then television—director of the Democratic National Conventions and presidential campaigns from 1944 through 1968. And before I resigned in 1969, I would help finalize the contract for the 1972 Democratic Convention in Miami Beach.

* * *

To attend my first convention in 1932, I had to pay what then was a small fortune for a ticket: $5. The Democrats came to Chicago Stadium, and Franklin Delano Roosevelt's strategists xii / GETTING ELECTED

succeeded in electing their own man as permanent chairman—despite opposition by the convention's organizers.

Chicago, 1932. It was the first convention in which a presidential candidate accepted his party's nomination in person. Little did I realize that 12 years later I would be a working member of the Democratic National Convention—as the radio adviser to three-time incumbent FDR, who used the radio about as resourcefully as Ronald Reagan uses television.

Radio and Roosevelt grew up together. The 1924 Democratic Convention was the party's first to receive national radio coverage—and FDR gave the nominating speech for Governor Al Smith. That convention is perhaps best remembered, however, for Alabama catching the nation's fancy by steadfastly announcing in a deep Southern drawl: "Al-a-ba-ma casts twenty-four votes for Os-cah W. Un-dah-wood!" on every one of the 103 ballots—the most ever cast in any convention.

Over the ensuing 20 years, radio would become an increasingly important tool for all politicians. Sheer numbers tell why: there were only 3 million radio sets in 1924; 48 million in 1944.

The first President to deliver a speech on radio was Warren Harding. The date: June 21, 1923. The President spoke on station KSD in St. Louis. His speech was relayed by long-distance lines to New York for simultaneous broadcast on WEAF, New York. As a courtesy to the President, other broadcasting stations across the nation stayed off the air.

But if any President's style was perfectly tailored for radio, it was that of Franklin Roosevelt. His fireside chats and warm greeting, "My friends . . . ," became etched into America's political consciousness forever.

As the Democratic Party's candidate in 1932, Roosevelt had learned of his convention victory by radio. With his flair for the dramatic, he asked the convention to stay in session while he flew to Chicago. There, he became the first presidential candidate to make his acceptance speech in person over nationwide radio.

Until Roosevelt broke the tradition, presidential nominees had stayed home during conventions. A committee notified the candidate of his nomination, calling on him several weeks after the convention. It was a perfunctory ritual, which required the nominee to be properly surprised and photographed with the notification committee. Not until then did the candidate give his acceptance speech.

Now, at the 1932 convention, I sat in the gallery and watched Roosevelt close his acceptance speech with a ringing declaration: "I pledge you, I pledge myself to a new deal for the American people!"

That same convention, incidentally, was the first to recognize "Happy Days Are Here Again," later to become the Democratic Party's official theme song. Actually, the song was chosen by happenstance. While another unknown tune was played by the orchestra, someone at party headquarters at the Blackstone Hotel angrily telephoned the convention hall: "For heaven's sake, get rid of that music! Play something else!" The "something else" was "Happy Days Are Here Again."

Thereafter, Roosevelt's fireside chats changed the course of history. I remember watching the President broadcast from the White House. Before air time, he was genial and relaxed. Once he got his "on the air" cue, he worked the microphone with the flair of a professional. He beamed at the mike. He grimaced. He smiled. He scowled. He was the consummate communicator.

To President Roosevelt, the microphone personified a single American listener. Unlike most politicians, FDR never forgot that radio listening was done by individuals and family groups, not by hordes who filled auditoriums. Using radio, Roosevelt parlayed his persuasive voice and personal appeal to sell his policies again and again. No American politician would use radio so effectively.

* * *

For me, it all began in 1944, when I was responsible for three radio stations owned by former presidential candidate James M. Cox, who also had been governor of Ohio. The stations: WHIO in Dayton, Ohio; WSB in Atlanta, and WIOD in Miami. My office was in WSB's studios, in Atlanta's Biltmore Hotel.

From the White House, President Roosevelt telephoned his close friend, James Cox (who, in the 1920 campaign against Harding, had selected Roosevelt as his running mate). "I want to borrow your 'radio man,'" the President told Governor Cox, gearing up for an unprecedented fourth successful run for the presidency.

Governor Cox asked me to meet him in his Biltmore apartment. "Would you be willing," he said, "to be the radio director of the Democratic Convention and the presidential campaign?"

I couldn't say "yes" fast enough. A formal announcement of my role was made on June 12, 1944. President Roosevelt had his "radio man."

SCENE 1

Stand By!
Here's Radio

CHAPTER 1

Chicago
Summer 1944

*"Fibber McGee and Molly" came into most American homes
by radio every week. . . . Bobbysoxers sang of their GI boyfriends
overseas: "He's 1-A in the Army and he's A-1 in my heart". . . .
Faster than the GIs captured Sicily, a young singer named
"Frankie" Sinatra captured millions of those bobbysoxers'
hearts. . . . In Washington, President Roosevelt appeared pale
and tired. The press corps was convinced that he didn't want to
run again. "All that is within me," FDR wrote to Bob Hannegan,
chairman of the 1944 Democratic National Committee, "cries out
to go back to my home on the Hudson River."*

AS RADIO DIRECTOR OF THE 1944 CONVENTION, I went to Washington to make preparations. There, I attended my first White House news conference in the Oval Office.

President Roosevelt enjoyed jousting with the news media. He was the consummate politician, gesturing and pontificating, sometimes with his elongated cigarette holder clasped between his thumb and forefinger. He was animated, but he could also become irritated. He didn't mind venting his anger.

As I stood there and watched, I couldn't help but be impressed with FDR's self confidence—and his ability to divert questioners to the subject he wanted to discuss.

Through it all, there was a deference that the reporters respected. Each was given a chance to ask questions in his own way, and the President—in a folksy, informal sort of way—made sure that everybody had an opportunity to question him.

This was a time, of course, when a handful of radio reporters—equipped only with pencils and notepads, joined the throng of print reporters in the Oval Office for a press conference. Seated at the left corner of the President's desk was the senior White House correspondent, Earl Godwin. The sparring for news—and the repartee between President and press—continued until Earl Godwin, on cue from the President, said, "Thank you, Mr. President."

Then everybody hurried to telephones and typewriters in the cramped press quarters, located in front of the White House executive wing, behind a small office for Secret Service agents.

From Washington, I traveled to Chicago to review arrangements for the convention at Chicago Stadium. George Allen, the program chairman, was in London. Bob Hannegan was busy behind the scenes, trying to assure the nomination of an obscure senator from Missouri, Harry Truman, as the party's vice-presidential candidate.

That left the responsibility for program details on my shoulders. I quickly learned a defensive gambit to protect any decision I made. My standard reply to questions was "This is the way the President wants it. You'll have to ask him to make the change."

After all, a President preoccupied with winning World War II wasn't readily available, and his press secretary, Steve Early, had agreed to back up any decision I made. As for decisions requiring political acumen, I deferred to Bob Hannegan and Paul Porter, the convention chairman and publicity director, respectively. Generally, I was told to use my best judgment. As a result, I found myself in the unusual position of having a relatively free rein over an event that would shape America's political process and affect millions of voters.

Print reporters were unhappy "in spades." They complained that radio network newsmen worked in the luxury of soundproof, air-conditioned booths. "The networks paid to build those booths," I told the print reporters. "You can do the same if you want to." They didn't.

The newsreel people were autocratic and difficult. They knew that politicians coveted newsreel publicity in moviehouses across the nation. Every time the newsreel people didn't like a camera position, or grumbled because a favor was denied, they threatened to pack up and leave. They stayed.

On Sunday afternoon, three days before he would deliver the keynote address, Senator Robert Kerr consented to stand at the rostrum, giving selected excerpts of his speech so they could be filmed by the newsreels. These excerpts would be released to theaters nationwide on Wednesday.

I was admonished to make sure that Senator Kerr wore the same suit, shirt and tie on Wednesday that he had worn for the Sunday shooting. I also had to be absolutely certain that there were no changes in the text. Little did these newsreel people—or anyone else—realize that two conventions later, they would have to battle for camera positions with an upstart known as television.

To anyone who runs a political convention, molehills become mountains. Who will sing the "Star Spangled Banner"? At which session? For invocations, a cross-section of religions must be represented.

* * *

Predictably, President Roosevelt was nominated. On the day of his nomination, Thursday, July 20, he was 2,000 miles away, perched on a towering California cliff, watching 10,000 U.S. Marines practice amphibious landings.

Broadcasting the President's speech from San Diego required delicate timing. My job was to make sure that everyone would receive the radio pickup from California. That meant switching the long-distance lines to Shangri-La, the President's railroad car, for his acceptance speech. It also meant that we had to allow enough time for the convention chairman, Senator Samuel D. Jackson, to formally introduce the President's speech.

When the President began his remarks, I relaxed—unaware that a major problem lay ahead. Like almost everyone else, I expected the convention to proceed with the nomination for Vice President.

However, during the applause after President Roosevelt's speech, I heard Bob Hannegan shouting at Senator Jackson: "You get up there right now and I mean now—and recognize Dave Lawrence, or I'll do it for you!"

Spitting out the words, Hannegan pushed a sluggish, reluctant Senator Jackson toward the microphones on the rostrum.

Since 1940, Bob Hannegan had been a determined supporter of Harry Truman. Jackson, from Indiana, was a backer of Vice President Henry Wallace, as were most of the galleryites. Almost all evening long, they chanted, "We want Wallace!" It had been alleged that counterfeit gallery tickets had been provided Wallace supporters.

Senator Jackson, the convention's permanent chairman, pounded the gavel in a vain attempt to gain the delegates' attention. Ed Pauley turned to me and asked for music. I telephoned Al Melgard, the Chicago Stadium's organist, and requested music—any music—as long as it was loud.

As shouts of "We want Wallace!" and organ music reverberated through the convention hall, Chairman Jackson shouted: "Ladies and gentlemen of the convention, we are packing the aisles until it has become dangerous. This has been a great day for the Party, a great day for the country!"

He paused, then added: "I recognize Delegate David Lawrence from the State of Pennsylvania for the purpose of making a motion."

Quickly, Dave Lawrence moved to the rostrum. "Mr. Chairman," he said, "I move that this fourth session of the Democratic National Convention recess until tomorrow, Friday, July 21, at 11:30 A.M."

Whereupon Chairman Jackson routinely said: "As many as favor will signify by saying 'aye.' Contrary 'no.' The 'ayes' have it. The meeting is recessed to reconvene at 11:30 o'clock Friday morning. . . ." And the convention recessed that night, shortly before 11 o'clock.

The foregoing illustrates a fundamental rule for success in a national convention: control the gavel and you control the convention, which is why an incumbent President wields such enormous power. He appoints the National Committee Chairman, who, with the President's approval, appoints the committees that control the structure of the convention.

That structure includes another important figure—the parliamentarian. He rules on challenged decisions. Since there is nowhere to appeal the chair's ruling (which is backed by the parliamentarian), the chairman and the parliamentarian control the convention procedures.

A Missouri congressman named Clarence Cannon served as parliamentarian of the 1944 convention. His Democratic Manual, published in 1936, 1940 and 1944, brought together all important convention rulings of the party.

It should be noted, too, that each national convention is a law unto itself. But each convention generally follows the rules and procedures of the preceding convention, including applicable rules of the House of Representatives.

Vice President Wallace's hopes ran high. He obviously was the front-runner for renomination to the Roosevelt ticket.

Only hours earlier—on that fateful day of adjournment— Wallace had made a rousing seconding speech for the President. Wallace, who headed the Iowa delegation, was interrupted nine times by applause and cheers, to say nothing of those almost deafening chants of "We want Wallace!"

Shortly before the roll call for the President's nomination, Chairman Jackson had announced: "Ladies and gentlemen of the convention, as the expected Permanent Chairman of this convention, I received a short time ago a letter which I regard it as one of my duties to read to the delegates. It reads as follows:

> Hyde Park, New York
> July 14, 1944

My Dear Senator Jackson:

In the light of the probability that you will be chosen as Permanent Chairman of the Convention, and because I know that many rumors accompany annual conventions, I am wholly willing to give you my own personal thought in regard to the selection of a candidate for Vice President. I do this at this time because I expect to be away from Washington the next few days.

The easiest way of putting it is this: I have been associated with Henry Wallace during his past four years as Vice President, for eight years earlier while he was Secretary of Agriculture and well before that. I like him and I respect him, and he is my personal friend. For these reasons, I personally would vote for his renomination if I were a delegate to the Convention.

(Applause and cheers)

At the same time I do not want to wish to appear in any way as dictating to the Convention. Obviously, the Convention must do the deciding. And it should—and I am sure it will—give great consideration to the pros and cons of its choice.

> Very sincerely yours,
> Franklin D. Roosevelt

(Applause)

Given the momentum of the President's letter, the enthusiastic response to Wallace's seconding speech, the mood of the spectators and the emotions of the convention, the Wallace forces had every reason to be supremely confident.

There could be only one block play—adjournment. Even so, a roll call postponed until the next day could make Wallace the vice-presidential candidate again.

All told, the President had sent three letters to the convention. The first—a customary formality—was sent to Bob Hannegan one week before the convention. Roosevelt stated that if the convention were to nominate him, "I shall accept. If the people elect me, I shall serve."

The second letter from the President was the foregoing, July 14 message, with its somewhat lukewarm endorsement of Wallace. But the President's third letter—dated July 19 and also sent to Bob Hannegan—became a big news story, thanks to deft maneuvering by Paul Porter, the DNC's publicity director.

Working behind the scenes, Paul fashioned an aura of mystery about this third letter. Rumors about the letter flooded the news media. Did it really exist? Was it all a smokescreen? Nobody knew for sure.

Reporters stormed Bob Hannegan's office, demanding a copy of this letter they weren't sure even existed. Finally, copies of the July 19 letter were made available. It read:

> Dear Bob:
> You have written me about Harry Truman and Bill Douglas. I shall, of course, be very glad to run with either of them and believe that either would bring real strength to the ticket. . . ."

Months later, after the 1944 election, Bob Hannegan would tell me that the President had positioned Bill Douglas' name first in the original draft of that July 19 letter. But Hannegan, true to his loyalties to Harry Truman, persuaded the President to lead off with Truman's name.

What nobody also knew during the convention was that the President, according to Hannegan, had scrawled a terse note in longhand to him during a pre-convention meeting of the President and Democratic leaders. This note was never made public and had been written long before the President had drafted those three letters that were read to the convention. The note, written on a scratch pad at the President's desk, simply said: "Bob, it's Truman."

I later also learned that during this same pre-convention meeting, Frank Walker (who had preceded Hannegan as DNC chairman) was instructed to advise James Byrnes that the President had decided in favor of Truman. Byrnes had a distinguished government career. He had resigned from the Supreme Court to become assistant to the President in charge of war mobilization.

Yet, oddly, even after Byrnes was notified that Truman was to be the President's running mate, Byrnes asked Truman to place Byrnes' name in nomination for Vice President!

Truman, apparently unaware of the President's inclination toward him, consented to Byrnes' wishes. He went to Chicago, expecting to nominate Byrnes for the No. 2 spot on the ticket!

In any event, Truman was stunned when told that he was FDR's choice. "My God!" he said. He didn't believe it—that is, not until the President told him so over the telephone. Then, with characteristic bluntness, Truman privately asked some of his friends, "Why the hell didn't he tell me in the first place?"

In 1944, a war-weary President Roosevelt lapsed into failing health. The drive to replace Wallace was initiated by Ed Pauley of California, with Bob Hannegan pushing hard for Truman as Wallace's replacement. Roosevelt, always the practical politician, had given up on Wallace long before the vice-presidential sweepstakes began.

The 1944 Democratic Convention had 1,176 qualified votes, which meant that 589 votes (a simple majority) were needed to win the nomination. It used to be that as many as two-thirds of the votes were needed, but the Democratic Party had scrapped its two-thirds rule in 1936—a rule that had stood for exactly one century. The Republicans never employed the two-thirds rule at their conventions.

(In 1836, President Andrew Jackson introduced the two-thirds rule to insure the nomination of his chosen successor, Martin Van Buren. Thereafter, the two-thirds rule became an obstacle to any candidate who couldn't muster support from the Solid South.)

When Franklin Roosevelt ran for President in 1932, he and Jim Farley, then chairman of the DNC, tried unsuccessfully to have the two-thirds rule eliminated so they wouldn't have to worry about the Solid South. They tried again in 1936—at a convention in which President Roosevelt was accorded 57 nominating speeches, as well as a 63-minute demonstration.

This time FDR succeeded in getting the two-thirds rule

scrubbed in a tradeoff with the South. The Southern states no longer would be granted delegates on the basis of population. Instead, they would be granted delegates according to the size of the Democratic vote in the previous election.

Friday, July 21, 1944. In the early morning, it was clear that neither Vice President Wallace nor Senator Truman could win on the first ballot.

All night long, supporters of Wallace and Truman battled for delegate votes, splitting states that weren't controlled by the unit rule.

Truman's forces deployed time-honored strategy: "If you can't vote for Truman on the first ballot, back your favorite son. Don't take chances with Wallace. Truman is sure to win—he is Roosevelt's choice." It was a busy night for the Truman strategists—Bob Hannegan, Mayor Ed Kelly of Chicago, Ed Flynn of New York, Ed Pauley of California and former DNC chairman Frank Walker of Pennsylvania.

Meanwhile, James Byrnes persisted in pushing for the vice-presidential nomination. His able advocate was Walter Brown, a broadcaster. But Byrnes' candidacy died when the head of the CIO, Sidney Hillman, came out against Byrnes.

By noon on Friday, July 21, the professionals knew there would be more than one ballot. Favorite-son pressure welled up all over the place. The first ballot went as expected:

Wallace	429½
Truman	319½
Favorite sons	393½

With Wallace falling far short of the 589 votes needed to be nominated, the Truman forces were jubilant. While the results were announced, Bob Hannegan whispered to Ed Pauley with the self-assurance of a professional politician, "Truman is in on the second ballot."

As the second ballot proceeded, the votes fell in place as the Truman forces expected. Eighteen states switched their favorite-son votes to Truman. The first to do so was Maryland, whose delegates had been introduced to Truman at a personal appearance. Senator Millard Tydings had introduced Truman as the "Maryland candidate for Vice President."

Soon it became apparent that Truman would win. The final tabulation:

Truman:	1,031
Wallace:	105

Scattered: 37
Absent: 3

The man who, in less than three months after the inauguration would become President of the United States stood at the
rostrum of the 1944 Democratic National Convention. Plain-
spoken and genuine as usual, Harry Truman thanked the convention for his nomination. "I accept the honor," he said.

Truman's brief acceptance speech would precipitate my first
argument with the radio networks about "equal time" for candidates.

The gavel fell to end the 1944 Democratic convention—the
last convention before television. It was the end of an era.

CHAPTER 2

Campaign 1944

FROM THE START, it was clear that Harry Truman had a speaking problem. He spoke much too fast, almost to the point of being unintelligible, with a flat Missouri accent.

I telephoned Tom Evans, owner of KCMO in Kansas City, and asked if I could obtain a secure studio, a control room and trusted employees for at least a day. Tom was a good friend of Harry Truman, and readily obliged.

I had listened to a transcription of a Truman speech given in Philadelphia weeks earlier. When I met the candidate one morning in the KCMO studios, I asked him why the speech was so long—almost one hour—and why his delivery was so hurried.

His answers were true Truman. Well, he said, the nice folks who wrote the speech would have been offended if he cut the length, and he didn't want to hurt their feelings. He said he delivered the speech rapidly to get it over with as soon as possible. "It wasn't very interesting," Truman commented.

Harry Truman belied his widespread public image as a caustic, shoot-from-the-hip politician. He also was kind and considerate, regardless of the status of anyone with whom he dealt.

Truman recognized that he had a speaking problem. He was exceptionally cooperative in trying to correct it. For several hours at KCMO, he patiently read and reread the material I placed on his desk or the music stand. We had him read aloud, sitting down. We had him read, standing. We also had him speak without notes. We discussed the ideal length of a speech, the proper delivery and words to avoid.

My objective was to get Truman to be his own natural self while speaking—albeit at a much slower pace—and let his Missouri accent be natural. To slow down his delivery, I devised a technique of placing only one sentence of his speech on a page—in the middle of the page. That way, the physical act of turning each page slowed him down.

In those days, Truman was no different from any other candidate—save FDR—when it came to speaking into a radio microphone. They bellowed into the mike as if they were addressing thousands of people in a convention hall. Radio, in a sense, was a more intimate medium between candidate and voter, and I told Truman so. "Imagine yourself talking only to members of a small family in their living room, back home in Independence, Missouri. Imagine them sitting by their radio console, listening to you talk to *them*."

Every ten pages or so, as Truman practiced his delivery, I placed a slip of paper in the text. Each slip contained only one comment:

"Take it easy"

or

"Slow down"

or

"Remember the living room"

Subsequently, I used this method on many speeches Truman would make as President.

I always kept an exact duplicate of Truman's speech notebook. I checked carefully to make sure that the pages were in proper sequence, that the light on the rostrum didn't cast shadows, that the notebook fit comfortably on the rostrum and that the drinking water did *not* have ice. Cold water can tighten up the throat and hamper speech delivery.

At the end of our daylong session at KCMO in Kansas City, Truman invited me to his home in nearby Independence for dinner. His wife, Bess, and daughter, Margaret, served a sumptuous Midwestern meal.

After dinner, I asked to use the telephone so I could summon a taxi. I was due in Chicago the next morning and I had a berth on the Santa Fe train that evening.

"No need to call a cab," Truman said. "You were nice enough to come here and help me. The least I can do is drive you to the station."

He insisted on driving, a trip of 17 miles each way. It was the first of several times during the 1944 campaign that I would be accorded Harry Truman's thoughtfulness.

* * *

"Equal time" became an issue early in the 1944 campaign. The networks gave 30 minutes to the acceptance speech by the Republican vice-presidential nominee, Senator John Bricker.

I argued that the Democratic candidate was entitled to the same air time. Not so, the networks countered. They asserted that Harry Truman had made *his* acceptance speech at the convention when he expressed thanks to the delegates.

Actually, I was mainly interested in obtaining radio time so Truman could make a trial run in front of the microphone in August. An acceptance speech wasn't expected to weigh on the voters, anyway. It was commonly felt that about 65% of the voters made their voting decisions at the time of the convention. Thereafter, 25% would decide on the week before the election—and 10% stayed undecided until they went to the polls.

Finally, after extended arguments, the networks agreed to give Truman 30 minutes for an acceptance speech. For the speaking site, he chose his birthplace—small-town Lamar, Missouri. The date: August 31.

The man scheduled to introduce Truman was Senator Tom Connally of Texas, a silver-tongued orator of the old school. Connally's official title was Chairman of the Committee to Notify the Vice-Presidential Nominee.

I knew Connally's introduction would be long. The problem was, it was longer than I expected. Since we had only 30 minutes of network time, I asked for a shorter introduction. Taking no chances, I got several members of Connally's notification committee to persuade Connally to shorten his remarks. Fortunately, he did. He delivered a fine, old-fashioned introduction, allowing Truman ample speaking time.

What pleased me most about Truman's acceptance speech was that he managed to speak more slowly. The only problem: a screeching noise called "feedback" from the local public-address system. From that day on, I always sent an engineer to a speaking site one day in advance to make sure the sound system worked properly.

* * *

From Lamar, I traveled back to New York to work out the details of buying radio time for the campaign. The Democratic Presidential Campaign Committee was headquartered in the Biltmore Hotel.

For reasons I never could understand, the Republican Party set up its national headquarters in, of all places, the Roosevelt Hotel. Just about everywhere you looked inside, you were reminded of FDR. Every time the Republican workers picked up a book of matches, a bar of soap, a towel or a menu, they saw the name "Roosevelt."

Most of the campaign money was allocated toward buying radio network time for both the presidential and vice-presidential candidates. We also bought time for other speakers such as Secretary of the Interior Harold Ickes and Senator Claude Pepper of Florida.

To help with the radio campaign, I brought in Tom Downing from our station WSB in Atlanta. To supervise the buying of time on stations in the agricultural belt at early hours, I appointed John Merrifield, agricultural director of WHAS in Louisville.

As a radio executive, I had developed program formats throughout my career. One of my major concerns was flow of audience—keeping the largest possible number of listeners tuned in from one program to the next.

In American politics, the 30-minute speech was as much a part of campaigns as whistle stops and Gallup Polls. But I didn't think the Democrats' 30-minute speech—with few exceptions—reached the undecided voters or Republicans. I said so to the national committee members. They agreed.

My plan was to position a five-minute political spot between the most popular programs—notably "Your Hit Parade," "Dr. I.Q." and others. Since radio programs in 1944 were live, they could be finished five minutes early without difficulty.

During those five minutes, we would present a Democratic message. That way, the radio listeners wouldn't bother to switch to another program since another of their favorite programs would begin in a few moments. American living rooms were familiar tableaus—families gathered around large radio consoles.

To my knowledge, this five-minute political spot on radio in 1944 was the genesis of the five-minute political insert that we accept as a common campaign tool today.

When Bob Hannegan accepted my idea, I asked John Hamm of the Biow Company—the Democratic campaign's advertising agency—to buy five-minute periods. But it wasn't all that easy. Our time buyers, Reggie Schuebel and Stanley Pulver, got a chilly reception from the networks.

The networks said the agencies and advertisers refused to cooperate in cutting their programs by five minutes. We countered with a promise not to buy 30-minute blocks for political speeches, except for the two major candidates. Still, we were told "no."

I countered by saying that the vice-presidential candidate, Harry Truman, wanted a five-minute period. This time we prevailed. We bought a number of five-minute spots. The first came at 10:55 P.M. on October 2, with Truman on the Blue Network (ABC), followed at 8:25 P.M. on October 3 on the Red Network (NBC).

At the same time, we negotiated for time on Election Eve. We reserved the hour of 10 to 11 P.M. (EST) on two networks. This blocked the Republicans. They had to settle for a later—and shorter—period: 11 to 11:15 P.M. (EST).

I worried that the hour might be top-heavy with ponderous political speeches—and the audience would tune out. Paul Porter and I developed a new concept in political programs— one that we believed would hold the audience and win Democratic votes.

We planned for pickups from several radio stations around the country. We sprinkled the scripts with lively, bright, human-interest material for all speakers. Our keynote feature was to be read by actor Jimmy Durante, doing what we hoped would be a heart-rending paean to the days of Herbert Hoover, when veterans across the country peddled apples at a nickel apiece. To write the script, we obtained the services of Norman Corwin, a foremost, innovative radio writer.

We battled with the networks again. The networks told us that the script was too long on drama and entertainment—and too short on political speeches. Paul Porter argued our case brilliantly. The battle went almost down to the wire—and we won.

*   *   *

In the pre-television campaign of 1944, newspapers and magazines wielded considerable influence in politics.

Franklin Roosevelt and the Democrats weren't popular with most of the press lords. Big-circulation newspapers, as well as national magazines constantly ran photos of a tired, old and haggard President.

To counter this impression, we decided that we needed more campaign appearances by the President. The party put constant pressure on the President to pick up the pace—but the President refused to give in. He said he wouldn't increase his speaking engagements beyond six—the number he had settled for immediately after the convention.

No one paid much attention, however, to the speech schedule of the vice-presidential candidate, which, I thought, was a mistake. I took particular pains to make sure that Truman got as much advantageous air time as possible.

Even as I doubled back and forth between both Democratic candidates, I went out of my way to serve the vice-presidential nominee. It was clear that Harry Truman was relegated to near-obscurity by the almost larger-than-life presence of President Roosevelt. The two men lunched together—in the glare of national publicity—on the White House lawn in late August. It was the only time they met formally during the campaign.

Clearly, most of the excitement rode with the President's campaign travels. Harry Truman's journeys, by contrast, were more relaxed and fun. President Roosevelt had asked Truman not to campaign by plane, but to stick to trains. Truman's train included a private railroad car, with a cook and meals-to-order.

My first network campaign assignment was the President's talk at Washington's Statler Hotel on Saturday evening, September 23. The air time was purchased by the Teamsters Union.

The maximum amount of money a presidential campaign committee could spend—by decree of the Hatch Act—was $3 million. The idea of limiting expenditures was sound, but it meant nothing. Other committees could legally spend money to support a presidential candidate, which meant that the campaign spawned an extraordinary number of committees.

Earlier that Saturday, I briefed the Teamsters Union board on broadcast arrangements. Teamsters president Dan Tobin, who was to introduce the President, handed me a copy of his introductory remarks. I was horrified. The remarks ran six minutes.

When the meeting ended, I rushed to the White House. I told the President that I was concerned that the introduction was too long. The President wasn't concerned. He jauntily waved his hand and dismissed the problem. "They're paying for the time," he said.

To make it easy for the President to reach the banquet room on the second floor, the Washington Statler constructed a special elevator. When the President entered the ballroom, the Teamsters gave him a standing ovation.

The pre-broadcast program moved along without a hitch—until 10 seconds before air time. There *was* a hitch. The light on the rostrum that was supposed to illuminate the speech text went out! Was it the bulb? Was the problem caused by one of the many electric wires scattered like spaghetti all over the floor? Fortunately, Dan Tobin had prepared a lengthy introduction.

Nervously, we traced the wires. We discovered that a new bulb wasn't the answer. We were lucky. As the President began his speech, the light flicked on.

The President gave one of the best written and best delivered speeches ever. He relished attacking the Republican Party and "that candidate of the other party." He clung to his strategy of previous campaigns: (1) Never mention the opposing candidate by name (in this case, Thomas Dewey), and (2) Wait for the opposition to make a mistake, then capitalize on that mistake.

FDR's speech is best remembered as the "Fala speech," because of the President's amusing remarks about his dog, Fala. "These Republican leaders have not been content with attacks on me, or my wife, or my sons," the President said. "They now include my little dog, Fala. Unlike the members of my family, he resents this. Being a Scottie, as soon as he learned that the Republican fiction writers had concocted a story that I left him behind on an Aleutian Island and had sent a destroyer back to find him at a cost to the taxpayers of two or three or twenty million dollars, his Scotch soul was furious. He has not been the same dog since."

The President thoroughly enjoyed the Fala remarks he had

written. For several days before that speech, he read the excerpt about Fala to just about everybody who visited the Oval Office.

For his part, Thomas Dewey had made the mistake of listening to Roosevelt at his best. Two days later, on September 25, in Oklahoma City, Dewey decided to attack the President head on. It was a fatal mistake. Dewey was coached by commentator Lowell Thomas and made a good presentation on radio. Strangely, though, Dewey's effectiveness as a radio speaker peaked early in the campaign, then fell off.

In a sense, the ratings told the campaign story. Roosevelt's "Fala speech" attracted 82.6% of the total radio audience. Dewey's speech two days later in Oklahoma City was heard by only 65.3% of available listeners.

I always felt that a correlation existed between a candidate's speech ratings on radio and voter support. Could this be true of television, too?

Let's look, for example, at the ratings—in this case, percentage of radio sets turned on—for the 1944 campaign: Roosevelt's highest rating was 40.6 (percentage share of homes with radios tuned in) on Saturday, November 4, for a speech he gave at Fenway Park in Boston. FDR's lowest was 27.0 on Friday, October 27, at Shibe Park in Philadelphia. Dewey's highest was the 24.4 he got for his September 25 speech at Oklahoma City. His lowest was 8.6 on October 3, from Albany, New York. What's more, throughout the campaign, Dewey wasn't helped by the comment of national columnist Dorothy Thompson. She tagged Dewey as "the little man on the wedding cake," and the tag stuck.

*　*　*

I rejoined Harry Truman on the train to St. Louis, where the candidate was scheduled to give two radio talks that night. We arrived in time to attend a World Series game between both St. Louis teams, the Cardinals and the Browns.

After Truman's broadcasts that night, I was exhausted. I had a tiring schedule shuttling between the two candidates and working in the New York office.

The person who made travel arrangements had booked Truman and me in a two-bedroom suite, with one bathroom. The next morning, we were supposed to get up early—for breakfast on the farm of a friend of Truman.

Suddenly I felt someone shake me awake. I gazed blurry-eyed at a man staring down at me, fully clothed. It was Harry Truman.

I was so embarrassed that I began blurting out apologies. But Truman would hear none of it. "Your schedule is worse than mine," he said, "and you looked like you needed the sleep. Anyway, I'm an early riser, so don't worry."

Then he paused, and added, "We'll have to get going shortly if we're to get to our breakfast on time."

* * *

President Roosevelt's political advisers were worried. They sensed that he was losing interest in the campaign, if not in politicking. They continued to press him to make additional speeches.

But the President was adamant. He insisted on sticking to six speeches—and no more.

By early October, with the 1944 election one month away, we introduced what I've always felt is effective strategy. After each address by the President, we cut away to various local stations across the nation. These stations, in turn, aired brief messages by Democratic candidates for senator and governor in their respective areas. Labor was most helpful in arranging local cut-ins through its radio adviser, Maurie Novik.

Across the country, about 125,000 voting precinct meetings were organized so voters could listen to broadcast messages tailored to their districts. A party worker in each district arranged a meeting of at least ten of his neighbors. It was painstaking work, but highly productive.

Meanwhile, on October 21, the President toured New York City on a cold, rainy and blustery day. He traveled more than 50 miles, greeting huge crowds from an open car. Along the way, he stopped in Greenwich Village to change clothes at Mrs. Roosevelt's apartment. It was an exhausting day, but the President was determined to prove he still was a robust campaigner.

That evening, the President addressed a lukewarm, Republican-oriented crowd—members of the Foreign Policy Association—at a dinner at the Waldorf Astoria.

During dinner, the famous Oscar of the Waldorf stood behind the President, refilling his wine glass after every sip. Whenever still photographers appeared on the scene, I discreetly moved the wine glass away from the President.

Soon the President turned to me and said, "Leonard, I know

what you are doing, but don't you think I earned it today?" I had to agree.

After the broadcast, I received a telephone call from Governor Cox. He asked if the President had too much wine. It was particularly apparent, Governor Cox said, during the first 15 minutes of the broadcast. He felt the President didn't have his normal delivery. The last 15 minutes, however, were superb.

* * *

One day the receptionist at our office called me: "Friends of Dan Mahoney are here to see you."

Dan Mahoney was the son-in-law of Governor Cox and a powerful political figure in his own right, living in Miami, Florida. After conversing with them for a few moments, I realized that they weren't friends of Dan Mahoney. They had used his name to gain access to my office.

As I tried to end our conversation, one of the men counted 100 one-thousand-dollar bills and placed them on my desk. "We want to make a contribution to the party," he said, "and we only want a small favor."

"You're in the wrong office," I said, steering them to the office of the treasurer, Ed Pauley. I subsequently learned that Pauley had tossed them out of his office.

The reason: in exchange for the contribution, they wanted what they called a "little fix" with the Internal Revenue Service.

* * *

The President's final campaign appearance occurred in Boston's Fenway Park—three days after Thomas Dewey had visited Boston and unleashed a personal attack on the President.

Frankly, I thought Dewey's attack built Roosevelt's radio audience. The President's speech at Fenway Park drew his highest rating of the campaign.

Meanwhile, between campaign trips, I had been working on the Democrats' one-hour Election Eve broadcast. Everything was in place, including comedian Jimmy Durante's five-minute sketch in praise of FDR.

On Monday morning, hours before the Election Eve broadcast, came a bombshell. We were notified by the William Esty Agency that Jimmy Durante could not appear. Neither the advertising agency nor his sponsor, R. J. Reynolds Co., would grant permission for what each termed a blatant Democratic political pitch.

It didn't take Paul Porter, John Hamm of the Biow Co. agency and me very long to realize that, without Durante, we couldn't provide alternate programming. Our broadcast had been timed to the second.

We decided to go ahead with the rest of the program and let the networks fill their schedules until 11 P.M. when the Republicans were scheduled to air a 15-minute broadcast.

Although we didn't yet know it, our decision to go with a shorter program turned out to be a brilliant political move.

Because the program closed with remarks by President Roosevelt, I joined him at his home in Hyde Park. The broadcast originated in the library, which contained shelves galore of documents and myriad other papers in cardboard file boxes. The President, noting my interest in these files, told me they contained material for books he intended to write.

After the President's on-the-air remarks, we signed off the program with seven minutes left to fill. To my surprise and delight, the network filled in the remaining minutes with somber, classical organ music.

The President was gleeful. "No one will keep their sets on to listen to the Republicans," he exclaimed, referring to the upcoming GOP broadcast. I had difficulty persuading the President that it wasn't our strategy, but the networks' low-cost program fill that provided the deadly organ music.

The Republicans came on at 11 P.M. Herbert Brownell, the GOP national chairman, said, "We have presented no campaign songs, shows or entertainment to distract the American people from the issues." The program droned on and on.

Fala, the President's dog, had been sitting alongside Roosevelt. During the Republican broadcast, Fala turned over on his side and fell asleep. President Roosevelt was amused. "They're even putting Fala to sleep," he chortled.

The pollsters envisioned a close election in 1944. They were wrong. Perhaps they should have looked at Roosevelt's dominance in the radio ratings.

As it was, the President was overwhelmingly re-elected to a fourth term. The official results:

Roosevelt: 25,602,505 votes (432 electoral votes)
Dewey: 22,006,278 votes (99 electoral votes)

The "FDR Wins Again" headlines were barely dry when speculation was rife, as usual, about new faces in the government. My name—and Paul Porter's—were mentioned frequently as possible designees for chairman of the Federal Communications Commission. I advised Paul that I intended to return to my work for Governor Cox. I also advised the White House that I sought no government appointment. Paul Porter did become chairman of the FCC.

Not long after Inauguration Day in 1945, Tom Pendergast—leader of a Kansas City political organization—died in disgrace, deserted by his family. The date: January 26.

Vice President Truman's sense of loyalty presented us with a problem. I discussed it with Matt Connelly, Truman's former administrative assistant, who later would become a key figure in the White House.

We knew that Truman owed his early political career to his backing by the powerful Pendergast organization. But we also knew that the Vice President would risk torrents of criticism if he went to Pendergast's funeral in Kansas City.

To avoid this criticism, we suggested to the Vice President that he not go to the funeral. He ignored the advice and went, anyway.

* * *

Traditionally, a Vice President is inundated by invitations to speak. I suggested that we select one speaking engagement per month for broadcast.

Each month, Vice President Truman spoke on a different network. His speeches, written by Ed Reynolds, were to be carefully crafted. They were to be rigidly neutral, with no strong position on any subject. We were at war, and the President—not the Vice President—made policy. Not surprisingly, Time magazine would comment, "It is impossible to tell from his speeches as Vice President where Truman stands on any issue."

On April 6, 1945, I traveled with Truman from Washington to Buffalo, where he would make his last speaking appearance as Vice President. On the train ride to Buffalo, Truman and I rode in adjoining compartments; I doubled as press secretary. The Vice President was accompanied by one Secret Service agent, George Drescher.

From Buffalo, I went to New York, a stopover on the way to

Washington, where I was to rejoin the Vice President for the Jefferson Day dinner at the Mayflower Hotel.

There, Truman was to introduce President Roosevelt, who was to speak from his convalescent retreat in Warm Springs, Georgia. The President had gone to Warm Springs on March 30 to relax after he had participated in the historic Yalta Conference with Joseph Stalin and Winston Churchill. Moreover, the President had addressed a joint session of Congress after he returned from Yalta. During his address, the President remained seated, complaining about the weight of his leg braces.

On Thursday, April 12, 1945, as I traveled from New York to Washington, I had my radio tuned in aboard a crowded railroad car. Suddenly the program stopped. The announcer said, "President Roosevelt is dead."

That evening, at 7:09, the man I had left in Buffalo as Vice President was sworn in as the 32nd President of the United States.

I arrived in Washington at 8 P.M. and immediately telephoned President Truman. It wasn't easy to get through, but I finally reached him at his apartment. He asked me to report to the White House in the morning.

On Saturday, April 14, the body of Franklin Roosevelt arrived in Washington by train from Warm Springs. The train was to depart at 10:15 that evening from Union Station for Hyde Park. I joined the official traveling party of 137, which included the President and Margaret Truman, Eleanor Roosevelt, Secret Service agents, assorted newspaper and radio correspondents—few with dry eyes.

Our departure from Washington was delayed. We had to arrive in Hyde Park at 8:40 A.M. Sunday and leave at 11:30 A.M., returning to Washington around 8 P.M. To stay on schedule, the engineer increased the train's speed. The right-of-way from Washington to Hyde Park was lined with mourners.

In the last car rode the President's flag-draped coffin, accompanied by an honor guard. The train surged on into the night, then into the sunrise. Destination: history.

CHAPTER 3

Spring 1945

PRESIDENT TRUMAN HAD SERVED 82 DAYS as Vice President. During that period, the President was away from Washington for 51 days. A student of history, Harry Truman was keenly aware of the Vice President's lack of authority, which raises a question: If Truman had been Vice President for a full term, what would he have made of the office?

It was said that John Tyler gave up his candidacy for the Senate in 1840 in exchange for the vice-presidential nomination. When William Henry Harrison died in the presidency in April of 1841, at the age of 68—after only one month in office—Tyler became President. (Incidentally, it was during the 1840 presidential campaign that the Democratic Party first used the donkey as its symbol. On occasion, cartoonists had portrayed the party with a rooster.)

As perceived by some, the No. 2 spot on the presidential ticket is inconsequential. Actually, it has been turned down several times.

In typically graphic fashion, President Lyndon Johnson once summed up how Presidents generally feel toward Vice Presidents. When asked what authority he would give his newly elected Vice President, Hubert Humphrey, Johnson replied: "The same amount of authority Jack Kennedy gave me. Not a god-damned bit."

* * *

Vice Presidents are an essential part of our political process. But, despite disclaimers to the contrary, no Vice President ever is prepared for the presidency.

From the moment of Franklin Roosevelt's death at the "Little White House" in Georgia, Harry Truman was thrust into a pressure cooker. The tasks faced by the new President were unmatched in history.

America was fighting World War II, and now Truman was Commander-in-Chief. Not only did he have to deal with the Allies, he had to cultivate personal relationships with Churchill and Stalin—to say nothing of making major decisions on the home front.

Like all Vice Presidents before him, Truman had no on-the-job training. Whoever was President made all the decisions, unencumbered by consultation or advice from his second-in-command.

For three weeks, I worked at the Truman White House, doing whatever I could to assist with the transition. It was a difficult time for human relationships in Washington.

Roosevelt people were emptying their desks and vacating offices that had become their second homes. No longer would they enjoy all those fringe benefits of working in the White House. No longer would they automatically make the exclusive lists for invitations to cocktail parties and dinners. No longer would they occupy the public stage, courted by the news media. Now they were former employees of a dead President. With numbing suddenness, they had to make a transition that wasn't easy.

Little did I realize, back in that spring of 1945, that one day I would participate in two more presidential transitions—the orderly one from Eisenhower to Kennedy in 1960, and the painful one in November of 1963, when Kennedy was felled by an assassin's bullet in Dallas.

*   *   *

Steve Early, who had served capably as press secretary for President Roosevelt, had left the White House to join the Pullman Company. Early's successor, Jonathan Daniels, was leaving.

Suddenly I found myself pinch-hitting as press secretary. One of my first tasks was to correct a problem encountered by photographers. They had trouble coping with reflection from

President Truman's glasses. The problem was solved by applying a transparent coating to the lenses.

Early in office, Truman prepared to make two speeches—an afternoon address on April 16 to a joint session of Congress and a five-minute talk on the evening of April 17 to armed forces around the world.

No announcement of the armed forces speech, however, was to be made until noon on April 17, ten hours beforehand. On Monday afternoon, April 16, Colonel Harry Vaughan, the President's military adviser, burst into the Oval Office, saying, "I missed a great chance to keep my big mouth shut."

It turned out that an alert reporter had asked Vaughan when the President's next speech was scheduled. Without thinking, Vaughan replied: "Tuesday night (April 17) to the armed forces." As a result, we had to make the official announcement ahead of schedule.

All of which was part of the learning process by the new administration. For every new presidential organization, it takes time to learn that everything that happens in the White House is an instant news story.

One morning at a staff meeting, General Vaughan (who had been given his second star as a general by the President) complained that the press was sniping at him. It should be mentioned that Vaughan was an easy target.

The President told Vaughan to forget it. Then, turning to the other staffers, the President said, "And that goes for all of you. You have to understand that the press isn't after you—they're using you to get at the President."

With his blunt down-to-earthiness, President Truman had difficulty adjusting to the security and ceremony that was essential to the presidency. For example, I happened to be in his office when the President was leaving for his first trip to the railroad station to meet Mrs. Truman. He asked me to come along.

A car containing Secret Service agents preceded us. Secret Service agents, of course, also occupied the President's car. All went well until the first car sped through a yellow light.

As the light turned red, the President told the driver: "Stop!" The driver stopped on the President's command, but then he accelerated and caught up with the first car. It all happened so quickly that no one except the Secret Service agents realized it.

They explained to the President that security required ignoring red lights. The President seemed surprised, but satisfied, with the explanation.

One thing was certain: the President never concealed his uneasiness with all the tight security. While rehearsing his April 16 speech to be delivered to the joint session of Congress, he paused and remarked, "I hope we don't have all those policemen on the hill when I go there today. They were always all over the place when Roosevelt visited the Congress."

* * *

During those first few days of his presidency, Harry Truman moved in a whirlwind of updating sessions, decision-making and briefing books.

After one briefing, the President returned to his office, visibly overwhelmed. His eyes betrayed a sense of urgency; he spoke in almost a whisper, his voice tense.

"Leonard," he said, "I have just been given some very important information. I am going to have to make a decision which no man in history has ever had to make."

He paused reflectively and went on: "I'll make the decision, but it is terrifying to think about what I will have to decide and the consequences of my decision."

As a broadcaster, I was naturally curious. I had an almost irresistible urge to say: "Well, Mr. President, tell me what *is* this important decision?"

But I resisted. After all, my work at the White House had thrust me into a different role. I wasn't a newsman; I was a "sounding board" of sorts—a trusted member of President Truman's inner circle. If the President had wanted to tell me, he would have done so.

"I wish I could talk to you about it," the President continued. "It's going to be tough, but I'll make the decision."

I responded by saying: "I know you'll make the right decision, and the country will support your decision."

It wasn't until four months later—in August of 1945—that I would realize that Harry Truman, the fledgling President, was weighing a decision that would change the course of history forever. He had said he would make the decision—and he did: in August, the United States dropped the atomic bomb on Hiroshima and Nagasaki, which prompted the surrender of the Japanese and brought an end to World War II.

The bombings claimed many lives, but they *saved* hundreds of thousands of more lives, simply by ending the war. As I look back now, I'm convinced that's what weighed most on Harry Truman's mind as he considered his historic decision.

Throughout his presidency, Truman made courageous decisions, but not until after he had pondered them with careful, painstaking study. It wasn't unusual to see the President leave the Oval Office each night with an armload of books and stacks of briefing papers. "This isn't the most interesting reading," he once told me, "but I have no choice if I'm to handle this job."

"Handling the job," as Truman put it, requires huge quantities of energy and intellect. The presidency is a marathon run and mental gymnastics all rolled into one. A President's appointment schedule demands that he shift gears—from one subject to another—all day long and sometimes far into the night.

Everybody who calls on the President has thoroughly studied his subject, and the callers may arrive only 15 minutes apart. That means that the President has to know when he may safely say "yes" and when he must respond with an emphatic "no"—or, in many cases, say nothing at all.

*   *   *

I had occupied the press secretary's office in the Truman White House for only a few days when I received a telephone call from Rose Conway, the President's secretary.

She said that Bess Truman had been talked into a press conference. I was told that as many as 88 reporters regularly covered the activities of Eleanor Roosevelt.

I telephoned Mrs. Truman. "Do you want to hold a press conference?" I asked.

Her reply was what I expected: "Absolutely not, but I thought it was expected and I had to do it."

I assured the new First Lady that she didn't have to hold a news conference if she didn't want to. I told her I would cancel this one—and I suggested that any further requests for a news conference be referred to me.

Bess Truman was much relieved and expressed her thanks. She didn't need press conferences to establish her place as one of the most admired First Ladies in history.

*   *   *

I already knew that the press corps traditionally held anyone in radio in bitter contempt. What I didn't know was how deep that bitterness ran.

Years later, of course, the press corps would scramble to appear on radio programs like "Meet the Press." Then, with the emergence of television as the most powerful of all media, most of the press corps pursued the camera—which, in turn, resulted in many worthwhile programs.

From the start, I encountered hostility among the press corps. Barely after I finished my first daily briefing, all three wire services—Associated Press, United Press and International News Service—endeavored to have me replaced on the spot. At least, their feelings toward me were unanimous and they were totally negative.

After one particularly rough day, I dragged disconsolately into the Mayflower Hotel lobby. There, I met an old-timer named Ralph Smith, a friend who reported on Washington for the *Atlanta Journal.* "Leonard," he said, "they're really going after you. Nothing personal—but a radio man cannot be a press secretary, even on a temporary basis. Watch yourself. The press corps is out to get you."

The resentment by the press against radio was echoed by some of my associates in broadcasting. "Washington Press (sure) Corps," headlined a *Broadcasting* magazine article about the problems of a radio man trying to placate the Washington press corps. When a major dinner for the press was held in the capital, *Broadcasting's* publisher Sol Taishoff, a veteran Washington newsman, was promptly uninvited.

My brief tour-of-duty as press secretary made me the target of constant verbal slings and arrows. Most of the press gave me a rough time. But, when I left that job to pursue other White House duties, veteran reporter Merriman Smith of INS consoled me. "Hey, you surprised me," he said. "You did a good job." His remarks were echoed, in a sense, by the AP's Tony Vaccaro, new to the White House beat. "We're going to miss you," he said.

* * *

On April 19, I received a telephone call from Governor Cox. "When are you going back to Atlanta?" he asked.

"I'm glad you called," I replied. "I hoped you would talk to the President about my relationship with the White House."

I had become more immersed in White House activities than I intended. I wanted to help in every way I could, but I didn't intend to become a permanent member of the White House staff.

Whereupon Governor Cox telephoned President Truman and sent the following wire the next morning.

April 20, 1945

My dear Mr. President:

Some time ago you made an appeal to me which I think I responded to at the moment in good spirit. Now I am going to make an appeal to you. Please let us have Leonard Reinsch back. When we gave our consent we were not sufficiently mindful of the tremendous tasks ahead of radio in connection with Television, Frequency Modulation and whatnot.

On special occasions for your personal uses his services could be available without embarrassment to us. It might not seem a patriotic impulse which prompts this message and yet, I am sure on reflection you will see it is justified.

Kind regards,
JAMES M. COX

Not long after Governor Cox wired the President, the following news story clattered across the teletypes:

When Mr. Truman first took office it was announced that J. Leonard Reinsch, managing director of three radio stations owned by James M. Cox, would act as secretary in charge of press and radio affairs.

The President explained at a special news conference that Cox had telegraphed him, making a special appeal that Reinsch be allowed to return to his post with the Cox stations because of the urgent need of his technical knowledge.

The President said that after receiving the appeal from Cox he called in (Charles) Ross, a reporter for the St. Louis Post-Dispatch, a friend since they went to high school together, and asked him to take the post. Ross agreed to this, saying he would be available on May 15 after he reports on the United Nations Conference in San Francisco.

With the arrival of Charlie Ross, I no longer had to provide the daily briefings for the press. No longer did my telephone ring off the hook with calls from reporters demanding information, confirmation and/or denials of reports heard in and out of Washington's 'round-the-clock rumor mill.

The press secretary was expected to be the President's alter ego, in a sense—to be knowledgeable about every thought and action of the President—in advance! And the press secretary was expected to field calls and requests from the press 24 hours a day, seven days a week.

In those times, it was especially difficult. The press secretary's staff was so small it occupied only two offices, which seems like a skeletal operation today—in these days of 100-member staffs and widened responsibility.

*   *   *

My new assignment thrust me into more familiar surroundings. I was to work closely with the President on all of his speeches and his broadcast appearances. At the same time, I was able to pursue my radio career. Both the President and Governor Cox seemed satisfied with this arrangement of my time.

It was the age of pre-television—and pre-tape recorders. Speeches were transcribed on wire recorders, which had a limited frequency response. I used a wire recorder to coach the President, so he could judge the pacing of his speech delivery.

While waiting to have lunch one day with President Truman, I let the servants speak into the wire-recorder microphone and then listen to themselves on the playback.

They talked on the recorder about their work in the White House. Some had served several Presidents. One old-timer provided a character analysis of two Presidents: "Mistah Hoover was a fine man. People come to see him. He give them everything they want, they go away mad. Mistah Roosevelt was a fine man, too. People come to see him, he give them nothing, they go away glad."

One of my first projects was to reduce the forest of microphones—each bearing network and radio station call letters—which hid the President during his speaking appearances at the House of Representatives. House Speaker Sam Rayburn agreed with removing most of the mikes. Of course, the radio networks and stations were unhappy to lose the picture identification of their call letters. Off the record, however, they agreed with my objections.

My next concern was the audio pickup of the President's words. I discussed this problem—the President's voice didn't come across strongly enough—in meetings with the networks, station representatives and newsreel executives. With the backing of the President and the House Speaker, I was in a "no-lose" position.

To improve the audio pickup, I arranged to have cables installed beneath the House floor. That way, only two or three unmarked microphones would appear in front of Speaker Rayburn and on the desk of the reading clerk. The cable would feed into an amplifier, from which the networks, stations and newsreels could get their pickups.

A similar amplifier, which we later used whenever the President spoke on the road, became known as the "presidential amplifier." Instead of requests for microphone positions, we got requests for a patch into the presidential amplifier.

Normally, we used only four microphones—one for newsreels, one for the public-address system, one for radio and one as a backup microphone in case one of the other three malfunctioned. We also used a rostrum that could be elevated or lowered, depending on the height of the speaker.

At one Democratic dinner in the 1950s, we didn't have such a rostrum. We had to obtain a Coca-Cola crate so shorter speakers could use it as a platform.

For every speaking appearance by President Truman, I made sure that the front of the rostrum bore the presidential seal—yet another highly visible reminder that he was President. It still was difficult for many political leaders to comprehend that America did, indeed, have a new President. The nation accepted Truman as President, but still imagined Roosevelt as occupying the Oval Office. Every reminder of Truman as President helped establish his identity in office.

*   *   *

President Truman was scheduled to address the closing plenary session of the United States Conference on International Organization in San Francisco on June 26, 1945. The honeymoon—enjoyed by all new Presidents—was still on.

Along the way to California, the President made a stopover visit to Washington State and stayed with Governor Mon Wallgren in the governor's mansion. From there, we took a nine-hour tour of the Puget Sound aboard the Coast Guard ship, the USS Grant. On this same cool, overcast day, the governor had arranged for a fishing trip in the Puget Sound.

After fishing with no luck, the President and most of his traveling party retired to try for better luck—at poker. But the

President's luck wasn't good. He began to write a check payable to one of the winners.

"Wait, Mr. President!" someone said. It was suggested to the President that no check be signed by him. We had visions of a presidential check—framed and mounted on somebody's office wall—with the inscription "In payment of poker losses."

Senator Warren Magnuson was worried about the presidential party returning to shore without having caught any of Washington State's famous salmon. The senator noticed a small fishing boat nearby.

"Any luck?" he hollered to the boat's occupants.

They hoisted a beautiful salmon.

"Could we have it?" the senator asked.

"What for?"

"For the President."

A doubtful "yes" came across the water, whereupon the senator boarded a rowboat and delivered the salmon back to the USS Grant. When the senator asked the President to pose with the salmon for photographs, the President replied, "Yes, but I'll say I didn't catch it."

There is a postscript to the foregoing salmon story, although I didn't know it until Senator Magnuson told me about it a year later. It seems that when the fishermen returned home, they were accused by their wives of taking a day off from the factory.

"Where did you go?" one irate wife asked.

"Oh, we went fishing," one of the men replied.

"OK, where are the fish?"

"We gave the fish to the President."

Whereupon one wife hauled off and belted her husband across the face. "The President?" she screamed. "What a story! Don't you lie to me!"

Finally, the distraught husband reached Senator Magnuson on the telephone—and the senator explained the whole episode to the fisherman's wife. The fish story was verified—and domestic tranquility was restored.

* * *

When Truman became President, he inherited a Cabinet that included his one-time political foe, Henry A. Wallace, as Secretary of Commerce. Wallace stayed in the Cabinet, that is, until he openly opposed the administration's foreign policy. On September 20, 1945, the President asked for Wallace's resignation.

Months earlier, I observed firsthand how our government squabbled with other governments. The President asked me to help arrange the V-E Day announcement on May 8, 1945. After much hassling, particularly with the British government, it was agreed that the United States, Great Britain and Russia would announce the victory in Europe at 9 A.M., Washington time.

This, of course, was 3 P.M. in London and 4 P.M. in Moscow. President Truman said Winston Churchill kept telephoning him in the wee hours of May 8, suggesting that Russia be ignored and that only the United States and Great Britain make the announcement—earlier than planned. Despite Churchill's urgings, the joint announcement was made as planned—by all three nations.

The V-J Day announcement wouldn't come until August 14, but now V-E Day was history. It also was a joyful celebration of President Truman's 61st birthday.

*   *   *

General Harry Vaughan, the President's friend and military counselor, was a graduate of Westminster College in Fulton, Missouri. This relationship resulted in an invitation to Winston Churchill to speak at the college.

When the President advised Churchill that he would introduce him if he accepted, the Prime Minister accepted. We left Washington by train for Jefferson City, Missouri, on March 4, 1946, arriving the next day.

We traveled to Fulton by car. When we arrived at the home of Westminster College's president, the Prime Minister was escorted to the second-floor main bedroom. There, while he changed clothes, we had an international crisis on our hands; the black bag containing the Prime Minister's brandy was missing!

Search parties were quickly organized. It was an unforgettable sight—the Prime Minister, in full regalia, sitting on the edge of a large double bed, hands folded across his vest. Obviously, he wasn't going to move until the precious black bag was found.

Soon, however, the crisis was over. The black bag was found—in one of the escort automobiles—and the brandy bottle was full. The bag was delivered to the Prime Minister. Only then did he make his entrance to a luncheon on the first floor. He was in fine spirits during the meal. Nodding to the entree, he remarked, "The pig has reached its highest point of evolution in this ham."

The official party for Churchill's speech included 31 newspaper and wire reporters, 13 radio reporters, four still cameramen and ten newsreel representatives, not to mention the local media from Central Missouri.

At the gymnasium, the site of the speech, Western Union hooked up 35 lines into the basement. The telephone company had installed a new cable with 600 circuits from the local telephone office to the gym. Plenty of borrowed typewriters were available, too.

It was stiflingly hot in the crowded gymnasium, and many complained of the heat that was added by the newsreel lights. During Churchill's speech, the newsreel lights were turned off—to the relief of everybody except the cameramen.

Even though my responsibility was radio, the newsreel crews pleaded with me. "Can't you get him to do something?" they grumbled, their words sprinkled with language not usually heard in a Presbyterian college.

"Him," it turned out, meant General Vaughan, who had ordered the lights shut off. I told the newsreel people I would see what I could do.

I couldn't get to President Truman, since he was seated in the middle of the platform, but I successfully reached General Vaughan. I argued on behalf of the newsreel people, but it wasn't easy. General Vaughan was adamant. No more lights, period.

Thus, Churchill's famous "Iron Curtain speech," as it was later called, never got on film in its entirety. His speech drew its theme from a key passage: "From Stettin in the Baltic to Trieste in the Adriatic, an iron curtain has descended across the continent. Behind that line lie all the capitols of the ancient states of central and eastern Europe . . . subject in one form or another, not only to Soviet influence but to a very high and increasing measure of control from Moscow."

That evening, on the return trip, we arrived at the St. Louis train station. Many in the official party had relaxed and donned pajamas and robes. Some played poker, and Prime Minister Churchill good-humoredly asked the other players if two ladies beat two knaves.

In the train station, a large crowd had gathered, hoping to get a glimpse of the President and the Prime Minister. The two world leaders didn't have time to dress, so I suggested that they put on overcoats.

I moved the still photographers and newsreel cameramen out of range of a full-length shot. The President and the Prime Minister waved from the rear platform of the rail car, Churchill flashing his famous "V" sign. Moments later, the two men returned to the car. They doffed their coats and resumed the poker game in pajamas and robes.

* * *

En route back to Washington, the President made a stopover at Columbus, Ohio. There, on March 6, he addressed the Federal Council of Churches of Christ in America.

Weeks later, I checked with the President about future speeches. He obviously was irritated.

"Do you know what the trouble is with this job?" he asked rhetorically. "You have to kiss too many asses to get people to do what they ought to do in the first place."

Later, I saw this statement in print. Or, words to that effect: "The principal power the President has is to bring people into the Oval Office and try to persuade them to do what they ought to do without persuasion."

* * *

For a long time, I thought the White House needed an auditorium. It could provide ample facilities for all media, including the writing press, still photographers, newsreel cameras, radio reporters and television cameras. Moreover, it could provide seating for a small audience. The President could hold press conferences, introduce foreign visitors and make official announcements—all in one place.

I told President Truman that such a facility could be built at the rear of the executive offices that adjoined the Oval Office. The addition could face the old State Department building, away from the view of Pennsylvania Avenue. The President liked the idea and called in Lorenzo S. Winslow, the White House architect.

On January 14, 1946, *Broadcasting* magazine reported that "complete broadcast and television facilities" would be built when the West Wing of the White House was expanded, later in 1946. The facilities were said to include six radio booths on the sides of the balcony, with windows at an angle to permit a view of the stage. TV cameras would be positioned in the photography room, across the back of the balcony. *Broadcasting*'s report went on:

> All Presidential broadcasts will originate from stage of 375-capacity auditorium. Movie and still cameramen can shoot from booths during broadcasts, saving President from agonizing half-hour under kliegs and flashlights.
>
> Interior Dept. has $1,650,000 appropriation for White House project, which also includes alterations to mansion, completion of East Wing and landscaping. Federal Works Agency will handle construction. . . . New rostrum likely will have concealed microphones. Stage will be 24 × 16 feet, with part of it disappearing to change props.

Unfortunately, the White House architect announced that the Interior Department funds included money for alterations to the mansion. In everybody's mind, the auditorium became an addition to the White House.

Objections poured in from everywhere. Wires containing hundreds of names protested the defacing of "our White House." Because of the hue and cry, the project was dropped.

The problem was nobody really stopped to analyze what I had proposed. The auditorium would not have detracted from the reverence of the White House and the Oval Office, for which I've never lost my feeling of awe. Actually, the proposed addition hardly would have been noticed. It was a practical extension of the working media quarters.

As it was, the President had to continue using the East Room in the White House, the conference room in the present Executive Office building or even State Department facilities. In ensuing years, it became increasingly apparent that the auditorium was needed more than ever.

*   *   *

Storm clouds gathered against President Truman in the spring of 1946, not even a year after he took office. Resentment against him was becoming fashionable, even among Democratic leaders. In fact, by the mid-term elections, most Democratic office seekers disowned Truman and extolled Roosevelt's presidency to buttress their campaigns.

It's hard to be popular and, at the same time, be a good President. In April of 1946, *Life* commented: "To reach the conclusion, as the nation obviously has, that Truman is not a great man, perhaps not even an exceptionally able one, is by no means reaching the conclusion that he will be a disastrous or even a poor President."

The President's unpopularity in some quarters was driven home with frightening reality in Chicago, where he was to attend Army Day ceremonies on April 6. Arriving by train that morning at Chicago's Union Station, we were asked to stay on board. The Secret Service had received a threatening, anti-Truman letter from someone identified in the crowd at the railroad station.

The purported letter writer was taken into custody. We streamed out of the station to waiting cars that whisked us to the Blackstone Hotel. Instinctively, while traveling with the President, you follow every order issued by the Secret Service agents. You never really think of a President being shot while you are part of his traveling party. The late 1940s seemed so innocent, in that sense, compared to later years, which would bring the assassination of President Kennedy and attempts on the lives of President Ford and President Reagan.

* * *

I continued to work on the President's speech delivery, still writing notes to him: "Remember the living room". . . . "Slow down. . . ."

President Truman still used chopping gestures, which came naturally to him, whenever he spoke. I wanted the President to be natural, to be himself, yet also easily understood. I didn't want him to be preoccupied with the mechanics of speaking, breathing and other details. In some ways, delivering a speech is tantamount to swinging at a golf ball. As the legendary golfer Bobby Jones once told me, "Don't worry about the mechanics of the swing. Hit the ball."

While working with the President's speaking technique, I also tried to get him to shorten his speeches—and to limit the number of speakers at official functions.

That, of course, was a sure path to unpopularity. As a rule, everybody who wrote—or contributed to—a presidential speech thought he was writing the modern version of the Gettysburg Address. The exception was Captain Clark Clifford, the president's naval aide, who was a top-notch speechwriter and who would go on to an illustrious government and legal career in Washington.

Unfortunately, every Democratic leader felt it was his or her right to give a speech at any affair the President addressed. These speeches always were too long.

Sometimes I won these battles in quest of shorter speeches. Mostly, I lost. As television began to flex its muscles, I redoubled my efforts to get shorter, more meaningful speeches—and fewer speakers.

In time, I acquired a reputation as someone who kept everybody on schedule. In broadcasting, you live—and sometimes die—by the clock.

At one Democratic dinner, three former First Ladies sat at the head table: Mrs. Woodrow Wilson, Mrs. Roosevelt and Mrs. Truman. Just as she approached the table, Eleanor Roosevelt saw me and said, "Leonard, I have to leave early to catch my plane. I am going to count on you to make sure I leave on time."

Seeing Eleanor Roosevelt at that dinner would remind me of my first meeting with her early in 1950, at her apartment in upper New York City. Chuck Palmer, an Atlanta friend, had asked me to go with him to see Mrs. Roosevelt. Chuck wanted to discuss his pet project, the "Little White House" at Warm Springs.

As we sipped tea, we were interrupted by a telephone call. Mrs. Roosevelt answered, then suddenly spoke French. It was, she said, a reporter from a Paris newspaper.

She reminisced fondly about her courting days with FDR. Before her marriage, Mrs. Roosevelt had done social work in some New York City tenements. When Franklin picked her up at the Social Service office, she said, he told her that he couldn't understand how people could live that way.

She said she told Franklin to come back the following week and she would arrange for him to tour some walk-up, cold-water apartments. "I didn't know it then," she said, smiling, "but I think I did some good that afternoon for a better housing program."

* * *

Whenever the President made an important speech outside Washington, I went along, bearing the title of "radio adviser to the President." I always received the President's confidential schedule well in advance, so I could plan for the trip.

My presence sometimes created protocol problems, particularly in Canada and Mexico. After all, what is the protocol ranking—at official luncheons and dinners—of a radio adviser? No other country had a radio adviser serving the head of government.

Before a goodwill trip to Mexico in March of 1947, Protocol Officer Stanley Woodward briefed the President on details of what would be a very tight schedule. When the briefing was over, President Truman looked at Woodward with a half grin.

"Do you mind if I ask you a question?" the President said.

"No, sir, Mr. President," Woodward replied.

"When do I get time to go to the men's room?"

CHAPTER 4

Philadelphia
Summer 1948

The Kinsey Report ushers sex out of the bedrooms and into America's bookstores and everday chit-chat. . . . A Hollywood starlet is fired by Columbia Pictures with the comment: "Can't act." Her name: Marilyn Monroe. . . . The dulcet voice of Nat King Cole sings "Nature Boy". . . . Millions of Americans say they're wild—or not wild—about Harry Truman. . . . And Americans aren't yet wild about television. By New Year's Day of 1948, there are only 172,000 television sets in use—many with hefty price tags and tiny (7-inch) screens.

TELEVISION MADE AN UNCEREMONIOUS ENTRY into politics at the Democratic Convention. Only a handful of bulky, cumbersome cameras were allowed into the convention hall at Philadelphia. They provided limited live coverage for the relative handful of viewers who owned TV sets and happened to live between Boston and Washington. National television of the conventions still was four years away.

Even so, television was about to bring dramatic changes in American politics. Radio, of course, already had inspired some of these changes.

In time, television would influence the location of conventions, the content of conventions and, later, even the choice of candidates. Gone would be the 40 and 50 ballots to determine a party's presidential nominee (a process changed, too, by the proliferation of primaries and altered party rules). Gone would be the 50-minute ovations. Gone would be all those drawn-out, New Year's Eve party-like demonstrations on the floor after a nominating speech. Gone would be the lengthy speeches so dear to a politician's heart. Gone, too, would be the leisurely notification of presidential nominees, the torchlight parades and the Election Night newspaper "extras."

Movie newsreels with demanding physical deadlines would be replaced by the more immediate coverage of TV newsreels. Live television pickups would be relayed by coaxial cable and microwave (in 1944, television cameras had filmed the proceedings, and the film was rushed to New York or Los Angeles by plane).

In 1980, satellite transmission would revolutionize television with an impact not yet fully realized. Cable, along with satellites and computers, would add new dimensions to politics. Like the rest of us, the average politician can't keep pace with these changes.

Even the traditionally powerful print media would feel the impact of the omnipotent television camera. Some national magazines with tough deadlines would fade in importance. So, too, would afternoon newspapers, which had to compete with the evening news on television.

In ensuing years, politicians would "play" to the cameras. Conventions no longer would be primarily timed or programmed to influence the delegates. Instead, greater consideration would be accorded to the potential impact of the convention on the television audience (also known as the electorate). Delegates and alternates would become merely the backdrop for the national television pickup.

The proliferation of primaries, dominated by television, would determine the presidential candidate long before the national party conventions. The convention would become nothing more than a political rally, often boring and rarely exciting.

Television also would influence the way we talked about politics. Words like "photogenic" and "charismatic" would come into vogue. And new computer techniques would bring an epidemic of public-opinion polls, which would present a new and still-difficult problem—election results known even before the local polls close, i.e., presidential tallies of votes available nationwide, hours before polling places in the Western states close.

At the same time, candidates would avail themselves of a

new and mushrooming breed—"professional political consul-tants," pollsters and fund-raisers armed with mailing lists extrapolated from computer printouts of demographics. The power of the old-time political bosses would inexorably give way to the power of television.

For political convention managers, too, television would usher in a new world. They would be concerned about things like line of sight, neutral backdrops, convention hall visuals and camera positions, including the solid camera platforms on the floor (which would provide head-on shots of each speaker). Ever present, too, would be another problem—camera-con-scious politicians bobbing and hovering around the platform, thereby providing unnecessary clutter and unwanted distrac-tion.

A prime consideration in the physical layout of each con-vention hall would be adequate lighting for television. In 1976, it would cost $200,000 merely to redistribute the existing lighting in New York's Madison Square Garden, scene of the Democratic Convention that nominated Jimmy Carter.

Every four years, the litany of problems raised by television would mount: Which state delegations were to be in easy camera range? How will pool coverage be handled? How to control floor coverage in the era of the small, hand-held cam-era, the long lens and the omnipresent microphone? Who will get floor privileges? How does one accommodate print media, radio and still cameras? Where does one position the televi-sion studios, control rooms, satellite dishes and special rooms needed for convention business?

At the 1936 Democratic Convention, only 40 representatives of the news media showed up. By 1940, that number grew to 294. Contrast these numbers with those for the 1980 con-vention: more than 4,500 represented TV and radio alone! In fact, one network covered the 1976 convention with twice the total number of media people who had covered the 1936 con-vention.

With the advent of the minicam TV camera and wireless radio for the audio side, control of the convention floor became difficult, if not impossible. For the first time, electronic cam-eras were used exclusively in 1976; floor cameras had been scrapped. One network alone, CBS, used as many as 30 cam-eras. Television had achieved maximum mobility.

Thanks to low-cost satellite transmission in 1980, the number of local television stations covering the convention multiplied. Today, the enormous space occupied by television—with its crews, technical equipment, et cetera—weighs heavily on where conventions will be held.

By 1952, political conventions would undergo many changes—some of which I managed to pioneer. And radio, while still important, would take a back seat to television. The year 1952 was the first time political conventions were telecast on a national basis. The first televised convention in 1948 came at a time of turmoil in the Democratic Party.

Nowadays, when you hear the almost universal comment, "We need another Truman to run for President," it's hard to imagine the years when Truman ran into heavy political turbulence. As the President plotted strategy for his 1948 campaign, many Democrats planned to thwart the President's bid for the nomination.

As opposition to President Truman welled up, he was consoled by his knowledge of history. No national convention has ever gone against the wishes of the incumbent President. He picks the officers of the national committee, and of the convention itself. He directs the program. He controls the convention's actions—no matter what the party's political leaders say or do.

Nevertheless, President Truman faced attacks from two—and possibly three—fronts: the Southern opposition to civil rights and the Progressive Party movement of Henry Wallace. A third front also seemed possible—the entry of General Dwight Eisenhower into the presidential sweepstakes, as a Democrat.

In 1947 and well into 1948, Eisenhower was being wooed by prominent Democrats to run for President with hopes of removing Truman from office. But Eisenhower didn't seem enamored with the idea. "The necessary and wise subordination of the military to civil powers," he wrote in January of 1948, "will best be sustained when lifelong professional soldiers abstain from seeking high political office."

As a result, the draft-Eisenhower front dissolved, but the Southerners were increasingly vocal against Truman's stand on behalf of civil rights.

As early as October of 1947, the President made his first move to control the 1948 convention. Senator J. Howard McGrath, three-time governor of Rhode Island and a Truman appointee as Solicitor General in 1946, was elected national chairman, succeeding Bob Hannegan, who was ailing.

At the same time, the national committee adopted a resolution which confirmed that the President was in control: " . . . The Democratic National Committee reasserts its support of the President and his program and his administration. . . ."

The Republicans already had chosen Philadelphia for their convention. Now it was the Democrats' turn to consider applications from cities that wanted to host their convention.

First, the national committee members in Washington heard the usual chamber of commerce-style sales pitches on hospitality, hotel rooms and transportation. Then Roger Clipp, general manager of WFIL-TV in Philadelphia, was introduced to discuss something called television.

This was the first presentation to a Democratic arrangements committee on the advantage of television. Clipp pointed out that live television would be possible from Boston to Washington, with fast air delivery of films to television stations around the country. One-third of America's population, he said, would be reachable by television—an area representing 168 electoral votes. Next door to the convention hall—in a space accommodating 25,000 people—would be enough TV sets so everyone could watch the proceedings.

As it was, the Democrats' desire for television coverage outran whatever problem they had with the quantity of available hotel rooms in Philadelphia. San Francisco withdrew its bid for the Democratic Convention because it lacked television facilities. So, like the Republicans and the Progressive Party, the Democrats settled on Philadelphia because of television—and television alone. The convention would open on Monday, July 12, 1948.

*　*　*

In the truest sense, Harry Truman was America's first television President.

He enthusiastically watched the televised opening session of the 80th Congress—on a 10-inch RCA set on his desk. Then, on Monday, January 6, 1947, the President achieved a historical milestone: his address to the joint session of Congress was the first ever to be televised. (President Jefferson had sent a written message to Congress; Woodrow Wilson was the first President to address the Congress in person).

For many years after Truman's televised address, Presidents spoke to joint sessions of Congress at 1 P.M., that is, until television asserted itself as the most powerful medium of all. That's when Presidents became conscious of prime time. Today, it's almost routine for the White House to ask for pre-emption of prime-time programming so that the American voters can be reached with *any* presidential message.

On October 5, 1947, President Truman established another precedent—a televised program from the White House. He addressed the nation on food conservation, speaking from the Oval Office.

* * *

The 1948 Democratic Convention ushered in a new era—and new problems. One was the problem of sponsorship of the conventions. The problem was academic back then; the convention paid for the TV installations, and the networks didn't have sponsors.

Where would the funding come from? The 1948 planners decided to sell advertising in a printed convention program. First, however, many companies asked for a legal review—to make sure that the ads were deductible as a business expense. Assured that such an expense was deductible, a small furnace company placed the first ad in the program.

* * *

At the convention, five television cameras were trained on the proceedings—all with lenses to provide closeups and long shots.

Politicians no longer could rely solely on voice coaches to teach them the nuances of speaking into a radio microphone. Television changed all that. As Edwin James wrote in *Broadcasting*, "This year's crop of candidates who may expect to be laid bare by television's merciless eye, may need to engage, as well, the professional assistance of dramatic teachers, cosmeticians, wig makers and clever haberdashers. The television camera is an uncompromising reporter—jowls droop and wrinkles deepen. . . ."

For the first time, the word "charisma" became etched into the political reporters' working vocabulary. Truman was reported to convey sincerity and determination. Dewey's moustache was considered a liability, but his voice quality was good. Eisenhower ranked high. Said one reporter, "He has an interesting and mobile face with an infectious grin."

An estimated 10 million viewers watched the Democratic Convention on television, with 62 million listening on the radio. That was quite a contrast with 1940, when two television cameras covered the Republican Convention that nominated Wendell Willkie. The audience then was generously estimated at 10,000.

In 1948, it wasn't just the public that watched television. So did other media. Mutual Broadcasting, a radio-only network, provided television sets for its reporters covering the convention. The Paramount Theatre in New York provided another first—live television of Thomas Dewey's acceptance speech from the Republican Convention. For television stations not interconnected, a 40-minute newsreel was provided by air delivery.

No one knew what to do about television. Although there were attempts to shorten speeches, political conventions weren't materially different from pre-TV days. Little attention was paid to things like floor layout and placement of slogans. At the time no one knew it, but the conventions became a promotional vehicle to sell television sets. Moreover, neither television commentators nor politicians realized how much television would influence their careers.

It was clear, however, that Thomas Dewey was mindful of television's intrusive eye. At the Republican Convention, he instructed his floor leaders not to be seen on camera talking to heads of delegations pledged to other candidates. He also advised them to keep as many delegates as possible within camera range and to watch their personal conduct.

Taking a cue from the Republicans, the Democrats issued words of caution to their convention delegates. "Television has a complete and merciless eye, shifting without notice," one memorandum read. "Reading of newspapers, yawning and other signs of boredom are to be avoided." A good reminder even to delegates today.

* * *

At noon on July 12, the Democrats gaveled their first session to order. A confident President Truman watched the convention on television at the White House.

One of the first speakers, Mrs. India Edwards, executive director of the Democratic National Committee's Women's Division, was keenly conscious of the television cameras. As a result, she got a place on the agenda in prime time. To emphasize a point she made about rising prices, she released balloons. To illustrate problems stemming from increasing prices, she pulled grocery items from a shopping bag. She brought a small girl named Sally Zimmerman to the rostrum and told how much each item of the girl's clothing had risen in price. India Edwards, then, became the first convention speaker to use props for television.

Harry Truman's first choice for his running mate was Supreme Court Justice William O. Douglas. But when Douglas declined to run, the President, with little enthusiasm, tapped Senator Alben W. Barkley of Kentucky. Barkley, as temporary chairman of the convention, gave an old-fashioned, "barn burner" speech that clinched his nomination as the vice-presidential candidate.

Vice-presidential candidates are usually older than the presidential candidates. Alben Barkley was the oldest, almost 71 years old when nominated.

Meanwhile, the President knew he would encounter problems with the South during the convention, but he also knew he would be the nominee. The Truman forces wanted a moderate civil rights plank, but they were defeated by the liberals. The evening session of Wednesday, July 14, would be anything but smooth and orderly.

Alabama, first in the roll call for nominations for President, immediately raised a point of personal privilege. Handy Ellis, chairman of the Alabama delegation, said that he and the other delegates intended to walk out of the convention—in protest of the liberal plank on civil rights. Ellis added that the Alabama delegates would be joined in their walkout by Mississippi's delegates.

Perhaps the first example of "staging" in television reporting occurred that evening. A director for Life-NBC got several Southern delegates to dramatize their walkout from the convention by ripping off their badges and tossing them into a pile in front of the TV camera. Then the delegates were interviewed. When the interviews ended, the delegates returned to their seats and put on their badges.

Senator Lister Hill of Alabama yielded to Georgia. Charles Bloch, vice chairman of the Georgia delegation, nominated Senator Richard Russell of Georgia for President. Suddenly a band struck up "Dixie," and Southern delegates kicked up their heels in a frenzied demonstration that almost got out of control.

Arizona yielded to Missouri. Governor Phil M. Donnelly of Missouri placed President Truman's name in nomination with a speech that the President himself heard on the radio while riding on the train to Philadelphia. After dinner on the train, the President arrived at the convention hall with his family and members of the White House staff, shortly before the roll call of states.

Three candidates had been placed in nomination—President Truman, Senator Russell and former Indiana Governor Paul McNutt. The roll call of states resulted, predictably, in an overwhelming vote for the President. The outcome:

President Truman:	947½
Senator Russell:	263
Paul McNutt:	½

Although the convention managers controlled the results, they didn't control the timing. During the nominating process, Truman and Alben Barkley were holed up in a suite beneath the convention hall. The wait seemed like an eternity.

Finally, it was 2 A.M. when President Truman appeared at the rostrum. The delegates had sweltered in the mid-July heat. They were tired. But they weren't wanting for entertainment.

Earlier in the evening, an enraged *Life* photographer had accosted Sam Brightman, then assistant publicity director for the Democratic Convention. "They won't let me take pictures of the dying pigeons," the photographer complained.

Brightman was unsympathetic. He couldn't see any connection between dying pigeons and the proceedings of the Democratic Convention. But it turned out that Emma Guffey Miller, national committeewoman from Pennsylvania, had brought in crates of white pigeons to portray doves of peace.

The pigeons were hot, too. As the pigeons were released from their crates, they soared toward the ceiling fans and the cool air. That, of course, distracted politicians and spectators, who suddenly had no interest in what was happening at the rostrum.

Nervously, they watched the pigeons fly overhead. A group of pigeons swooped toward the rostrum. Speaker Rayburn's shiny pate appeared a likely target. Voices yelled and arms flailed, scattering the pigeons. A second group of pigeons zeroed in on Rayburn. Waving his arms frantically in defense, the speaker-convention chairman shouted, "Get these goddamned pigeons out of here!"

It was probably another first for television, if not for radio. Rayburn's angry words were heard on coast-to-coast radio—

with the picture and words on television from Washington to Boston.

When order was restored, President Truman was fighting mad, too—not at the pigeons, but at the Republicans. His audience was hot, weary and discouraged. Everybody anticipated going home to wage a losing battle against the Republicans. But Truman delivered a speech in those wee hours of July 15 that some have compared to the soaring oratory of William Jennings Bryan.

Speaking extemporaneously, the President said, "Senator Barkley and I will win this election and make those Republicans like it. Don't you forget that. We will do that because they are wrong and we are right and I will prove it to you in just a few minutes."

The delegates perked up. The President went on the offensive against the Republicans, calling them the party of privilege. The 80th Congress wasn't spared the President's scathing words, either.

"Everybody likes to have low taxes, but we must reduce the national debt in times of prosperity," the President said, "and when tax relief can be given, it ought to go to those who need it most and not to those who need it least, as the Republican rich-man tax bill did, as they did when they passed it over my veto on the third try.

"The first one of these tax bills that they sent me was so rotten that they could not stomach it themselves. They finally did send one that was somewhat improved, but it still helps the rich and sticks the knife into the backs of the poor."

Harry Truman had delivered a stemwinder of a speech, but it had played to a limited audience. At 2 A.M., most television viewers and radio listeners had long since gone to bed.

CHAPTER 5

Campaign 1948

THE LAST GAVEL OF THE DEMOCRATIC CONVENTION had barely
fallen when campaign battle lines were drawn on other fronts.

In Philadelphia, the Progressive Party also met in convention (choosing the site because of television, too). As expected, Henry A. Wallace was nominated to run for President,
with Senator Glenn Taylor of Idaho his running mate.

In Birmingham, Alabama, irate Southern Democrats nominated Governor Strom Thurmond of South Carolina and Governor Fielding Wright of Mississippi as the ticket of the States'
Rights group, dubbed the "Dixiecrats." The Dixiecrats posed a
serious threat to the Democrats' chances of winning the 1948
election.

On Monday, July 25, the President addressed the special
joint session of Congress. He outlined an extensive program for
action. Despite pleas from Republican strategists, the Re-
publican-controlled Congress adjourned two weeks later without taking any action on key bills.

That, in turn, set in motion President Truman's campaign
strategy. He branded the legislators the "do nothing" 80th
Congress—and never let up.

At the same time, the President knew he could count on
little, if any, support from the news media. He had to reach out
to the people in person. That meant he would mount one of the
best-known train campaigns in history. Truman traveled
31,473 miles by train in 36 states, giving 351 speeches and
rear-platform talks.

The 1948 campaign was the last in which candidates for President relied heavily on train travel. Truman's rear-platform technique became increasingly successful. "Whistle stops," they were called. And they suited the President's style just fine. Even though the President's approval-poll rating was only 36, he was supremely confident of victory—and his spirit was contagious.

With few exceptions, President Truman didn't use a prepared text from May until the election. The President's new "off the cuff" approach suited his personality and his mood. But then again, off-the-cuff remarks by a President can be dangerous. Fortunately, foreign policy was largely ignored during the campaign.

Meanwhile, Thomas Dewey's style was pallid alongside Truman's fighting words. The Republicans believed everything they read and heard about their upcoming "victory." Dewey even was said to have already picked his Cabinet.

For the first time, television advertising was used to promote presidential candidates. But in 1948, it was merely a toe-in-the-water approach.

The water was tested on October 5, 1948, with the election almost one month away. President Truman spoke in Jersey City, New Jersey, and his remarks were telecast by Newark's WATV (Channel 13). It was the first paid political television appearance by any presidential candidate.

*   *   *

On election night, November 2, 1948, an editor in the *Chicago Tribune's* newsroom looked at his watch. It was 7:45 P.M. The deadline for the bulldog edition stared at him. The paper was going to press early—so it could hit the streets and greet Chicagoans pouring out of moviehouses and theaters.

The editor needed a page 1 headline. It was too long before the final votes would be tabulated. He knew the headline couldn't say something so bland as "Voters Go to Polls." Everybody knew that. He knew that Truman was leading, but those early votes really meant nothing because they came from scattered hinterlands. He knew that the crush of votes would come from the big cities.

Would that turn the tide in favor of Dewey? Probably. The editor wrote: "DEWEY DEFEATS TRUMAN."

Hans Kaltenborn, the radio commentator, shared the editor's inclinations—and those of many other pundits across the nation. In his distinctive voice, Kaltenborn repeatedly told his listeners: "Truman is ahead, but when the country vote is counted, Dewey will be the winner."

The pundits and the headline writers were wrong. Truman swept to victory, and the Democrats carried both houses of Congress. The vote:

President Truman:	24,105,812
Thomas Dewey:	21,070,065
Strom Thurmond:	1,169,021
Henry Wallace:	1,157,172

The electoral college vote:

Truman:	303
Dewey:	189
Thurmond:	38

The President had the last laugh. At Democratic gatherings, he reveled in doing impersonations of Kaltenborn's radio delivery and his election-night forecast. The President also posed for pictures with a winning smile, holding aloft a copy of the *Chicago Tribune's* bulldog edition headlined: "DEWEY DEFEATS TRUMAN."

After Truman's surprise victory, a torrent of contributions surged into Democratic National Committee headquarters. The money was accompanied by letters that struck a common theme: "My secretary forgot to mail this letter." They climbed onto the Truman bandwagon—*after* it crossed the finish line. "Tuesday Democrats," someone dubbed them. They were personally resented by the President.

On January 20, 1949, Chief Justice Fred Vinson administered the oath of office to President Truman. It was another television "first"—the first inaugural ceremony to be televised.

* * *

Things got rockier for President Truman in his new term. Approaching his work in ways that differed from when he first became President in 1945, he emerged, at long last, from the giant shadow cast by Franklin Roosevelt.

Along the way, the President had to deal with the June 25, 1950, invasion by North Korean forces into South Korea. He continued to make tough decisions, such as the widely unpopular decision to fire General Douglas MacArthur as supreme commander of the Allied, United Nations and American forces during the Korean War (on advice of the Joint Chiefs of Staff). He had to cope with the nagging problems involving Senator Joseph McCarthy of Wisconsin and the rise of young Richard Nixon. Truman also was confronted with alleged corruption in his administration. On November 1, 1950, he even survived an assassination attempt at Blair House (where the Trumans lived while the White House was renovated).

For all these troubled waters, the President found time to offer gracious hospitality. While visiting Washington with my wife, my daughter Penny, then 10, and son Jim, 9, during the summer of 1949, I was invited to introduce them to the President in the Oval Office.

There, the President pointed to a painting on his office wall. "Do you know who that is?" he asked.

Penny and Jim shook their heads.

"That's Simon Bolivar," the President said. He was an admirer of Bolivar. He gave the children a 10-minute history lesson on Bolivar's home continent, South America.

*   *   *

On January 4, 1951, President Truman made history when he addressed the Japanese Peace Treaty Organization in San Francisco. It was the first television program broadcast live—from coast to coast—and 107 stations were available for the pickup.

Soon the President turned his attention to politics again—to the 1952 Democratic Convention. Would he run for President again? He mulled it over in April of 1951, while vacationing in Key West, Florida. Returning to Washington, the President told the media that he had made up his mind about the 1952 race, but he said he wasn't yet ready to make an announcement.

At a Democratic National Committee meeting in May, everybody buzzed about a 1952 election pitting the President against Senator Robert Taft of Ohio. (Philadelphia bid to host the convention again, pointing out that it had a time-zone advantage for television. Miami also bid. But the committee picked Chicago.)

When the committee met again in October of 1951, its leadership changed. William M. Boyle, Jr., resigned as chairman because of ill health. The President hand-picked Boyle's successor, Frank McKinney, a successful banker from Indianapolis.

In November, the President called his staff together and said he would not run in 1952. His decision was a well-kept secret for months, during which the President privately asked Chief Justice Vinson if he would become the Democratic Party's candidate in 1952. Vinson responded with an irrevocable "no."

Finally, the decision was made public on March 29, 1952, when President Truman addressed the Jefferson-Jackson Day Democratic dinner at Washington's National Guard Armory. Gasps of surprise rippled across the room when he told the guests: "I shall not be a candidate for re-election."

The Sunday newspapers, meanwhile, missed the story in their early editions. They had gone to press with a previously released—but incomplete—copy of the President's speech.

The field was wide open. Nobody had a head start. The President had difficulty settling on a candidate. Most politicians felt the field wasn't very inspiring: Vice President Barkley (age 74), Senator Estes Kefauver of Tennessee, Senator Robert Kerr of Oklahoma, Senator Richard B. Russell of Georgia, Averell Harriman of New York and a most reluctant governor of Illinois, Adlai Stevenson.

On January 22, 1952, the President invited Adlai Stevenson to the Blair House. Stevenson wouldn't say "yes" or "no." Additional talks with Stevenson were equally non-productive. Some felt that Stevenson wanted no ties to Truman; he believed he could finesse the nomination without being labeled "Truman's man."

As for the other prospects, party officials wanted no part of Kefauver. Although Kerr belonged to the "club," he was too closely associated with the oil lobby. At the last minute, Vice President Barkley lost labor's support, so he wasn't in contention. Harriman was a Democrat with experience, but he lacked delegate support and had never run for an elective office. Of all the prospects, Senator Russell probably was best equipped to be President, but he lacked backing outside the Solid South. Just about every discussion pointed to the reluctant candidate: Adlai Stevenson.

While the Democrats searched all over the landscape for a candidate, the Republicans lined up in two sharply defined camps: the well-organized forces of Robert Taft, and the anti-Taft group that was trying to woo General Eisenhower as the party's standard-bearer.

Eisenhower was getting restless. From Europe, he sent a

message in January of 1952, saying that he would run for President if he received a "clear-cut call." That, of course, was a 180-degree turn from his position in 1948.

Reporters questioned Eisenhower, and the man who commanded the NATO armies coyly reversed his field again. "Under no circumstances," he said, "will I ask for relief from this assignment in order to seek nomination to political office and I shall not participate in the pre-convention activities of others who may have such an intention with respect to me."

By late spring, however, Eisenhower sought relief from his NATO command. He returned to the United States and engaged in a strenuous, pre-convention campaign against Taft.

Why did Eisenhower reverse his 1948 stand? Was it because he disliked Truman and all he stood for? If so, where did his intense dislike for Truman originate? Was it the firing of MacArthur? Was it contempt for a man he felt wasn't capable of being Commander-in-Chief? Was it because of the striking difference in their personalities?

Certainly Truman went out of his way to express his admiration of—and confidence in—Eisenhower. Whatever Eisenhower's reason for tossing his hat into the ring, the enmity was deep-seated and lasting. In his book, *Tumultuous Years*, Robert Donovan would quote Eisenhower as saying that the reason he had run for President was to prevent the Truman Administration from "continuing in power." Eisenhower also would tell Donovan that he wouldn't have run if he'd known that Stevenson would be the Democratic nominee.

* * *

Television would, for the first, time, cover the New Hampshire primaries in 1952. So many radio and TV reporters descended on some New Hampshire towns to cover the nation's first primary election that it all bewildered party pros. In one town, party officials sent out extra ballots for the reporters.

On primary day, March 11, NBC originated ten radio and television film broadcasts from New Hampshire. Cameramen often waged losing battles trudging through 20-foot-deep piles of snow to the polling places.

It was clear that the national political convention was being nudged aside as the device for selecting presidential candidates. Did the power of television cause this change? Or did the electorate's desires change?

One problem with primaries is that they generally center on

a single emotional issue. Those relatively few people who participate in them impose their will on the majority because the majority don't show up at the polling places.

Even though it would be a new experience, the 1952 New Hampshire primary was covered with comparative ease. The battle lines were sharply drawn: Kefauver, a spokesman for the Truman forces, went up against Harold Stassen (Eisenhower's spokesman) and Robert Taft (MacArthur's candidate). In the end, the primary winners were General Eisenhower and Senator Kefauver.

President Truman's name had been entered without his authorization. "All these primaries," he complained, "are just eyewash." Indeed, back in 1952, Truman was right. The primaries didn't really wield their full power in dictating the choice of the conventions until 1976, when Georgia's Jimmy Carter came out of nowhere to win the Democratic nomination and run against incumbent Gerald Ford.

One irony about television back in those early years was that the medium was expected to make campaigning easier. But television, in a sense, has contributed to more primaries—and thereby made running for President an often impossible test of stamina and resources.

SCENE II

Fade Out Radio—
Cut to Television

CHAPTER 6

Chicago
Summer 1952

Johnnie Ray sang "Cry," the No. 1 hit on "Your Lucky Strike Hit Parade," which peddled cigarettes with "fine tobacco," years before they became "hazardous to your health". . . . For $5, you could "fill er' up" at the gas pumps. . . . Tract homes in suburbia sprang up all over the place for less than you can buy a compact car today: $6,000. . . . Gary Cooper rode to an Oscar in "High Noon," and Dwight Eisenhower went around whistling the theme song for months. . . . Americans crawled out of their bomb shelters, entertained over their barbecues and could see prosperity forever.

THE DEMOCRATS CHOSE TO FOLLOW THE REPUBLICANS into convention so they'd know whom—and what—they'd be up against in the presidential sweepstakes. The year 1952 would bring the first nationally televised convention.

Before the convention in Chicago's International Amphitheatre, the Republican National Committee waged a crucial battle over credentials. The meeting was scheduled for the Grand Ballroom of the Hilton Hotel. But the scene of the battle was moved to a night club called the Boulevard Room. Reason: Uninvited TV cameras, newsreel cameras and radio microphones were all over the Grand Ballroom.

The Boulevard Room offered tight security. Or did it? No one except members of the credentials committee and the writing press was admitted. That angered TV executives, who demanded equal rights for television. But Taft's supporters distrusted television; they voted to keep the TV cameras out. The pro-Eisenhower-Dewey forces voted in favor of television. In the end, the Taft forces won. No TV or newsreel cameras were allowed.

Meanwhile, a WBBM radio engineer remembered that a "hot" mike connection existed inside the Boulevard Room—to be used for band pickups. Soon the recorders were humming. Within 20 minutes, CBS went on the air with a half-hour program showcasing the bitter, blow-by-blow credentials fight over the selection of the Texas and Georgia delegations. The credentials battle between the Taft and Eisenhower forces over the naming of the members of the Texas and Georgia delegations was crucial to the vote for the nomination. The Eisenhower people won this battle.

Television carried its fight for equal access to every meeting, long after the convention began. On Tuesday, July 8—the second day of the convention—the credentials committee voted unanimously to open its proceedings to television and newsreels. The battle for equal access was over. Television—the new kid on the block—had won.

Several days before the Republican Convention, I arranged for a Hilton Hotel room to be equipped with four television sets and four radios. With several assistants, including Elmo Ellis from WSB in Atlanta and Bob Swan of the Katz Advertising Agency, I monitored the GOP convention from start to finish.

This was the beginning of the television era, and it was marked by on-the-job training for everybody involved—convention programmers, candidates, all other politicians and all of the news media, especially the TV networks.

On July 8, one day after the convention began, NBC faced a difficult decision—to continue carrying the convention or switch to the All-Star baseball game. The network switched to the game—after Senator Styles Bridges was introduced—at 12:28 P.M. Two hours later, the convention adjourned.

For the most part, the Republicans conducted the convention as if television didn't exist. One speaker, however, did play to the TV audience—the wily senator from Illinois, Everett Dirksen. He was a natural showman, with the flair of a Shakespearean actor.

Dramatically, he paused in his speech. The hall fell silent.

The spotlight trained on Dirksen, an orator from the old school. Slowly, with the rapt attention of all, he raised his arm. He pointed to Governor Dewey, who sat with the New York delegation. The cameras suddenly focused on Dewey.

"Twice," Dirksen said, his mellifluous voice rising, "twice you led us down the road to defeat. You shall not do it again!" The drama crescendoed with a chorus of boos.

Meanwhile, things heated up during a session that dealt with credentials. But an exchange between the floor and the podium helped provide comedy relief. When the three-member Puerto Rican delegation asked for a poll of its members, the delegation chairman, Judge Marcelino Romani, spoke with a heavy Spanish accent.

Romani's words weren't always understood by the man who pounded the gavel—former House Speaker Joseph Martin, the convention chairman, who hailed from Massachusetts. Their exchange was reminiscent of Abbott and Costello's "Who's on first?" routine.

Most of the politicking, however, went on backstage and in smoke-filled rooms, far from the prying eye of the TV cameras. Political strategists suggested to Eisenhower that he pick, as his running mate, a young senator from California—Richard Nixon. The argument was that Nixon added a good geographic mix to the ticket. He spoke out loudly against communism. He was young and had an attractive wife. Eisenhower was sold: He chose Nixon for the No. 2 spot on the ticket.

* * *

The networks made the most of the limited equipment available in 1952. For the first time, they gave the voters an intimate view of the convention process of choosing a presidential candidate. An estimated 60 million viewers watched the 1952 conventions on black-and-white TV screens (about 18 million television sets were in use); 1,200 radio stations provided coverage for 106 million radio sets.

The television pool, under Robert Doyle's direction, used seven cameras. The radio pool installed and operated the convention's central audio system, furnishing microphones that served the platform and each State's delegation. Television used the same audio facilities.

Microphones on the convention floor were controlled rigidly by the presiding officer. No one was heard without the chairman's approval. The audio engineer, George McElrath of NBC, sat near the front of the rostrum and turned on the delegation microphones only when directed by the chairman.

To add to the drama, we paid attention to small details. For instance, to make the pounding of the gavel more emphatic, we installed a "peanut mike" on the gavel sounding board.

It was soon apparent that long-accepted convention procedures needed streamlining. It would be necessary to scrap the lengthy nominating speeches, the innumerable seconding speeches and the demonstrations, often carried out by paid demonstrators. Many techniques aimed at exciting everybody in the audience at conventions in the early years became uninteresting—and often boring—to the voters who watched from their living rooms.

* * *

Monitoring the Republican proceedings paid off for the Democrats. The Republicans had handed the Democrats a great publicity play when they barred all cameras and microphones from the national committee meeting that included the fight over credentials. Frank McKinney, chairman of the Democratic National Committee, announced that the Democrats were the "party of the people." All committee meetings, he said, would be open to the media at all times.

Radio and television were allocated 50,000 square feet on the Amphitheatre's second floor for operating facilities. They also had been given space at the Hilton Hotel, the convention headquarters.

In 1948, the convention committee paid for radio and television installations. By custom, convention officials had provided all media space free. But, with nationwide television making inroads, the physical requirements of TV became too costly for the convention to underwrite. After considerable haggling over the matter, the networks agreed to assume all their installation costs.

Those financial burdens, of course, were lightened when both the Democrats and the Republicans agreed to let the networks run commercials during their convention coverage. That paved the way for Betty Furness' appearances on those Westinghouse spots on CBS. Philco and Admiral were sponsors for NBC and ABC, respectively. To present these commercials, studios were built on the Amphitheatre's roomy second floor.

The 1952 conventions were "media events" and created new logistical problems. Space had to be provided for newspapers, periodicals and press associations. Still photographers needed dark rooms, which required special plumbing. Space was provided for the railroad lounge, the airline lounge, a telephone center, Western Union and a post office. Police and fire stations were provided, as were 24-hour emergency medical facilities. AT&T installed 670,000 miles of teletypewriter circuits serving 7,500 press locations. Illinois Bell put in 1,000 telephones, 30 telephoto channels, 25 radio channels, 70 audio-visual channels and 12 microwave dishes.

Caucus rooms at the convention hall were always important. For convention business, several rooms had to be available on demand for a state caucus. Behind the rostrum was a layout of offices for convention operating personnel, including a private office for the chairman.

I also pushed for a large waiting room for upcoming convention participants. I preferred that participants relax with soft drinks, tea or coffee 30 minutes before their appearance. Then, moments before their appearance, they were asked to stand, out of sight, at the rear of the platform. That way, no time was lost between the introduction and the appearance.

By custom, the press had 500 seats on either side of the rostrum. In these areas, most seats stayed vacant most of the time. It was difficult to explain away those vacant seats when party regulars complained that they couldn't get seats. To head off party regulars' complaints, we placed large signs over the press seating area: "Reserved for Press," The empty seats, clearly shown on television, were a nagging irritation despite the signs.

If television changed the way conventions went about their business, it also prompted changes in the way conventions were reported in the news media. Pen-and-pencil reporters soon came to lean on television. The wire services, large newspapers and periodicals all provided their desks with television receivers. Editors told reporters to write about the proceedings with more depth and background because, after all, their readers had watched it all on television.

We arranged for each network's studios to be positioned high above the convention floor, behind the rostrum. Designated originally as radio studios, they quickly were converted for television. NBC started the changeover by squeezing a television camera into its radio studio. To supplement its live and film coverage, NBC also used a Polaroid camera to deliver developed pictures in only one minute. The network hired a laboratory staff to process film.

Few issues raised the blood pressure of convention planners more than the one pertaining to fixed camera stands on the convention floor. The Republicans solved the problem easily: No cameras could interfere with any seating.

Because of this arbitrary decision by the Republicans, television's style was cramped. The cameras were able to focus only on side-angle shots of the speaker's rostrum. Moreover, these side views presented annoying distractions in the background. The depth of focus for each camera gave a cluttered picture of news people, politicians and messengers moving throughout an area that seemed to be alongside the speaker.

I talked to Frank McKinney about getting a clean, head-on shot of the Democratic Convention rostrum, which would add immeasurably to the effectiveness of the speaker on television. The camera would be mounted on a stand 55 feet from the front of the rostrum. That posed two disadvantages: The loss of seats with a clear view of the speaker, and the pre-empting by television of seats that had been reserved for important guests.

How to remedy the problem? I proposed putting several television sets behind the new camera stand, so delegates could watch on the monitors what they were missing in person. Everybody was irritated by the location of that central-camera stand. Everybody, that is, except the TV audience, which responded enthusiastically to the head-on shots.

My next problem was allocating space on the new camera stand. We ordered a stand built with three decks: still photographers on the first deck, newsreels on the recessed second deck and TV cameras on the top deck. The long lens in use at that time was sensitive to even the slightest movement. Therefore we made arrangements for a stand that wouldn't vibrate. We stationed guards all around the stand and gave the photographers and cameramen specific instructions: Once they got on that stand, they had to stay until the session finished.

I also got approval from the Democratic National Committee to scale down invocations and benedictions to two minutes. Most religious leaders willingly cooperated. A few said, quite bluntly, that I must be a son of Satan to dare tamper with the Lord's message. My reply to them: "It's still two minutes, if you want to stay on the program." They stayed.

Not the least of our problems, too, was the little red light on each TV camera, telling whoever was on camera that they were, indeed, on live television. As a result, everybody in the camera's line of sight with a red light at the Republican Convention instantly became actors and actresses. For the Democratic Convention, I got the networks—at CBS President Frank Stanton's suggestion—to move the red light alongside the camera's viewfinder, so it was visible only to the cameraman.

*   *   *

Taking cues from the Republicans' trial-and-error convention, we wanted to make every participant in the Democratic Convention as television-conscious as possible. We sent them mailings in advance of their journey to Chicago. When the participants arrived, we distributed reminder sheets. At the convention hall, we placed reminder cards on each seat. We urged everybody to remember that the TV camera was an all-seeing eye. We cautioned them that a closeup shot might provide information by lip reading. We asked that they refrain from reading newspapers while the convention was in session—a habit that wasn't broken during the 1952 convention.

The important thing, we told the participants, was to conduct themselves with decorum and dignity, as if they were on camera all the time. We cautioned speakers about proper clothing; we advised women to avoid flashy jewelry; we tried to shorten the speeches, but we were bucking a political tradition of long-windedness, and we asked the delegates to leave the floor if ever they got into a heated argument. That was wishful thinking.

For the most part, the participants cooperated. But habits acquired from having attended many political conventions weren't going to be changed by a few reminders about conduct.

It didn't take long, meanwhile, for the delegates to realize that if they challenged their state's vote and asked for a poll of their fellow delegates, they had a good chance of being on coast-to-coast TV. That set off a rash of requests to "poll the delegation." I sensed it might happen, but I couldn't get the rules changed fast enough to head off the problem before the Democratic Convention.

We did, however, succeed in changing the rule after the 1952 convention. Thereafter a request for a poll of the delegation automatically passed the state in the roll call. A representative of the chairman went to the delegation and handled the poll—off camera. In subsequent conventions, the requests for polls of delegations declined back to normal.

Common convention installation costs were split with the Republicans. They had used a plain board front for the rostrum area. For the Democratic Convention, I managed to obtain wallpaper, which gave a three-dimensional effect to the rostrum—a pictorial improvement on black-and-white TV. At the same time, the back door was decorated to provide a good backdrop for television pickups of important people who entered the convention hall.

We also planned the decorations with TV in mind. In an immense amphitheater, there is only so much you can do with red-white-and-blue bunting and flags. So we arranged the decorations, mindful of the camera locations. We put up several large signs with easily read slogans. The largest sign stretched high across the back of the rostrum. It read: "20 YEARS OF PROGRESS." Five large illustrations were placed in easy camera range: Presidents Jefferson, Jackson, Wilson, Roosevelt and Truman. The Republicans had put up only one picture: President Lincoln.

To avoid unnecessary reflection and glare in the TV cameras, the wooden floors, chairs and writing benches in the press section—which were unpainted during the Republican Convention—were painted gray by the Democrats.

Arrangements for music weren't left to chance, either. The Republicans had chosen to position conductor Lou Breeze and his orchestra on one side of the hall—across from the rostrum. They lost contact—and control—of the orchestra. By contrast, we managed to synchronize the music with the program at the Democratic Convention. We moved the orchestra directly behind the rostrum, up one flight of stairs. That way, the soloist could appear at the rostrum in full view of the convention.

And by controlling the music, we controlled the demonstrations. I didn't want the Democrats to do anything like the Republicans did, for instance, after Eisenhower won the nomination. Apparently unaware of what had happened, the orchestra played "Only Make Believe."

At the Republican Convention, too, the speakers had to fight their way to the speaker's podium, which created distractions on the television screen. For the Democrats, we built a 6-foot staircase, properly carpeted, directly behind the speaker's platform. The area was kept clear so the speaker could walk unrestrained to the podium, thereby making a good picture for the head-on cameras.

For each wire service and the networks, we also provided fixed desks on the rostrum. They were convenient to my desk in front of the rostrum, where I had telephones to keep everybody advised of schedule changes. I followed television on four monitors.

We ran such a tight schedule at the Democratic Convention—especially during the early sessions—that the networks complained they didn't have enough time to insert commercials. I told them to relax because sooner or later they'd have more time than they needed. In fact, during the Republican Convention, the networks discovered that some of the routine business of the convention wasn't very entertaining. Indeed, it was boring, all of which led to the increased use of camera gimmicks and commentary.

At the 1952 conventions, one newsman with only a year's service at CBS delivered particularly effective commentary. His name: Walter Cronkite. The CBS staff also included Edward R. Murrow, Eric Sevareid, Lowell Thomas, Robert Trout, Douglas Edwards and Charles Collingwood.

NBC's convention-reporting team included John Cameron Swayze, Dave Garroway, H. V. Kaltenborn, Morgan Beatty, Earl Godwin, Richard Harkness and Robert McCormick. Two relative unknowns also had joined the NBC team: David Brinkley and Clifton Utley.

ABC operated with a lean staff, but one that was most aggressive and innovative: John Daly, Elmer Davis, Martin Agronsky and Austin Kiplinger.

For its listeners on radio, the Mutual Broadcasting System assigned the following team: Bill Henry, William Hillman, Gabriel Heater, Fulton Lewis, Jr., and Frank Singiser. Another reporter who covered the 1952 conventions would one day establish his own syndicated radio and television commentary which, more than 30 years later, is still going strong. His name: Paul Harvey.

*   *   *

On the convention floor, the Republicans had considerable trouble with walkie-talkies used by members of the news media. The Republicans constantly had the sergeant-at-arms throw out the walkie-talkies. Then, after the networks complained, they were readmitted. For the Democratic Convention, I tried to solve this problem by limiting each network to no more than two walkie-talkies on the floor at any one time.

Credentials, too, were a problem—and will be at conventions forever. After numerous meetings with the media, we divided media credentials into three classifications: "Go Anywhere," "Go Most Anywhere" (allowing the bearer access to all areas except the platform) and "General" (allowing access to everywhere except the floor or platform).

Even today, there remains a powerful, animal urge by all media people, all politicians and all self-styled dignitaries and guests to get on the convention floor and the platform. I managed to control access to the platform. The convention floor was another problem.

To gain access to the convention floor, people of otherwise reputable character resorted to all sorts of subterfuge, including bribery. One delegate would collect a dozen floor badges from fellow delegates already on the floor, then go outside and distribute these admittance badges to friends or, even worse, to avowed supporters of a contending candidate. At one convention, a specially cut red-white-and-blue ribbon was the admittance badge to the floor. By the second session, vendors outside the hall were hawking these ribbons at $1 apiece.

Human nature being what it is, I'm convinced that there's no easy and sure way to control admittance to the convention floor completely. If top-security methods were imposed, the delegates probably wouldn't tolerate it.

Even so, I knew we'd need tight security in some areas. While planning for the 1952 convention, I suggested that we put guards at vulnerable locations—such as those where somebody could cut off the air conditioning. Frank McKinney laughed, but he agreed that a breakdown of air conditioning—especially on a sweltering July night in Chicago—would force the convention to adjourn.

History tells us that forced adjournments have caused problems. At the 1876 Republican Convention in Cincinnati, the favorite to win the nomination was Maine's James C. Blaine, former Speaker of the House. Because he was a shoo-in on the first ballot, his opponents frantically tried to force an adjournment. They didn't have the votes to obtain an adjournment.

They had someone cut the main gas pipe to the convention hall, causing the lights to go out. The session was adjourned.

The next morning, Blaine couldn't rekindle the enthusiasm that he had built up the night before. The winner of the nomination was Governor Rutherford B. Hayes of Ohio. In 1952, Frank McKinney approved the additional security-guard service.

I also placed guards in key areas of the public-address system to avoid a recurrence of the 1940 "voice from the sewers" episode. With President Roosevelt bidding for a third term, Mayor Kelly stationed his superintendent of the Chicago sewers in the basement of the Chicago Stadium. There, the superintendent was given a microphone that was wired to the PA system. On cue, he chanted into the microphone—and delegates, alternates and guests throughout the hall heard those chants blasting through the loudspeakers: "We want Roosevelt! Roosevelt! Roosevelt!"

I assured Frank McKinney, too, that we would have the roll-call ballots printed and available when needed. In the 1860 Republican Convention, the first roll call was about to begin when the necessary tabulation sheets were discovered missing. So was the printer. The roll call had to be postponed.

As for seating arrangements on the rostrum, I was careful to avoid any distracting movement. At my desk, I watched four television monitors, one for each network and the pool. I had a telephone line to the office behind the platform, another to the orchestra, another to the entrance (for use by the chairman, in case a VIP had a ticket problem). I also talked on separate phone lines to each network production manager, the pool production manager and the lighting director.

Seated alongside the speaker's podium was the Democratic Party's veteran parliamentarian, Missouri Congressman Clarence Cannon, who had served the party since 1920. By the second session's end, stacks of telegrams had arrived from people who wanted to know who the "ugly guy" on the rostrum was.

Tactfully—or, so I thought—I moved Cannon's chair to the side, out of camera range. The parliamentarian promptly moved his chair back to its original position. He turned to me and said, "I know why you're moving me—I admit I don't take a good picture, but I must hear what is going on." Whereupon he clasped his right ear and said, "This is the only ear that works." For the rest of the convention, we kept Clarence Cannon's chair in its original position.

* * *

The TelePrompter of 1952 was primitive and cumbersome. Today, clear glass outriggers show the speaking text in an easy-to-follow fashion.

At the 1952 GOP Convention, most speakers used the Tele-Prompter. The equipment below the platform was operated by hand. The operator turned the speaking script, which rested on the rostrum. During former President Herbert Hoover's speech, the TelePrompter operator rolled the text too slowly. Hoover was heard to say, in exasperation, "Move it on, move it on!"

From their perches high behind the rostrum, the network television cameras—equipped with long lenses—zoomed in on the text. Viewers at home could watch the words roll into— and out of—view. At one point, they saw a word that looked out of place in the script. Actually, the word specified that there should be audience reaction at that point in the speech. The word: "Cheers."

Because of these and other problems, we decided to bar the TelePrompter at the 1952 Democratic Convention. That didn't stop Irving Kahn, the enterprising president of the Tele-Prompter Company. He prevailed upon several speakers to use the prompter in spite of our ban.

* * *

Who would give the keynote address?

Because the permanent chairman, Sam Rayburn, was from the Congress, custom dictated that we turn to a governor to be temporary chairman and keynoter: Governor Paul A. Dever of Massachusetts.

I first met Dever in a Mayflower Hotel suite. Frank McKinney and I wanted to know what he would say in his keynote address so we could make sure all Democratic Convention speeches would carry a uniform theme.

I sat in the back of the room, studying Dever, listening to his remarks, watching his facial expressions. Television was so new—and this man was to represent the Democratic Party on the popular "Meet the Press" program later that day. The program's hosts, Lawrence Spivak and Martha Roundtree, had made a successful transition with the program from radio to television. "Meet the Press" was then, as now, a "hot vehicle" for politicians.

As our meeting ended, Frank McKinney asked if I had any suggestions for Governor Dever's appearance on "Meet the Press." McKinney explained to the governor that I was the Democrats' television expert.

Reluctantly, I began: "In the first place, don't let them use any side-angle shots."

A deadly silence fell over the room.

"Why not?" Dever asked coldly.

For the moment, I was tongue-tied. Apparently the governor wasn't accustomed to negative suggestions. Finally, I replied: "To get the full character of Governor Dever, you need to use head-on shots—and *only* head-on shots."

I didn't have the heart to tell the governor that his drooping jowls—photographed from the side—only reinforced the public's impression of tired, shoddy politicians. We didn't need that impression on coast-to-coast television. Unfortunately, "Meet the Press" used side-angle shots of Dever. The reaction was predictably negative.

With the first gavel only 24 hours away, I checked the facilities throughout the hall, which was empty, except for a few workmen and Governor Dever and his aides. The air conditioning was going full blast. I told one of Dever's aides that the governor would have throat problems if he rehearsed too much in the chilly convention hall. Despite our suggestion, Dever went on rehearsing.

When he delivered the speech the next night, Dever's voice gave out. Too many rehearsals in the cold indoors had caught up with him. What's more, the speech was too long. Dever died as a keynoter.

Right after Dever's speech, there was a lull in the convention. Behind the platform, I walked through the chairman's office. There, a lonely disheartened man sat with his head in his hands. "I missed my great opportunity," he said forlornly. "I missed my great opportunity."

It was Governor Dever. He went on to lose his next election.

* * *

It was soon evident that television told the viewer at home more about what was happening at the convention than the delegate could learn on the convention floor. Most of the delegates had little or no information about crucial committee meetings that went on at the headquarters hotel while the convention was in session at the amphitheater. For the first time ever, those at the convention called home to find out what was going on at the convention.

With television in mind, we suggested several resolutions calling for changes in procedure before the next session. At the daytime session on Wednesday, July 23, the convention adopted these changes to streamline the program:

1. Nominating speeches limited to 15 minutes, seconding speeches to five minutes each, and total time in seconding speeches not to exceed ten minutes.

2. All floor demonstrations restricted to duly elected delegates and alternates—and limited to 20 minutes. No paid demonstrators. (This resolution gave us some control over convention-floor traffic. It was said that during the GOP Convention, about 150 paid demonstrators worked for all candidates and that they merely switched banners for each demonstration.)

3. All music for demonstrations to be provided by the convention orchestra—and limited to 20 minutes.

To speed up the proceedings, too, we tried to push through a resolution limiting nominations only to serious candidates. But that effort failed.

*   *   *

President Truman had said he wouldn't go to the Democratic Convention until after the party's presidential candidates were nominated. But the President showed up ahead of time, anyway. He arrived in Chicago by plane at 3:30 on Friday afternoon, July 25.

The Democrats weren't even close to picking a nominee. One thing was certain: The President was not an Estes Kefauver man. He felt the senator from Tennessee was ignorant of history, an amateur in politics and not deserving of the nomination. The President sent word to Averell Harriman, suggesting that he withdraw and throw his support to Governor Adlai E. Stevenson of Illinois.

Many others felt that if Senator Richard Russell of Georgia

had been from a Northern state, he could have been nominated and perhaps elected.

At the start of the Friday evening session, Paul Fitzpatrick, chairman of the New York delegation, read a message from Averell Harriman that signified that the drums were beating for Stevenson. Harriman withdrew as a candidate and asked his supporters to vote for Stevenson. Governor Dever also withdrew and he, too, asked his backers to rally behind Stevenson.

The roll call was well in progress when Kefauver sensed that the convention was marching to a different drum—not Kefauver's, but Stevenson's. Kefauver strode purposefully to the platform, followed closely by Senator Paul Douglas of Illinois.

At Kefauver's request, I escorted Chairman Rayburn to the rear of the platform. Kefauver wanted to break into the roll call and withdraw. No way, Rayburn said. The chairman pointed out that roll calls couldn't be stopped for anybody withdrawing his candidacy. Parliamentarian Cannon agreed.

Kefauver was furious. Douglas, a Kefauver backer, shared his pique. Muttering complaints, they paced the floor at the rear of the platform. I guessed that they got limited camera coverage. They had no authority to be on the platform, but I decided to leave them alone and not force them off the platform.

Besides, I was busy getting in touch with Senator Russell to make sure he would be present at roll call's end. Russell rushed to the convention hall and arrived on the platform, just as the Canal Zone cast two votes for Stevenson.

When the roll call was over, Senator Kefauver had cooled off. He asked his followers to join him in working to elect Governor Stevenson as President. Senator Russell joined the pro-Stevenson chorus. The rush was on.

Utah switched its 12 votes to Stevenson, which gave him the number he needed to win: 617½. The chairman of the Minnesota delegation then moved that the convention cast a unanimous ballot for Stevenson. The convention concurred with cheers and applause. The Democrats had their nominee, at last.

Would Stevenson have been nominated on the first ballot if he had accepted President Truman's invitation in January of 1952? Would Eisenhower have consented to be a candidate if Stevenson had declared his availability as early as January? Would Stevenson have been elected President if he had accepted the Truman Administration's record and worked in harmony with President Truman?

* * *

During a lull in the proceedings prior to the presentation of the candidate, we arranged the platform seating, and a Secret Service agent placed a fresh glass and bottled water on the rostrum for the President.

Then the band struck up "Hail to the Chief." President Truman entered the hall, accompanied by Adlai Stevenson and members of his family. They made an impressive entrance, but not many television viewers saw it. Again, it was far past midnight, and most TV sets had been turned off.

Addressing the convention, the President said, "I pledge to you now I am going to take my coat off and do everything I can to help Adlai Stevenson win."

Several times during his speech, the President reached for a glass of water. To my horror, he clasped the glass used by everyone—not the sterile glass provided by the Secret Service. Apparently no harm was done.

It was 2:10 A.M. when President Truman introduced the Democratic Party's presidential nominee. I winced at the late hour for such an important event. I said to myself: "Will we ever learn?"

The last previous acceptance speech away from the convention had been televised. Back in 1928, Governor Al Smith accepted the Democratic nomination in the assembly chamber of the state capitol in Albany, New York. His speech was broadcast by the General Electric television station in Schenectady, New York.

* * *

After candidate Stevenson's acceptance speech, everybody gathered on the platform for picture-taking. Stevenson posed at the rostrum with President Truman. They were joined by Vice President Barkley and his wife.

Mrs. Truman remained in the presidential box. I had to choose between placing Mrs. Barkley out of camera range or putting Mrs. Truman next to the President. I asked Mrs. Truman to join the group at the rostrum, but she demurred.

I told her that Mrs. Barkley had pushed herself up front and that we needed the President's wife in the picture. She finally consented and moved slowly to a place alongside the President.

The convention session adjourned at 2:25 A.M. A tenth session was called for Saturday morning at 11 o'clock—to nominate the vice-presidential candidate.

Adlai Stevenson hadn't chosen a running mate. Richard Russell declined to run in the No. 2 spot. He was asked to submit a list of prospects: Lyndon Johnson of Texas, George Smathers of Florida, Albert Gore of Tennessee and John Sparkman of Alabama. Senator Sparkman had been endorsed by President Truman.

In the end, Sparkman was chosen. His fellow Alabama senator, Lister Hill, asked to place Sparkman's name in nomination Saturday morning.

I worried about that Saturday session. Two previous late-night sessions—and the mere formality of the Saturday session—portended sparse attendance. And a bad television picture.

My worst fears had materialized when I arrived at the convention hall one hour before the scheduled 11 A.M. opening. Empty seats were everywhere. Even the delegate area was deserted. For the first time I hoped that not many television viewers would be watching. I advised the networks to forget 11 A.M. and to plan on a noon start.

I had brought stacks of resolutions to the hall that day. And when we started at noon, we passed and passed and passed resolutions, hoping that most of the seats would fill up. Finally, the chairman—with a generous head count—decided that we had a quorum.

Senator Sparkman was put in nomination. So were two women—India Edwards, vice chairman of the Democratic National Committee, and Judge Sarah T. Hughes. After the nominating and seconding speeches, the two women withdrew.

By prearrangement, James A. Farley, the veteran Democratic leader from New York, moved for suspension of the rules and for the nomination of Senator John J. Sparkman by acclamation.

Introduced by Stevenson, Sparkman wisely kept his acceptance speech short. It was 2:20 P.M. when the gavel pounded the 1952 Democratic Convention to a close.

And so ended the age of innocence in televised political conventions.

CHAPTER 7

Campaign 1952

WHY NOT BOOK THE PRESIDENTIAL CANDIDATES, both Republican and Democratic, on the same television program—hopefully in the same studio—together?

To me, the idea was so appealing that I couldn't wait to suggest it to my friends in politics and the networks. I first went to Frank Stanton, the president of CBS.

"Look," I said, "the Republican candidate's remarks generally make page 1 of the major newspapers. The Democratic candidate often appears on page 10. And more than 80 percent of the newspapers in this country favor the Republicans. If both candidates appear on the same TV program, we could reach Republican voters—and undecided voters."

I had long been convinced that Democratic broadcasts reached, for the most part, Democrats. If the Democrats were to win in 1952, they'd have to reach more than Democrats.

Frank Stanton agreed. He, too, had been thinking about a joint appearance of the Democratic and Republican presidential candidates. He thought the networks would cooperate if only the Section 315 problem could be resolved. Section 315 of the Communications Act of 1934 is an "equal-time" statute which states, in part:

> . . . If any licensee shall permit any person who is a legally
> qualified candidate for any public office to use a broadcasting
> station, he shall afford equal opportunities to all other such
> candidates for that office in the use of such broadcasting station:
> Provided, that such licensee shall have no power of censorship

over the material broadcast under the provisions of this section.
No obligation is hereby imposed upon any licensee to allow the
use of its station by any such candidate. . . .

In other words, if the networks gave free time to the Democratic and Republican candidates, they had to give the same
free time to all other qualified presidential candidates in 1952,
including 18 from such parties as the Vegetarian, Church of
God Bible, Greenback, Socialist Labor, Spiritual and Poor
Man. During one gubernatorial race in Georgia, Atlanta station
WSB-TV had to give free time to 12 other candidates to present
the two major candidates on free television time.

In 1960, the debates between John Kennedy and Richard
Nixon would be made possible by a temporary suspension of
Section 315 as it applied to presidential candidates. In 1976,
the League of Women Voters would be able to stage a "debate"
between President Ford and his Democratic challenger, Jimmy
Carter. This was made possible by a liberal interpretation of
the news-event portion of Section 315. The same interpretation
made possible the televised confrontation between President
Carter and Governor Ronald Reagan, the Republican challenger, in 1980. But these presentations by the League of
Women Voters in 1976 and 1980 weren't a satisfactory solution
to the problems of Section 315.

Frank Stanton, joined by other industry leaders over the
years, had waged an unsuccessful campaign to repeal Section
315.

In ensuing years, Congress has been strangely reluctant to
give the television industry any relief from the equal-time
restrictions, even when they pertain to major presidential candidates. Broadcasters generally feel that since the equal-time
provision benefits incumbents, it's extremely difficult to get
officeholders to repeal Section 315.

In 1952, I tried to line up the presidential candidates on the
networks and worry about Section 315 later. After all, we did
have a Democratic Congress, so we could reasonably expect
some relief.

When I suggested the idea to Adlai Stevenson, he liked the
prospect of appearing with Eisenhower on the television networks. That same day, I put out feelers. Soon, however, I
learned that I was considered "a Truman man" and therefore
my ideas weren't acceptable to many in Stevenson's organization.

NBC President Joseph McConnell invited candidates Stevenson and Eisenhower to appear together on his network. Stevenson's headquarters office in Springfield, Illinois, turned down the offer of free television time.

As expected, Eisenhower turned thumbs down on the idea. When asked about NBC's offer of a television debate, Eisenhower's campaign manager Arthur Summerfield said, "The Republican Party is perfectly capable of conducting its own campaign." Summerfield's reasoning: "Eisenhower is better known to the American public and would have more to lose than gain." Perhaps Richard Nixon should have taken Summerfield's words to heart in 1960.

During the 1952 campaign, Stevenson faced a largely hostile press. Large partisan newspapers not only blacked out Stevenson's side on their editorial pages, but used biased headlines and buried Democratic activities on the back pages. The larger news weeklies were, for the most part, pro-Eisenhower.

As we would find out when John Kennedy debated Richard Nixon in 1960, a joint appearance by Stevenson and Eisenhower on national television would have added up to the publicity break needed by the Democrats.

In time, I would reminisce with Adlai Stevenson, during his tenure as U.N. Ambassador, about the 1952 campaign. "Leonard, I believe I would have been elected President," he said, "if you had been successful in getting me the television debate with Eisenhower." I had to agree.

* * *

After the 1952 convention, I visited Frank McKinney, the Democratic National Committee chairman, in his suite at the Broadmoor Hotel, Colorado Springs. We were rehashing the convention when the telephone rang.

McKinney answered, and whoever was on the line didn't exactly impart good news. McKinney tried to control his temper, but he slammed down the receiver.

"I've just been fired," he said. That was Governor Stevenson. He doesn't want me as National Chairman since I'm so closely tied to President Truman. He's going to appoint Steve Mitchell, a lawyer from Chicago."

McKinney telephoned President Truman. The President was incredulous; he told McKinney that was the first he'd heard of any change. Candidate Stevenson hadn't given the President the courtesy of a call before he fired McKinney.

A short time later, I was in the Oval Office with President Truman. Stevenson's schedule indicated that he was campaigning in Baltimore. The President asked the operator to call Governor Stevenson. A few minutes later, the operator said that Stevenson was busy and couldn't return the call.

The President was hurt. "I guess the candidate doesn't want any part of anyone named Truman," he said.

"Join the club, Mr. President," I said. Like all Truman associates, I, too, was on the outside looking in.

*   *   *

The Democratic National Committee had left Stevenson's organization a money-saving legacy. Long before the convention, the DNC had contracted for 25 hours of network radio and television time between Labor Day and Election Day.

We chose the time carefully to ensure the maximum available audience and to avoid any pre-emption charges. Since most programs were live, late scheduling required payment of talent costs, as well as payment for air time. Time charges were about $28,000 per half hour, while talent charges added another $28,000 to the cost of pre-emption.

In August, Steve Mitchell, a bright, energetic successor to McKinney, presided over his first DNC meeting—and the first such meeting he'd ever attended. He announced that the DNC offices would stay in Washington and not be moved to New York. All Republican activity was centered in Washington.

Stevenson's national campaign headquarters, Mitchell announced, would be in Springfield, Illinois. Stevenson, while running for President, was still governor of Illinois.

That made for awkward coordination of Stevenson's campaign, even with the best communication arrangements. Confusion between the two staffs—in Washington and Springfield—was inevitable. Lost in the choice of Springfield was the instant access to media headquarters, as well as television and radio network facilities. And getting to and from Springfield wasn't easy.

*   *   *

Adlai Stevenson kicked off his campaign on Labor Day in Detroit. He appeared on 60 CBS stations from 1 to 1:30 P.M.

As governor of Illinois, Stevenson was accustomed to using television to report to the voters regularly. But that was free time. When he learned how costly the campaign would be on television, he was appalled. He wanted Eisenhower to agree to a ceiling on television expenditures. The idea was sound in theory, but not in practice. As usual, the Democrats were scrambling for campaign money.

For his part, Eisenhower opened his campaign on 65 NBC television stations, as well as 165 NBC radio stations. His talk was broadcast from Philadelphia between 9:30 and 10 P.M.

"Simulcasts," as the combination of radio and television broadcasts was called, became increasingly popular as the campaign wore on. You had to lean on radio to achieve blanket coverage. Television still was a stranger in many parts of America. There were 108 VHF television stations in 33 states, but only 12 stations west of the Mississippi River. The only television station not connected to the network was KOB in Albuquerque, New Mexico. Thirty-nine percent of the homes in America (representing 442 electoral votes) had television sets.

Getting television coverage wasn't easy. The basic problem was that 32 cities had only one television station. You could buy time on a television network and miss many cities.

With the 1952 election about a month away, I accepted the Democratic National Committee's request for help during the stretch run of the campaign. One of Stevenson's problems was that his speeches invariably exceeded the broadcast time. His powerful, closing punch lines never got on the air.

Stevenson was one of the three great wordsmiths I've known. The others: Prime Minister Churchill and Governor James M. Cox. Stevenson was so precise in his use of words that no speech draft was ever finished. He wrote and edited and polished right up to the moment of delivery, which was his problem.

It wasn't until much later that I lucked into a solution. While timing Stevenson's speech before it was delivered, I gave him a longer time figure than what the speech actually clocked. That night, the candidate's punch lines got on the air. From then on, I deliberately misled Stevenson when we timed his speeches during rehearsals. I usually allowed for a two-minute cushion.

I've long felt that conscientious speech writers worry too much about squeezing every last second out of the broadcast period. Actually, it's better for a candidate to run short—to give a good speech with a smashing close—than to risk getting cut off the air. Only speech writers for the President can ignore the clock because it's not likely the President will be cut off. Speech writers for anybody else must be clock watchers.

*   *   *

The 1952 campaign hinged, for the most part, on only a handful of issues—notably "the mess in Washington," the Korean War and high prices. As GOP vice-presidential nominee, Richard Nixon thrived on the issue of communism and rarely neglected to bring up the Alger Hiss spy case (in which Nixon was instrumental in bringing about a conviction against Hiss, a former State Department employee).

The Republicans were troubled by the split between Eisenhower and Robert Taft, who represented the GOP's Old Guard. If allowed to fester, this rupture with the Eisenhower-Dewey Eastern wing could spell defeat for the Republicans.

In a move to bury the hatchet, Eisenhower invited Taft to his home in New York City for a meeting on September 12. Later, it was announced that Eisenhower had agreed with a Taft manifesto, although they still didn't always see eye-to-eye on foreign policy. The candidate also promised Taft that Taft's supporters would be appointed to their fair share of public offices. He also continued to mend fences by endorsing every GOP candidate, including the controversial Senator Joseph McCarthy of Wisconsin and Senator William E. Jenner of Indiana.

For his part, Stevenson reached into his repository of dry humor whenever the subject of the Eisenhower-Taft meeting came up. "Unconditional surrender at Morningside Heights," Stevenson called the meeting. Taft, he said, must be a six-star general because he dictated to a five-star general. "Taft lost the nomination, but won the nominee," Stevenson said.

*   *   *

On Monday, September 18, the New York Post—one of the nation's few pro-Democratic newspapers—charged that Richard Nixon had available an $18,000 fund for personal use, provided by admirers from California.

The news set off sparks all over the campaign front. DNC Chairman Steve Mitchell demanded that Nixon be dropped from the ticket. Republicans debated the ethics of the fund. Eisenhower wavered in his support of Nixon, but agreed not to take final action until Nixon explained everything.

A political career was at stake. Nixon turned to radio and, more important, television to make his case. The Republican National Committee spent $75,000 to provide for time on 62 NBC television stations, 194 CBS radio stations and 560 Mutual radio stations. NBC estimated 25 million viewers with 18.5 million TV sets; Mutual estimated that 90% of America's 46 million radio homes were tuned in, and CBS placed the "probable and possible" audience at 60 million.

For Richard Nixon, it was "do or die." Either Nixon gave a successful explanation—or he became a has-been politician.

The show—it really was a show—was meticulously prepared. Nixon spent very little time discussing the fund. He simply stated that "not one cent or any other money of that type went to me for my personal use." He cited a legal opinion to prove his innocence and an audit to prove his honesty. Then he quickly moved away from the fund question. In true soap-box-opera form, he talked about his financial hardship as a youngster, the rise to fame of a poor but honest boy. Then, with a dramatic flourish, he said, "What I am going to do—and, incidentally, this is unprecedented in the history of American politics—I am going to, at this time, give to this radio and television audience a complete financial history; everything I've earned; everything I've spent; everything I owe."

Nixon's wife, Pat, was present in the studio. She owned only a Republican cloth coat, Nixon said, "not a Democratic mink coat (a not-so-subtle reference to the mink coat received by a secretary at the White House)." The candidate then introduced Checkers, his children's dog, which led to his remarks being called the "Checkers Speech."

"I have no apologies to the American people for my part in putting Alger Hiss where he is today," Nixon said, referring to the man who had been accused of being a Communist and of passing confidential State Department documents to the Soviets through Whittaker Chambers.

Then, Nixon said that whether he resigned from the ticket was up to the Republican National Committee. He asked his viewers and listeners to send their opinions to the RNC, where his fate would be decided. It was an excellent appeal to the voters' emotions. The slush-fund issue became so blurred that it got lost in the dramatics.

More than 100,000 calls and 110,000 letters poured into Republican National Committee headquarters. With few exceptions, they were favorable. Dwight Eisenhower decided that his running mate had been subjected to "a very unfair and vicious attack." Richard Nixon was vindicated as a man of "courage and honor."

* * *

In 1952, political campaigning relied on an innovation: the widespread use of televised spot announcements. Serious political observers took a dim view of them. "How is it possible," they asked, "to explain any issue in one minute, let alone 30 seconds?"

The Republicans came up with a gimmick: filming people asking questions, with Eisenhower giving pre-recorded answers, to wit:

"Mr. Eisenhower, what about the high cost of living?"

Eisenhower: "My wife, Mamie, worries about the same thing. I tell her it is our job to change that on November 4th."

"Mr. Eisenhower, I need a new car, but I can't afford it at today's high prices."

Eisenhower: "Yes, a low-priced car today includes $624 in hidden taxes. Let's start saving the billions now wasted in Washington and get those taxes down."

Those Republican spots offered no specific solutions—only the inference that Eisenhower had the solution to all problems, whether it was the high cost of living or high taxes.

* * *

With the increasing use of television, it became obvious that you couldn't measure shifting political winds simply by counting noses at rallies. The TV and radio ratings were a far more effective barometer.

Even so, with the exception of Nixon's "Checkers Speech," campaign television viewing was relatively light. No speech during the 1952 campaign reached the 10,161,000 homes reached during the Democratic Convention.

That should have told us that the campaign was too long. It should have been shortened to the four weeks immediately preceding the election. The traditional Labor Day start set in motion a September of campaigning that was expensive, tiring and unproductive.

Twenty percent of television expenditures in 1952 came during the last three days. On election eve, President Truman, Vice President Barkley and vice-presidential candidate Sparkman joined Governor Stevenson in a telecast demonstrating Democratic solidarity. The Republicans outspent the Democrats; they paid $267,000 for Eisenhower's final appearance as a candidate. Election eve was the only time when simultaneous time was purchased on more than one television network.

On election eve, television got a peak audience of 13,977,000 homes. The public-opinion polls predicted an Eisenhower landslide, but pollsters—remembering 1948—were wary of publicizing results of their polls.

It was, however, a time when projected computer results made their debut. CBS, in a deal with Remington Rand, used a Univac computer programmed by Dr. Max Woodbury, a mathematician. Shortly after 8:30 P.M., Univac projected returns almost as precisely as they eventually turned out.

But it was obvious to the pros that Dwight David Eisenhower was winning in a landslide. The final result:

>Eisenhower: 33,936,252 votes
>Stevenson: 27,314,992 votes

The electoral college vote:

>Eisenhower: 442 votes
>Stevenson: 89 votes

The next morning, President Truman wired his congratulations to General Eisenhower. The President added a line: "The presidential plane *Independence* will be at your disposal if you still desire to go to Korea."

CHAPTER 8

November 1952

THE CIVIL WAR HAD PRODUCED FOUR GENERALS who became
President: Grant, Hayes, Garfield and Harrison. Now, America
liked Ike—and felt cozily secure with another general in the
White House. At 62, Dwight David Eisenhower became the
first President to emerge from World War II, although some of
his peers had aspired to the Oval Office.

At the same time, a new source of presidential timber—the
United States Senate—would be cultivated, thanks to television's ever-widening influence. In the first half of this century,
only two senators became President—Warren G. Harding in
1920 and Harry S. Truman in 1945. By 1969, three more senators would be sworn in as President—John Kennedy, Lyndon
Johnson and Richard Nixon.

What was television's impact on the 1952 campaign? Television made Adlai Stevenson widely known in only three
months. Television was also credited with the high voter registration and a large turnout at the polls.

Television also snatched Richard Nixon from the jaws of
political oblivion. Few politicians mastered the use of television more quickly than Nixon.

Most media experts agreed that television hadn't been used
properly in 1952. The campaign was too long—and inor-
dinately expensive. Estimates ranged up to $82 million.
Eisenhower made 228 speeches and traveled almost 50,000
miles; Stevenson gave 203 speeches and covered 32,500 miles,
about the same distance that Harry Truman had traveled in

1948. The difference was that Stevenson plane-hopped about the country (as well as rode trains), while Truman campaigned mostly by train, which allowed him to catch up on sleep in the afternoons.

* * *

Adlai Stevenson became ex-governor of Illinois on January 8, 1953. He was succeeded by William G. Stratton, a Republican.

Shortly after he became a private citizen, Stevenson opened a law office in Chicago. William McCormick Blair stayed on as his assistant. But along with his law practice, Stevenson made countless speaking appearances at Democratic Party fund-raisers. As titular head of the party, Stevenson differed from most of his losing predecessors: He felt a personal responsibility for the party's estimated debt of $800,000. "Being titular head," Stevenson told me then, "gives me all the responsibility and no authority."

Worse yet for the Democrats, a major source of income was lost in 1953. For the first time since 1936, there was no Jefferson-Jackson Day national dinner, an event that had cleared about $500,000 in 1952.

By today's inflated standards, an outstanding debt of $800,000 in 1953 looks paltry. In the wake of the 1980 campaign, for example, Senator Edward M. Kennedy of Massachusetts had slashed his $2.2 million debt to $190,000. Former Texas governor John Connally's presidential committee was in debt to the tune of $1.6 million. The committee of the incumbent Jimmy Carter-Walter Mondale ticket owed $634,000.

"Federal laws don't generally require candidates to pay these bills," the *Wall Street Journal* reported in 1982. "The debt can sit there 100 years and all you have to do is report it to the Federal Election Commission. . . . The most recent campaign reports show that losers often overspend and then can't raise the money to pay their bills. . . ."

Since 1952, campaign costs have skyrocketed every year. The major culprit is television. In the state of Georgia, for example, Joe Frank Harris, the 1982 Democratic candidate for governor, was reported to have spent $3 million in his winning campaign.

* * *

President Truman held his last weekly press conference on January 15, 1953, and commented that these conferences provided a very necessary contact between the White House and the people. But would they continue as frequently under Dwight Eisenhower? The President-elect said he was uncertain about holding news conferences on a weekly basis.

For some time, it was plain that news conferences reflected a President's style and philosophy. Herbert Hoover required all questions to be in writing—and submitted in advance; only a small percentage of questions were answered. Franklin Roosevelt accepted verbal questions. The only restraint placed on reporters during the Roosevelt-Truman regime was that the President couldn't be quoted without specific permission.

* * *

On the eve of 1953 inaugural festivities, the Republicans were swept up in the excitement of the occasion. President-elect Eisenhower and his family checked into the Statler Hotel in Washington.

The dress-rental merchants, however, weren't overjoyed. The incoming President had selected a homburg, instead of a high hat, for the inaugural style of dress.

President-elect Eisenhower declined an invitation from President Truman to attend a small informal luncheon at the White House before the inaugural ceremonies on January 20. At 11:30 A.M. that day, Eisenhower left the Statler for the ride to the White House, where protocol dictated that the incoming President makes a courtesy call on the outgoing President.

Eisenhower and President Truman were supposed to ride together to the Capitol. But Eisenhower stayed in his car, and forced the President to join him in the car under the portico. The ride to Capitol Hill apparently was made in cold, stony silence.

* * *

It was another "first" for television. An estimated 75 million viewers watched the inauguration of Dwight Eisenhower as President and Richard Nixon as Vice President.

The event was carried on 118 stations in 75 cities. The Voice of America supplied kinescopes for television transmission in Holland and Japan. The telecasts began with the swearing-in ceremonies at 11 A.M. and closed with the Inaugural Ball at 12:50 A.M. Wednesday, January 21.

* * *

From Day One, it was obvious that White House strategists really weren't sure about the best way to present President Eisenhower on radio and television. They worried mostly about television and groped for a suitable format by trial and error.

On May 19, 1953, Eisenhower made his first report to the nation as President—on radio only. Television was allowed only brief filmed excerpts at the end of the broadcast.

James Hagerty, the President's capable press secretary and man on the spot, promised that TV would be allowed full access next time, probably in two weeks.

On June 8—from 9:30 to 10 P.M.—the President and four Cabinet members appeared in a simulcast discussion of domestic and world affairs. It was the idea of Ben Duffy, president of the BBD&O advertising agency. An estimated 50 million viewers watched the program, which was carried on all radio and television networks and boasted the week's top ratings.

The program drew mixed reviews. "I've seen better vaudeville shows," wisecracked Wayne Morse, the Independent senator from Oregon. Republican Senator William G. Saltonstall of Massachusetts countered by saying that the show was excellently rehearsed and carried out." *Broadcasting* magazine called it "a chatty, easy talkfest."

It wasn't until close to the end of Eisenhower's first year in office—December 16, 1953—that the President's staff felt comfortable enough with a news conference to allow the entire proceedings to be broadcast. However, in those days, presidential news conferences weren't aired live. This one was recorded and broadcast seven hours later, with the President fielding questions for 32 minutes on topics such as sharing atomic bombs with other nations, juvenile delinquency and his own feelings about the nickname "Ike."

Even though all four networks taped the news conference, nobody was forewarned that the White House would make the tapes available for broadcast. The President, Press Secretary James Hagerty and his assistant, Murray Snyder, and other staff members had reviewed the tapes and decided by mid-afternoon to free the morning news-conference tape for on-the-air consumption. "Since we have been in here, we have been figuring out some way to expand coverage of a press conference," Hagerty told reporters. Then, he made a dramatic announcement: "Today at 6 o'clock, we are sending the entire press conference to the networks to use as they see fit." (Television was allowed sound-only excerpts).

Some members of the print media complained about the impromptu announcement. "Everybody is, of course, glad to be able to use it in direct quotes," Marvin Arrowsmith of the Associated Press said, "but it will mean each time that the wire services—and, I suppose, a lot of others—will have to completely scratch their early stories, and it will infuriate a lot of editors."

That same week, two filmed versions of Eisenhower's statements to a legislative conference were released by the White House on December 17 and 19. At that time, the White House also announced that the President would report to the people on January 4, 1954, on both radio and TV.

Robert Montgomery, the actor and producer, became the unpaid radio-TV adviser to the Eisenhower White House and was provided an office in the White House. Since the Democrats were considered the "poor man's party," I was soon dubbed "the poor man's Robert Montgomery."

Nowhere was the disparity between the two parties more visible than in budgets for the 1954 mid-term election campaigns. The Republican National Committee approved a budget of $3.8 million—twice the amount spent in 1950—with most of it earmarked for radio and television. By contrast, the Democrats countered with only $475,000.

* * *

Presidential press conferences had been the exclusive domain of pad-and-pencil reporters. But tradition was shattered on January 19, 1955, when TV and newsreel cameramen, as well as still photographers from newspapers and magazines, covered President Eisenhower's news conference.

A few hours later, millions of Americans—via television—watched most of what went on during the news conference. Again, live TV coverage had not been permitted, in keeping with established procedure in which the President is quoted directly only when he authorizes such quotes. About two-thirds of the news conferences was cleared immediately for TV and newsreel use. Four cameras served both TV and newsreels jointly.

When it was over, CBS correspondent Charles von Freund rejoiced in the event. "What occurred today," he said, "is a historic milestone and a convincing victory for television."

*   *   *

When would the Democrats hold their 1956 convention? I favored a late convention; Paul Butler wanted a July date, or early August. It depended, of course, on the availability of a site.

We were certain that President Eisenhower would remain at the top of the Republican ticket, which meant that we weren't concerned about when the Republicans would convene. We figured, however, that the Republicans would follow the Democratic convention. If the Democrats selected a late August date, we might force the Republicans into a September date that might overlap the Jewish holidays.

The TV networks cared very much about convention dates and space. We were advised that because of the needs of color and expanded coverage, the radio-TV networks would require 75,000 square feet of space. Not many places in the nation could provide that much room.

As it was, the Democrats selected the week beginning August 13, 1956, at Chicago's International Amphitheatre again. The Republicans, despite vehement protests from the networks, opted for the week of August 20 at the Cow Palace in San Francisco. It would be the first time since 1920 that a political convention would be held west of Denver. It was said that the Republicans didn't want to return to Chicago because of the two "Ms"—McCarthy (senator from Wisconsin) and McCormick (publisher of the *Chicago Tribune*).

What's more, it would be the first time since 1888 that the Democratic Convention preceded the Republican Convention.

The only Democratic Convention to be held so late began on August 29, 1864. In theory, a late convention should provide continuing momentum into the campaign. In practice, a late convention doesn't allow for enough time to organize the campaign. At one time, the ideal period for a national political convention would have been in late June or early July. This no longer is true since the candidates selected by the primaries usually are known long before the convention is called to order.

It became clear, too, that television began to figure in campaign strategy. In 1955, GOP Chairman Leonard Hall investigated why the Republicans lost a congressional seat in New Jersey in the 1954 election. He concluded that television had helped elect a Democrat in a normally Republican district—presumably Harrison Williams, elected by the largest plurality ever in traditionally Republican Union County. Hall suggested that the Republicans hereafter pick candidates with "attractive television personalities."

*　*　*

Even though he hadn't intended to, Adlai Stevenson established himself as the front-runner for the 1956 nomination. With each passing month, it became apparent that Stevenson would be the nominee.

Meanwhile, Eisenhower's popularity reached a new high as a result of the 1955 Big Four summit in Geneva in July. Stevenson's candidacy got a boost one month later when 20 Democratic governors called on him at his Libertyville, Illinois, farm and endorsed him for the nomination. "I'm for Stevenson all the way," Governor Averell Harriman of New York said in response to a reporter's question.

But soon Harriman wavered. Although he said he was for Stevenson, he said he didn't necessarily favor him for President, which rankled Stevenson: "What does he think I'm running for, County Coroner?"

Nevertheless, Stevenson was convinced that the Democrats wanted him as their candidate again. When and where should he formally announce his candidacy? He had been invited to be the keynote speaker at the Democratic National Committee meeting in November at Chicago's International Amphitheatre.

Everybody agreed that it was a proper setting for the announcement of Stevenson's candidacy. This time he would gear up for the campaign with carefully conceived attacks on the Eisenhower Administration, and attacks on the Republican Party, which he felt traditionally stood for isolationism in foreign affairs, for high tariffs and for other business subsidies—the party of Big Business.

But then came a bombshell on September 23, 1955, wrecking all the Democrats' best-laid plans. From Denver came an announcement that the President had suffered a "coronary thrombosis." When the stock market reopened on Monday, September 26, Wall Street plunged, with losses estimated at more than $12 billion.

The best assumption was that the President couldn't seek a second term. The Democratic nominee, accordingly, could probably win the 1956 election with Democrats sweeping the Congress. Four Republicans—all from California—suddenly became presidential prospects: Vice President Nixon, Senator William Knowland, Chief Justice Earl Warren and Governor Goodwin Knight. Due to a quirk in one of California's voting laws, all four had run on both Republican and Democratic tickets at one time or another.

In the Democratic camp, Estes Kefauver and Averell Harriman suddenly decided that Stevenson was not their man, after all. Favorite sons began weighing their odds of success.

Stevenson, meanwhile, was forced to change his announcement plans. He pushed the date to November 15, at a location to be determined. Early in October, I had received a call from Stevenson. He asked me to handle the arrangements for the announcement, and I accepted.

Where to make the announcement and achieve maximum media coverage? We settled on the Hilton Hotel in Chicago, the headquarters hotel for all political conventions in the Windy City. There, we would set up an office in the Boulevard Room—a simple set with an American flag and ample space for cameras, technicians and reporters.

When Stevenson was ready to begin, he turned and asked me: "How much time do I have?" He had become accustomed to time limits on all his speeches.

"You have all the time you want," I said. "It's your announcement and your news conference."

Stevenson read from a single-page announcement, which closed with two brief paragraphs: "The task of the Democratic Party is to make 'prosperity and peace' not a political slogan but an active search for a better America and a better world.

"I am ready to do what I can to that end either as a worker in the ranks or at the top of the ticket if my party sees fit to so honor me."

In Washington, the White House issued medical bulletins that were carefully worded with politics in mind. "Operation

Candor," the White House called it, in hopes of assuring everyone that President Eisenhower was perfectly capable of running for re-election. Dr. Paul Dudley White, the eminent heart
specialist, was called upon to issue bulletins about the President's health. The theme: The President is rapidly becoming as
physically fit as ever.

On November 11, the President returned to Washington. The
date had been purposefully chosen. Washington was hosting a
veterans' parade, and the streets were crowded. White House
strategists played it safe. They continued to give the President
maximum coverage with minimum exposure. As a result,
America liked Ike more than ever.

In the summer of 1956, the President recovered rapidly. But
along the way, the press no longer was treated to "Operation
Candor." Instead, reporters had to depend on Press Secretary
Hagerty's version of the President's recovery.

* * *

The Stevenson for President Committee, meantime, bought 30
minutes on NBC radio for a Stevenson speech February 4,
1956, in Fresno, California.

For its part, the White House still refused live television
coverage of President Eisenhower's news conferences. NBC's
request for live TV coverage of the President's first news conference since August of 1955 was met with an emphatic "no."

An inept presidential utterance could have international
implications, the White House argued. The opportunity to kill
remarks before broadcast still remained, thanks to editing of
film and tape. But NBC pointed out that newsmen with fast
pencils would catch flubs, anyway.

The White House did agree, however, to a radio-only pickup
of the President's speech to fund-raising dinners in 53 cities
only via closed-circuit television. Republican National Chairman Leonard Hall expected the dinners to gross $10 million.

At his news conference on February 29, 1956, President
Eisenhower announced that he would run for another term. He
turned aside questions. He said he would provide answers to
questions in a broadcast that evening, whereupon he explained his decision to run again before a prime-time audience
estimated at 70 million.

The President said he wouldn't engage in extensive traveling
and whistle-stop speaking. He said he would reach the Amer-

ican people through mass communications. He added that he might have to transfer some of his nonessential duties to others in the White House during a second term. He closed his remarks by introducing the First Lady, Mamie Eisenhower.

The "Robert Montgomery production" was accomplished with a single camera, but it was flawed at the end by indecision, with no one apparently knowing what would come next.

Requests for equal time poured into the networks. The networks refused. DNC Chairman Paul Butler argued that the President's speech was strictly political and that the Democrats wanted equal time in accordance with established procedures. Again, the networks said "no." Whereupon Butler contended that the networks were morally obligated to grant the time. He pointedly hinted that Congress (controlled by the Democrats) might want to change the law to assure fair treatment to both major political parties.

CHAPTER 9

Chicago
Summer 1956

Actress Grace Kelly goes to the French Riviera to make "To Catch a Thief." She catches a husband—and becomes Princess Grace of Monaco. . . . Israel and Egypt shoot from the lip, then at gunpoint, in a battle for control of the Suez Canal. . . . A young rebel named Fidel Castro calls on President Batista of Cuba to get out or face revolution. . . . Negroes in Montgomery, Alabama, boycott and kick Jim Crow off city buses. . . . A 21-year-old Tennessee truck driver sings, strums and shakes his way to fame and fortune ($17,000 per appearance) on "The Ed Sullivan Show." His name: Elvis Presley. . . . On August 6, 1956, the Gallup Poll shows President Eisenhower leading Adlai Stevenson, 61 to 37.

TELEVISION NOW WAS A FACT of political life that couldn't be ignored. The cameras roamed the convention wherever the networks decided news was breaking. If you held stormy credential or platform hearings during convention sessions, it meant that TV snubbed the convention sessions.

To avoid any head-on collision of hearings and the convention, I recommended that the committees meet a week in advance of the convention in the host city, thereby giving the Democrats an additional week of publicity—hopefully favorable.

* * *

The crush for media credentials at the Democratic Convention was heavier than ever.

All told, 2,600 radio and television representatives covered the 1956 Democratic Convention. The networks brought crews of caterers, cooks, maids, helicopter pilots, chauffeurs for VIPs and commercial plane pilots. To revive the sweltering staff, NCB imported the ultimate in convention luxury—a plastic swimming pool.

Betty Furness returned with CBS, opening and shutting those refrigerator doors again. This time, she brought a card index—to keep track of when she wore each of the 31 dresses she had carried to the convention.

For CBS convention coverage, Walter Cronkite and Bob Trout were the TV and radio anchors, respectively. John Daly, vice president of ABC, headed a group of 30 from his network. NBC presented a tandem anchor team that would go on to win acclaim on the "NBC Nightly News": Chet Huntley and David Brinkley.

*　　*　　*

To insure as large a crowd as possible for every session of the convention, we overprinted tickets for general seating on the mezzanine. Now and then, we miscalculated, and some ticketholders weren't admitted. They were bitterly unhappy. I really couldn't blame them, but we had to overprint tickets because, after all, we wanted the biggest possible audience for (what else?) television.

The floor plan for 1956, meanwhile, was rearranged. For the first time, we scrapped the wide center aisle and put in two side aisles. That protected the center camera position—and was designed to reduce confusion on the convention floor.

Telephone connections were improved, too. We had lines installed between each delegate and alternate group. It made the alternates feel important, but the phones were rarely used. Direct phone connections also linked the rostrum to the delegates. Each delegate chairman assigned someone to watch a red light on the phone, indicating a call. Even so, we usually had to send a runner to get the delegations to answer the phone.

To aid the line of sight for each camera—and reduce clutter—we did away with the traditional state placards, which were horizontal. In their place, we introduced triangular, red-white-and-blue standards designating each state, the letters arranged vertically.

For the first time, air conditioning was installed at the rostrum. We adjusted the height of the rostrum to give each speaker the same camera position. Lights were installed in the rostrum to eliminate facial shadows on each speaker. A Tele-Prompter, much improved over 1952, was placed under glass on the rostrum.

To provide a strong gavel sound effect, we installed a heavy post alongside the rostrum. Unfortunately, the habit of gaveling in one direction couldn't be broken. The heavy post was ignored. Sooner or later a strong gavel straight ahead broke the glass in the rostrum practically every session. Cost per pane of glass: $20.

To control the band and avoid distractions on the rostrum, we placed the band in a well, behind the rostrum. The audio engineer, who sat next to the chairman and in front of my desk, controlled the delegation microphones. That gave the chairman ultimate control on who would speak.

At my desk were 12 telephones. Singly, or all at once, I could talk to anybody at Democratic headquarters, the orchestra, the entrance to the platform, the television pool, the lighting controller, the public-address announcer, the court reporter, Gate 2, the stage entrance, the projection booth, the newsreels and chief usher Andy Frain's office. The Associated Press, reporting on my desk layout, commented: "Leonard Reinsch, the convention manager, must be a joy to the Bell System."

Paul Butler, meanwhile, had demanded better seats for the delegates than the customary, but uncomfortable, wood or metal chairs. We located 2,800 opera-type seats that were being removed from the Paradise Theatre, which was being demolished. These seats were purchased by the Chicago Host Committee. Our publicity release read: "The delegates will have comfortable cushioning, thus enabling them to concentrate on the important decisions of the convention."

For a better television picture, we added blue slipcovers on the seats. Because the pictures were in black and white, we abandoned the traditional red-white-and-blue bunting for decorations. Painted areas were soft blue.

The set was built by a crew headed by Lewis Gomavitz, one of television's most capable directors. He worked a feverish production schedule to have the convention hall ready for the first gavel on August 13.

Midway through construction, Gomavitz telephoned me, terribly upset. He had completed construction in an area where a wrestling show was booked for August 3. We had no choice but to tell the Amphitheatre management that it must cancel the wrestling show.

Soon the promoter showed up in my office. He was a former heavyweight wrestler. We exchanged words that threw more heat than light on our predicament. Several times I feared that the promoter would jump my desk and eliminate me in one fall. Finally, the promoter, Ted Kohler, agreed to postpone the wrestling card. Saved by the bell.

As a courtesy to *Life* magazine, we provided an advance layout of the seating of delegations. A few days later, someone from *Life* telephoned.

"Why," he asked, "are certain states closest to the front?"

"You must have been reading about the 1860 Republican Convention in Chicago," I replied.

My explanation for 1956 was easy: Illinois is in front because it's the host state. Tennessee is in front because it's the home state of the temporary chairman. Texas occupies a favored spot because Sam Rayburn is permanent chairman. Indiana was favored, too, because it's Paul Butler's home state.

And Georgia? Well, Georgia also occupied the front section because I was from Georgia and, after the convention, I would go back home and live with Georgians.

*   *   *

Former President Truman called a news conference on August 11, two days before the convention. Truman said he wasn't jumping on the Stevenson bandwagon. His choice for President was Averell Harriman. "He has the ability," the President said, "to act as President immediately without risking a period of costly and dangerous trial and error."

It was apparent that Stevenson was Truman's second choice. Which reminded me of an old political story: The country voter was asked to support the candidate for county sheriff. But the country voter replied, "He's my second choice."

"Who's your first choice?" someone asked in exasperation.

"Anybody else."

Truman was prepared to fight Stevenson all the way. The

Harriman forces, buoyed by the President's endorsement, began dreaming of a deadlocked convention—and maybe, just maybe—a Harriman victory.

On August 13, the first session of the 1956 Democratic Convention was gaveled to order. Five-hundred television stations would carry the proceedings to 40 million TV sets. The networks geared up for intensive floor coverage by equipping their troops with new back-pack transmitters and hand-held cameras. The cameras had special-lens attachments.

To cover this convention, the networks had sold $14.5 million in commercials to six national advertisers. Later, the networks estimated that they lost $5 million.

To usher the Democratic Party into the age of television, I had suggested to Paul Butler that a documentary film, rather than the keynote address, be shown to home viewers. Paul liked the idea. He enlisted the help of Dore Shary, then a top executive at Metro-Goldwyn-Mayer, and Norman Corwin, a script writer *par excellence*. The title was "Pursuit of Happiness." The narrator was a young senator from Massachusetts: John F. Kennedy.

Since the film was part of the convention program, the cost could legally be borne by the convention committee. Thus, we had, without charge, effective campaign material.

I had planned to substitute the film for the keynoter. But I should have had better sense. We had the film *and* the keynoter—Governor Frank Clements of Tennessee, a powerful orator often likened to his good friend, the Reverend Billy Graham.

I gave prints of the film to each network well in advance of the evening session. We assumed that each network would carry the film, since it was an integral part of the convention program.

But CBS chose not to run the film. Paul Butler was justifiably furious. He was ready to castigate CBS. I tried to calm him down, without success. When the film ended, Butler told the conventioneers: "I am sorry to say that one of the major networks has failed to keep its commitment to present this documentary film to the American people."

Booing rippled across the convention floor.

Butler pressed on: "I want to at this time express our thanks to the National Broadcasting Company and the American Broadcasting Company for keeping their commitment."

Applause.

It would not be a restful night. Arguments over the CBS snub of the film kept many of us up most of the night.

* * *

The nominating session of the 1956 Democratic Convention began at noon on Thursday, August 16.

After the nominations were concluded, the vote count progressed quickly and smoothly. In fact, it was the shortest on record for a convention in which more than one candidate contested for the nomination.

Finally, Pennsylvania threw 67 votes to Stevenson, clinching the nomination for him—again. He became only the third Democrat—previously defeated as a presidential candidate— to be renominated.

As his nomination was being made official, Stevenson called an impromptu meeting in the Stockyards Inn. I left Jack Christie, my assistant, in charge of music and resolutions and joined the meeting. There, a smoke-filled room was filled with politicians, including Paul Butler, Sam Rayburn, Mayor Daley, David Lawrence and James Finnegan of Pennsylvania, Governor Abraham Ribicoff of Connecticut, Jack Arvey of Illinois and John Bailey of Connecticut, among others.

(The term "smoke-filled room" originated in 1920. Leaders of the Republican Party met in Rooms 408, 409 and 410 at Chicago's Blackstone Hotel. Out of this meeting, in a room filled with cigar smoke, came the agreement that Warren G. Harding would be the Republican candidate for President.)

The meeting was tense. Stevenson looked at everyone in the room. He said emphatically that he wouldn't pick his running mate. The choice would be made, instead, by the convention delegates. The Democrats would have a free choice, unlike the strict control that would steamroller President Eisenhower's choice the following week.

Tempers at the meeting were short. At one point, an exasperated Sam Rayburn demanded a decision: "God damn it, Adlai, name a candidate and we'll get this convention over!"

Stevenson didn't budge. "The convention will pick the candidate in a free choice," he said.

Some opponents of Stevenson said later that he couldn't pick one man as his choice because he had promised the vice-presidential spot on the ticket to each of four candidates.

Stevenson, however, had given considerable thought to his decision. He felt it would make a favorable impression on the voters—and it did.

Back in the convention hall, Stevenson addressed the delegates: "I have decided that the selection of the vice-presidential nominee should be made through the free processes of the convention." His words drew applause. At 11:27 P.M. the convention adjourned and would reconvene at noon the next day.

* * *

Television introduced to the viewers instant running totals of balloting. Those in the convention hall still were dependent on keeping their own scorecard of the balloting results—an almost impossible task for anybody except veteran politicians.

In the 1956 convention, I introduced a "tote board"—a large board in back of the rostrum designed to show vote by vote updates in the balloting. It was cumbersome, but it kept everybody in the convention hall informed of the unofficial count of each candidate's totals.

As it turned out, we didn't need a tote board for Adlai Stevenson's one-ballot victory. But, for the first time, we did need a tote board for the hectic vice-presidential race, in which the candidates stacked up like the Hollywood Freeway at 5 P.M.

Unfortunately, the tote board was dismantled and removed after the presidential vote, even though I had instructed no one to do it. I was furious. The tote board couldn't be reinstalled in time for the vice-presidential balloting.

It took two ballots to nominate Senator Kefauver, with Senator Kennedy—backed by strong Southern support—nipping closely on Kefauver's heels.

This raises a question: In view of the close count, would Kennedy have won the nomination if the results had been posted on a tote board? There had been considerable confusion about the official tally. Some argued that Kennedy had reached the magic total of victory by a few votes, but those votes weren't recorded in time to make the result official.

Friday evening, August 17, was a celebration and unity night for the Democrats. Former President Truman spoke, as did Estes Kefauver, the vice-presidential nominee. In his acceptance speech, Adlai Stevenson was interrupted 53 times by applause. He paid tribute to "that great young American states-man, Senator John F. Kennedy."

The session closed with Mahalia Jackson singing "The Lord's Prayer."

* * *

A total of 93,831,000 persons had watched at least part of the Democratic Convention on television, according to the American Research Bureau.

A. C. Nielsen Company reported that the peak viewing occurred on Thursday—from 11 to 11:30 P.M.—when people in 17.8 million homes watched the balloting for the presidential nomination. The second highest viewing took place on Friday, between 10:30 and 11 P.M., when 15.4 million homes were tuned into the acceptance speeches. Surprisingly, more than 4 million homes watched the predawn fight on Tuesday over the civil rights plank.

The following week, Nielsen reported that Republican peak viewing occurred during the arrival of President Eisenhower at San Francisco—19.2 million homes. The President's acceptance speech attracted viewers in 18.3 million homes, almost 3 million more than the number watching the Stevenson and Kefauver acceptance speeches. All told, the Democratic Convention reached 40.9 million homes and the Republican Convention 39.5 million homes, according to Nielsen.

On August 20, *Broadcasting* magazine would report that the 1956 Democratic Convention was "generally acclaimed as the best managed and physically planned in history."

* * *

Six hours after the 1956 Democratic Convention closed, each of the three networks loaded 10,000 pounds of equipment in a pool plane bound for the Republican Convention in San Francisco. Deadlines were met in San Francisco, but the pressures of the big move exerted a strain on the networks.

On August 20, the 1956 Republican Convention was convened with 1,328 delegates and 1,328 alternates. Harold Stassen's move to replace Vice President Nixon with Christian Herter went nowhere.

Because of the three-hour time difference, sessions in San Francisco were scheduled for 5:30 P.M. to reach prime-time audiences in the Eastern time zone.

For radio and television, the Republican Convention's big

event took place on Wednesday, August 22, in the Italian Room in the St. Francis Hotel. With less than 30 minutes' notice, Press Secretary James Hagerty announced that President Eisenhower would make journalism history by giving the first "live" press conference on both radio and television. The President earlier had set the precedent of putting White House presidential news conferences on radio and TV by delayed recording and film, after clearance by the White House staff.

The history-making news conference lasted 17 minutes, with the President reporting on his meeting with Harold Stassen. A question-and-answer session with reporters followed.

CHAPTER 10

Campaign 1956

WITH THE NOMINATION OF PRESIDENT EISENHOWER, the 1956 election—for the first time since 1900—matched candidates who had run against each other in the previous election.

The 1956 campaign rekindled flashbacks of 1944. But this time a Republican President in uncertain health, approaching his 66th birthday, was seeking re-election.

Barely after the conventions ended, novelty salesmen across America rushed into business. Buttons of all sizes, colors and types sprang up everywhere. So did bumper stickers and posters, not to mention soap cakes with wrappers reading "Clean Up the Mess in California." A seed company sold seeds with a candidate's name on packets. Sales started sluggishly with violets and petunias, but then they picked up dramatically with forget-me-nots: 7 million packets sold.

A manufacturer of inflatable swimming pools cranked out inflatable donkeys and elephants, three and four feet tall. Commemorative plates available at the conventions vied with jewelry of all sorts—tie bars, cuff links and earrings—even an elephant made of 67 rhinestones.

At the same time, a famous 1952 photo of Adlai Stevenson with a hole in one shoe sole inspired miniature silver shoes—each with a hole in the sole. The names of Eisenhower and Stevenson were emblazoned on pillows, ballpoint pens and cigarettes. And a candy maker suggested a lollipop—to keep Ike's name on everybody's tongue.

* * *

Television's impact weighed heavily on the 1956 campaign. Instead of easing travel, it complicated it. No longer could a presidential candidate take a day's respite from the campaign trail. Daily exposure on television news programs became imperative.

By 1956, campaigning was so frantic that it dredged up stories of the grandmother who once told her traveling-executive grandson: "That sounds very exciting, but tell me—when do you have time to think?"

In the rush to send the candidate everywhere at once, there is little or no time to think, to plot strategy, to calculate how the campaign may be won. Not enough time was one of the problems with Stevenson's 1956 campaign.

Presidential campaigns are based on mathematics. Each party calculates the sure states, the undecided states and the unlikely states. In swing states, crucial counties are pinpointed.

Campaign time is budgeted in myriad ways: To travel in small groups; with political leaders; with the news media; to formal functions; to private meetings; to national TV appearances; to pretaping spots and programs for radio and TV; to joint radio-TV programs; to interviews with the national media, the local media and columnists; to TV commentators; for personal appearances in key counties and precincts; to strategy meetings; to studying progress reports; to reviewing and writing speeches; to reviewing the opposition's campaign strategy, and to sizing up the public-opinion polls.

Some campaign activities may be delegated. But to win, a candidate must be informed, kept physically fit and make the most effective use of all 24 hours of every campaign day. There is absolutely no letup—and no prize for finishing second.

Each local appearance hinges on the competence of the "advance" people. Their job: To coordinate and supervise all local arrangements for a candidate's appearance. Selecting and training advance people is a monumental task. Unless it's done well, local appearances will encounter trouble—and trouble means fewer votes.

In 1952, for example, the trouble with Stevenson's campaign was spelled with a capital "T." As one internal campaign memo pointed out: "In New York, an advance man, who was unknown to the campaign headquarters in Springfield, 'took charge' of Stevenson's impending visit, countermanded instructions previously issued and alienated scores of local politicians. In California, a cocktail party was scheduled entirely on the initiative of an advance man without approval from headquarters, without provision for funds and included as guests some controversial, if not questionable, persons."

The advance person must pay painstaking attention to detail. He or she must brief the local media, make sure the right political leaders are on the reception committee and arrange for enthusiastic crowds so the candidate comes across well on the national evening news (this means obtaining time off for schoolchildren and workers).

And if that weren't enough, the candidate and his or her staff must be supplied with plenty of telephones and copies of local newspapers. If it's an overnight stop, the media must be provided with every accommodation—pre-registered rooms, a schedule of events, names of local officials and other background information, along with phones, typewriters, power outlets and even suggestions of where to set up the best TV camera shots.

For the candidate, the advance person must also provide for a hideaway suite with limited phone access. And proper settings should be arranged for—including signs and flags. That means checking things like lighting, the public-address system, signs (to be in camera range), the height of the rostrum, the speech area and readily available water without ice (if water is too cold, it can tighten up vocal cords and impair speaking).

The advance person must be innovative and ready for sudden changes in schedule or—heaven forbid!—explanations if a cancellation occurs.

* * *

Using a radio-TV saturation technique, the Democrats opened the 1956 campaign on September 13 with a prime-time address by Adlai Stevenson.

Three-hundred fifty-four TV stations on three networks, as well as 1,230 radio stations on four networks, carried Stevenson's talk from 9:30 to 10 P.M. The costs: $180,000 for time, $16,000 for television facilities and $3,000 for TV-production items.

Stevenson's talk achieved an impressive rating—No. 4 in the week's ratings, right behind such heavyweight programs as "The $64,000 Question," "The $64,000 Challenge" and "What's My Line?"

Mostly, however, political programs came packaged in five-minute spots. The Democrats scheduled 89 of these five-minute spots on the radio and television networks. Spot announcements were an increasingly favored advertising vehicle.

Both political parties had learned the hard way from 1952. They discovered that you don't bump popular programs like "I Love Lucy" and hold the audience's attention. (Eisenhower bumped "I Love Lucy" for a campaign talk. Only one-fourth of the normal audience tuned in the political program.) In fact, viewers can resent a substitute political talk—so much so that about half of them will switch to other programs.

* * *

To the voters, the whole 1956 campaign was one big yawn. There were no real issues—only the same faces as in 1952. Even the international crisis like the Suez Canal dispute left President Eisenhower unscathed.

Behind the scenes, it was rumored that Richard Nixon had been offered a Cabinet post in exchange for not seeking the vice presidency again, and that he refused. Eisenhower, it was said, felt that Nixon could acquit himself better by settling for a Cabinet post, rather than the vice presidency. The President believed that Nixon would want to seek the presidency in 1960.

In the Democratic camp, Kefauver was a tireless campaigner, pressing the flesh almost around the clock. By contrast, Stevenson was plagued by a schedule that was too crowded. He argued that Eisenhower's political stock-in-trade was ambiguity. He hoped for dialogue between the two candidates, but it never happened.

President Eisenhower stayed aloof—that is, until the polls showed gains by Stevenson. Then the President suddenly got interested in campaigning and meeting the people. The Gallup Poll of October 26 showed Stevenson running strongly—with a 41 against 51 for Eisenhower.

October 29 was a fateful day in a crisis involving control of the Suez Canal. In keeping with his agreement with Britain's Anthony Eden, Israeli Prime Minister David Ben-Gurion ordered troops from Israel to attack Egypt. On that same day, Hungarians in open revolt seized control of Budapest. The Russians faced a tough decision—withdraw or brutally suppress the revolt. They chose the latter by unleashing troops and tanks against Hungary.

With the presidential election only a few days away, the United States was forced to take sides. The President chose the moral high road as the safest course. In the United Nations, the U.S. abandoned its normal allies and joined Russia in a condemnation of the Suez action. The U.S. position: To ask for an immediate cease-fire in Hungary and Egypt.

Nevertheless, Secretary of State John Foster Dulles continued bitterly denouncing the British and French action. America was confused. Even the admiral of the Sixth Fleet wired Washington and asked: "Who is the enemy?"

The day before the election, Stevenson made a last-ditch attack on the Eisenhower Administration. "The Administration," Stevenson charged, "has assured us there will be no war in the Middle East. . . . When Egypt took over the Suez Canal in July, the President was at Gettysburg. On August 4, when the *New York Times* called the Suez impasse the 'gravest challenge to the West since Berlin and Korea,' the President played golf. On August 11, when Britain rejected Communist proposals for a Suez conference, the President played golf. As the crisis mounted toward the end of August, the press reported that the President, now at Pebble Beach, California, golfed happily at one of America's toughest and most beautiful courses. . . ."

Stevenson's speech fell on deaf ears. The voters had long since determined their choice for President. On Election Day, November 6, the British and French landed their troops—in accordance with the agreement with Israel. But the attack occurred much later than planned; it also wasn't well organized.

After the British seized control of the entrance to the Suez Canal, Dulles again went on the attack. The constant pressure by the United States finally forced Great Britain to pull out. It wasn't a shining moment in the history of America's relationships with foreign powers.

If the international cauldron had boiled over during the first week in October—rather than November—would the ensuing events have made possible a Stevenson victory?

As it was, the popular vote totals were:

Eisenhower:	35,590,472
Stevenson:	26,029,752

The electoral vote:

Eisenhower:	447
Stevenson:	74

*   *   *

Eisenhower had won in a bigger landslide than the one in 1952. But political pundits were stunned by the congressional results. Eisenhower's coattails weren't long enough to help Republicans running for Congress. After the votes were tabulated, the Democrats controlled the Senate, 49 to 47, and the House, 234 to 201.

Later, someone reported that Eisenhower was miffed at what he considered a delay by Stevenson in making a concession statement. The President was about to leave his suite in New York's Park Sheraton Hotel when Stevenson appeared on television with his concession statement. The President didn't stay to watch. "I haven't listened to that fellow yet," he said, "and I'm not going to now."

It was shortly after noon on November 7 when Stevenson read his concession message to his followers in the Grand Ballroom of Chicago's Hilton Hotel. Then he thanked his supporters and friends across the country. He closed by saying, "Be of good cheer, and remember, my dear friends, what a wise man said: 'A merry heart doeth good like a medicine, but a broken spirit dryeth the bones.'"

Former President Truman dictated a letter to President Eisenhower, but he never mailed it. The letter would appear in a book published in 1982, entitled *Strictly Personal and Confidential: The Letters Harry Truman Never Mailed:*

My dear Ike:
  You are elected again and this time without a Congress of your own choosing. A record with only one precedent, back a hundred and eight years ago—1848 when old Zach Taylor, another professional General, was elected with Millard Fillmore, who was the know-nothing candidate in 1856. Your V.P. (Richard Nixon) is not that far advanced.
  I am sincerely hoping you'll pray as loudly and as long as you did in 1953—January 20th. I also hope you'll go to Egypt and Palestine and perhaps to Hungary and Poland in order to surrender to the Kremlin as you did in Korea in 1953.

Meanwhile, the Democrats in 1956 entered a new age in politics without realizing it. Gone forever was the suspense of a convention that required roll call after roll call to pick a candidate. Gone were the days when political bosses made deals in smoke-filled rooms and, in turn, made the candidates.

No one knew, in 1956, that he or she had participated in the last of the old-time political conventions. Television, as it had changed the convention procedures, also was changing the whole manner of picking presidential nominees.

For better or worse, television begat the primaries as a way of selecting presidential candidates. Do these primaries—by replacing the importance of convention procedures—produce better Presidents? The jury is still out.

CHAPTER 11

January 1957

THE VOICE ON THE TELEPHONE belonged to Senator John F. Kennedy. He asked me to visit him on my next trip to Washington.

When we met in his office, Kennedy asked me about convention procedures. I interrupted by saying, "I don't want to know all about your 1960 plans, but it would help if I knew whether you were running for Vice President or President."

Kennedy replied tersely: "I've already run for the vice presidency."

From there, Kennedy and his alter ego, Ted Sorensen, peppered me with questions, even though they already knew some of the answers. Weeks later, Kennedy sent a representative to Atlanta, where we spent an entire day discussing convention preparations.

John Fitzgerald Kennedy, quietly and behind the scenes, had laced on his running shoes and climbed into the starting blocks. The finish line was nearly four years away, but Kennedy and his brothers, Robert and Ted, were off and running.

They lined up political operatives—usually lawyers—to cultivate potential delegates in cities and suburbs across the country. They overlooked no contacts. They enjoyed at least one advantage: John Kennedy continued to lead in all the public-opinion polls. The Kennedys ran hard and fast—right up to the crack of the first gavel at the 1960 Democratic Convention.

* * *

Former President Truman's library in Independence, Missouri, was to be dedicated on Saturday, July 6, 1957. He asked me to handle media arrangements and the seating of political leaders on the platform. "You know all about protocol, Leonard," he said. "Go ahead and seat my guests."

The invited guests included luminaries such as Senators Lyndon Johnson of Texas and William Knowland of California, Chief Justice Earl Warren, Mrs. Franklin Roosevelt and former President Herbert Hoover.

I solved part of the protocol problem by restricting the first row of seats to participants in the program and former occupants of the White House. This eased any status problems relating to proper seating. Well, somewhat.

Truman turned over to the library 3.5 million documents for indexing and maintenance. At the same time, he presented to the government 10,000 books, as well as gifts and mementos of historical significance he received while in the White House.

During the ceremony on an open platform, a short letter from President Eisenhower to President Truman was read under a blistering hot Missouri sun. I thought the letter dripped icicles.

President Truman had asked me to escort 82-year-old former President Hoover to Truman's home in Independence after the ceremonies. As we drove, I remarked that I thought President Eisenhower's letter was too impersonal and unnecessarily cold.

Hoover responded: "You know they didn't want me to come today. They even threatened me with reprisals if I attended."

It was obvious that "they" were top-ranking Eisenhower White House officials. "I told them," Hoover went on, "that the President (Truman) was a friend of mine and I intended to attend his library dedication regardless of what anybody in the White House thought or said—so I came."

At that moment, I recalled a discussion in the Oval Office, where President Truman, a great student of history, was discussing how our country discarded former Presidents and neglected to use their experience. As an example, he cited Herbert Hoover, who had been tossed aside even by the Republicans—a forgotten ex-leader of the party.

"I am going to put Hoover's talents to work," Truman said. Thus was born the Hoover Commission. Subsequently, Hoover was invited to Republican functions and, on a few occasions, was asked to speak.

Hoover never forgot that call from Truman. They remained good friends through the years.

* * *

On September 8, 1957, President Eisenhower signed the first civil rights law in 85 years. The law, however, lacked the substance desired by the Democratic Advisory Council, formed by the Democratic National Committee chairman, Paul Butler. The Congress, however, was going to make its laws without any help from the Advisory Council.

Then the United States was caught off guard when the Russians, on October 4, 1957, shot into orbit the first man-made satellite. They called it "Sputnik."

In a press conference, President Eisenhower shrugged off the satellite. Presidential aide Sherman Adams, however, angered many Americans when he contemptuously referred to the space race as an "outer space basketball game."

Adlai Stevenson offered a measured response to the space question in a speech to the National Conference of Christians and Jews at New York's Waldorf Astoria on November 12. "The basic issue is not supremacy of one nation over another, but the supremacy for good or evil, for survival or suicide," he said. "Sputnik should be a call to decision, not a portent of disaster."

In 1958, America fell into a steep economic decline, with unemployment rising along with consumer prices. The turn finally came in June, but the recession's impact would reverberate in the November mid-term elections.

* * *

At the Democratic National Committee meeting in Washington, February 21, 1958, I influenced the approval of new rules for bids as the convention's host city. The DNC's Site Committee would visit each city at the expense of the city making a bid. No longer would the decision be made on the basis of a Washington presentation alone. We felt the Democrats would receive additional favorable publicity, as well as knowledge of the issues, both nationally and in each city we visited.

The Site Committee of only five members visited San Francisco, Los Angeles, Chicago, Miami, New York and Philadelphia. Two other cities were ruled out, Buffalo and Atlantic City. Beforehand, we had sent a detailed questionnaire to each city. We requested information about hotel rooms and rates, asking for a guarantee that the rates wouldn't be increased. We also wanted to know about the number of taxis, cab fares, available bus transportation and many other pertinent items. We also requested each city's bid in dollars, as well as plans for specific fringe benefits like free hotel space for the convention staff.

It all was a far cry from the way some convention sites had been selected. In 1944, President Roosevelt simply telephoned Mayor Ed Kelly of Chicago and suggested that his city host the Democratic Convention.

It was also a far cry from 1987 when more than one hundred members of site committees visited contending cities, expecting full scale entertainment. Actually, the sites for the 1988 conventions were selected, as always, by the incumbent president—in this case, President Reagan—and chairman of the National Committee of the opposing party—in this case, Paul Kirk.

* * *

Both the Democrats and the Republicans were served notice about the way the networks would cover future conventions.

In a speech to the Overseas Club in New York, Sig Mickelson, vice president of CBS News, predicted that the networks would unshackle themselves from gavel-to-gavel coverage. He described his plan to condense, on tape, a 45-minute speech into no more than 90 seconds.

"A day's activities will be wrapped up in an hour," Mickelson predicted. "The networks, however, would continue their activities on the convention site as if they were actually broadcasting it, so that instantaneously, should an unforeseen bit of excitement creep into the session, we'd be able to throw our coverage on the air live. The balloting session would, of course, be covered in its entirety."

Would such scaled-down coverage run counter to the public interest? "No," Mickelson said, adding that most pre-balloting activity is spent in smoke-filled rooms, which are off-limits to cameras. The networks might antagonize the mass viewer, he said, by depriving him of the staple programming on which he has come to depend.

"Television," he said, "is uniquely a live medium. We believe in live coverage where warranted. But we will not waste the viewer's time with hour after hour of deliberations in which the significant developments are only a small part of the proceedings.

"Videotape recording will enable network news editors to pare pre-balloting coverage to the bone and thus keep commercial pre-emptions to a minimum."

CHAPTER 12

Los Angeles, Summer 1960

Americans wiggle in hula hoops and dance to "The Twist" by Chubby Checker. . . . Alfred Hitchcock shakes up moviegoers with the shower scene in "Psycho". . . . Four black college students in Greensboro, North Carolina, set off a string of Woolworth lunch-counter sit-ins that rock the segregated South. . . . The U.S. Food and Drug Administration lifts the curtain in yet another theater of social change by approving the Pill. . . . Forty million American families—or 88% of them—own at least one TV set.

LOS ANGELES WAS NEW TO POLITICAL CONVENTIONS. It had many favorable attributes and a few new features. The Democratic Party convened in a larger arena, but we had to put up a large air-conditioned tent outside for the media. Hotel space was scattered across metropolitan Los Angeles—from Santa Monica, by the sea, to Pasadena, east of downtown.

This was the largest convention ever hosted by Los Angeles, with the possible exception of the Shriners' convention in 1950. Allen Pollack, general manager of the Los Angeles Convention Bureau, provided 75% of all first-class hotel rooms in a five-mile radius of the city's core—11,319. By contrast, in Chicago, we could house 30 delegations in just two hotels, not counting the headquarters hotel, the Hilton.

Now, in sprawling Los Angeles, we had to consider expansive distances and make sure that adjacent hotel assignments didn't favor one candidate over another. We also had to furnish frequent bus service (500 buses), since Los Angeles had only 1,800 taxicabs, compared with 4,500 in Chicago and 13,000 in New York.

*   *   *

The Los Angeles Sports Arena, which, incidentally, had been dedicated by Vice President Nixon on July 4, 1959, was a bright, airy, modern facility. However, it presented a problem in acoustics, which we had to solve. Temporary walls and TV lights created another problem—a heat load that could possibly set off the automatic sprinkler system. We provided makeshift solutions—and hoped for the best.

Since we weren't allowed to drill holes in the floor, a new type of adhesive held the temporary walls in place. We did find solid support in the ceiling for the walls. We were lucky. Nobody leaned against a wall hard enough to cause problems until after the nomination.

Meanwhile, the decor of the arena didn't lend itself to the usual oversized photos of former Democratic leaders. One reporter wrote that the absence of pictures had broken tradition and signaled a break with the old-line leadership. Actually, it was only a decoration problem. We used, instead, colorful shields containing the mottoes of the 50 states, as well as U.S. territories.

Next door, the Memorial Coliseum—scene of the 1932 and 1984 Summer Olympics—was being used temporarily as the home ground of the Los Angeles Dodgers, who were newly transplanted from Brooklyn. If the convention were to last longer than expected, we knew we'd have to cope with excessive crowds and traffic.

Just before the convention began, we discovered that four caucus rooms under the rostrum had been planted with electronic eavesdropping devices. We never did find out who did the bugging.

By 1960, television's space requirements were recognized by the other media. Sharing camera stands was a way of life. We provided eight camera positions shared by TV, newsreel and still photographers. ABC television was responsible for the pool feed, with six camera positions. CBS handled the audio for the pool and the convention. In addition to network space, 12 sound studios were provided for independent TV and radio stations.

The Pacific Bell Telephone Company installed a closed-circuit TV system to alert convention officials and delegates to incoming calls. A 24-hour maintenance crew was on call.

A telephone at each delegate chairman's seat bore a red light, indicating an incoming call. As in 1956, we had to send a runner to most delegations to remind them to answer their phones. Again, we used those three-sided vertical, red-white-and-blue state placards that worked so well on television in 1956. Each placard was topped by a golden eagle.

The convention was, as usual, a communications nerve center. Western Union set up two offices capable of handling 6,500 words a minute. The press occupied two floors in the arena, plus a 12,000-square-foot, air-conditioned tent adjacent to the arena.

Public relations experts were available to each delegation. They were on call to help file localized stories for hometown media—press, radio or television. Photographers, as well as videotape and audio tape, were available. An information bulletin I wrote suggested the types of material that would "play" to editors and news directors back home.

A five-foot aisle separated the press seats from the rostrum area. "Leonard's moat," someone dubbed it. It kept anyone from jumping from the press section to the platform. We placed the band 11 feet above the platform so the head-on television shot showed only the speaker. Our operating offices were out of sight, to the rear of the rostrum. Again, I watched multiple TV monitors that covered the pool pickups and the three networks.

As in 1956, we used an elevator in the rostrum to keep the speaker's head height at a constant 11 feet, 4 inches above the floor. Herb J. Schlafly, Jr., vice president of TelePrompter, helped design the new rostrum. Again, we installed a separate air-conditioning unit for the rostrum and a special spotlight to eliminate shadows on the speaker's face. A specially constructed camera built into the podium enabled a speaker looking at the manuscript to gaze into the lens of a camera, which kept each speaker constantly in full view of the audience.

My telephone switchboard was expanded and improved. At the push of a button, I could talk directly with the musical conductor, band curtain operator, organist, central camera position, the public-address announcer, projectionists, chief electrician, maintenance superintendent, information booth, police and fire chiefs, head of ushers, rear-screen operators, those in charge of the television monitoring system and audio checkpoints, committee office workers behind the rostrum, party headquarters at the Biltmore Hotel and long-distance to any city in the 50 states.

In the area occupied by the networks and wire services, we arranged a section wherein interviews could take place away from the roving eye of the camera. The presentation platform design was new—an elevated 40-foot-long walkway.

A special stairway operated like the drop-down ramp of an airplane and was hidden by a curtain when not in use. When political officials and entertainers were introduced, they made a dramatic entrance. It helped, too, that the man who directed the brass band and handled entertainment was Johnny Green, musical director of MGM Studios and conductor of the Hollywood Bowl orchestra.

At the Biltmore Hotel, we had new problems—too many candidates and not enough acceptable space. Media representatives were located in the Biltmore Bowl and the Rex Room, one floor below the main level. We set up a joint news-conference facility in the Biltmore Bowl. The speaker occupied what was normally the band platform, facing 250 seats, six fixed camera positions and several small camera platforms. Radio and television studios were provided on the fourth floor. NBC's "Today" show originated from the foyer of the ballroom.

Candidates offered free goodies to anyone who visited their public headquarters: lollipops at Symington's; candy kisses bearing the slogan "Choose Lyndon" at Johnson's; soft drinks at Stevenson's. At Kennedy's headquarters, some items sold like hotcakes: Kennedy's book *The Strategy for Peace* ($1); Frank Sinatra's recorded hit, "High Hopes," adopted as the JFK campaign tune (25 cents), and a tie clasp shaped like a PT boat (25 cents).

Serving as volunteer hostesses for the convention were 263 "Golden Girls," who were assigned to all groups visiting the convention. The girls were charming and attractive, an instantaneous hit. They wore white shirtwaist dresses, skimmer straw hats with red-and-blue organza streamers, white pumps and white gloves—and each carried a white purse. "Only in California!" one delegate commented.

Nobody can say the Golden Girls weren't appealing. A CBS correspondent married the one assigned to his group.

*   *   *

When the convention opened on July 11, Kennedy led all candidates in every poll, even as he had before the primaries. For Kennedy, that was a good omen. History shows us that three other candidates led in the polls *before* they were nominated: Alf Landon and Thomas Dewey by the Republicans in 1936 and 1944, and Adlai Stevenson in 1956. In 1968, Richard Nixon followed suit. (In 1972, Edmund Muskie led in the Democratic polls, but lost the nomination to George McGovern.)

Only in 1960 was the incumbent President constitutionally ineligible to run for another term. In 1952, President Truman withdrew after the primaries were under way, as did President Johnson in 1968.

Meanwhile, 10,000 people—the largest crowd ever to assemble at Los Angeles International Airport—had greeted Adlai Stevenson on his arrival. Stevenson remained noncommittal. "If selected, I will, of course, run," he told California Lieutenant Governor Glenn Anderson.

When Kennedy arrived, 3,000 well-wishers cheered him. Many of his followers were trying to win over delegates.

In the hours before the first gavel, all the candidates attended state caucus meetings, bouncing furiously from one group to another like a badminton bird, from Beverly Hills to Hollywood to Pasadena and back. An indefatigable John Kennedy continued the grueling pace, appearing before every necessary caucus. He never dodged a question and obviously won votes with every appearance. It became apparent that Johnson and Symington recognized that Kennedy led in delegate votes.

The strategy of Kennedy's opponents was to finesse a deadlock. Johnson counted on a fifth-ballot victory, Stevenson a sixth or seventh-ballot win. Symington hoped for an overall deadlock, banking on former President Truman delivering the big-city bosses of the large states.

The headlines of Tuesday morning, July 12, proclaimed that Kennedy had the necessary 761 votes to win. Headlines always have an impact on delegates, particularly if they still have a free vote.

In the end, Kennedy won the nomination on the first ballot. The tally read:

Kennedy:	806
Johnson:	409
Symington:	86

```
Stevenson:      79½
Meyner:         43
Humphrey:       41½
Smathers:       30
Barnett:        23
```
            (Humphrey had not been nominated)

* * *

John Fitzgerald Kennedy was the seventh person younger than 44 to be nominated for the presidency. His first-ballot victory by a new candidate was the first since 1928, when the Democrats nominated Governor Al Smith of New York, also a Catholic.

Kennedy's staff unanimously opposed his appearance at the convention right after the balloting. But Kennedy himself insisted on going, anyway. With a police escort, he left his hideaway apartment for the arena while the balloting wound to a close. When Kennedy arrived at the arena, he was officially the nominee.

Kennedy went immediately to his arena headquarters. After exchanging remarks with his brother, Robert, and brother-in-law, Sargent Shriver, he visited with a few political friends. A large crowd of well-wishers slowed Kennedy's walk into the arena. He spoke briefly to the convention, referring to Johnson and Symington. He made no mention of Stevenson. Afterward, a bone-tired John Kennedy returned to his apartment, and the convention session adjourned at midnight.

* * *

Who would be the vice-presidential nominee?

The best guess was either Symington or Senator Henry (Scoop) Jackson of Washington. No one really knew, but perhaps the turning point came when Kennedy received a friendly telegram of congratulations from his once-bitter opponent, Lyndon Johnson.

On Thursday morning, Kennedy went alone to Johnson's suite in the Biltmore. Meeting followed meeting. Telephone calls piled up. Party leaders streamed into Kennedy's suite. Labor strongly opposed Johnson, but it decided it wouldn't back Nixon, regardless of who ran for the vice presidency.

Johnson was busy on the phone. Should he exchange his position as majority leader with a vote for a gavel? He apparently received mixed advice.

Finally, to the surprise of many, Kennedy made his decision—Johnson. Few expected Kennedy to select Johnson, and even fewer expected Johnson to accept.

The political reality of the Electoral College votes probably swayed Kennedy to pick Johnson. Lady Bird Johnson may have been the determining factor in Johnson's acceptance. Several times she had said that Johnson's job in the Senate was too strenuous, particularly after her husband's heart attack.

* * *

Meanwhile, Democrats gleefully pointed out the parallel of the Kennedy-Johnson ticket to the winningest Democratic ticket of modern times—the 1932 Harvard-educated millionaire Easterner, Franklin Roosevelt, and a Texas vice-presidential candidate, John Garner.

A rally in the Coliseum started late Friday afternoon with a two-hour spectacular featuring entertainment stars. Long before the session was called to order, the hastily constructed wooden platform for the speakers posed a problem. In their enthusiasm over the victory, several members of Kennedy's organization had sent telegrams inviting VIPs to be on the platform for the acceptance speeches. Each recipient was an important Democrat who had helped in Kennedy's victory drive. They came in droves, each with an invitation in hand. There was no way even a small number could be added to the platform, which already was overloaded.

We were forced to turn back an untold number of invitees. At one point, the crush became so bad that both the police and fire departments blocked the entrance to the platform.

At 4 P.M., the program got under way with the reading of a telegram from former President Truman, pledging his support to the Democratic ticket.

Stuart Symington introduced Lyndon Johnson for his acceptance speech. "The Republicans know," Johnson said, "as I know, and as you know that a new star has been born in the leadership skies of the nation here in Los Angeles. I know when I see a political genius, and I have seen it in my friend, John F. Kennedy."

Chairman Collins introduced Adlai Stevenson to present Kennedy. Stevenson received a standing ovation. By now, 50,000 spectators, far short of the number promised, had arrived, leaving the Coliseum with vast open spaces. I couldn't help but think what a massive overflow crowd we could have had next door, inside the Sports Arena. Speaking from the platform in the Coliseum was extremely difficult. The speaker could feel no empathy with the audience, which was scattered and too far away. Helicopters overhead caused major distractions.

Even under ideal circumstances, John Kennedy would have found it impossible to deliver a forceful call to arms and a stirring promise of victory. He had had little sleep during the week, and his reflexes had been stretched to the breaking point. He felt not only the strain of battling for votes in Los Angeles, but the effects of strenuous campaigning with no letup for an entire year. Time and again, he had to call on reserve strength until there was little left. He was haggard from total exhaustion.

According to A. C. Nielsen, Kennedy's acceptance speech was seen in 17.6 million homes. Two weeks later, Richard Nixon's impressive acceptance speech in Chicago reached 17.2 million homes.

At home in Washington, Vice President Nixon watched Kennedy's tired performance, which was picked up by distant TV cameras under unfavorable conditions. It probably was the first time a Republican candidate-to-be watched an acceptance speech by his opponent. Richard Nixon commented privately to his friends that John Kennedy did a very poor job. Then he said, "I can take this man."

CHAPTER 13

Campaign 1960

ACCORDING TO AN A. C. NIELSEN SURVEY, 38,736,000 television homes out of 45,200,000 were tuned into the Democratic Convention at one time or another. More than 20 million persons watched the balloting. John Kennedy's acceptance speech drew 41,760,000 viewers. At least 108 million saw part of the convention.

Of all adults who had access to television, 79.2% watched the Democratic Convention, compared with 69.1% for the Republicans, according to Albert E. Sindlinger of Sindlinger surveys.

On the day after the convention, Saturday, July 16, the new Democratic National Committee met in the Grand Ballroom of the Biltmore Hotel.

As one of his final tasks, outgoing Chairman Paul Butler (who soon would retire) requested all National Committee members to sign a statement saying "that in the performance of my duty as a member of the Democratic National Committee, I hereby affirmatively declare my support of John F. Kennedy and Lyndon B. Johnson, the nominees of the 1960 Democratic National Convention for the office of President and Vice President of the United States, respectively."

Not signing the new loyalty oath could subject a National Committee member to removal from the committee. Ninety-two of 93 committee members signed the oath immediately—a far cry from the bloody battles over the oath in previous years.

The introduction of Lyndon Johnson brought standing applause. After a few remarks, Johnson introduced John Kennedy, who was given a rousing reception.

Kennedy included in his remarks suggestions about officers of the National Committee. He recommended Henry Jackson to replace Butler as chairman. Jackson had hoped to be selected for the vice presidency. He enjoyed a fine relationship with Kennedy, but the politics of necessity ruled him out of the No. 2 spot. Jackson was a good soldier; he agreed to become national chairman.

Normally, the national chairmanship went to a Catholic. With a Catholic candidate for President, it was felt that the custom should be changed. For the first time in 28 years, a Protestant, Henry Jackson, became chairman of the DNC, which now looked forward to a rough-and-tumble campaign—and victory in November.

We had to clear out hotel offices quickly and discard banners. Leftover souvenirs, once coveted, were destined for the wastebaskets. Pacific Bell Telephone had to remove 4,000 telephones, 250 teletype machines, 25 switchboards, 20 telephoto channels, 48 television-sending antennae, 350 public telephones and 70,000 feet of cable. (Western Union had transmitted 6.8 million words during the convention.)

An organization carefully built over the months was dismantled overnight. The pressure cooker was shut off. All of us had trouble returning to normal lives.

With my wife, Phyllis, and daughter, Penny, I headed for the seaside resort town of Carmel, California, for some "R and R." We had just unpacked when the telephone rang. Hyannisport, Massachusetts, was calling.

I was told that John Kennedy, who had returned home to Hyannisport on Sunday, two days after the convention, would like me to handle the television and radio part of the campaign. I was happy to accept.

"How soon can you get here?" the voice on the phone asked.

I explained that my wife and daughter were with me.

"Bring them along. Let us know your plane arrival in Boston. A private plane will meet you and fly you to Hyannisport."

On July 20, my assignment was officially announced in Hyannisport. There, a few days later, I attended a meeting in Kennedy's home. With the candidate were his brother, Robert; Ted Sorensen (speech writer and adviser), Pierre Salinger

(press secretary) and Henry Jackson (the new DNC chairman).
We plotted strategy for the 1960 campaign.

* * *

The 1960 Republican Convention in Miami Beach, Florida,
introduced two large screens, each 750 square feet and 80 feet
above the rostrum. They were designed to give everyone a clear
picture of the proceedings. Additionally, a computer projected
voting totals for the presidential and vice-presidential candidates.

The networks used the same equipment they used in Los
Angeles, although the fact that the conventions were held in
separate cities added about $2 million to their total cost.

The Nixon Volunteers provided a news trailer as a staging
area for radio-TV interviews. It was equipped with soft chairs,
air conditioning, telephone, typewriters and other amenities.

On Wednesday, July 27, Richard Nixon was nominated to
run for President. Arizona had placed Barry Goldwater in
nomination, but he graciously withdrew, setting the stage for
1964.

Then, after consulting with party leaders, Nixon selected
Henry Cabot Lodge of Massachusetts as his running mate.
Lodge, who had been in the Senate since 1936, had been
defeated by Kennedy in 1952, despite the Eisenhower landslide. Kennedy had become a Congressman in 1946, defeating
nine opponents in the Democratic primary. After three terms
as a U.S. Representative, Kennedy had decided in 1952 to run
for the Senate.

The national campaign of 1960, then, would match two
Senators against two former Senators (and two Senators would
head up the National Committees of both parties).

Members of the Senate were amused as they contemplated
an unusual campaign—the Republican candidate for President
presiding over a Senate that included a majority leader as the
Democratic vice-presidential candidate and a Massachusetts
Senator as the Democratic presidential candidate.

Robert Kennedy, a young man with a razor-sharp mind,
would direct his brother's drive for the presidency. He was
more experienced in presidential campaigns than many realized.

In 1956, Bobby Kennedy was assigned to travel with Stevenson, but his responsibilities were zero. He had plenty of time

to observe and take notes. The lessons he learned were re-flected in the strategy for 1960.

Politics is simple arithmetic. Two-hundred sixty-nine elec-toral votes are needed to win. Of these, 237 electoral votes come from nine states—Massachusetts, New Jersey, New York, Pennsylvania, Ohio, Michigan, Illinois, Texas and California. These numbers were very much on the minds of Kennedy strategists after a post-convention Gallup Poll showed Ken-nedy leading Nixon, 52 to 48.

But, after the Republican Convention, the Gallup Poll flip-flopped and gave Nixon a 53-to-47 lead. For the first time, Nixon was the front runner, due in part to a superlative accept-ance speech.

Kennedy's schedule was a model of efficiency in the use of the candidate's time. Unfortunately for Kennedy, it also be-came a test in stamina. Sleep and meals were not top priorities. Kennedy would concentrate on seven of the large states; Johnson would be responsible for Texas and Stevenson for California.

Pierre Salinger handled media arrangements. I coordinated the broadcast schedule; but most important of all, I argued over a debate schedule with Nixon's representatives so dates and sites of debates would fit into schedule-maker Kenneth O'Donnell's master plan.

John Kennedy pursued a campaign schedule as grueling but not as expansive as that of Richard Nixon, who would fulfill his vow to visit all 50 states. During one 10-day span, Kennedy traveled 17,000 miles. Arrangements were handled clumsily; schedules were ill-timed, and advance men faltered and made mistakes. Kennedy's success, however, would hinge on three things:

—Meeting the religious issue head on, with a televised talk and question-and-answer session before the Ministerial Asso-ciation of Greater Houston on September 12.

—The first debate, on September 26.

—The successful effort in the waning days of the campaign to gain the release of the Reverend Martin Luther King, Jr., from the Reidsville prison in Georgia.

As it was, the vicious attacks on Kennedy over the Catholic issue surprised Kennedy's forces. First, someone circulated a fake anti-Kennedy oath by the Knights of Columbus, of which Kennedy was a member. In July, the Stanley (North Carolina)

Bruington Baptist Church published in its weekly bulletin a denunciation of Kennedy as a member of the Knights of Columbus. According to the oath, members of the Catholic group purportedly disowned allegiance to "any heretical king, prince or state and obedience to any of their laws." The oath also called upon members to answer only "to the Pope" and "wage relentless war, secretly and openly, against all heretics, Protestants, and Masons."

Actually, the first paragraph of the real oath states: "I swear to support the Constitution of the United States. . . . I pledge myself as a Catholic citizen and Knight of Columbus, to enlighten myself fully upon my duties as a citizen and to conscientiously perform such duties entirely in the interest of my country and regardless of all personal consequences."

The bogus oath was used in propaganda against Kennedy during the primaries and in mailings to delegates attending the Democratic Convention. The Masonic Order called the phony oath "scurrilous, wicked and libelous and the invention of an impious and venomous mind."

Soon the church pastor, the Reverend James C. Honeycutt, Jr., renounced the article as incorrect, saying that he was sorry it had been published in the church bulletin.

The Republicans, too, had problems with the religious issue. Nixon refused to discuss it and ordered his campaign workers not to talk about it either. But Republicans with long memories couldn't forget what happened in 1928, when the anti-Catholic outburst in the South caused Northern Catholics to switch to the Democratic Party. As a consequence, the Republicans lost their traditional control of the big cities—control which, in 1960, they still hadn't regained.

Kennedy had to face the religious issue in a public forum. An invitation was arranged for him to appear before the Greater Houston Ministerial Association on September 12. His address was carried live on statewide Texas television:

"I believe in an America that is officially neither Catholic, Protestant nor Jewish—where no public official either requests or accepts instructions on public policy from the Pope, the National Council of Churches or any other ecclesiastical source—where no religious body seeks to impose its will directly or indirectly upon the general populace or the public acts of its officials—and where religious liberty is so indivisible that an act against one church is treated as an act against all.

". . . contrary to common newspaper usage, I am not the Catholic candidate for President. I am the Democratic Party's candidate for President who happens also to be a Catholic. I do not speak for my church on public matters—and the church does not speak for me."

One questioner, whose questions were obviously resented by the group, quoted from books 10 and 11 of the *Catholic Encyclopedia* and the official Vatican newspaper. Kennedy replied he had never read the *Catholic Encyclopedia*, but he would do his best to give direct answers, even though the quotations were incomplete and apparently unrelated.

The moderator had to ask the audience to refrain from applause because time was limited, but Kennedy's forthright answers drew extended applause.

After Kennedy's remarks in the heart of Baptist country, his strategy was not to mention the religious issue, but to emphasize tolerance.

I edited the tape of Kennedy's Houston speech to comply with the requirements of half-hour political programming on television. From Texas to Minnesota, we ran a saturation campaign in the Baptist belt. Forty states were given ample opportunity to see Kennedy deal with the religious issue.

The program created so much excitement that some stations responded to viewers' requests by repeating the program without charge.

Campaign issues throughout September, were overridden by the religious issue, bigotry and venomous printed propaganda—i.e., Harvey H. Springer, a cowboy evangelist, was listed as the author of a pamphlet entitled "Kennedy Cannot Win." The illustration on the pamphlet showed an octopus (the Vatican) grabbing the White House, with the caption: "If we get there first, we'll soon own all the rest."

On September 14, the Reverend Norman Vincent Peale, a nationally syndicated columnist and radio commentator, author and a fervent Nixon supporter, called a secret meeting of 150 Protestant ministers and laymen in Washington. The group called itself Citizens for Religious Freedom. It warned of Vatican control if Kennedy became President—and it released a manifesto which was pointedly anti-Catholic.

But Peale's meeting backfired. Some people began to say the Roman Catholic Church is not standing for election any more than is the Religious Society of Friends.

The attacks on Kennedy continued. The Reverend W. A.

Criswell of the First Baptist Church of Dallas preached a sermon critical of Kennedy, whom he referred to as "that Roman Catholic from Massachusetts." Criswell went on: "Roman Catholicism is not only a religion, it is a political tyranny. It is a political system . . . like an octopus, covering the entire world and threatening those basic freedoms . . . for which our forefathers died."

Criswell's sermon was printed and distributed to Baptists in Texas, where 1½ million Baptists reside (Methodists and Catholics are a distant second).

A Church of Christ ad, prior to the election, stated: ". . . Americans cannot afford to elect a 'loyal son' of a religio-political church into the highest office in our government for the perilous days that lie ahead of us."

The Department of Justice, meanwhile, identified 144 producers of anti-Catholic literature during the campaign. It was reported that the Republican Party had no connection with the printing or distribution of the anti-Catholic material.

In all the uproar over Catholicism, few noticed that Kennedy opposed federal aid to parochial schools. The Republican candidate for Vice President, Henry Cabot Lodge, strongly supported aid to parochial schools.

CHAPTER 14

Campaign Debates 1960

SINCE 1952, I HAD BEEN EAGER to match the Democratic and Republican presidential candidates on the same television screen. Frank Stanton, president of CBS, and I had discussed the joint appearance of the two major presidential candidates on the television networks. Stanton had spearheaded the fight for repeal of Section 315 (requiring equal time for all candidates). His was a voice of experience; he said we'd have an easier time with the networks than we would with the Congress.

As it turned out, we not only had trouble with Congress in 1952 but also the Democratic candidate. What's more, in 1956, with Eisenhower as President, we didn't stand a chance. The Republicans didn't even reply to my wire suggesting a presidential debate. One of my friends at the Republican National Committee called and said: "Do you think we're crazy? Forget it."

To me, the frequency or length of the debate programs didn't really matter. I just wanted both candidates together on television screens across America. That way, for the first time, the Democrats would get front-page coverage in every newspaper in the country.

Most important, we would reach Republicans and undecided voters who otherwise ignored the Democrats' appearances. We would receive the kind of exposure that is absolutely essential to winning modern elections.

This was especially true in 1960. Here was a highly articulate, personable candidate in John Kennedy, who, in the eyes of extremists, had Catholic horns; who, in the eyes of Republicans and some Democrats, lacked experience; and, in the eyes of many, was much too young to be President. In a joint appearance with Richard Nixon, Kennedy had nothing to lose and everything to win.

As Kennedy, Ted Sorensen, Scoop Jackson, Pierre Salinger and I conferred over clam chowder at Kennedy's Hyannisport home on July 25, 1960, Kennedy tossed me a telegram and said: "What do we do about this?"

Robert Sarnoff, president of NBC, was inviting Kennedy and Nixon to appear on the NBC radio and television networks for free. I couldn't contain my excitement. I almost shouted, "Accept at once without any qualifications. Agree to meet Nixon any time, anywhere. We'll work out the details later."

Remembering my frustrations in 1952 and 1956, I added, "Have Pierre release your unqualified acceptance to all media several hours before you send your reply to Bob Sarnoff. We want everyone to know you have accepted without any restrictions. . . . I'm sure Nixon will include some qualifications."

Herb Klein, Nixon's communications adviser, accepted for Nixon on July 29. Three days later, Nixon announced his acceptance. In the meantime, Kennedy also accepted invitations from CBS and ABC, as did Nixon.

I was designated to represent Kennedy at a meeting with network executives on August 9 in New York. Whenever possible, Ted Sorensen attended other meetings with me. Before the first meeting, I asked Kennedy if he had any instructions.

"Just one," he said. "Don't let him get off the hook."

Having waited eight years for this opportunity, I wasn't about to let that happen. Before we completed all negotiations for the four debates, I would attend 15 meetings.

To make the debates possible, we still needed repeal of the equal-time provision, Section 315 of the 1934 Communications Act. We assumed correctly that the Democratic-controlled Congress would cooperate. Congress repealed Section 315 and sent the bill to the White House on August 22. Two days later, President Eisenhower signed the bill into law. The way was cleared for the Kennedy-Nixon debates.

The repeal also allowed the Democratic and Republican presidential and vice-presidential nominees to appear on other broadcasts not paid for by political organizations. NBC immediately announced that Nixon would appear on the Jack

Paar "Tonight" show August 25, and Kennedy would be invited to appear at a later date. Nixon had asked to be on the program; Kennedy had appeared on it in June.

Additionally, the repeal gave radio and TV stations the right to broadcast speeches and other appearances by the major candidates for President and Vice President without being required to grant equal time to minority parties. In 1960, there were 16 other presidential candidates, representing such groups as the Socialist Workers Party, the Tax Cut Party, the National States Rights Party, the Greenback Party, the Socialist Labor Party, the African American Unity Party and the American Third Party.

Unfortunately for broadcasters and the voters, the equal-time provision was suspended only for the 1960 campaign.

We had to hammer out the details of the joint appearances. At our first meeting in New York, the networks discussed who would sponsor the debates. Several members of Congress declared that "Congress does not expect networks to accept commercial sponsorship of programs on which candidates appear that are covered by the new law." That resulted in network sponsorship.

How much time for each debate program? We all agreed that they should last one hour. The networks had offered eight hours of free time. Because the debates would use up only four hours, we argued about what to do with the other four hours. We wanted to control the air time, but the networks said "no" and demanded editorial control.

It also was agreed that all networks would broadcast the debates simultaneously—an agreement we felt was most important and could only help Kennedy all the more.

At the second arrangements meeting on August 31 in Washington, we agreed to four debates. I had argued for five, but happily settled for four. My argument for five debates was interpreted as a sign of weakness and lack of confidence on Kennedy's part. Nixon's people expected him to knock Kennedy out of the ring in one debate—apparently debate No. 4. We were concentrating on debate No. 1.

Ted Sorensen and I worked out a schedule with Fred Scribner (who represented Nixon) for the four debates:

1. Chicago (September 26).
2. Cleveland (October 7), later changed to Washington.
3. Kennedy in New York and Nixon in Los Angeles (October 13).

4. New York (October 21).

I pushed for a later date in October for debate No. 4, but the Republicans were adamant. Democratic Congressmen were unhappy that the final debate wasn't closer to Election Day. We figured that Nixon wanted to keep the last weeks open for his planned blitzkrieg down the stretch.

The sites of each debate posed an intriguing problem. Neither side wanted to divulge campaign strategy by revealing the candidates' travel schedules. Before the first debate, Kennedy was in Cleveland. We reluctantly agreed to Chicago as the location for debate No. 1 (actually, Chicago had been our first choice).

Scribner asked for our cooperation on the second debate, so we selected Cleveland. Kennedy was scheduled in Cincinnati the previous day. There was no way we could coordinate the two candidates' schedules for the third debate, so they appeared 3,000 miles apart, Kennedy in New York and Nixon in Los Angeles.

Later, we learned that President Eisenhower was upset about the debates beginning on September 26. That was the date he was scheduled to speak on national television at a dinner of the Catholic Charities in New York. He lost his television appearance to the two presidential candidates.

Everyone agreed that we didn't want a straight-out debate. That would be too deadly—a real ratings killer and an audience loser. Sig Mickelson of CBS pushed for a format in which the two participants gave opening statements, then questioned each other. Neither side liked that idea. Both Nixon's people and ours wanted a panel of newsmen to ask questions of both candidates, which would, in turn, play to Kennedy's strong suit.

Nixon's representatives, apparently acting under instructions, wanted to confine at least two debates to only one subject apiece. They insisted on foreign policy—a strong area for Nixon—as the subject of the last debate. Nixon's rationale was: "Start in low key and work to a crescendo in the last two weeks." Debate No. 4, on foreign issues, was counted on by Nixon's planners as the one that would obliterate Kennedy.

Frankly, we were delighted to make domestic issues the subject of debate No. 1, although we weren't overly concerned about any topic. We felt that the first debate was the most important of all. Succeeding debates could be anti-climactic. So we concentrated on getting every concession and arrangement we felt important for debate No. 1.

Since the networks bore all costs of the debates, they logically concluded that they should provide the members of the news panel. Both Pierre Salinger and Herb Klein came under an immediate barrage from the print-media members asking to be on the panel. After considerable wrangling, it was agreed that the television networks could furnish the panel for debate No. 1; panels for other debates would include members of the print media.

The format was set for debates No. 1 and 4; each candidate would open with an eight-minute statement; answers to the questions would be limited to 2½ minutes, with responses by the opponent limited to 1½ minutes. The questioning would alternate, with the first question asked of the candidate making the opening statement. Each candidate would conclude the program with a three-to-four minute statement. The candidate who opened the program would speak last.

We liked this format, but needed only one more thing to make it entirely workable—Kennedy to lead off and close debate No. 1. I worried about this problem for days. The rotation was to be decided by a coin toss. Some of Nixon's representatives said they didn't care if he went first or second—he would win, anyway.

I countered, "Why bother with a coin toss? We'll go first."

"No, sir," I was told. "We'll toss the coin for rotation."

Finally, Ted Rogers of Nixon's staff and I faced each other, with a neutral observer tossing a coin. I called "heads." As the coin spun in the air and then landed, I held my breath. Heads it was! We had won the opening and closing positions.

We turned to other details. It was agreed that each side would approve its own lighting.

And would the candidates sit? Or stand? Since Nixon's leg (injured when he struck a car door during a campaign stop in North Carolina) still caused him problems, I wanted the candidates to stand for the entire hour. If Nixon had to shift his weight every now and then, it would give the impression that he was uncomfortable and ill at ease. I expected Nixon's people to resist. But, to my surprise, they readily agreed that both candidates should stand.

For debate No. 1, the networks announced that the panel would consist of: Stuart Novins (CBS), Robert Fleming (ABC), Sander Vanocur (NBC) and Charles Warren (MBS). Designated as moderator was Howard K. Smith of CBS.

The day of debate No. 1, Monday, September 26, was clear of all meetings for Kennedy, except a 2:30 P.M. appearance before a friendly carpenters convention at Chicago's Morrison Hotel.

Twenty-four hours earlier, the Kennedy "brain trust" gathered in another hotel: Ted Sorensen, Richard Goodwin, a brilliant young lawyer, and Mike Feldman, who had been Kennedy's chief of legislative research in the Senate. They carried armloads of documents on domestic issues, from which they distilled 14 subject areas. Each subject area was updated.

We had agreed that domestic issues should be the topic of debate No. 1 because Kennedy was so familiar with them. He had served in the House and Senate, as a Labor Committee member, and he needed only to be brought up to date on key points.

I didn't go on Kennedy's Wyoming-Colorado-Utah swing on Thursday, Friday and Saturday. I wanted to make sure that the setting for the debate on Monday would be correct. The set was being built in CBS's New York studios and had to be transported to Chicago. Lou Dorfsman of CBS coordinated the set design. We wanted a gray scale of 5 for the backdrop because we were on black-and-white television. The curved, rear wall of the set measured 9 feet high and 39 feet long.

By Saturday night, the set was in place in Chicago's WBBM studio, an ideally equipped facility. In the middle of the backdrop was a large molded eagle. On Monday, the day of the debate, the eagle was discarded.

The day before, photographs of the set were sent by pre-arrangement to Chicago's Midway Airport for Kennedy's approval. He discussed production details with CBS producer-director Don Hewitt and me. We all agreed; all systems were "go."

*   *   *

Don Hewitt, an outstanding veteran of 13 years at CBS and who would go on to produce the network's widely acclaimed "60 Minutes," prepared for debate No. 1 in a state of sophisticated calm.

Hewitt's demeanor contrasted sharply with frenzied loss of composure by those who would produce and direct the succeeding debates. In the Chicago studio, Hewitt found that the set was too light. He ordered it repainted to reach the No. 5 gray scale originally intended.

There was some hassle about where chairs would be positioned for the candidates and the moderator. We requested a small table with a carafe alongside each candidate. The "music stand" rostrums for the candidates were approved. Against CBS's objections, both sides insisted that the moderator should sit at a desk—to provide more separation between the candidates.

Don Hewitt, who had a good feel for television audiences and what appealed, arranged the panel of media members so that they would sit with their backs to the camera. To the home audience, they looked like front-row spectators.

In any confrontation, whether it's a debate or a sporting event, reaction shots of the contestants are an absolute must because they lend so much depth and meaning. At the control panel, Hewitt didn't have a wide array of camera angles for reaction shots—a calculated decision reached by both sides before the telecast. That meant Hewitt had to make frequent use of reaction shots from very few vantage points.

As Hewitt said later about the reaction shots, "I made no conscious effort to balance (between each candidate). I just called them as I saw them." Actually, there were 11 reaction shots of Kennedy totaling 118 seconds and nine of Nixon totaling 85 seconds.

Nixon's staff requested no pictures of Nixon's left profile, which made no difference to us. And during the program, neither candidate was to see himself on any in-studio monitor.

At noon Monday, Frank Stanton, ever the perfectionist, checked the set. He said it looked too "busy," so a gauze scrim was ordered and then applied on the curved-wall back-drop. We gave Robert Barry, CBS's senior lighting director, a hard time when we moved the two "music stands" farther apart. Barry, too, had favored a darker background; he adjusted the lighting to provide 125-foot candles of intensity, which was fine with me.

Nixon's people, however, constantly changed the lighting on their side of the set. Despite later reports to the contrary, I had nothing to do with the lighting on Nixon. His advisers added two 500-watt spotlights and, at the last minute, they continued to request lighting changes. I sensed that too many people were making decisions on lighting for Nixon.

At 5:30 P.M., both sides approved the set and the lighting. I rechecked the shade of Kennedy's dark-blue suit and was satisfied that it contrasted well with the background (earlier I suggested that he change from gray to dark blue). We changed Kennedy's shirt to light blue, instead of the off-white he wore to the studio. I also brought along a pair of long socks, in case his regular socks detracted from his grooming while he sat at the start of the program.

During the day, Kennedy and his "board of strategy" sweated out questions and answers. Kennedy didn't like the first draft of his eight-minute opening remarks; he dictated his own remarks. All morning, questions were hurled at Kennedy. His answers often were greeted by somebody saying, "Why did you say that?" or "You're weak on that answer." It was a grueling give-and take rehearsal in an informal setting.

At times, Kennedy paced the floor. Or he gazed out the window. Or he sprawled on a bed. The barrage of questions never let up. Nor did the critique of his answers. Now and then, somebody approved by saying, "That's great! Be sure to remember that one." As each topic was exhausted, cards inscribed with facts were left on the floor. Bobby Kennedy, Pierre Salinger, Ken O'Donnell and Kennedy pollster Lou Harris drifted in and out of the suite. But John Kennedy stayed on, fielding questions that came at him in rapid-fire succession.

After lunch, Kennedy went to the Morrison Hotel for his short talk to the United Brotherhood of Joiners and Carpenters. When he returned to his suite at the Ambassador East, he took a scheduled nap until 5 P.M. Then came more questions and answers.

By contrast, Nixon's advisers wanted Nixon to rest all day Sunday in Chicago. He remained virtually inaccessible. Advisers traveling with him didn't return telephone calls.

Arriving late Sunday at the Pick-Congress Hotel, Nixon looked tired. He spent most of Monday alone in his suite. Against the advice of his "brain trust," Nixon spoke in the morning to a hostile union—the same group Kennedy addressed after lunch. Returning to the hotel, Nixon remained incommunicado. He took only one telephone call—from Henry Cabot Lodge.

Not until he got into a limousine to ride to the television

studio were any of his TV advisers allowed to intrude. The ensuing ten-minute ride apparently was the only time Nixon was briefed for the crucial first debate. Then, alighting from the limousine, Nixon struck his sore knee. He quickly recovered, but the pain showed on his face.

*   *   *

The arrival of each candidate that Monday evening at WBBM smacked of a heavyweight championship fight, in which the challenger always makes the first entrance. We hoped Kennedy would arrive after Nixon. We might also pick up a slight psychological edge if Nixon had to wait for Kennedy. We were lucky. Kennedy arrived 15 minutes after Nixon.

CBS offered the services of its professional makeup director, Frances Arvold. Nixon declined. Instead, a Nixon adviser, Everett Hart, applied Lazy Shave, a pancake makeup designed to cover a stubble of beard.

Kennedy constantly used a sun lamp. When we ran the pre-broadcast test, I noticed a shiny spot on his forehead. Taking no chances, I applied ordinary pancake makeup to the area. I had purchased the makeup that afternoon.

Nixon paced the studio floor, waiting for Kennedy's arrival. He beckoned the producer and requested, as a personal favor, that he not be on camera if he happened to be mopping sweat from his face.

For Kennedy, I had specifically requested two things: (1) that the red light atop the camera (indicating that the camera is in use) be removed, and (2) that the program would include a substantial number of reaction shots—of Nixon when Kennedy spoke, and vice versa.

We had coached Kennedy to watch Nixon at all times while Nixon was speaking. We also suggested that Kennedy talk to the television viewer—not Nixon—and, if advisable, use each question as a springboard to another topic.

CBS, meantime, had to cope with almost twice as many reporters as expected. Two studios had to be cleared for 340 reporters. Both studios were equipped with TV monitors, telephones, teletypes, on-going transcript facilities and food. Separate VIP quarters were provided guests of each participant; Kennedy's space adjoined the studio where the debate took place.

With security provided by the Secret Service and the Chicago police department, the studio was kept clear of visitors except for the pool coverage by reporters and photographers. The control room was off limits to everybody except representatives of both candidates and working personnel.

* * *

At 8:30 P.M. (CDST), a hush fell over millions of living rooms across America. This was the moment that everybody had waited for.

Howard K. Smith, after short introductory remarks, introduced John Kennedy. A confident Kennedy delivered his eight-minute opening remarks and closed by saying, "I think it is time America started moving again."

Nixon startled his backers by opening with conciliatory remarks: "The things Senator Kennedy has said many of us can agree with. . . . I subscribe completely to the spirit that Senator Kennedy has expressed tonight."

The first question went to Kennedy from ABC's Bob Fleming: "Senator, the Vice President in his campaign has said you were naive and, at times, immature. On this issue, why do you think people should vote for you rather than the Vice President?"

Kennedy pounced on the question. "Well," he said, "the Vice President and I came to Congress together—1946 . . ." He closed by saying: "The question before us is: Which point of view and which party do we want to lead the United States?"

Surprisingly, Nixon said he had no response. He threw away 90 seconds of valuable time early in the debate.

As the program moved on, it was clear that Kennedy had done his homework, given his fresh, ready answers. Watching from the control booth, I wasn't happy, however, with the pictures of Nixon. I leaned over Don Hewitt's shoulder and whispered, "We're short of reaction shots of Nixon." Later, I got the picture I wanted—not for as long as I would have liked, but the picture was there—Nixon wiping his sweaty brow with a handkerchief.

Each candidate used three minutes and 20 seconds for closing statements, with Kennedy appearing last. When Howard K. Smith said, "Good night from Chicago," all of us heaved a huge sigh of relief, particularly everyone from CBS. One down, three to go.

As I headed for Kennedy's VIP quarters next to the studio, Chicago's Mayor Daley hardly could contain himself. "Leonard," he asked, "how many of these debates do we have?

Buy the time for more if you don't have any free ones. These debates will make Kennedy President."

It was estimated that 75 million people watched the debate—a much bigger audience than that which watched regular prime-time entertainment. In a public-opinion survey, most television viewers polled picked Kennedy as the winner. But most of those polled among the 8 million listeners on radio thought Nixon had won.

Hundreds of miles away, in Hot Springs, Arkansas, the debate was watched with keen interest by 11 Southern governors during their annual conference. The only strong Kennedy booster among them was Luther Hodges of North Carolina. Kennedy's vigorous, crisp debating style, however, won the support of nine more Southern governors. Hodges sent Kennedy a telegram of enthusiastic support. It was signed by ten Southern governors. The tide was turning.

Kennedy's air of self-assurance, his intense concentration and his engaging smile dissipated the Republicans' charges that he was "immature" and "too young." By contrast, Nixon looked haggard, tense, tired and seemingly awed by Kennedy. Shifting his weight because of the sore leg, he only contributed to his image as an ill-at-ease candidate.

The next day, few could recite exactly what was said during the debate. But Kennedy projected the "feel" of a winner. He had enhanced his image—and image won out over content.

The first TV debate was the most publicized single event in the 1960 campaign. Large headlines Tuesday trumpeted the story in all the population centers. Editorials, for the most part, gave Kennedy the edge. The Schwerin Research Foundation announced that its poll showed Kennedy the winner, 39 to 23.

*   *   *

Everywhere John Kennedy went, the crowds swelled—and so did cash contributions to his campaign. Kennedy's debate performance had made him a television celebrity, a politician touched by stardust.

He moved across center stage now, mobbed by squealers, squeezers, touchers, grabbers, autograph hounds and souvenir hunters. Women with babies in their arms jumped up and down, screaming for Kennedy. Crowds surged toward Kennedy like groupies clutching rock musicians.

At Charleston, West Virginia, I overheard two women talking. One ecstatically said: "I touched his car!" In Springfield, Illinois, a Kennedy worker held aloft a towel and shouted, "I got it! This is the towel he used. I'm gonna frame it!" As one dazed girl touched Kennedy's sleeve, her companion shrieked, "You touched him! Quick, Mary! Let me touch your hand, then Sally can touch mine!"

You had to see all this Kennedymania to appreciate it. But many still wondered: how much of it would translate into votes?

*   *   *

Debate No. 2 presented a problem with the site. Cleveland was the agreed-upon city, and NBC was the producer. But a tour of all available facilities in Cleveland convinced us that they were inadequate. We had to find another originating point. After more verbal sparring, we settled on Washington and its NBC-owned television station.

A few rule changes were adopted. At the request of Nixon's people, all cameras would be equipped with red lights that worked. The panel would include two members of the print media, chosen by their peers. They were Alvin Spivak of United Press International and Hal Levy of *Newsday*. They would join Paul Nivin (CBS) and Edward P. Morgan (ABC). The moderator would be NBC's Frank McGee.

Robert E. Kintner, president of NBC and a veteran political observer and broadcasting executive, carefully outlined the network's procedures and policies to William McAndrew, NBC's executive vice president of news. McAndrew had full authority for production of the program, but he would yield to the candidates' representatives on questions of lighting and makeup. No changes in the set were allowed, unless they were approved by the producer, Julian Goodman (NBC vice president of news), or the director, Frank Slingland, of NBC's Washington Bureau.

For the second debate, the rules called for Vice President Nixon to be questioned first—and to be given 2½ minutes to answer. Each candidate had 1½ minutes to respond to his opponent's answer. Questions could touch on any subject. As time began to run out, Nixon was asked the last question, leaving Kennedy to close the program by commenting on Nixon's answer.

Frank Slingland, who had produced "Meet the Press" for five years, set the stage at WRC-TV with a medium-brown grass-cloth as a backdrop. A hole was cut into the backdrop so that a camera could take head-on pictures of the panel reporters, who sat behind a gently curved desk with a low wall at their backs. Reporters who covered the event worked in a large storage area adjacent to the main studio.

Slingland planned to use 6-to-1 zoom lenses on the main cameras, but they provided too sharp a picture to suit either side. We agreed, instead, to keep the same lens arrangement used in Chicago.

When I arrived at the studio early on the day of the debate, Friday, October 7, it was "meat cooler" cold. I looked at the thermostat: 60 degrees. It was apparent that Nixon's people were trying to keep the studio cool so Nixon wouldn't perspire. I always felt that Nixon was a psychosomatic perspirer, but I wasn't going to settle for a refrigerator-cold room.

I asked someone about changing the thermostat.

"It operates with a key," he replied, "and no one is here who has a key."

I was getting upset. I went to the maintenance rooms downstairs. No one was around. I opened every door and finally found a man who looked worried.

"Where's the key to the studio thermostat?" I shouted.

"Don't know," he said.

I had a hunch that he knew, so I persisted. Soon we exchanged loud words, and he discovered the key. We returned to the studio and reset the thermostat. Despite the added heat of studio lights, the studio didn't get comfortable right away. When the program ended at 8:30 P.M., the thermostat read only 69 degrees.

In the meantime, Kennedy's schedule had been kept clear all day, allowing for him to prepare for the debate. When Kennedy arrived first at the studio by prearrangement, Bobby Kennedy was edgy. "What are they trying to do?" he said. "Freeze my brother to death?"

I explained that I had taken care of the temperature problem. The candidate and his brother checked the lighting, a detail that everybody talked about in the wake of Nixon's problem with lighting during the first debate.

This time, Nixon brought along his own professional makeup man, Stan Lawrence. Kennedy didn't need makeup.

As the debate progressed, I noticed that the monitor showed no reaction shots. I complained to Julian Goodman: "RCA, the parent company of NBC, is pro-Republican. They are trying every way possible to help Nixon, including the meat-cooler temperature." When still no reaction shots appeared, I went to Frank Slingland, the director.

"Where are the reaction shots?" I asked.

"This program doesn't need any," he said.

I was upset. "Frank," I said, "we either get reaction shots or I'm going into the reporters' studio and tell them the Democrats have been framed."

"You don't dare!" Slingland retorted, while busily calling the camera shots.

"Try me!" I shot back.

A few minutes later, reaction shots flashed on the TV screens. I finally got the one I wanted—Nixon mopping his brow. Through it all, Frank Slingland was mindful of the continuing imbroglio over reaction shots. He meticulously timed each one with a stopwatch.

* * *

From the start, the Kennedy-Nixon telecasts were compared by the news media with the Lincoln-Douglas debates. I tried hard to call the telecasts "joint appearances" by Kennedy and Nixon, but the Great Debate tag had more appeal—and it stuck.

For debate No. 2 between Kennedy and Nixon, the total viewing audience dropped from 75 million for the first appearance to 61 million. The audience had held steady for the entire hour during debate No. 1, but it dropped off sharply in the second half-hour of debate No. 2.

Although Kennedy was a clearcut winner in debate No. 1, most surveys indicated that he won narrowly in debate No. 2. The Schwerin Research Foundation poll, however, gave Kennedy a commanding edge, 44 to 28. A Hearst poll showed Kennedy winning, 44 to 38.

Now many newspaper columnists sensed that the debates were working to Kennedy's advantage. "Issues aside, it now seems clear that Vice President Nixon got caught in a bear trap when he decided to meet Senator Kennedy on television," Eugene Patterson wrote in the *Atlanta Constitution*. "The medium is good to Kennedy and most unkind to Nixon. It makes Kennedy look forceful. It makes Nixon look guilty."

Debate No. 3 on Thursday, October 13, was a two-city program produced by ABC. Kennedy was in New York, Nixon in Los Angeles.

ABC took great care that both studios were exact duplicates—right down to the sets made of warm-toned gold fabric and wood-grained panels, the L-shaped standing desks for podiums (the heaviest so far) and the bookcases to the right of each candidate. Some books were stage dressing; some were not. One book was entitled: *Things That Matter Most*.

The technological marvels that made debate No. 3 possible in 1960 are taken for granted today. The New York pickup was transmitted to Los Angeles, to be mixed with the West Coast pickup. The combined picture and sound was sent back to New York—there to be fed to all networks. There was a lag of $\frac{1}{36}$ of a second in Kennedy's picture from New York but it couldn't be detected by television viewers.

The studio where Nixon stood in Los Angeles was cooler (58 degrees) than Kennedy's in New York (72 degrees). When the candidates were shown on a split screen, the picture was technically perfect. Rather than risk technical problems, ABC didn't bother with reaction shots. For the first time, too, the candidates were provided with monitors.

Again, Frank McGee of NBC appeared—this time as a panelist, not as moderator. Bill Shadel of ABC moderated the panel, which included three new faces: Charles Von Freund of CBS, Douglas Cater of *Reporter* magazine and Roscoe Drummond of the *New York Herald-Tribune*.

The format was the same as in debate No. 2, but Kennedy fielded the first question. Soon a touch of humor showed up for the first time. Kennedy was asked whether, as the Democratic presidential candidate, he should apologize for Harry Truman having said that Texas Democrats who vote Republican "ought to go to hell."

Kennedy replied that he'd be hesitant in trying to admonish the former President on anything. "Maybe Mrs. Truman can," Kennedy said, "but I can't."

* * *

After the debate, I retreated for a quiet dinner with my wife in Manhattan. Little did I know that a storm brewed around me.

For debate No. 3, Kennedy had expected to give some direct quotes while on camera. He had come to the studio in New York with photostats of an Eisenhower letter, a page from a book from Army General Matthew Ridgway and a quotation from former Secretary of State Dulles.

During the warmup picture-taking, Nixon evidently observed the papers on his television monitor, on the rostrum in

New York. He publicly complained that Kennedy used notes in violation of the agreement for the debates. Nixon had proposed that the debates be held "without prepared texts or notes."

In truth, our lengthy talks that led to the joint appearances contained no mention of any rules about notes. We didn't agree to Nixon's proposal. Nor were we asked to agree to any proposal like it.

With Republicans charging that Kennedy "cribbed," the *Washington Post* editorialized, as did many other newspapers, that mountains were being made out of molehills. "The Republican charge that Senator Kennedy was 'cribbing' when he read a statement from President Eisenhower . . .," the *Post* commented, "is an offensive characterization of what, at worst, was a minor violation of an understanding which Mr. Kennedy obviously did not spell out in the same way that Mr. Nixon did. . . ."

When we returned to our hotel, I found a stack of telephone messages. I couldn't reach Kennedy until early the next morning. I explained to his satisfaction where we stood on Nixon's outburst. By nightfall, Nixon's bluster was lost in more topical developments of the campaign.

Many felt, however, that Nixon had come away with a slight edge in debate No. 3. I attributed this, in part, to the fact that there were no reaction shots. Moreover, Nixon was inclined to be more sure of himself away from Kennedy's presence.

Kennedy, meanwhile, wasn't about to let Nixon's complaints fade into oblivion. In Johnstown, Pennsylvania, he said, "When he (Nixon) said to Mr. Khrushchev on the occasion of the famous debate (in 1959 at an exhibition in the Soviet Union), 'You may be ahead of us in rockets, but we are ahead in color television'—and I quote him accurately because I have the notes. . . .

"I understand Mr. Casey Stengel (New York Yankees' manager) wants the seventh game (of the 1960 World Series) played over again because the manager of the Pittsburgh Pirates had notes. I believe that when we quote the record, we ought to quote it accurately, especially when discussing things with Mr. Nixon. It is a very wise thing to do, to bring the record with you, because it sounds a lot different when he gives it frequently, both mine and his. . . ."

With the election less than a month away, the two candidates still ran almost neck-and-neck. The Gallup Poll showed Kennedy 49, Nixon 46 and undecided 5.

The audience for debate No. 3 was about the same as that which saw the first half-hour of debate No. 2—61 million. But the audience in debate No. 3 increased slightly during the second half-hour, when 65 million tuned in.

*　*　*

Friday, October 14. Debate No. 4 was only a week away, but now we also had to map plans for debate No. 5, which was being discussed in the media.

Three senators who had voted for the repeal of Section 315 sent a wire to the networks. Senators John Pastore, Mike Monroney and Warren Magnuson called for a fifth debate, close to Election Day.

The networks moved to implement the idea. Kennedy had wired an unequivocal acceptance shortly before debate No. 3. Nixon was in favor, too, but with qualifications. He also favored stretching debate No. 4 to two hours, with the second hour consisting of phoned-in questions from viewers and three-minute answers from the candidates.

When debate No. 3 became history, Kennedy urged Nixon to agree to a fifth debate late in the campaign—to cover issues that might crop up unexpectedly. But Nixon said "no," explaining that his travel schedule would prevent the additional debate.

Nevertheless, Kennedy scored again by accepting Nixon's two-hour proposal for debate No. 4—and criticizing Nixon's rejection of a fifth debate. "I wanted this debate," Kennedy said in a prepared statement. "The networks were willing to give time for this debate. The American people want this debate. Only Mr. Nixon stands in the way. . . . If he did not want a fifth debate, it is equally difficult to understand why he would not permit postponement of the fourth debate into the final ten days of the campaign. . . .

"I call upon Mr. Nixon to reconsider his refusal and permit the American people another opportunity to hear us discuss issues—many of which change from a day-to-day basis as we near the election. . . ."

On October 20, Fred Scribner, Nixon's representative, met with the network executives and me. We issued a joint statement saying that we explored the idea of extending debate No.

4 to two hours, but that there wasn't enough time to develop the format.

At the meeting, I asked Scribner, "Is the fifth debate still open?"

"No," he said.

* * *

ABC drew the fourth debate, which was held as scheduled on October 21 in New York. Both Kennedy and Nixon asked for monitors with clocks. Each candidate's monitor would be turned off while he spoke.

Again, the candidates appeared in a new set—six feet apart. The media panel—moderated by Quincy Howe of ABC—was moved closer to the candidates. The panelists: John Edwards (ABC), Walter Cronkite (CBS), Frank Singiser (MBS) and John Chancellor (NBC). And this time we didn't have to argue for reaction shots. The director, Marshall Diskin, punched up reactions with one-shot and two-shot cameras.

The format was the same as that in debate No. 1, except that Nixon opened and closed. The subject was foreign affairs. Kennedy again shunned makeup. Nixon wore heavy makeup.

As in the second debate, the audience declined during the second half-hour—this time from 65 million to 62.5 million. The outcome of debate No. 4 was close, with both sides claiming victory.

Would there be a debate No. 5? Kennedy hoped so. He stayed on the attack, charging that "Mr. Nixon is willing to answer any question—only if no one questions his answer. . . . Some say his wild charges lately prove there never was a new Nixon anyway—it was just the old Nixon with new lighting."

Again and again, Kennedy asked, in effect, "Why is Nixon afraid to meet me in a fifth debate?" Something had to give. On Sunday evening, October 23, it did. Kennedy received a wire from Nixon, who suggested not only a debate between both vice-presidential candidates, but a Kennedy-Nixon debate focusing only on what to do about Communist Cuba.

Kennedy sent a reply telegram to Nixon in hopes of arranging a fifth debate. The text, which addressed Cuba, read in part:

> . . . Your telegram to me tonight clearly indicates I was right in calling for such a debate—for the distortions of the record concerning my position on Cuba exceed any others you have made during this campaign. You have developed the technique of

having your writers rewrite my statements, using those rewritten statements and attacking me for things I have never said or advocated. . . .

I have never advocated and I do not now advocate intervention in Cuba in violation of our treaty obligations and in fact stated in Johnstown, Pennsylvania, that whatever we did with Cuba should be within the confines of international law.

What I have advocated is that we use all available communications—radio, television and the press—and the moral power of the American government—to let the forces of freedom in Cuba know that we believe that freedom will again rise in their country. I will be pleased to discuss the whole record of Cuba with you—how this island only 90 miles from our borders fell into Communist hands and the sorry record of Administration inaction with regard to Cuba. . . .

I think the American people want and deserve to hear us discuss all the important problems which face our country and to limit the subject of the fifth debate to one country would be to subvert the purpose of such a debate.

I have instructed Mr. Leonard Reinsch of my staff to meet with your staff and attempt to further work out details for this important fifth debate.

John F. Kennedy

We started negotiations for the fifth debate on Monday, October 24, in Washington. With little sleep as a result of having to travel all night, I was matched against an excellent negotiator in Fred Scribner. I was never quite sure that Nixon wanted the fifth debate. I wondered whether Nixon had accepted the idea of a fifth debate for no other reason than to shut off Kennedy's attacks on him.

The next day, the networks suggested a format for a fifth debate. The candidates would open with a statement on an agreed-upon topic; they would rebut each other, then interrogate each other. A moderator would keep peace and time. There would be no panel.

Both sides issued charges of bad faith, but we zeroed in on Monday, October 31, as the probable date and Philadelphia the site. We had met all the Republican conditions, except for limiting the subject to Cuba. We still couldn't get a definite answer on the Monday night date.

The negotiations dragged on all week. On Friday, October 28, I wired the networks, saying that we'd been unsuccessful in trying to arrange the debate. My telegram read in part:

. . . Apparently the Republican candidate was not acting in good faith in his acceptance of the fifth debate in his belated and much publicized Sunday telegram, and is not willing to meet Senator Kennedy again face to face before a seventy million television audience in the final days of this crucial campaign. . . .

As you will recall, the Republican candidate placed several stipulations in his acceptance which included: the appearance of the vice-presidential candidates, and a limitation of subject to a discussion of Cuba. Although we felt the vice-presidential candidates' debate should be a separate appearance, we were willing to agree to this stipulation. It became evident, however, that public interest called for a broad discussion of many other vital issues besides Cuba in the closing days of the campaign. While we felt one hour was sufficient for the fifth appearance, Senator Kennedy was willing to agree to the longer period if the Republican candidate insisted on a longer period as a requirement for his appearance. . . .

Senator Kennedy appreciates the willingness of the networks to provide facilities for this important fifth debate. He remains available to meet the Republican candidate face to face on the television and radio networks at any time and any place and has asked me to continue to make myself available to bring the discussion of arrangements to a successful conclusion.

J. Leonard Reinsch

Pushing hard for a decision, Kennedy wired Nixon on October 28, asking for an acceptance or refusal by midnight. The next day, UPI reported that Nixon had broken off negotiations for a fifth debate. The wire service also carried charges and counter charges by both sides.

On Sunday, October 30, the *Chicago Tribune* headlined: "GOP CUTS OFF PLANNING OF FIFTH DEBATE." It was virtually all over but the balloting. Almost lost in the shuffle was an Associated Press report on October 29 from Las Vegas:

Senator John F. Kennedy was being quoted as favorite in man-to-man betting to defeat Richard M. Nixon for the presidency, according to a consensus of six licensed Las Vegas bookmaking establishments.

CHAPTER 15

Election 1960

WITH THE FIFTH DEBATE A LOST CAUSE, I concentrated on the campaign and the Democrats' final television program.

The stretch drive for the Oval Office heated up like never before. For John Kennedy and Richard Nixon, the long, punishing marathon was almost over—the finish line at 1600 Pennsylvania Avenue was breath-takingly within reach.

Whenever possible, I joined the Kennedy campaign trail. Kennedy and his most trusted advisers rode in the Convair known as the "Mother Ship." Two other American D-6 airplanes carried the staff, reporters and photographers.

When I wasn't needed on the "Mother Ship," I preferred to ride with the photographers. They were refreshingly laid-back, with little to do until the next stop. On presidential campaigns, you'd better learn to relax, to catch up on sleep and meals, if at all possible. The world suddenly becomes a blur of long hours, jackrabbit arrivals and departures, crash deadlines and stale sandwiches on the run.

Still, it all adds up to memories, to a wonderful camaraderie with reporters and photographers, to an emotional rush that you suddenly miss when Election Day arrives.

You miss the reporters who, just like that, are reassigned to the other candidate, then return to cover your candidate again. You miss hearing them tell you that they're glad to be back with the Kennedy entourage, that ours is a more carefree campaign and that they had better access to our candidate. You wonder if they tell Nixon's people the same thing.

Early in the campaign, some reporters complained that they had trouble obtaining printed copies of Nixon's remarks. There was, I was told, an adversary position taken by Nixon toward everybody in the news media. Herb Klein did his best to patch things up, but it was a struggle all the way.

* * *

The campaign trail of John Kennedy read like a Rand-McNally atlas: Salt Lake City . . . Duluth, Minnesota . . . Miami . . . Teaneck, New Jersey . . . Bridgeport, Connecticut . . . Lewiston, Maine . . . Albuquerque . . . Toledo . . . Roanoke and Norfolk, Virginia. . . . And yes, you do get to know the way to San Jose, too.

East Coast, West Coast, all across the land, you live with the constant reality that in politics there isn't any second place. Everybody loves a winner, and nobody cares about who loses. About all second place can get you is maybe an audition on those American Express commercials that say "Remember me?"

In a race as blisteringly close as the one in 1960, one misstep can knock you out of the running forever. You worry around the clock that the other guys are cooking up some secret strategy that, at the eleventh hour, will swing pivotal votes. You push yourself to your limit of endurance. Then you drive even harder and faster. You have time only to make snap decisions—and it's usually by reflex only.

Years later, the memories of lighter moments flash back— first in a trickle, then a rush.

In Duluth, too many microphones—badly placed—cause an audio problem for Kennedy's speech. En route to the next town, Kennedy asks, "Who's responsible for those microphone problems?"

"I don't know," I tell him. "I have only broadcast responsibilities."

"How about you being responsible?" he asks.

How can I say "no" to a candidate for President?

On a campaign flight out of Chicago, Frank Stanton hands me a stack of photographs of debate No. 1 for Kennedy to autograph. Kennedy happily obliges. When he finishes, I place my autographed photo in the stack of other pictures.

"Look what I wrote on your picture," Kennedy says.

The photo is inscribed: "To Leonard Reinsch, whose great debates made the great debates possible, John F. Kennedy."

On a Kennedy campaign trip, reporters are constantly stripped of pens, pencils and combs. The guy who always seems to ask to borrow them is John Kennedy.

In 1960, shopping centers become a new phenomenon of political campaigning—necessary to reach a population that is shifting from America's cities to her suburbs.

The pace sometimes becomes so furious that even junk food is a luxury. Kennedy usually runs behind schedule, so the first item scratched from the schedule is—what else, but—lunch. All of which brings wisecracks from Kennedy's staff: "The Senator has said 17 million Americans go to bed hungry at night, and he expects you to do your part."

Never one to duck the religious issue, Kennedy sometimes treats it light-heartedly. At the Al Smith dinner in New York, Kennedy cracks: "Cardinal Spellman is the only man so widely respected in American politics that he could bring together amicably at the same banquet table, for the first time in this campaign, two political leaders who are increasingly apprehensive about the November election, who have long eyed each other suspiciously and who have disagreed so strongly, both publicly and privately—Vice President Nixon and Governor Rockefeller. . . ."

Then Kennedy tells his audience that he doesn't regard former President Truman's strong language lightly. "I have sent him the following wire," Kennedy says.

Dear Mr. President: I have noted with interest your suggestion as to where those who vote for my opponent should go. While I understand and sympathize with your deep motivation, I think it is important that our side try to refrain from raising the religious issue.

John Kennedy had passed two important tests in his campaign with flying colors. He deftly fended off the uproar over his Catholicism, and clearly emerged the winner in the debates.

The third major event that tested him in 1960 almost went unnoticed, if not unappreciated. On October 19, Martin Luther King, Jr., a hero in his fellow blacks' struggle for equality, was arrested in the Magnolia restaurant of Rich's department store in Atlanta. Also arrested were 52 other blacks.

Five days later, all except King were released. On a legal technicality, King was sentenced to four months at hard labor.

He was sent to Georgia's Reidsville state prison, where at times an inmate is left for dead.

Sargent Shriver, Kennedy's brother-in-law, who with Harris Wofford was in charge of the campaign's civil rights section, learned of King's arrest and telephoned Kennedy in Chicago to tell him about it. Richard Nixon knew about it, too, but chose to ignore it.

Without hesitation, Kennedy telephoned King's wife, Coretta, in Atlanta. He assured her of his interest and willingness to intervene. Mrs. King, who was expecting a child, advised friends about Kennedy's call. Two Southern governors weren't so enthusiastic; they warned the Kennedys that they would lose the South if they intervened in King's case.

Bob Kennedy promptly telephoned Judge Oscar Mitchell, who had set the sentence, and inquired about the right to bail. On October 27, eight days after the arrest, King was released on $2,000 bail, pending appeal.

Kennedy's campaign strategists seized on King's release from one of the nation's most notorious prisons. On the Sunday before Election Day, more than 1 million pamphlets describing the episode—and Kennedy's role in it—were distributed outside every black church in America.

* * *

As the days of campaigning dwindled to a precious few, the pace picked up. So did the crowds who flocked to $100-a-plate dinners and massed at railroad crossings and airports to meet John Kennedy.

In the wee hours of Saturday morning, November 4, Kennedy and his entourage arrived to a spirited welcome in Bridgeport, Connecticut, after a frantic day of campaign stops in Virginia, Ohio and Illinois (and a national television talk in Chicago Stadium).

A chill autumn rain fell in Bridgeport, but Governor Abraham Ribicoff and John Bailey, a powerful Connecticut Democrat, had mustered a huge crowd and a high school pep band. Waterbury, our stop for the night, was 27 miles away.

Along the way, thousands of cheering admirers gathered at every crossroad, their torchlights and red flares flickering in the predawn rain. At 3 A.M., a throng estimated at more than 30,000 screamed greetings to Kennedy when we arrived at the Roger Smith Hotel in Waterbury. There, a dog-tired Kennedy stepped out on a balcony and said, almost by reflex, "My name is Kennedy, and I have come to ask for your support." It was 4 o'clock when Kennedy went to bed.

With three hours of sleep, Kennedy began his final two days of the campaign—at places like Wallingford, New Haven, Suffolk County, Providence, Burlington and Manchester—all across New England. His journey ended in Boston, where preparations were under way for an Election Eve national telecast.

Kennedy had been indefatigable in stumping the nation. (The word "stumping" stems from a candidate who hopped onto a stump to deliver his speech to farmers and backwoodsmen who had complained that they couldn't see him.) Nixon's schedule was no less arduous. He was building to a crescendo. The Harris polls for Kennedy showed a frighteningly close election—and a surge to Nixon in the final ten days. It was only during those last days that Nixon called on President Eisenhower to breathe more life into his campaign. Although the Democrats spent $2.6 million during the last three weeks of the campaign, the Republicans outspent them in every category. Vast chunks of the money went to television. Nixon made televised speeches at 7 o'clock each evening during the final week of the campaign.

Twenty-four hours before the election, the Republicans unveiled their secret television strategy—a four-hour telethon from Detroit over ABC. Theirs was a slick, excellent production, albeit "cornball" at times. The program featured big-name entertainers, as well as questions and answers (carefully screened) from across the country.

We had scheduled a 15-minute telecast from Manchester, New Hampshire, on the eve of the election. Bob Kennedy was concerned about the impact of the Republicans' telethon; he asked me to buy 15 more minutes on another network. Those back-to-back telecasts created production problems. Ted Sorensen and I flew in a small chartered plane from Boston to Manchester to help put the telecasts on the air.

The Republicans culminated their televised get-out-the-vote drive with a three-way hookup among President Eisenhower, Nixon and Lodge at 11 P.M. on CBS. They repeated the program a half-hour later on NBC and ABC.

Nixon then returned to the West Coast, the final leg of a campaign that had carried him 65,500 miles in the air, to appearances in 188 cities for 150 major speeches. His staff estimated that he had been seen in person by 10 million people.

For his part, Kennedy signed off his television campaign with a late-night program on CBS after appearing at a huge, boisterous rally in the Boston Garden. He also spoke from historic Faneuil Hall, with Lyndon Johnson appearing in Austin, Texas, and Jacqueline Kennedy in Hyannisport. The announcer said "Good night" at 11:29:20. The campaign was over.

Even foreign leaders expressed wonderment and dismay at the frenetic pace of the 1960 presidential race. So did Douglas Cater, who wrote in the *New York Times*: "We want the contest to be a vigorous one. Yet, when all is said and done, it is not a whirling dervish we seek to elect, but, hopefully, a wise and unwearied leader."

* * *

On Tuesday morning, November 8, Senator Kennedy voted in Ward 3 in downtown Boston. Like most of my colleagues, I was an absentee voter. I mailed a ballot to my hometown, Atlanta.

We left for Hyannisport to begin the long, suspenseful hours of watching the returns—and the waiting. A command post was set up in the compound at Bobby Kennedy's home. My responsibility: To handle television and radio arrangements at the Armory, the site of press headquarters.

And so began an interminable, nerve-wracking night, consisting only of a few catnaps, but no sleep; of countless doughnuts and cup after cup of coffee.

It was clear that it would be a close—oh, so close—election that could go either way. At the command post, telephone lines bristled with up-to-date information and vote counts, but still no clear hint as to the winner. The long-distance bill that night exceeded $10,000.

As the hours dragged on, Secret Service agents arrived on the scene. They were organized to protect the elected President and his family—in either Hyannisport or Los Angeles—as soon as a winner was determined.

At 3 A.M., it was announced that Nixon would make a televised statement. We all expected a concession. Appearing before cameras at the Ambassador Hotel in Los Angeles, Nixon wore a fixed smile; his wife, Pat, brimmed with tears.

"If the present trend continues," Nixon said, "Senator Kennedy will be the next President of the United States. I want Senator Kennedy—and I want all of you to know—that certainly if this trend does continue and he does become our next President, he will have my whole-hearted support, and yours, too."

One hour later, Herb Klein, Nixon's press secretary, cautiously stated that the election remained undecided.

At the Armory 3,000 miles away, 300 journalists watched Nixon on television. They all were professionals, but physically and emotionally drained. You can go only so far on missed meals and sleepless nights. When Nixon refused to concede, just about everybody vented emotions with words that couldn't appear in most publications and certainly not on any broadcast.

At 3:50 A.M., John Kennedy returned to his house and tried to catch some sleep. He, too, was disappointed that Nixon hadn't conceded.

For the key states of California, Michigan, Illinois, Minnesota and Pennsylvania, the returns still were not in. Hours later, however, Michigan went to Kennedy, boosting his unofficial electoral vote total to 285—enough to win.

Shortly before 6 A.M., Chief of Secret Service Urbanus E. Baughman directed his Hyannisport agents to move to the Kennedy home. Soon 16 agents under the direction of Inspector Burrell Petersen established tight security around the President-elect.

Nixon had hoped to carry Illinois, Pennsylvania, Texas, Ohio and California. By 9 A.M., however, Republican leaders conceded that Kennedy's wispy lead in Pennsylvania and Michigan was unassailable. Kennedy had won, and the other states he carried would be merely frosting on the cake.

When John Kennedy was awakened, he was told that the arithmetic victory in the Electoral College was assured. He later wandered in the crisp November air outside for several hours. He was at the command post at 12:54 (EST) when Nixon's press secretary went on television to read the concession wire from Nixon:

"I want to repeat through this wire the congratulations and best wishes I extended to you on television last night. I know you will have the united support of all Americans as you lead the nation in the cause of peace and freedom in the next four years."

The Vice President never made a personal appearance and

evidently considered his remarks the night before a virtual concession, although he never used the word "concede." Kennedy certainly didn't view it as a concession speech.

As soon as Nixon's wire was read on television, we went to work preparing for Kennedy's appearance on nationwide television at the Armory. Less than an hour later, at 1:45 P.M., the President-elect arrived at the Armory, accompanied by his wife, mother and father, and brothers and sisters. It was his father's first public appearance with him since the first primary.

Elated correspondents, 300 in number, who had drawn the winner, crammed into the Armory among the TV cameras, microphones and spectator stands. It was much easier to control the media crowds, now that I had the backing of the Secret Service.

Kennedy read the wire from Nixon, then a wire from President Eisenhower. He closed his brief remarks by saying, with a grin, "My wife and I now prepare for a new administration— and a new baby." (The baby was due in three weeks.)

When asked which state put him over the top, Kennedy replied tactfully, as only a master politician can. "All the ones we carried," he said.

And so ended a night and morning when 83 million viewers—many without sleep—watched the election returns on television.

* * *

John Kennedy became the youngest President ever elected, and the first President born in the 20th Century. Worldwide reaction to Kennedy's victory was enthusiastic. Even Soviet Premier Nikita Khrushchev sent a wire to the "Esteemed Mr. Kennedy."

The 1960 election will go down as one of the closet ever. Of the 68,836,385 votes cast, Kennedy clung to a lead of only 119,450 votes, a plurality of only one-tenth of 1%. The Electoral College vote was as follows:

> Kennedy: 303
> Nixon: 219

All told, Nixon won 26 states and Kennedy 23, with Mississippi voting for Senator Harry Byrd of Virginia. Kennedy's strategy for victory—conceived back in August—worked to near perfection. With few exceptions, such as Ohio, the electoral votes fell in place as planned.

Kennedy's victory margin of approximately two votes per precinct was the closest vote since 1880, when James Garfield won the presidency with 4,454,416 votes to Winfield S. Hancock's 4,444,952 votes.

What's more, the 1960 election spawned a wave of might-have-beens and what-ifs. For instance, Kennedy carried Illinois by only 8,858 votes—out of more than 4.7 million votes—for 27 electoral votes. In New Jersey, Kennedy's margin was only 22,091—for 16 electoral votes.

What if Illinois and New Jersey had tipped the other way? That would have subtracted 43 electoral votes from Kennedy—and Nixon would have won in electoral votes, 262 to 260!

And what if the Republicans had called on their biggest gun—President Eisenhower—earlier in the campaign? What if Nixon had concentrated on the largest states, instead of visiting all 50 states? What if Nixon had refused to debate? What if Nixon had come to the rescue of Martin Luther King, Jr.? (In Illinois, blacks had cast 250,000 votes for Kennedy.) The Monday-morning quarterbacking goes on and on. . . .

* * *

Of all the campaign issues, religion was the biggest in 1960, according to the University of Michigan Research Center, whose surveys showed that Kennedy lost 1.5 million more votes than he gained, as a result of his Catholic faith.

Even so, the Catholic issue helped Kennedy in the large states. Of ten states with the largest number of Catholics, Kennedy won seven—for a total of 103 electoral votes.

It was clear, too, that our radio and television buying helped Kennedy. Air time was purchased, for the most part, in states with large numbers of electoral votes: New York (45), New Jersey (16), Pennsylvania (32), California (32), Illinois (27), Ohio (25), Texas (24) and Michigan (20). These states provided a total of 221 electoral votes out of the 269 needed to win. Of these states, too, Kennedy lost only Ohio— a surprise loss, since Governor Michael DeSalle was an early booster of Kennedy.

Of course, no one can minimize the significance of the Kennedy-Nixon debates to Kennedy's victory. John and Robert Kennedy themselves said they were the biggest factor. All pollsters agreed—using different figures—that Kennedy was the overall winner in the debates, and that Kennedy achieved his biggest gain after debate No. 1.

A Roper survey for CBS showed that 57% of those who voted believed that the televised debates had influenced their vote. Another 6% said their final decision rested on their reaction to the debates. Of that 6%, a total of 73% said they voted for Kennedy and 27% for Nixon.

At the same time, one Gallup Poll showed that 85 million people watched one or more of the debates. NBC claimed a figure of 115 million, while CBS showed 120 million watching one or more of the debates.

All of which is a distant cry from the turn-of-the-century, when Democratic presidential candidate William Jennings Bryan set out on the campaign trail. His journey carried him only 18,000 miles in three months, during which he gave as many as 19 speeches in one day. In the end, he reached an audience of fewer than 5 million.

What a difference television makes.

Leonard Reinsch tests the effectiveness of the elevator in the rostrum at the 1960 Convention. It was designed to keep the speaker's head height at a constant 11 feet, 4 inches above the floor.

President Truman dines with friends on June 27, 1945, at the home of Independence Mayor Surman.

Truman and Reinsch pose for the press at NAB Board meeting arranged at the White House by Leonard Reinsch.

Candidate Adlai Stevenson and Reinsch consider strategy in Atlanta.

Adlai Stevenson fields questions from reporters.

Jim Farley, on right, veteran Democratic leader from New York moved for suspension of rules and the nomination of Sparkman at the Chicago convention during the summer of 1952.

The rostrum area at the 1956 Convention had air conditioning and lights to eliminate facial shadows, as well as a TelePrompter under glass.

The architect's rendering of the floor plan for the 1960 Convention shows the rostrum and dias at left center with press galleries on each side of the rostrum and stepped platforms for the press photographers.

As he leaves Atlanta for the 1960 Convention, Reinsch tests the back of the Democratic donkey with the aid of stewardesses.

Reinsch cleans up
on the day after the
1960 Convention.

Shirley McLaine was a hostess at the 1960 Los Angeles convention.

All conventions are hectic for the men coordinating them, but here Reinsch looks like he enjoys it.

Candidate Kennedy and brother Robert prepare for debate.

As sparklers are set ablaze on over-sized cake, distinguished guests look on at birthday party for President Kennedy.

Leonard Reinsch turns over to the President the Radio-TV Executive Society Gold Medal which Reinsch received on behalf of the Chief Executive in New York.

Broadcasting executives join Kennedy and Reinsch.

Reinsch, Johnson, and Kennedy share a laugh.

Lyndon Johnson never was totally comfortable with Reinsch's role in the conventions or in the White House.

The Atlantic City convention hall was the site of the 1964 Democratic Convention where Senator Pastore (here with Reinsch) was the keynoter.

President Nixon shares a laugh with Reinsch and, on right, James M. Cox, Jr., and Senator Richard Russell at a reception for Senator Russell.

During the Campaign of 1968 the nomination of Senator
Hubert Humphrey was practically assured. He had not lost a
partisan election in 20 years.

Reinsch jokes with Walter Cronkite and Hale Boggs.

Leonard Reinsch and Governor Carter entertain Amy.

Senator "Scoop" Jackson walks with Reinsch at television station WSB in Atlanta.

Senator Edward Kennedy fought Carter in the 1980 primaries and on the convention floor tried to persuade the convention to nullify a delegate rule in a bid to upset the vote for Carter.

Ambassador Edwin O. Reischauer speaks with Reinsch in Tokyo about the growing exchange of cultural and educational television programs with Japan.

CHAPTER 16

December 1960

CLARK CLIFFORD, A LONG-TIME WASHINGTON ATTORNEY, took charge of President-elect Kennedy's transition team. He had to fill 204 government jobs by December 1 and another 406 by New Year's Day of 1961.

While John Kennedy went to Florida for a much-needed rest, his staff members busily perused what was known as the "blue book," which listed all presidential-appointed jobs. Most of Kennedy's staffers vigorously looked for government appointments. The "blue book" was so well-thumbed that the pages all but fell out.

When Kennedy returned from his vacation in Palm Beach, his life at home in Hyannisport resumed at a hellfire pace. Clifford's transition work had been thorough—and had received superb cooperation from President Eisenhower—but now Kennedy tackled one problem after another. The most pressing: Whom to appoint to his Cabinet?

I met with Kennedy at his Washington home on December 2, and told him that he didn't need to worry about appointing me to any government post. Kennedy's deeply tanned face expressed surprise. I explained that I preferred to stay in the broadcasting business, although I agreed to continue as a radio-TV consultant—on call as needed.

The President-elect gave me my first assignment—to coordinate all radio and television arrangements for the inauguration. Most of us think of inaugural ceremonies as quick and uncomplicated. The swearing-in of the new President and Vice President is the most important item on the agenda. But inaugurations consist of hordes of activities that stretch into the wee hours of the morning-after.

On Thursday, January 19, 1961, Washington ground to a standstill with the inauguration only 24 hours away. Eight inches of snow made most streets impassible. All night long, regiments of men and snow machines cleared the parade route on Pennsylvania Avenue from the Capitol to the reviewing stand in front of the White House.

During the snowy day, Kennedy walked across the street from his home on N Street to the residence of Helen Montgomery and her father. They had allowed newsmen to use their home as they awaited statements from the President-elect. Kennedy presented a plaque which read:

"In the cold winter of 1960–61, this house had an important role in history. From it was flashed to the world news of pre-inaugural announcements by President John F. Kennedy. Presented by grateful newsmen who were given haven here by Miss Helen Montgomery and her father, Charles Montgomery."

* * *

Inauguration Day, January 20. At 10:55 A.M., John and Jacqueline Kennedy, accompanied by Speaker Sam Rayburn and Senator John Sparkman, departed for the White House. There, they chatted over coffee with the Eisenhowers before leaving at 11:31 for Capitol Hill.

The sweeping political transition on this day wasn't lost on those of us who are fond of counting noses. When Eisenhower was inaugurated in 1953, there were 26 Republicans occupying governors' mansions and 22 Democrats. As he was leaving office, the total of governors was: 34 Democrats and 16 Republicans.

Historians, too, were kept busy all day reaching into the archives for inaugural trivia:

—Of the 43 presidential inaugurals from 1879 to 1957, there were 26 in clear weather, ten in rain and seven in snow. When William Howard Taft was inaugurated in March of 1909, Washington was buried in ten inches of snow. The ceremony had to be moved indoors to the Senate chambers.

—The first President to be inaugurated in Washington? Thomas Jefferson, in 1805—back when the capital was a shabby village on the Potomac's north bank.

—The first President to have an inaugural ball in his honor? James Madison, in 1809.

—The first Presidents to ride together to the inauguration? Martin Van Buren and Andrew Jackson, in 1837.

—The first inauguration to be photographed? The swearing-in of James Buchanan, in 1857.

—The first Presidents elected while serving in Congress? James Garfield of the House of Representatives in 1880, and Warren Harding of the Senate, in 1920.

—The longest inaugural address? By Benjamin Harrison—9,000 words, in 1889.

—The first to ride to his inauguration with his wife? Woodrow Wilson, in 1913.

—The first to ride to and from the Capitol in an automobile? Warren Harding, in 1921.

—The first to be inaugurated on radio? Calvin Coolidge, in 1925.

—The first to be inaugurated on January 20? Franklin Roosevelt, in 1937.

—The first to be inaugurated in front of television cameras? Harry Truman, in 1949.

On this Inauguration Day in 1961, more history was made. The ceremony was attended by four former First Ladies: Mrs. Woodrow Wilson, Mrs. Franklin Roosevelt, Mrs. Harry Truman and Mrs. Dwight Eisenhower.

The skies were sunny, but the air was scathing cold—22 degrees, with an 18-mile-an-hour wind blowing in from the north. More than 50,000 spectators turned out for the swearing-in ceremony; another 1 million-plus lined the parade route.

The program didn't begin on time. Under provisions of the 20th Amendment, Eisenhower's term ended at precisely 12 noon, and Kennedy's began. With the ceremonies delayed past noon, Kennedy was President without constitutional authority until he took the oath of office.

Finally, the program began at 12:20 P.M., with music from the U.S. Marine Band. Richard Cardinal Cushing, the Catholic archbishop of Boston, pronounced the invocation—one which reporters said was extraordinarily long.

As Cardinal Cushing prayed on, smoke began rising around the rostrum. I quickly looked for the origin of the smoke. Had paper been set on fire below the platform? No, just smoke from the motor that raised and lowered the rostrum.

But which connection? Which wire? There were eight connections and more than 30 wires tangled on the platform. What happens if I pull the wrong wire? If I pull the connection from the public-address system, the crowd will complain. If I pull the heater connection, everybody on the platform could catch pneumonia. If I yank any wires that hook up radio and television, the networks will scream at me forever. I could see the trivia books already: "First person to knock an inaugural off the air: Leonard Reinsch (whose job was to make sure it stayed on the air)."

While I frantically tugged at the electrical wires, Eisenhower whispered to Kennedy, "You must have a hot speech today." David Brinkley commented on NBC: "Leonard Reinsch seems to be the chief fireman."

There was nothing left to do but pull one of those eight wires—and hope for the best. Success! I had pulled the plug to the rostrum motor! My 1-in-8 shot was unbelievably lucky! The smoke stopped, and Cardinal Cushing went on as if nothing had happened.

First, Lyndon Johnson was administered the oath of office by Speaker Rayburn. Then, at 12:51 P.M., John Kennedy began repeating the oath given by Chief Justice Earl Warren. At the end of the swearing-in, the Marine Band struck up "Hail to the Chief"—and Kennedy was accorded a 21-gun salute.

And history again was written: Dwight Eisenhower, at 70, the oldest President to occupy the White House, was succeeded by John Kennedy, at 43 the youngest inaugurated after an election. (Some historians listed Kennedy as the 35th President. They counted Grover Cleveland twice, as the 22nd and the 24th President.) At the same time, Kennedy became the first President since Andrew Jackson to have served in both the House and the Senate.

For the oath of office, Kennedy provided the family Bible once owned by his grandfather—the Douay version used for centuries by English-speaking Catholics. Harry Truman, too, had laid his left hand on a Catholic Bible—a Gutenberg.

Kennedy's inaugural address of 1,300 words lasted 14 minutes—and it was one of the most eloquent in American history. The most oft-quoted line: ". . . and so my fellow Americans: Ask not what your country can do for you—ask what you can do for your country."

Kennedy went on: "My fellow citizens of the world: Ask not what America will do for you, but what together we can do for the freedom of man. . . . Let every nation know, whether it wishes us well or ill, that we shall pay any price, bear any burden, meet any hardship, support any friend, oppose any foe to assure the survival and success of liberty. This much we pledge and more."

The entire inauguration was beamed worldwide by the Voice of America in 36 languages (Radio Free Europe transmitted the event to countries in Eastern Europe). Press releases were written in 56 languages.

After the ceremony, the new President, according to custom, lunched at the Capitol with VIPs and other dignitaries. He first signed two documents of nomination—one with the names of ten Cabinet officers; the other for the new Ambassador to the United Nations, Adlai Stevenson.

At 2 P.M., Kennedy and his official party rode to the reviewing stand in front of the White House. Again, electric heaters were provided; but this time there was no smoke. In nearby Lafayette Park, NBC carried the program via four RCA color cameras—the first color ever for an inaugural parade.

Former President Eisenhower, meanwhile, had left the inaugural stand for a private luncheon at the F Street Club hosted by Lewis Strauss, former chairman of the Atomic Energy Commission. At about 3:30 P.M., private citizen Dwight Eisenhower drove to his farm in Gettysburg.

The parade, late in starting, lasted until shortly past 6 P.M.—after dark and long after the networks had shut down. That evening, 25,000 people jammed into five locations for the inaugural balls—each one attended by President Kennedy, who had to push his way through snow and ice.

One of my responsibilities was to make sure television viewers got a good picture of the President and his wife, together with the Vice President and his wife. It sounded simple, but it became almost impossible. Whenever I got three of them in place, it took awhile to find the fourth. Then when I put the fourth in place, two more were missing.

I finally persuaded Mrs. Kennedy and Mrs. Johnson to stay put, then I retrieved Vice President Johnson and asked him to promise he wouldn't wander away. Hurriedly, I enlisted the help of General C. V. (Ted) Clifton, the President's new military aide, to open a wedge through the crowd so that we could drag the President to the first row of seats. There, all posed for the required picture.

It was 2 A.M. when President Kennedy went to the home of

columnist Joseph Alsop to relax and finish the long, long hours of festivities. At 3:30 A.M., Kennedy left to go home—to 1600 Pennsylvania Avenue.

* * *

Saturday, January 21, Kennedy's first full day in office, was get-acquainted day. It was clear that Kennedy's style would differ sharply from Eisenhower's. Under Eisenhower, Sherman Adams was responsible for keeping problems off Eisenhower's desk if someone else could resolve them. Kennedy, by contrast, didn't want predigested solutions that needed only his initials; he wanted problems brought to him—to be hashed over again and again—before he made a decision.

Moreover, Kennedy expected to receive from each government department a twice-weekly report on its current problems and impending decisions.

At noon on January 21, the Democratic National Committee was gaveled to order by Chairman Henry Jackson, who shortly would be succeeded by John Bailey, 56, the Democratic state chairman of Connecticut who was fulfilling a lifelong ambition.

Kennedy addressed the committee at 12:30 and asked everybody to stand up and cheer Jackson. "Scoop automatically loses his share of the $4 million debt," Kennedy quipped. "We're not going to let him in on it. . . ." For a change, the meeting adjourned with everybody happy.

* * *

President Kennedy set a pattern that would be followed by all of his successors—news conferences on live television. Kennedy opened each news conference with a statement or statements, then fielded questions from reporters.

The President's first news conference—at 6 P.M. on January 25—reached 17 million homes, almost three times the audiences claimed by each of the top network news programs.

From the start, Kennedy's style was very much an indelible trademark—a quick reply, a ready smile, a gracious manner that disposed of tough, irritating questions.

John Kennedy would hold 62 more televised news conferences—and make nine televised reports to the nation. His intelligence and wit, together with his command of each session, invited contrasts with his predecessor. As Tom Wicker of the *New York Times* wrote, "Ike had conveyed the impression of calm, fatherly competence. Kennedy represented the keen executive of the computer age."

*   *   *

Kennedy's razor-thin margin of victory meant that he had to deal with the old coalition of conservative Democrats and Republicans in the Congress. That spelled trouble for what Kennedy hoped would be a liberal program of legislation.

Congress responded sluggishly to Kennedy's proposals, although it did approve the Peace Corps barely two months after Kennedy moved into the Oval Office. The Peace Corps' purpose: "enlisting the services of those with the desire and capacity to help foreign lands meet their urgent need for trained personnel." Kennedy appointed his brother-in-law, Sargent Shriver, as Peace Corps director. And Shriver recruited hundreds of college students who turned the Peace Corps into an enduring tribute to Kennedy's vision.

With Kennedy asserting himself on television, the Republicans countered with a program of their own—hosted by Senator Everett Dirksen of Illinois and House Minority Leader Charles Halleck of Indiana. "The Ev and Charlie Show," some called it. Together, they mixed humor and facts with their partisan views—and television once again became a star in the political arena.

In March of 1961, the Radio and Television Executives Society honored both Kennedy and Richard Nixon. I accepted a gold medal on Kennedy's behalf for "his notable contributions to bringing to maximum fulfillment the potentials of radio and television as instruments of public service, education and information during presidential campaigns."

*   *   *

I had learned never to go to the White House without being thoroughly up-to-date on all current events. If I met President Kennedy in a corridor, he might ask my reaction to a report on television or radio, in *Time* or *Newsweek*, in the *New York Times* or the *Washington Post*.

No one could plead ignorance. You were expected to know about the news—and offer a specific reaction. You were kept on your toes. Some of my friends in government were startled every now and then to receive a call from the President, asking them, "What do you think about. . . ?"

The space race shifted into high gear. The Russians' cosmonaut, Yuri Gagarin, became the first man to orbit the earth. One month later, in May, the United States sent its first astronaut into space—Alan Shepard—for a suborbital flight. John Kennedy proclaimed that America would be the first nation to land a man on the moon.

In June, Kennedy met with Khrushchev at the Vienna summit. They discussed Communist East Germany's threat to control supply routes to West Berlin. But no conclusion was reached. Two months later, the Communists put up a high wall—topped by barbed wire and monitored by armed guards—to keep East Berliners from escaping to West Berlin.

Also in June, Kennedy appointed me to the Advisory Committee of the U.S. Information Agency. Famed CBS commentator Edward R. Murrow was head of the U.S.I.A. Membership on the Advisory Committee was a non-paying job but professionally fulfilling in every way. In 1962, I was named the committee's chairman. Twelve years later, some of my colleagues were surprised when I was appointed to the USIA committee again—this time by President Nixon.

*   *   *

On October 15, 1962, American U-2 planes returned from flights over Cuba with pictures showing that launching sites for Soviet-built missiles were under construction in Cuba. Behind closed doors, the executive committee of the National Security Council held meetings that would last all week.

I received a call on Sunday, October 21, to report to the White House immediately. I was asked to draw up a list of American stations with coverage of Cuba.

On Monday evening, President Kennedy addressed the nation on television. Afterward, the Voice of America programmed the selected stations that reached Cuba. Telephone lines from Washington to these stations were installed, unbeknownst to the stations.

I telephoned WGBS, WMIE and WCKR in Miami; WSB in Atlanta; WCKY in Cincinnati, WKWF in Key West, Florida, and WWL in New Orleans. I also reached two short-wave stations—WRUL in New York and KGEI in San Carlos, California. We added KAAY in Little Rock on Wednesday.

I explained to each station's chief executive that the President needed help. Starting with the President's 7 P.M. (EST) address, I said, the government would like to take over each station's programming indefinitely. Everybody answered "yes" without hesitation.

Right after Kennedy finished his address in English, a translation in Spanish went on the air at each of these stations—much to the bewilderment of thousands of radio listeners. Each hour, an announcement in English stated: "In cooperation with the United States government, the programming of (call letters of station) is provided by the Voice of America."

The radio barrage by the Voice of America went on 80 separate frequencies in ten languages. Videotapes of the President's address, with overlay translations in Spanish and Portuguese, were flown by express to those countries in Latin America that used videotape. Two hundred prints of Kennedy's speech, dubbed in multiple languages, were shipped overseas for showing in theaters.

On Tuesday, the Soviets huffed and puffed about U.S. piracy, but took no military action. On Wednesday, word came that the Soviets' missile-bearing ships had stopped or turned back from Cuba. "We're eyeball to eyeball," Secretary of State Dean Rusk remarked, "and I think the other guy blinked." Khrushchev called for an emergency summit meeting with Kennedy. The President said "no meeting" until the missiles are withdrawn from Cuba.

On Thursday, television showed a dramatic confrontation at the United Nations between Ambassador Adlai Stevenson and Soviet Ambassador Zorin.

"Do you, Ambassador Zorin, deny that the U.S.S.R. has placed and is placing medium and intermediate-range missiles and sites in Cuba?" Stevenson asked loudly. "Yes or no? Don't wait for a translation. Yes or no? . . . I am prepared to wait for my answer till hell freezes over if that's your decision! And I am also prepared to present evidence in this room!"

On Friday, 5 million leaflets in Spanish were printed—to be used in case of an air strike on Cuba. At 6 P.M., a letter from Khrushchev arrived at the White House.

All day Saturday, all of us in the White House fidgeted, in a waiting game that could erupt into war. A response to Khrushchev's letter was sent to Moscow.

The stalemate between the two mightiest superpowers of the world lasted all night—until Sunday, October 28, when Khrushchev backed down. The Soviet premier's reply read: "In order to eliminate as rapidly as possible the conflict which

endangers the cause of people . . . the Soviet government . . .
has given a new order to dismantle the arms which you describe as offensive and to crate and return them to the Soviet
Union."

Millions of Americans, many of whom nervously had
stocked up on food and supplies, breathed sighs of relief. The
Cuban missile crisis was over, and radio and television had
served the government well.

On December 5, 1962, President Kennedy presented certifi-
cates of merit to representatives of each station that carried the
Spanish translation of the President's address. Before the presentation, Ed Murrow gave the President a draft of suggested
remarks that Murrow and I had composed. The President
asked a few questions about the stations. He left the suggested
prepared remarks on his desk. He made even better remarks on
his own.

* * *

Television continued to flex its muscles in American politics
in 1962.

In Massachusetts, Edward (Ted) Kennedy, the President's
youngest brother, ran in the Senate Democratic primary against
Edward McCormack, nephew of Speaker of the House John
McCormack. In a debate, McCormack unleashed an acri-
monious attack on Kennedy, but the attack backfired—and
Kennedy won. From there, Kennedy went on to defeat George
Cabot Lodge, son of former vice-presidential candidate Henry
Cabot Lodge, and win a seat in the Senate.

In Michigan, Republican George Romney challenged Governor John Swainson to television debates. Swainson declined—
and lost.

In Pennsylvania, Republican gubernatorial challenger
William Scranton engaged in an exceedingly brutal televised
debate with incumbent Governor Richardson Dilworth. Scranton won.

In Arizona and Illinois, incumbent Democrat Carl Hayden
and incumbent Republican Everett Dirksen refused to meet
their opponents for the Senate on television. Hayden and Dirksen, both Senate veterans, won. Of course these senators were
practically fixtures in the Senate.

Also in Pennsylvania, incumbent Senator Joseph Clark
couldn't get his opponent into a television studio with him.
Clark won.

In Wisconsin, Democratic Governor Gaylord Nelson challenged incumbent Senator Alexander Wiley to television debates. Wiley refused—and Nelson won.

In Ohio, incumbent Democratic Senator Frank Lausche was reelected despite a television trick by his opponent, who spliced his own remarks among clips of Lausche speeches. It all was reminiscent of Senator Arthur Vandenburg's shadow debate with President Franklin Roosevelt in the heyday of radio. Vandenberg debated with excerpts from Roosevelt's previously recorded speeches.

In New York, Governor Nelson Rockefeller made a joint appearance on television with Democratic challenger Robert Morgenthau.

In California, Richard Nixon challenged Democratic incumbent Edmund (Pat) Brown, both appearing together on television. Near the end of the campaign, both candidates made verbal flubs. Nixon lost, complaining that the media had "dutifully" reported his mistake and ignored Brown's.

In a bitter farewell to public life, Nixon scolded the press at a news conference. "I think it is time that our great newspapers have at least the same objectivity, the same fullness of coverage that television has," Nixon said. "And I can only say thank God for television and radio for keeping the newspapers a little more honest." Then, he told the reporters: "You won't have Nixon to kick around any longer."

Also introduced in 1962 was CBS's computer analysis of voting—developed by CBS, Lou Harris and IBM at a cost of $250,000. Using selected samples of voters, the computer often correctly predicted the winner—even before the polls closed. That set off a torrent of arguments over whether computer results should be aired. The uproar has continued even to this day—and now it's compounded by exit polls introduced in the 1980s.

As 1962 all but dissolved into history, President Kennedy's historic association with television was underscored by an unprecedented special interview of him on the three major networks. The program, "After Two Years: A Conversation with the President," was taped on the morning of the broadcast, December 17. The panel of interviewers included White House correspondents George Herman of CBS, William Lawrence of ABC and Sander Vanocur of NBC. The program was edited for the one-hour telecast.

Broadcasting magazine commented favorably on the telecast, calling Kennedy "possibly the most articulate chief executive in our history and certainly the most exposed." The magazine said the program was an "amalgam" of FDR's "fireside chats," the news conference and the Great Debates of 1960. "The President," *Broadcasting* went on, "made international news in a relaxed, informal and forthright manner. Mr. Kennedy is using to the fullest his mastery of broadcast journalism and his expertise in the give-and-take of the news conference."

In January of 1963, John Kennedy looked forward to the 1964 presidential election. The President said he was eager to debate whomever his Republican challenger would be.

At the same time, the marriage of television and politics continued to look more like a merger. The Federal Communications Commission calculated that political parties and candidates spent $20 million in broadcasting their views across America during the primary and general election campaigns of 1962. Of that sum, $12.5 million went to television, $7 million to radio.

* * *

If "Camelot" was the Kennedys' symbol, then "class" was their household word. The First Family brought to the White House not only a touch of class, but a feeling of tasteful elegance and style. Jacqueline Kennedy carefully and tastefully redecorated; she succeeded in getting the loan of fine art for hanging in all the right places. The President brought in a widely acclaimed chef.

John Kennedy strove to polish his administration's image to a high sheen, too. In August of 1963, I suggested to Pierre Salinger and the President that White House luncheons should also include leaders in television and radio. I was told to prepare several guest lists. Those on the first list received the following wire sent on August 12:

"It would be useful to me to have an exchange of views with you on state, regional and national problems. Therefore I would be most pleased to have you as my guest at luncheon on Thursday, August 22, at 1 P.M. . . . John F. Kennedy."

Nineteen broadcast executives attended the luncheon hosted by the President and assisted by Andrew T. Hatcher, White House associate news secretary. Over roast beef and California rosé wine, the President made it clear to the broadcasters that he thought radio and television stations on the whole did a better job than newspapers. Weeks later, in September, the "CBS Evening News," anchored by Walter Cronkite, became the first network television news program to expand from 15 to 30 minutes.

* * *

Texas and Florida loomed as pivotal states in 1964. President Kennedy had traveled to Florida in 1963, a trip that wasn't exactly a resounding political success. Vice President Johnson urged Kennedy to travel to Johnson's home state of Texas, in hopes of saving the Longhorn State's 25 electoral votes for 1964.

Not all the smoke had cleared in Texas from the 1960 election. Kennedy and Johnson had carried the state in a squeaker. Of Texas' more than 2.3 million votes cast, the Democrats won by slightly more than 46,000 votes. They also had lost in Dallas. Moreover, Texas in 1961 had elected a Republican senator for the first time since Reconstruction.

A liberal faction of a largely conservative group called the Democrats of Texas (DOT) rallied around Senator Ralph Yarborough. Because he supported Kennedy in 1960, Yarborough had been denied a seat in Texas' delegation to the Democratic Convention.

Governor John Connally, leader of the Democrats of Texas, was determined to destroy Yarborough and his followers politically. That thrust Vice President Johnson into a crossfire. To carry Texas in 1964, the Democrats needed a united front and every vote they could muster. Somehow the warring factions had to be brought together.

John Kennedy was called upon as the man to heal the party's wounds in Texas. On Thursday, November 21, he left for Houston—reluctantly and in a dour mood. The only bright spot was the doctor's OK for Jacqueline Kennedy to accompany him. Since the tragic death of their prematurely born son on August 9, Mrs. Kennedy had restricted her activities severely.

At 11:05 A.M. (EST), the President's plane left Andrews Air Force Base for San Antonio. At about the same time, my wife, Phyllis, and I left Atlanta by car for Augusta, Georgia. Our son, Jim, was to leave the Army's Camp Gordon, near Augusta, on Friday, November 22, for San Antonio.

After saying goodbye to Jim on Friday, Phyllis and I began

our drive back to Atlanta, stopping for lunch along the way. When we resumed our journey, I routinely turned on the radio. It was 1:40 P.M.

Suddenly we heard shocking news. A voice on the radio said: ". . . The President has been seriously wounded, perhaps fatally, by an assassin's bullet."

Shortly after 2:30 came the horrible news from Dallas: "Two priests who were with Kennedy say he is dead of bullet wounds."

I sat there, numb and heartbroken. An enormously popular President, to say nothing of a good friend, was gone—just like that. After a long, choking pause, I turned to Phyllis and said, "I must get to the White House as soon as possible."

We learned by radio that Vice President Johnson was sworn in as President on Air Force One at 3:30 P.M. by U.S. District Judge Sarah T. Hughes.

A succession law had been passed in 1947. The Constitution was vague about succession in the event of a President's death. It doesn't say specifically that the Vice President shall succeed the President. John Tyler established the precedent when William Henry Harrison, who had caught a cold during his inauguration, died after only a month in office. The line of succession was assumed by constitutional custom.

The plane bearing the new President—and the body of a former President—landed at 6 P.M. at Andrews Air Force Base. There, President Johnson met the media and said, "I'll do my best. That is all I can do. I ask for your help and God's."

Another plane carrying Cabinet members and Pierre Salinger to Japan turned around and returned to Washington. Salinger had accompanied the official party to make preliminary plans for a visit by President Kennedy to Japan.

Many of us worried about the possibility of a coup d'etat or a Communist plot, with subsequent assassinations of Lyndon Johnson, House Speaker John McCormack, 72, and the President Pro-Tem of the Senate, Carl Hayden, 86. The line of succession then moved to the Cabinet, with the Secretary of State first in line. If the line of presidential succession were broken, the government could be thrown into disarray. Fortunately, the gun shots in Dallas that killed John Kennedy and wounded Governor Connally were the last in the tragedy.

Kennedy was the fourth President to be assassinated. The others: Abraham Lincoln, James A. Garfield and William McKinley. Four Presidents have been targets of unsuccessful assassination attempts: Andrew Jackson in 1835, Harry Truman in 1950, Gerald Ford (twice) in 1975 and Ronald Reagan in 1981.

In 1912, someone attempted to kill then-former President Theodore Roosevelt. An early attempt on the life of Lincoln, after he was elected, was caught in the plotting stage. In February of 1933, an attempt was made against President-elect Franklin Roosevelt.

For months after John Kennedy was slain in Dallas, many Americans mulled over a series of coincidences, such as the "20-year cycle." Presidents elected in the years 1840 (William Henry Harrison), 1860 (Abraham Lincoln), 1880 (James A. Garfield), 1900 (William McKinley), 1920 (Warren Harding), 1940 (Franklin Roosevelt) and 1960 (John Kennedy) either died or were killed while in office.

And the parallels between the slayings of Kennedy and Lincoln are startling: Both were assassinated on Friday; both were slain in the presence of their wives; both were succeeded by Southern Democrats who had served in the Senate (both named Johnson). Andrew Johnson was born in 1808, Lyndon Johnson in 1908. Kennedy had a secretary named Lincoln; Lincoln had a secretary named Kennedy. John Wilkes Booth shot Lincoln in a theater and hid in a warehouse; Lee Harvey Oswald was accused of having shot Kennedy from a warehouse and hid in a movie theater. Booth and Oswald were murdered before they could stand trial. The bodies of Lincoln and Kennedy were carried on the same caisson. And in the center of the Capitol rotunda, Kennedy's coffin was placed on the Lincoln catafalque.

Many Americans wondered about the President's Secret Service protection. The Secret Service dates back to the Civil War, when the Treasury Department established it to suppress counterfeiters and restore confidence in federal currency. In 1913, protection was extended to President-elect Woodrow Wilson, then four years later to Wilson's immediate family. In 1951, Congress passed a law granting the Secret Service authority to protect the Vice President, if he makes the request.

In 1963, Secret Service agents were responsible for the safety of John Kennedy in Dallas. What went wrong? On November 29, President Johnson appointed a commission headed by Chief Justice Warren to study the Kennedy assassination.

* * *

Friday night, November 22. I joined a dazed Kennedy staff at the White House. We moved in a world that suddenly seemed unreal, as if we were in a nightmare. We made decisions by instinct and reflex.

I was put in charge of coordinating television, radio and still cameras. Within minutes, I was conferring with network executives, who hastily made plans to set up remote facilities, getting cameras and cable from the entire Eastern seaboard.

For the media, the tragedy posed a stupendous logistical problem. They had to cover the White House, the procession route to the Capitol, the route to the Cathedral, the services at the Cathedral, the line of march to the cemetery and the services at the cemetery, along with myriad other locations.

My job was to obtain schedules and other details from the Kennedy family and Pierre Salinger, approve locations for cameras and microphones (and lights where needed) and be in charge of obtaining security clearances everywhere.

Bob Kennedy helped a grieving Jacqueline Kennedy with difficult personal decisions. Sargent Shriver was on the phone, arranging for world and national leaders to come to the funeral. Shriver's wife, Eunice, helped with funeral arrangements for her slain brother. Steve Smith also was busy making telephone calls.

My immediate role was to plan coverage of the arrival of Kennedy's coffin at the White House. We had arranged for the coffin to lie in state in the East Room. Late Friday night, Kennedy family members discussed whether the coffin should lie open or closed. Bob Kennedy opted for a closed coffin, which is what Jacqueline wanted.

It wasn't until 4:30 A.M. Saturday when the coffin arrived from Bethesda, Maryland, and was carried to the East Room. It was accompanied by Jacqueline Kennedy, still in the blood-stained suit she had worn in Dallas.

I returned to the Statler Hilton for a short nap, a cold shower and breakfast. By 6:45 A.M., I was back at the White House. The crowd that had gathered in Lafayette Park early Friday evening still watched mournfully over the White House, many with transistor radios held to their ears.

To satisfy the flood of requests for pictures of the coffin, we set a time for picture-taking in the East Room: 9 to 9:15 A.M. As I left the East Room, I met Sargent Shriver, who said he had the responsibility of talking to 2-year-old John-John, the President's son.

Suddenly little John-John appeared on the steps and bounded cheerfully into the arms of his uncle. Words are inadequate to describe the wrenching sorrow I felt at that moment. A youngster had lost a loving father. I was furious at the senseless killing, frustrated at my helplessness.

Maybe if I hit my head on the wall it would all go away and I would be back home in Atlanta with my wife and children. Grief-stricken and numb, I glanced again at John-John and murmured again and again, "God help this poor child."

I told Sarge "good luck"—words he probably didn't hear as he scooped up John-John. Then I hurried back to my office to answer questions about camera locations in the church.

Across the hall, inside the White House, President Lyndon Johnson was the focal point of an incident I later learned about from one of the participants. The new President apparently was content to continue living at his home, Elms in Spring Valley, but he was anxious to move into the Oval Office.

Shortly after 8:30 A.M. Saturday, Lyndon Johnson asked Evelyn Lincoln, President Kennedy's personal secretary, to clear the Oval Office by 9:30 and plan to vacate her office at the same time. His order was rescinded a short while later.

Nevertheless, the removal of John Kennedy's personal possessions from the Oval Office began at 9 A.M. Long before noon, everything was out, except two white-covered sofas. The last items to go were the two Kennedy rockers that John-John loved so much. Later, as I passed Evelyn Lincoln's desk in the outer office, I noticed a conspicuous wall hanging. It was a portrait of Lyndon Johnson.

As I review my notes of that somber weekend, I notice that it rained on Sunday. Although I made several trips to the church and a preliminary journey to the cemetery, I haven't the vaguest recollection of rain.

*   *   *

John Kennedy's parish church, St. Matthew's Cathedral, was built in 1898. It contained a magnificent high altar of white marble, carved in India. The customary white candles on the altar were replaced by candles of unbleached yellow wax—the sign of a funeral.

Television coverage of the funeral was to be unobtrusive. We added only two lights to the cathedral's regular lighting. Microphones were concealed behind the altar rail, but they were able to pick up voices clearly.

Meanwhile, Pierre Salinger, Andy Hatcher and others on the press secretary's staff fielded rapid-fire questions on just about every detail. Their announcements spelled out the agenda of mourning: "The President's body will be moved from the White House in an official cortege to the Rotunda of the Capitol at 1 P.M. Sunday" .... "The public will be permitted to file past the bier at the Rotunda shortly after its arrival" .... "The body will be moved Monday at 11 A.M. to the St. Matthew's Cathedral for a Pontifical Requiem Mass at 12 noon" .... "Seating arrangements for the mass will be assigned by the White House. . . ."

Robert Kennedy had selected the gravesite in Arlington Memorial Cemetery, across the Potomac in Virginia. On Sunday morning, Jacqueline Kennedy checked the location of the plot and gave her approval.

Memorial services were held all over the world. In Moscow, 500 diplomats and Russians crowded into the little Roman Catholic church of St. Louis le Francais to attend memorial rites. Expressions of sympathy poured into the White House— from Pope Pius VI to Fidel Castro.

While the world was joined in grief, the hard realities of politics were explored by both the Democrats and the Republicans. On Sunday, headlines read: "Capitol Weighs Political Effect" and "Associates of Johnson Slated for Special Posts."

In the Republican camp, party pros weighed the 1964 ticket value of Goldwater, Rockefeller and Nixon. The early consensus was that Goldwater had slipped badly and that Rockefeller was questionable because of his divorce and remarriage. Nixon, on the other hand, looked like a good bet. Many Republicans feared that Goldwater would galvanize Democrats behind Lyndon Johnson. Any other Republican candidate might have a chance against President Johnson and a badly split Democratic Party. Even so, Goldwater quietly authorized a $100,000 poll to test his chances.

Sunday, November 24. A nation that found it still hard to believe that its President had been murdered had to deal with another unbelievable murder.

At 11:20 A.M., Lee Harvey Oswald was being transferred to a maximum-security prison. Jack Ruby, a 50-year-old bachelor and owner of two Dallas strip joints, burst through a cordon of policemen and fired one shot at Oswald. Oswald winced and crumpled to the floor. A murder had occurred on live television.

Two hours later, Oswald died at Parkland Hospital, where President Kennedy had died 48 hours earlier. Like many others at the White House, I had one eye cocked toward the television set. When Oswald was pronounced dead, some remarked, "I can't take any more. At least turn off the sound."

On Monday, Senator Everett Dirksen delivered a eulogy to John Kennedy in the Senate chambers. Meanwhile, I had gone to the Cathedral to make sure all cameras were in the correct locations—and to escort television crewmen inside, under strict security measures imposed by the Secret Service.

Photographers for *Life* magazine were upset. They demanded a camera position facing the grieving Kennedy family. I said "no." *Life's* photographers would have a camera stand set aside for them at the rear of the church.

"Why is television getting a camera to the side of the altar?" they asked.

"Because," I shot back, "I'll be in the truck and will determine what shots will be put on the air. There won't be any tight shots."

I was running out of time—and patience. "You either go to the allocated spot," I told them, "or you're out of the church!"

We had 30 minutes before the funeral procession arrived at the church. Suddenly something crashed in the alley outside. Swarms of security men sprang from everywhere to check the building. Nerves still were very much on edge. Nobody was taking any chances. It turned out that the sound was caused by a flower pot falling from a window sill.

At 10:48 A.M., the funeral procession that had started at the Capitol left the White House. Jacqueline Kennedy chose to walk in the procession from the White House to the Cathedral, a distance of six blocks. A riderless horse named Sardor, a Pakistani thoroughbred belonging to Jacqueline Kennedy, followed the caisson, bearing an empty saddle (with stirrups reversed) and empty boots.

Few who watched the procession in person—or on television around the world—will forget the thump-thump-thump of the muffled drums, at a cadence of 100 per minute. They drove home the terrible reminder that our President, a man so vibrant and alive, really was dead.

Inside the Cathedral, Cardinal Cushing of Boston conducted the low mass service in black vestments. "Ave Maria" was sung by Luigi Vina, a Boston tenor who had sung at Kennedy's wedding. In a poignant moment captured on television, Cardinal Cushing stooped to kiss little Caroline Kennedy.

After the service, Jacqueline Kennedy, attired in black suit and black-lace mantilla, stood at curbside in front of the church, waiting for her limousine. She held Caroline by her left hand and John-John with her right. The children were clad in twin pale-blue coats and red shoes. It was John-John's third birthday. Caroline had turned 6 on Wednesday, two days before her father was slain. In Caroline's hand was a memorial card from the church. John-John grabbed for it and fussed over it. In ladylike fashion, Caroline gave the card to her brother.

So many dignitaries attended that it was impossible for the media to identify all of them. One who stood out in the crowd, however, was General Charles de Gaulle, president of France, a towering man in an olive-drab uniform and a black armband.

It took an hour for the procession to reach the burial site, on a grassy slope in Arlington National Cemetery. We had carefully chosen camera sites so that millions of people around the world could share in the Kennedys' grief without intruding on their privacy. Head-on shots were avoided. The only camera designed to shoot closeup pictures was equipped with an 80-inch Japanese lens—for head-on shots only of Cardinal Cushing as he delivered the graveside prayers. The Cardinal had been wired for sound so that no microphones were visible.

In addition, seven NBC cameras fed the media's pool coverage from the cemetery. They were positioned 250 feet from the gravesite where John Fitzgerald Kennedy was laid to rest, 46 years young. He joined 126,000 military personnel and other heroes interred in Arlington National Cemetery (the only other President buried in Arlington: William Howard Taft).

At 3:15 P.M., Jacqueline Kennedy lit the eternal flame that would burn at the head of her husband's grave. She was handed the United States flag that had draped the coffin. Then she was escorted to her limousine by President Johnson.

Television coverage of the funeral ended with the lowering of the coffin at 3:34 P.M. A troubled nation now tried to return to normal. On the eighth floor of the State Department, President Johnson received chiefs of delegations from other countries. He assured them of the continuity of American foreign policy. As I returned to the White House, the network crews were busy untangling and dismantling the equipment that had served them so well—44 mobile cameras, 33 taping machines and countless miles of cable.

On that fateful Friday afternoon in Dallas—which now seemed like an eternity ago—the television audience had doubled in 30 minutes. Television coverage was beamed to 23 countries with a combined population of more than 600 million. CBS, ABC, NBC, and UPI sent newsfilm to countries on every continent.

During those 3½ dark days in American history, the average U.S. family watched television 34 hours. The networks' coverage ranged from 55 to 71 hours. Ninety-three percent of the homes with television in the United States watched the Requiem Mass at the Cathedral and the services at the cemetery. Radio coverage was carried worldwide in dozens of languages.

It was commercial television's finest hour. More than 2,100 network personnel participated, in one way or another, in the coverage of what may well still stand as the largest shared experience in the history of the world.

Historians have another what-iffer with the assassination of President Kennedy. In my opinion, in 1964, President Kennedy would have won another close election but with a different vice-presidential candidate. The course of the Democratic Party would have been completely changed.

CHAPTER 17

November 1963

LYNDON BAINES JOHNSON, a tall, drawling, proud man from the Texas hill country, may have been the most prepared politician ever to become President. Not since James Monroe had a President known so many of his predecessors.

However, just as John Adams presided in the shadow of George Washington, so would Lyndon Johnson labor in the almost larger-than-life legacy of John Kennedy. John Adams, who never was known for tact, called his predecessor "an old muttonhead." Even Lyndon Johnson, never one to mince words himself, showed more restraint.

The new President was eager to address a joint session of Congress. He suggested Tuesday, November 26. Bobby Kennedy was bitterly opposed to a presidential address so soon after his slain brother's burial. After considerable discussion, Johnson finally agreed on Wednesday. This was a forerunner of many other arguments that showed the hard feelings between the Kennedy and Johnson camps.

Bobby Kennedy had opposed his brother's selection of Lyndon Johnson as a running mate at the 1960 convention. He didn't hold Johnson in high regard. For that matter, Johnson apparently feared the Kennedy mystique personified in Bob Kennedy. They were natural adversaries.

For several days, editorials and news stories on John Kennedy dominated America's consciousness. They consisted of comments like "The crime of November 22, 1963, removed from the White House one of the most intelligent and attractive of our 35 Presidents" and "Intelligence was the keynote of Kennedy's short presidency and with it came a flair and excitement which has not been seen in the office for many years. . . ."

Predictably, these editorial sentiments spawned comparisons between Kennedy and Johnson. "Earthy and flamboyant," the *New York Times* said of Johnson.

Actually, from where I sat, Johnson operated as President as if the ghost of John Kennedy constantly looked over his shoulder—even after Johnson's overwhelming victory in 1964.

Kennedy was, to the manner, born; Johnson was self-made. Born in 1908 and reared in rural Texas, Johnson won his first congressional seat in 1937 in a special election. From there, Johnson emerged as a shrewd, cautious politician who didn't always remember his friends but never forgot his enemies. He loved power and knew how to use power. He used the telephone compulsively.

During the Eisenhower Administration, Johnson was the second most powerful man in the country. His credo: "There ain't nothing the government can't fix. It is our obligation to resolve issues, not to create them." Johnson, a member of the Christian Church of the Disciples of Christ (a sect with 1.8 million members), was fond of quoting from Isaiah 1:18: "Come now, let us reason together. . . ."

After Johnson's first presidential physical, Dr. Willis Hurst, a famed heart surgeon, pronounced him "very active" and "vigorous." "From a health standpoint," he said, "I would say he has no problem."

If Johnson had any problems at all, they were political. As Vice President, he had expected to work in partnership with President Kennedy. It wasn't to be. Although Kennedy treated Johnson with consideration, the hard facts of politics lived on: The Vice President simply has no power, except those delegated to him by the President.

For a man so accustomed to power, Johnson was frustrated and unhappy as Vice President. He spent much of his time overseas, representing the President. In fact, Johnson was out of the country so often that many speculated that President Kennedy was trying to keep him out of the White House's way. At one press conference, Kennedy had to deny a report that he was planning to dump Johnson in 1964.

Johnson's pride was wounded even more when Kennedy's staff members ignored him. "Forget him," some said. "He doesn't mean anything. He's only the Vice President." Rivalries flared openly between the staffs of Kennedy and Johnson.

Customarily, whoever was Vice President was content with his suite of offices at the Senate. Not Lyndon Johnson. He became the first Vice President to request an office inside the White House. He was refused. Johnson then asked for offices in the Executive Office Building, across a private street from the White House. The request was granted, and a disgruntled Johnson moved in with his inner circle: George Reedy, his press secretary; Walter Jenkins, his chief administrative officer, and Bill Moyers, fresh from the Peace Corps and one of Johnson's most brilliant aides.

As November faded away, the Johnson Administration's byword was "continuity." The President and his aides succeeded in keeping the Ship of State on a steady course.

One couldn't help but contrast the smooth transition and clearcut direction of Lyndon Johnson with the turbulence and recriminations that faced Andrew Johnson after the assassination of Abraham Lincoln. At that time, the nation was kept in ignorance of the full facts of Lincoln's death for weeks and, in some cases, months.

Early on, however, Lyndon Johnson caught heat from back home. When he appointed the Warren Commission to investigate the Kennedy assassination, Johnson ignored demands by Texans that the commission be composed entirely of Texans.

Meanwhile, 50 pieces of legislation were before the Congress. The most prominent were the Civil Rights Act and the Tax Bill. Within 12 weeks, a tax-cut bill was passed. The new President stirred up activity in Congressional committees. The Great Society was under way.

Yet even as Johnson plunged into the business of strong-arming legislation on Capitol Hill, he was sensitive to all those constant comparisons with John Kennedy. He cajoled the media with anger and humor. He told television producers in no uncertain language that he wanted only his left profile exposed to the cameras. He hungered for the attention so long denied him as Vice President.

At the same time, Johnson was a sharp observer of television news and major newspapers and magazines. He was quick to telephone CBS President Frank Stanton to complain about a news story on the network. He not only complained to editors, but vented his displeasure to reporters, too.

*   *   *

As President Johnson looked forward to 1964, he could count on a welter of inherited problems.

The Supreme Court was under fire for its decisions on civil rights. The John Birch Society was leading a revolt on the extreme right. Activists demanded that the United States withdraw from the U.N. and the U.N. withdraw from the United States. Movements sprang up all over the place—to impeach Chief Justice Warren, to sever diplomatic ties with Communist countries, to restore state sovereignty, to limit the federal government's power. It was enough to fragment any political party; but politics were the new President's lifeblood.

With Ted Sorensen, I had developed preliminary plans for the convention in Atlantic City, to begin the week of August 24. When I made my first report to President Johnson, he was particularly pleased about the date. His birthday was August 27, during convention week. He thought we picked the convention date to coincide with his birthday.

In January of 1964, the Democratic National Committee met in Washington. The committee passed resolutions paying tribute to the late President Kennedy and to other prominent Democrats who had died in the previous few years, notably Estes Kefauver. Colonel Jacob Arvey of Illinois read what committee members regarded the most important resolution of all—the apportionment of delegate votes for the 1964 convention. In other years, this resolution could have ignited a nasty floor fight; this time it was approved unanimously by voice vote. The party's loyalty-oath resolution also passed without dissent.

*   *   *

Early in January of 1964, the Republicans began to press for a joint appearance of the Republican presidential candidate and President Johnson on national television. Johnson was lukewarm to the idea.

HJ 247, a resolution that would suspend Section 315 (equal-time provision) for presidential and vice-presidential candidates in the fall of 1964, had been passed by the House and approved in a slightly amended version by the Senate in 1963.

It awaited further action. In August of 1964, the Democratic majority in the Senate tabled a resolution suspending the equal-time law in its application to the candidates for President and Vice President.

I told President Johnson, as I did President Kennedy, that I felt strongly that no President should appear with an opposing candidate. I was concerned about national security. It would be tantamount to fighting with one arm tied behind your back. Either the questions would be innocuous or the President would have to hold back on some of the answers.

Johnson was noncommittal about the debate question. He did, however, state that he planned to make full use of television in the months ahead. He said he wanted television to cover some of his news conferences. One of Johnson's problems was that he had a tough television act to follow in John Kennedy.

On Saturday, February 1, Johnson agreed to a televised news conference in the White House theater—a long, narrow room which made hearing difficult. The news conference was forgettable.

Later, the President held more successful news conferences in other locations, including the White House lawn. He improved and, for once, accepted critical reviews from close members of his staff. After one televised news conference, he told me that he much preferred sitting in a rocking chair in the Oval Office and holding court with a handful of reporters.

Television, however, was hardly to be denied. The networks later wired, at their expense, the Fish Room, adjacent to the Oval Office. While not suitable for a news conference, the Fish Room provided a comfortable setting for presidential announcements. The Fish Room was ideally located because the President often made impromptu decisions to go before the cameras with a statement.

In the early days of his administration, I felt that Johnson, while not comfortable with television, knew full well television's enormous power. The President quickly learned to use television. He made effective use of the glass TelePrompters placed on either side of his podium. In a few months, he became a near-professional performer.

* * *

As Barry Goldwater took the lead in his pursuit of the Republican nomination, his campaign strategy relied heavily on statewide live television hookups in prime time. A major staple of Goldwater's drive was a 30-minute documentary on his life: "A Choice Not an Echo—the Barry Goldwater Story."

In the meantime, I was busy fine-tuning plans for the Democratic Convention. President Kennedy had appointed me executive director of the convention. When I met early in 1964 with President Johnson to review convention plans, I asked if he had someone in mind to run the convention. He grinned and replied, "Yes, I do—you."

So now I was at work on my sixth convention. At the same time, I sensed that Johnson still had no intention of appearing on television with the Republican candidate. The House of Representatives would take no action on the repeal of Section 315 without a push from the Chief Executive. Without that push—no debates.

Nevertheless, television increasingly made its presence felt in the political process. In May, the networks announced that they would, for the first time, sell one-minute political announcements during entertainment programs.

That same month, the Democratic National Committee introduced a new campaign wrinkle: Sound-actuality tapes of news-making Democrats were made available to reporters calling the party's new automatic-tape telephone system in Washington. The media's response was so great that Wayne Phillips, director of *Democratic News*, doubled the facilities a week later.

In June, we bought ten campaign segments—each lasting five minutes—on CBS. They followed such highly rated programs as "The Ed Sullivan Show," so a large audience was guaranteed. The race for desirable television time was on.

*   *   *

The Republican Convention opened on July 13 in the Cow Palace in San Francisco, which had won out over six other cities vying to be the host city.

Since Cox Broadcasting Corporation, of which I was president, owned a television station in Oakland, across the bay from San Francisco, I visited the station just before the convention. Sig Mickelson, my long-time friend from CBS, was the convention's television director. As a result, the Republicans opted for a more streamlined convention than before. Sig, however, couldn't overcome political habits, and the

Republicans had some interminable sessions that served no political purpose and lost audiences.

For this convention, the Republicans attracted 2,700 radio and television personnel—far exceeding the 1,700 who covered the 1960 convention in Chicago. At the Cow Palace, the convention floor sometimes became a madhouse, with reporters and photographers fighting delegates for breathing and elbow room.

The crush became so severe during the second night of the convention that police from Daly City (where the Cow Palace is located) moved onto the floor. Perhaps the height of levity for this convention—or, for that matter, *any* convention—occurred when an officer ordered NBC correspondent John Chancellor to leave the convention floor. The moment was rekindled in an NBC News-produced book entitled *Somehow It Works*—and it began when co-anchor David Brinkley asked Chancellor to "come in" with his interview in the Alaska delegation:

CHANCELLOR: I'd come in if I could, David, but I may be under arrest. They have been trying to clear the aisles here—an understandable problem at a place like the Cow Palace, with all the people on the floor. We were waiting to do an interview in the Alaska delegation when two sergeants-at-arms came along and said, "You'll have to clear the aisle." We said we were working, and they said that didn't make any difference to them, so I sat down. Whereupon a policeman, Badge No. 21, from the Daly City police, tried to eject me forcibly. Am I going to be carried out?

ANSWER: You'll be removed by orders of the sergeant-at-arms.

CHANCELLOR: I wonder if I could get your name?

ANSWER: My name is Gary Kidwell.

CHANCELLOR: Okay. I don't want to debate this with you, Mr. Kidwell—let's get on with it. I'm about to be removed. Go ahead, gentlemen, remove me. Mr. Kidwell doesn't have a very nice job trying to get the reporters out. I can never remember a Convention staff being asked to clear the aisles of the press. . . .

There's another policeman here, Badge No. 38; he's got a hand on my elbow, and there's a sheriff's policeman coming forward. Here we go, down the middle aisle. It's hard to be dignified at a time like this. Well, I don't know what to say. What do you say? I'm in custody. I've been promised bail, ladies and gentlemen, by my office. This way, officer? Up this way. And for those of you who are watching, I want to assure you that NBC is fully staffed with other reporters who are not in the custody of the Daly City police and the San Mateo sheriff's office.

I formally say this is a disgrace. The press, radio and television should be allowed to do their work at a Convention. I'm being taken down off the arena now, by these policemen and I'll check in later. This is John Chancellor, somewhere in custody.

BRINKLEY: (laughing)	John, call us when you can, and let us hear from you, often. That's the silliest thing I've ever seen in my life, and I've seen a lot of silly things. The aisles are clogged from one end of the hall to the other with every kind of obstruction—and the only one they can find to arrest is John Chancellor, who really is a mild and inoffensive fellow.
CHET HUNTLEY:	I think this was a first, a man broadcasting his own arrest on television.
BRINKLEY:	And I hope a last.

A tightly controlled convention was not interesting to the television audience. Three independent television stations with only average-quality programming drew better ratings. They attracted more than half of all television sets between 7 and 11 o'clock during three nights of the GOP Convention (Monday 52%, Tuesday 56.6%, and Thursday 54.0%). On Wednesday, the night of the nomination, entertainment programs drew 44.2% of the audience.

Barry Goldwater's convention organization, directed by F. Clifton White, was reminiscent of John Kennedy's in 1960. Only 45 days earlier, Goldwater had been labeled weak and powerless by most experts. But now, as the front-runner, Goldwater was in a position to chide his party's moderates—and get away with it. Addressing the convention, the 55-year-old, white-haired senator delivered an unforgettable passage: "Extremism in the defense of liberty is no vice! And . . . moderation in the pursuit of justice is no virtue!"

Goldwater chalked up an overwhelming victory for the nomination—and soon he would challenge President Johnson to debate him on television.

For Goldwater's running mate, the convention nominated Representative William E. Miller, a Catholic from upstate New York and the party's retiring chairman. A vice-presidential candidate's lack of importance was never better illustrated than by a television commercial many years later. American Express featured William Miller in its series that carried the question: "Do you know me?"

CHAPTER 18

Atlantic City
Summer 1964

Four mop-topped kids from England take America by storm by singing "Yeah! Yeah! Yeah!" . . . Bathing suits go topless, and miniskirts go up, up, up . . . . Racial rioting erupts in Harlem, Chicago and Philadelphia with the battle cry "Burn, baby, burn!" . . . UCLA, with no starter taller than 6-foot-5, wins the national college basketball title, beginning one of sport's mightiest dynasties. . . . Three civil rights workers are slain in Mississippi, and the Civil Rights Act passes in Washington. . . . A jury finds Jack Ruby guilty in the murder of Lee Harvey Oswald, and the Warren Commission decides that Oswald, acting alone, murdered John F. Kennedy.

THE NETWORKS GRUMBLED as they tore down their expensive sets in San Francisco and shipped them to Atlantic City, 3,000 miles away. They still longed for back-to-back conventions in the same city, which hadn't happened since 1952.

For all their power, the networks hadn't been able to force the site committees of both major political parties to choose the same city for their conventions. Political strategy traditionally overrides all other considerations, including costs.

In 1964, it was estimated that NBC alone spent $5.6 million for equipment, studio construction, transportation and expenses for coverage of both the Republican and Democratic conventions. It wasn't until 1972 that the two conventions were held in the same city. The Republicans originally opted for San Diego, but were forced to move. They followed the Democrats to Miami Beach.

* * *

As we prepared for the Atlantic City convention, we geared up for potential trouble—mass picketing of the convention and plans by minority groups to block the seating of "all-white" delegations from Alabama, Louisiana and Mississippi.

From time to time, I was summoned to meetings with law-enforcement authorities. New Jersey's state police commander and deputy superintendent had attended the Republican Convention in San Francisco. There, demonstrators blocked traffic from the Cow Palace parking lots. We didn't have to worry about that tactic in Atlantic City; all the hotels were within walking distance of the convention hall.

Nevertheless, New Jersey assigned 400 uniformed state troopers to the convention, augmenting 187 local police officers, 50 sheriff's deputies and 200 Secret Service agents, along with 40 firemen stationed inside the convention hall around the clock.

Civil rights groups planned to picket the Democrats in force. They included the Congress of Racial Equality (CORE), the National Association for the Advancement of Colored People (NAACP), Christians for Social Action, the Convention Committee for Civil Rights and the Student Non-Violent Coordinating Committee (SNCC).

These groups weren't alone. Two militant groups on opposite poles of the political spectrum said they would demonstrate—the Black Muslims and George Lincoln Rockwell's neo-Nazi party. In addition, a Jimmy Hoffa-led teamsters Union contingent threatened to picket Attorney General Robert Kennedy.

The president of Philadelphia's NAACP chapter, Cecil Moore, promised demonstrators from CORE that his group would furnish 3,000 to 4,000 pickets. "We can make the line so long and so black," Moore said, "that they would think it was midnight in midday. We can give them enough pickets to block every entrance into the convention hall."

Convention-goers could enter the hall only through the front doors on Atlantic City's famed ocean-front Boardwalk. To avoid any blocking of the entrance, I instituted a so-called "cattle run"—a wide entryway that gradually narrowed to a single-file passage through the turnstiles. Uniformed state troopers were strategically placed, and we had very little trouble.

We knew we had to cope with five major dissident groups, none of them compatible. We assigned each group a section of the beach facing the convention hall. Each group respected its own territory and avoided the other groups like the plague.

One key to controlling the dissidents was the use of walkie-talkies, which were just coming into vogue. Everybody—including dissidents—used walkie-talkies. We monitored all conversations of all groups. I checked a monitor at my control desk on the rostrum. I also had a direct phone to New Jersey state police headquarters.

When one dissident leader advised his group to stand by and await his signal to storm the building, he was overheard and immediately picked up for questioning. The plan of operations for the New Jersey state police was so thorough that we had no untoward incidents.

Our security precautions, however, were complicated by a presidential order. Tickets for the convention were to be purchased from a printer in New Jersey. Unfortunately, the printer used ordinary stock for the tickets. If anyone had wanted to, he could have duplicated the tickets in 30 minutes in almost any print shop in America.

On the TV ratings battlefront, most of the talk centered on the shakeup at CBS News. NBC's Chet Huntley and David Brinkley had been winning the ratings war. CBS decided that it, too, would post a double-anchor team at the convention. Walter Cronkite, who had covered conventions for CBS since 1952, was out. In his place, CBS sent Robert Trout and Roger Mudd. Dallas Townsend replaced Trout as CBS's radio anchor.

Trout and Mudd were excellent newsmen, as was Townsend. The news fraternity, however, felt that CBS had done Cronkite an injustice, that he was a victim of ratings (which, during the Republican Convention, were dominated by NBC). Ironically, Walter Cronkite later returned to become CBS's sole anchor, pre-eminent in his field and, according to one public-opinion survey, "the most trusted man in America."

* * *

Many felt that the Republican Convention had dragged, that viewers and participants alike suffered from terminal boredom. A bigger audience, in fact, watched Dr. Milton

Eisenhower's nominating speech than Barry Goldwater's acceptance speech.

I had persuaded the Democratic National Committee that we should go with compact, single, nighttime sessions. After all, we had only one question to be resolved—the vice presidency. And everybody knew how he would be picked—by the President. It's not easy to sustain interest in a convention when the outcome is already predetermined. The Republicans learned that in 1956. Even so, despite the cut-and-dried nature of the 1964 Democratic Convention, it attracted a bigger news force (estimated as large as 6,000) than the Republican Convention did.

* * *

Atlantic City's convention hall is among the most massive indoor facilities in America. It measures 488 feet by 288 feet. The catwalks are 137 feet overhead. Even football games have been played inside it.

In a sense, it was made-to-order for Lyndon Johnson's Texas-sized way of doing things. The President was interested in every detail of the convention. He set up committees. He moved people from Washington to Atlantic City and back to Washington with free-wheeling abandon.

Johnson's aides decided that when Johnson was nominated, millions of paper stars would be dropped from the rafters, 137 feet up.

We all agreed that Johnson's 56th birthday—which would fall on the day of his acceptance speech—offered marvelous opportunities for a celebration on national TV.

This would be a convention in which the delegates would do no decision-making. They really could do very little about the basic issues that tormented the country in 1964. The President was preaching harmony, with three keys for the platform—peace, preparedness and prosperity. Wisely, he would avoid any civil-rights squabbles that could tear the party into pieces.

The 1964 convention of Lyndon Johnson would stress national unity. Johnson wanted desperately to outdo his mentor, President Roosevelt, by winning overwhelmingly without dividing the country. His personal standing was so high that whoever became the vice-presidential nominee could offer little, if any, political clout to the ticket.

* * *

In Atlantic City, the convention hall was so long that many delegates needed binoculars to see a speaker at the rostrum. We put up a gigantic, 37-by-27-foot TV screen above the rostrum. As usual, delegates complained that their view was blocked by the stand bearing cameras that took the television pictures. We installed TV sets at the back of each camera stand, but nobody was entirely happy. As we had learned in 1956, when we pioneered the head-on camera stand, politics in the 1960s confirmed that good television pictures were more important than happy delegates.

In 1964, we introduced another wrinkle to political conventions—closed-circuit TV by cable. Hugh McGinty operated a cable system in Atlantic City, reaching all the hotels, motels and public places, as well as private homes. He willingly leased a channel for full-time use by the Democrats. We originated all programs either from our studio in the convention hall, the hall itself or by tape. We secured Channel 2 on the sets receiving the cable picture.

I persuaded Mark Bartlett, an experienced program executive, to take a leave of absence from WSB-TV in Atlanta to direct the cable telecasts of the convention. He gave the Democratic presentations on cable a highly professional look. We ran an ambitious schedule: 3 to 11 P.M. on Sunday, August 23; and 8 A.M. to midnight, Monday through Thursday.

More than 50 U.S. Senators, House members, governors and Cabinet members came to the studio to appear on these almost 'round-the-clock cable TV programs. The cable shows became widely popular with viewers who felt left out of the convention proceedings—and with politicians who got more exposure on cable Channel 2 than anywhere else.

It all convinced me that cable, if available, should be part of every convention. Sadly, even today, most people in public life don't know how to use cable effectively. They must learn. In the future, cable television will be used as direct mail is used today. It is entirely possible that cable will reshape politics in the future as television reshaped politics in the past.

Meanwhile, at Atlantic City, we still had pressure to add entertainment stars to the convention program—and I still resisted. I told party pros that the television viewers, delegates and alternates are watching and participating in a political convention, not a variety show. I reminded everybody in a memo that the Republicans erred by trying to brighten up their otherwise dull 1956 convention by importing Ethel Merman and other big-name entertainers for the program.

My memo went on: "When the networks picked up the show, the audience was negative. The networks, however, generally switched to their own commentary at the time entertainment was presented. Today's television audience is more sophisticated and watches top names every night in the week presented under ideal studio conditions."

Just about everybody agreed with me, but the pressures persisted. As a last resort, my response was remindful of 1944, when I said: "You'll have to clear it with the President." That ended the arm-twisting for entertainment.

* * *

Lyndon Johnson never was totally comfortable with my role in both the conventions and the White House. He somehow identified me as one who was close to the Kennedys. In 1964, Johnson sent Marvin Watson to Atlantic City to make sure I didn't rig the convention in favor of Robert Kennedy.

That was a totally implausible thought, but the President wasn't one to leave anything to chance—especially his convention. As it was, Marvin Watson and I struck up a good rapport, and I tried to keep him fully informed of what I was doing.

Our relationship, it turned out, led to a story by national columnist Drew Pearson at the start of the convention. Pearson, unhappy with his hotel accommodations, decided that I was to blame. He used my association with Watson as background for a published story reporting that I had been fired as convention director because President Johnson didn't like the way the convention was handled.

John Bailey, the DNC chairman, issued an immediate and emphatic denial of Pearson's assertions. I laughed at all the commotion over the Pearson story and went about my work.

On Wednesday night, the eve of his 56th birthday, the President showed up unexpectedly at the convention. He put his arm around my shoulder and said, "Leonard, I hope you didn't pay any attention to that lying Drew Pearson. You and I have been friends too long to have anything like that come between us. I like the way you are handling the convention and I want you to know how much I appreciate your fine work."

"Mr. President," I replied, "like you, I've been around Washington too long a time to pay any attention to that type of story." He nodded contentedly and moved onto the platform, there to receive a standing ovation.

* * *

Every election year, both the Democrats and the Republicans took a "the more, the merrier" approach to their conventions. In Atlantic City, the seating of delegates and alternates required a whopping 5,398 tickets—far too many participants in any political convention.

How ideal, I thought again, to seat only 1,500 delegates (the number suggested by a Brookings Institute study)—and keep it that way for every convention.

The more participants, too, the greater the security problems. On the week before the 1964 Democratic Convention, I was visited at my office by a Secret Service agent. He said the President wanted me to have a shredder so important documents wouldn't be tossed into the wastebasket.

I thanked the agent and later thanked the President. Frankly, I couldn't see any need for a shredder. It was obvious to everybody what we had to do—and were doing—in the way of strategy. All the moves were plotted at the White House, not in the convention hall. Still, to keep everybody happy, we used the shredder.

The President, meanwhile, manipulated the political news with all the skill of an old pro. He created a contest for the vice presidency. He alone would pick his running mate. For weeks, he tossed up names like a circus juggler keeping several balls in the air at the same time. He raised hopes—and dashed hopes.

He worked the media for all he could get, creating story after story that he was "considering" this candidate, that candidate, all candidates. He reveled in all the speculation. He gave the vice-presidential nominating process a splash of razzmatazz, even though the No. 2 spot on the ticket would mean nothing in the 1964 election.

When the merry-go-round stopped, Johnson picked Hubert Humphrey.

* * *

On Monday night, August 24, John Bailey gaveled the first session of the 1964 Democratic Convention to order. To streamline the program, we omitted the reading of the names of all delegates and alternates, as well as an explanation of how votes were distributed. The information was given to everybody in printed material. Score one for the television audience.

With TV in mind, President Johnson wanted political films shown to the convention each night. They included "Quest for Peace," in which the President talked about America's strength and preparedness and "The Road to Leadership," which sang more praises of Lyndon Johnson.

The next film would be introduced by Attorney General Robert Kennedy. President Johnson had moved early to remove Kennedy as a possible running mate. He announced that no Cabinet member would be considered for the vice presidency. Many interpreted the announcement—correctly, I think—as anti-Kennedy.

The week of the convention, Robert Kennedy made his move in a different direction. He would run for Senator in New York (and would go on to win in November of 1964, the first Senate victory by a Democrat in the Empire State in ten years).

All eyes focused on the convention as Senator Henry Jackson introduced Robert Kennedy, who in turn would present a film tribute to the late John F. Kennedy. Originally, the film was scheduled to be shown on Monday, but it was rescheduled—for obvious reasons—*after* Johnson's nomination. The President didn't like the idea of a Kennedy film, but he couldn't block its showing. He could—and did—make sure the film wasn't shown until after he was nominated.

When Robert Kennedy was introduced, the convention burst into a thunderous ovation. Kennedy admirers danced in the aisles and wildly cheered. For 13 minutes, Kennedy tried in vain seven times to restore quiet so he could introduce the film. Johnson's adherents weren't impressed. "He's milking the audience," somebody grumbled.

Finally, Chairman John McCormack brought the crowd under control. In tears, Robert Kennedy introduced the film, "A Thousand Days." Earlier I had reviewed the film. I knew it would be long remembered. I also sensed that there would be few dry eyes in the audience.

The soundtrack filled the convention hall with actor Richard Burton singing the theme from "Camelot." On the huge screen above the rostrum, John Kennedy walked on the beach at Hyannisport, hand-in-hand with Caroline. Many in the convention wept openly. President Johnson was shown offering his reminiscences at the close of the film.

As the film was shown, I sat next to Bobby Kennedy on the platform steps. He was under an enormous emotional strain. He sat rigidly, riveted to every word and motion on the screen. Now and then, moisture came to his eyes. When the film ended, he left the rostrum. An Ohio delegate later remarked that Robert Kennedy was not seen once in the film.

*   *   *

As part of the Convention program, the late Eleanor Roosevelt was paid tribute in an address by Ambassador Adlai Stevenson. Then James A. Farley spoke in memory of Speaker Sam Rayburn. Hubert Humphrey gave his acceptance speech to a standing ovation. Then the President was escorted to the rostrum by a committee headed by Georgia Congressman Carl Vinson, who had served longer than anyone else in the House of Representatives. A wire from former President Harry Truman was read to the convention.

Addressing the convention, Lyndon Johnson accepted his party's nomination for President, having been welcomed by a standing ovation and a sustained demonstration. The networks commented favorably on the air about Johnson's speech.

About all that remained was the celebration of Johnson's 56th birthday. Actually, the celebrating had begun earlier that evening, with a regatta of 200 yachts, an ethnic parade on the Boardwalk with 15 marching bands and drill teams. Four pavilions sported red-white-and-blue bunting.

Seven birthday parties were given in honor of the President, as was a midnight supper at the Shelburne Hotel with Johnson and Humphrey as guests of honor. Post-convention fireworks crackled with a spectacular display of a birthday cake and portrait of the President.

Watching it all from the front balcony of the convention hall, Lyndon Johnson savored every moment. Several times he turned to me enthusiastically and said, "Thanks."

Later he enjoyed the parody by actress Carol Channing of "Hello Dolly," the theme song from the year's smash Broadway musical, sung with the words "Hello Lyndon." Cynics muttered that a spoof of the song about "Lola" was more appropriate: "Whatever Lyndon wants, Lyndon gets. . . ."

Before the post-convention weekend was over, the convention hall would be the scene of more music—a concert by the Beatles. A week later, the Miss America contest moved in. I was one of the judges—a totally new experience. The winner was a Republican from Arizona.

For a party whose presidential nomination was a foregone conclusion, the Democrats did amazingly well in the TV ratings war with the Republicans. The Democrats outdrew the Republicans every convention night, much to the delight of President Johnson, who now was more conscious than ever of television ratings. The results:

Monday
28.9 Democrats
25.9 Republicans
Tuesday
27.2 Democrats
24.1 Republicans
Wednesday
31.8 Democrats
28.0 Republicans
Thursday
33.4 Democrats
24.6 Republicans

What's more, the peak period of television viewing during the Democratic Convention attracted 35% higher viewership than during peak viewing of the Republican Convention. The Democratic peak attracted 41,490,000 viewers. Not too shabby, when you consider that a typical episode of the popular comedy series, "Beverly Hillbillies," drew 54,657,000 viewers.

With President Johnson's flair for showmanship, the Democrats had won over millions of viewers, if not potential voters. It was a good omen for November.

CHAPTER 19

Campaign 1964

AFTER THE CONVENTION, I had to make some tough professional decisions. The Atlanta-headquartered Cox Broadcasting Corporation, of which I was the president and chief executive officer, had gone public in April—listed over the counter. In August, Cox Broadcasting Corp. was listed on the New York exchange. Financial analysts wanted to hear from the company's officers.

Jim Cox, Jr., and I had ambitious plans. During the convention, I had negotiated the purchase of a Pittsburgh television station for $20 million.

Because of my business obligations, I suggested to the President that I be available on a when-needed basis. He thanked me—and that was that.

Just as certain as death and Texas, the President looked like a shoo-in to be re-elected. The campaign between conservatives backing Barry Goldwater and liberals supporting Lyndon Johnson shaped up as no contest.

The Johnson campaign was impeccably organized. The agency—Doyle, Dane & Bernbach—was to report to Team A in control of the news media. This team included Bill Moyers, Lloyd Wright, Abe Fortas and Dick Goodwin. Team B consisted of Clark Clifford, Abe Fortas and James Rowe. Team C was the Kennedy operational team; Team D the Five O'clock Club, and Team E the Democratic National Committee.

Passing judgment on television activity was John Hayes, president of the Post-Newsweek stations, who reported directly to the President. As John told me, he approved TV strategy only when he was certain that the President would approve, too.

Regardless of the campaign structure, the President followed every last detail. Under my breath, I hummed, "Whatever Lyndon wants, Lyndon gets." An incumbent President can control the flow of news from the White House; because he is President, the media consider that just about everything he does is newsworthy.

* * *

The Lyndon Johnson presidential campaign purchased TV spots in 17 states. His pride alone would dictate that he would accept no less than an overwhelming victory in Texas. Taking no chances, Texas topped the list by purchasing 1,345 national campaign spots, compared with 823 spots in California and 410 in New York. It turned out that Johnson would carry Texas with more than 63% of the vote.

Meanwhile, the absurdity of the equal-time law (Section 315) was never more clearly shown than in 1964. The Federal Communications Commission—by a vote of 4 to 3—ruled that stations carrying presidential news conferences "live" during the campaign were subject to demands for equal time from other presidential candidates.

CBS's Frank Stanton, who had battled mightily for repeal of Section 315 throughout his career, said the FCC's ruling was yet another illustration of the need to repeal or suspend the equal-time provision.

At times, Johnson and Goldwater slugged it out in rough-and-tumble campaigning. Two Johnson TV commercials aroused universal negative reaction, even though the photography was irresistible; the copy written with big-league craftsmanship, the visuals and audio weaved with consummate editing skill.

One Johnson commercial opened with pictures of a small girl picking petals off a daisy while she counted: "One, two, three, four." As she continued to pluck off the petals, she was interrupted by another voice delivering a countdown: "Five . . . four . . . three . . . two . . . one." Then the commercial cut quickly to footage of an atomic-bomb explosion, followed by the visual message: "Vote for President Johnson on November 3."

The other Johnson spot showed a little girl eating an ice

cream cone. A female voiceover explained that nuclear explosions in the atmosphere were contaminating foods, especially milk. The nuclear explosions must be suspended by the test-ban treaty, which Goldwater opposed.

The message was clear in each commercial: If Senator Goldwater were elected President, all little girls would be incinerated or doomed to eat lethal radiation in their ice cream.

When countless Americans protested, the daisy commercial was withdrawn after only one showing. I called the President after seeing both spots. I suggested that both commercials would cost him votes.

Still another dispute over Section 315, meanwhile, wound up in the courts. On Sunday, October 18, all three major networks granted President Johnson time to address the nation on the extraordinary international events of the preceding week: The fall from power of Nikita Khrushchev in the Soviet Union, and the explosion of a nuclear device by Communist China.

The networks denied equal time to candidate Goldwater. The FCC backed the networks. Goldwater's campaign organization appealed to the U.S. Circuit Court of Appeals in Washington. Six members of the nine-man court heard the appeal—a process usually performed by three judges. The appellate court voted 3-3, upholding the FCC. When Goldwater's group appealed to the Supreme Court to take jurisdiction in the case, the high court refused—by a 6-to-2 vote.

Goldwater's campaign manager, Dean Burch, didn't exactly endear himself to the press, meantime, when he said he much preferred free television time to free newspaper space.

Soon NBC retreated from its no-reply stance and gave Burch 15 minutes of free time to reply. Burch used the time to attack the President and the FCC—and to appeal for funds. It wasn't exactly a reply.

The Democrats' John Bailey kept the dispute alive. He asked for reply time to reply to the reply. He was turned down. It was all another example of the silliness of Section 315.

Soon the Republicans found themselves in political hot water over television campaigning. They produced a 30-minute film entitled "Choice," which showed a strip tease, a fig-leafed male and a generously endowed girl in a topless bathing suit.

An internal memorandum by Russell Walton, the GOP campaign's public relations director, spelled out what the Republicans wanted: Depict scandal in government, crime, immorality, mob violence to "remind these people what is happening."

"Take this latent anger and concern which now exists," the memo went on, "build it up, and subtly turn and focus on the man who drives 90 miles an hour with a beer can in his hands, pulls the ears of beagles and leave them charged up to the point they will want to do something about it—vote for Senator Goldwater."

The party was getting rough. They didn't play political softball in 1964. Fortunately, Barry Goldwater wouldn't let the film be shown. One-hundred prints of the film were hastily snapped up around the country. One was purchased for $55—by the Democrats.

*   *   *

In September of 1964, I received a telephone call from Senator Pierre Salinger of California. *Senator* Salinger?

Indeed, Salinger had been appointed Senator and was running for re-election against another friend of mine, George Murphy, an actor who long had been active in Republican politics.

Pierre said he was under pressure to appear in television debates with George.

"Don't!" I said.

"I thought you were a television man," Pierre shot back. "How come you say 'no' to television debates?"

"Pierre," I said, "in campaigns, sometimes it is wise for the candidate to stick with radio and newsprint. This is what you should do—stay away from television."

Pierre Salinger (now with ABC News and one of Europe's most able television correspondents) was the embodiment of the politician who is hurt by television—cigar-chomping, heavy jowled, a tendency to scowl. Not exactly the right chemistry against a suave, Hollywood-trained actor.

Pierre went on television against George Murphy, anyway. Whatever the reason, Pierre lost the election. He wasn't able to ride the coattails of President Johnson, who swept to victory in California with close to 60% of the vote.

*   *   *

On November 2, the day before the election, *Broadcasting* magazine estimated that $40 million was spent on radio and television for national, state and local campaigns. In 1960, the total was only $14 million. The main reason for the colossal increase—in only four years? The government's refusal to suspend the equal-time law.

On Election Night, the television networks—using computers—provided the fastest coverage and analysis of an election in American history. Lyndon Johnson was elected by a landslide. The popular vote totals:

Johnson:	43,129,484
Goldwater:	27,178,188

The electoral vote:

Johnson:	486
Goldwater:	52

Back in 1963, Johnson had acted cautiously, familiarizing himself with his role as the most powerful leader of the free world. Because the tragedy that made him President remained chiseled in the American psyche, Johnson retained John Kennedy's associates on his staff.

One year after the election, Johnson, flushed with his resounding victory over Goldwater, was deeply resentful of any reminder of Kennedy. He became infuriated at the sight of anyone wearing the Kennedy PT-boat lapel pin.

Inside the Oval Office, I was with President Johnson when somebody asked him about how much power and authority he would grant his Vice President, Hubert Humphrey.

"The same amount Kennedy gave me," he said. "Not a goddamned bit."

CHAPTER 20

January 1965

LYNDON JOHNSON RODE TALL in the saddle. He reached the zenith of his political life on Inauguration Day. As he took the oath of office he saw a shining future with only one ominous cloud—Vietnam.

The President's hopes were best reflected by his quotation on the front page of the inaugural souvenir program: "All that has happened in our historic past is but a prelude to the 'Great Society.'"

Already Johnson had achieved one ambition—to amass a greater popular vote than President Roosevelt did in 1936. Now Franklin Roosevelt's New Deal would be outdone by Johnson's Great Society, which was given life by a rubber-stamp Congress. In 1964, the Democrats piled up their biggest majority in the House of Representatives since 1936.

With no tax-increase proposals or anything else to muddy the waters on Capitol Hill, nothing diverted Congress from passing bill after bill after bill. By 1966, the President had pushed programs galore through Congress. They included 21 on health, 17 on education, 15 on economic development, 12 on urban aid and 4 on manpower training. Of these programs, only one failed—the short-lived one on model cities. In all, these programs required 10% of the federal budget—a budget that, for the first time, felt a strain from having to finance activity in the Vietnam War.

In 1965, the Voting Rights Act passed in the wake of the historic march by thousands of demonstrators in Alabama from Selma to Montgomery. The bill followed passage the year before of the Civil Rights Act. But now, cynics began calling the President's legislative packages nothing more than a "second New Deal." His guns-and-butter philosophy now began to raise questions about the budget. The President was adamant: "There will be no increase in taxes."

* * *

Early in 1965, a series of closed-door meetings at the White House resulted in a decision that would reverse the President's high tide of popularity—and ultimately sweep him to political oblivion.

The turning point came as early as February 6, when Viet Cong terrorists killed eight American soldiers in an attack on their barracks at Pleiku. The burning question: retaliate or not retaliate? Only George Ball, Undersecretary of State, and Vice President Humphrey opposed retaliatory strikes. For his opposition, Humphrey for several months received the Johnson silent treatment.

The President agreed to a policy of retaliation. Escalation of the war was inevitable; negotiations for peace were impossible. A Democratic President became inexorably tied to war, not peace. Was Johnson's decision one of ego and not the head?

* * *

The Democrats lost a great statesman on July 14, 1965. Adlai Stevenson died of a heart attack in London.

Eight months later, Congress finally authorized $750,000 for a mansion for the Vice President on the Naval Observatory grounds. The GOP dismissed it as "a teepee for the veepee," but joined in approving the bill.

Came the 1966 mid-term elections. When President Johnson delivered a televised address, the networks selected a Republican to reply: Richard Nixon. The former Vice President suddenly was anointed as spokesman and spear carrier for the Republican Party.

His rigorous campaigning made it possible for him to claim credit for the Republicans' numerous victories in 1966. In California, Republican Robert Finch, running for lieutenant governor, outpolled even the Republican who won the governorship by a plurality of nearly 1 million votes in his first try for public office. The new governor: Ronald Reagan.

As candidates lined up for the 1968 presidential race, Governor George Romney of Michigan was the early front-runner. Romney had survived the Goldwater calamity of 1964. For awhile, he even topped the President in the national polls by eight points.

But then, in one statement, a tired George Romney demonstrated how a political malady called "foot in the mouth" can kill a presidential candidacy. Returning from a visit to Vietnam, Romney decided to grant his friend, broadcaster Lou Gordon, an interview on Detroit television. Romney arrived at the studio alone, tired and in a hurry to return to Lansing.

During the broadcast, Romney was asked about Vietnam: "Isn't your position a bit inconsistent with what it was? And what do you propose we do now?"

Romney replied: "I have been brainwashed by generals and diplomats in Vietnam."

Later, those ten words set off a public outcry and editorial backlash of millions of words. Backers of Romney insisted that the media had distorted his words and taken them out of context. As it was, Romney hadn't stayed at the television studio to hear a playback of the interview, which Lou Gordon needed to peddle his own new interview program to sponsors. Since the program was on tape, editing could have been arranged.

It turned out that the national media ignored Romney's ten words on Vietnam until Gordon began pushing them publicly, hoping to sell his own show. The damage was lethal. On February 29, 1968, Romney withdrew, a promising political career killed by a single inadvertent remark.

What happened to George Romney provides food for thought to any political candidate. The lessons add up to the following advice:

—Don't give an interview when you're tired and in a hurry.

—Never appear on a televised question-and-answer program when you're exhausted.

—Always listen to a playback if the program is on tape.

—Always have at least one politically-savvy, articulate aide present at every interview.

—After a live interview, review the questions and answers privately, as soon as possible.

—Treat every interview as a major event, regardless of how trivial it may seem.

—Take time to be briefed before the interview.

—Don't be afraid to say "no comment" or "I don't know" or "I'll answer your question in detail at a later time."

—Don't hesitate to use the time-honored technique of saying, "I'm glad you asked that," and proceed to give an answer that gets across the points that you want to develop, even though your answer isn't entirely relevant to the question.

—Be in command, at ease and, if possible, appear relaxed. Don't be afraid to smile or gently josh the reporter about a question.

—Regardless of the wording of the questions, be sure you get across your important points.

* * *

With George Romney out of the race, Nelson Rockefeller, who had backed Romney, became a reluctant candidate.

If Rockefeller had put up a determined fight, he could have been the front runner and secured the nomination. Instead, on March 21, Rockefeller called a news conference at the New York Hilton Hotel to announce his withdrawal from the presidential race.

But then, on April 30, Rockefeller reversed himself. In Albany, New York, he declared his candidacy again. Massachusetts responded by giving him a victory in the primary—and 34 delegates.

In California, Governor Ronald Reagan was a late starter. By the spring of 1968, he hired a staff seeking delegates. His slate of delegates prevailed in the June primary. He planned to go to the convention as a compromise candidate. And for the umpteenth time, Minnesota's Harold Stassen jumped into the fray—with a minimum of enthusiasm in his favor, as usual.

Richard Nixon's energetic campaigning for Republican candidates in 1966, meanwhile, began to pay off in the 1968 primaries. In every section of the country, he'd picked up blank checks and political IOUs. In every primary that didn't run a favorite son, Nixon was the winner.

* * *

Anticipating the Tet offensive and knowing of our country's military preparedness in Vietnam, President Johnson gave his State of the Union address on January 17, 1968, and talked about victory over the enemy.

On January 29, Johnson's approval rating in the public-opinion polls reached 48%, which turned out to be his highest point in the cataclysmic year ahead. On that same day, we first learned of the Viet Cong's Tet offensive.

Two days later, the unbelievable happened. A suicide squad of Viet Cong stormed the grounds of the American Embassy in Saigon. All the agonizing, bloody details were carried into American homes by television.

Our armed forces, which had dug in for the Tet offensive, were well-prepared. They demolished the Viet Cong forces and scored an impressive military victory.

For his part, President Johnson felt that his re-election was assured. Hadn't he, as Commander-in-Chief, scored a colossal military victory in Vietnam? The Viet Cong, however, chalked up a more important psychological victory that was never offset.

It was the Tet offensive that breathed life into the candidacy of Minnesota Senator Eugene McCarthy. Allard K. Lowenstein, who was devoted to the cause of defeating President Johnson, latched onto McCarthy as a candidate who just might do it. Blair Clark, a man with good media credentials, volunteered to be McCarthy's campaign manager.

McCarthy's anti-war stance struck responsive chords with millions of American college students and young voters. On January 3, McCarthy had announced that he would enter the New Hampshire primary. The "youth quake" of McCarthy campaign workers hit New Hampshire with astonishing results: McCarthy (who attracted votes from Republicans as well as Democrats) polled 28,791 votes and finished an eyelash behind President Johnson, who had 29,021. In some quarters, McCarthy was branded a "stalking horse" for Robert Kennedy.

* * *

In December of 1967, Robert Kennedy had visited his friend, Robert Troutman, in Atlanta. I arranged for an interview of Kennedy at WSB-TV. I wasn't satisfied with the lighting for the interview. I made some changes.

Whereupon Kennedy commented, "That's good." Then Kennedy told those in the studio, "You know what Leonard did for my brother. Without television, my brother would never have been elected President."

The aftershocks of the New Hampshire primary, meanwhile, forced Lyndon Johnson to do some soul-searching about his political career. And just when the results of McCarthy's marvelous showing in New Hampshire were being broadcast, Robert Kennedy announced that he was reassessing his position about the presidential race.

With a cutoff date for filing in California fast approaching, Kennedy had to make a decision. It was a hectic week of meetings, long-distance phone calls and more meetings. On March 16, Robert Kennedy stood in the Senate caucus room and said, "I am announcing today my candidacy for the presidency of the United States. I do not run for the presidency merely to oppose any man but to propose new policies."

President Johnson apparently became concerned about my "Kennedy connection." The President appointed John Criswell of Oklahoma as executive director of the 1968 Democratic Convention. I was named consultant. My job was the same as ever. Criswell, who was Johnson's man as treasurer of the Democratic National Committee, and I worked together without any problems. Shades of 1964.

Meanwhile, a proud President fell under constant abuse. He was vilified daily on television. At the White House, he assessed his position, but, more important, the position of his country and the overwhelming desire for peace.

The President scheduled a major address on television for Sunday evening, March 31. The thrust of his speech was an announcement about bringing a halt to the bombing of Vietnam, except for defensive purposes in certain cases.

The President's closing paragraph was unexpected—and known in advance only by a few:

". . . I have concluded I should not permit the presidency to become involved in the partisan divisions that are developing in this year. . . . Accordingly, I shall not seek and I will not accept the nomination of my party for another term as your President."

Those of us who were in Chicago, preparing for the Democratic Convention, had no prior knowledge of Johnson's sudden pullout. We had plenty of company in high places.

* * *

On April 4, 1968, Martin Luther King, Jr., who had gone to Memphis to march for striking garbage workers, stood on a balcony outside Room 306 of the Lorraine Motel. He was about to leave for dinner with several of his closest advisers.

Suddenly gunshots crackled. King crumpled to the deck. Dead at 39. Witnesses said the shots came from a boarding house across the street. Shock waves rippled all over the world. Mobs of blacks went on angry rampages of rioting, looting and burning in 168 cities and towns across America. Again, as they had in the wake of John Kennedy's assassination, Americans turned to their television sets. More than 120 million watched a funeral march in Atlanta that lasted three hours—twice as long as Kennedy's.

On April 27, Vice President Humphrey announced his candidacy for President. He didn't enter any primaries. Nor was he involved in any planning for the convention in Chicago, where he expected to be nominated.

Robert Kennedy's drive in the 1968 primaries carried him to victory in Indiana and Nebraska. He lost in Oregon, but won the big one in California in early June. The victory was his last.

The cheers of his supporters at a victory speech in Los Angeles' Ambassador Hotel still rang in his ears as Kennedy exited through a back hallway outside the kitchen. There, Robert Kennedy was felled by an assassin's gun. The gunman was wrestled to the floor by angry bystanders. Two Kennedy aides, Olympic decathlon champion Rafer Johnson and 300-pound Los Angeles Rams lineman Roosevelt Grier, broke up the skirmish. Someone screamed: "Let's not have another Oswald!" Johnson seized the gun.

Hours later, Robert Kennedy died in a Los Angeles hospital. He was 42. Once again, America and the world plunged into mourning.

A continent away, I was attending a Harvard business seminar when I was called to the telephone. I was asked if I would go to New York immediately and coordinate the television, still pictures and radio arrangements for the funeral in St. Patrick's Cathedral.

It was a dreary task, threaded with memories of John Kennedy's assassination. During one moment of solitude, Kennedys' brother, Edward, sat alone in a pew inside the cathedral. I was readying the sanctuary for television. Our eyes met. We exchanged nods. It's impossible at times like these to know what to say. Maybe it's better to say nothing at all.

* * *

Robert Kennedy's followers turned to Senator George McGovern of South Dakota. He declared his candidacy for President, only 16 days before the first gavel in Chicago.

The Republican Convention opened first, in Miami Beach. Richard Nixon was just shy of the 667 votes he needed to win the nomination. Again, cable television was used. South Florida closed circuit fed two channels into 20,000 hotel rooms and apartments in Miami Beach. Before the convention, Nixon and Rockefeller used one of the cable channels.

In early discussions about media arrangements, Vice Chairman Donald Ross of the Republican National Committee exchanged harsh words with the networks about where to place cameras and microphones. The Republicans and the media were, from the start, fierce adversaries.

The Miami Beach GOP Convention of 1968 clearly magnified the problem of the increased mobility of TV cameras and microphones. The fine line between *reporting* news and *making* news got fuzzier as confusion reigned on the convention floor.

Example: Overly eager reporters quizzed one state chairman, "Our network has just announced that State A has switched its votes to Nixon." (Actually, there had been no public announcement.) "Are you going to switch your state's vote?" And then, "Can I quote you as saying you are going to switch?"

Unless you've experienced firsthand the chaos on a convention floor, you can't fully realize how difficult it is for delegates and their chairmen to deal with persistent questioning, glaring lights, a TV camera and microphone, putting them on center stage before millions of viewers and radio listeners.

At one crucial point in the convention proceedings, Romney wanted to call Rockefeller for a private political discussion. No sooner did Romney pick up the phone than microphones were shoved in his face while a camera lens practically brushed his eyeballs. Rockefeller had the same experience. There could be no confidential political conversation.

The Republicans' nominating session lasted nine hours while 12 candidates were placed in nomination. It was ridiculously long. Nixon's demonstration lasted 25 minutes. Even before anybody switched votes during the roll call, Nixon amassed 692 votes, 25 more than needed.

It should be noted that Rockefeller's earlier slight of a Rockefeller booster, Spiro Agnew of Maryland, threw Maryland into the Nixon camp. Without Maryland's vote, Nixon could have been stopped from winning on the first ballot.

In politically shrewd fashion, Nixon held four meetings with party leaders before picking his running mate. It was Spiro Agnew, who had made the nominating speech for Nixon.

Agnew was the first Marylander to run for national office since Joshua T. Levering was the Prohibition Party's presidential nominee in 1896. Later, Agnew became the first Vice President to resign under fire. He was replaced by Congressman Gerald R. Ford of Michigan.

Moments after Nixon's first post-nomination news conference, CBS hand-delivered a letter to Nixon from CBS President Frank Stanton. The network offered time and facilities to Nixon and the Democratic nominee for a series of broadcast discussions of the issues during the campaign.

Nixon quickly accepted. Stanton noted that CBS's offer was "contingent only upon repeal of Section 315 . . . and the agreement on time, place and format."

* * *

Within hours after the nomination of Richard Nixon by the Republicans, President Johnson telephoned his congratulations. He invited the Republican nominee to visit him at the LBJ Ranch, ostensibly to be briefed on presidential affairs. It was a big media event.

A hastily arranged, last-minute visit brought Hubert Humphrey to the ranch a few hours earlier than Nixon. It was a non-media event. It was as if Johnson hoped for a Republican victory, which somehow would restore his greatness.

For Richard Milhous Nixon, everything was going as planned. The nomination now in hand, he mapped plans for the 1968 campaign with his 1960 experience in mind: Ample money to buy whatever television time he wanted; to produce whatever TV spots he needed; and there was no need to visit 50 states. This time, unlike 1960, he concentrated on key states with the largest number of electoral votes.

At the same time, Nixon wisely decided that he would avoid any mention of Vietnam. His strategy: Let the Democratic candidate stand alone in discussing the "no-win" issue of the war in Southeast Asia.

In the meantime, Governor George Wallace of Alabama entered the presidential sweepstakes as candidate of the American Independent Party. He ran on a platform of "law and order." Wallace's electors signed pledges to support Wallace or "whomsoever he may direct."

It was clear very early that George Wallace was gearing up for a balance-of-power vote in the Electoral College, which, in turn, could throw the government into turmoil.

CHAPTER 21

Chicago
Summer 1968

"Make Love, Not War" bumper stickers crop up across America. . . . Jacqueline Kennedy marries Aristotle Onassis, and Bob Hope wisecracks: "Nixon has a Greek running mate, and now everybody wants one". . . . Nixon's running mate, Spiro Agnew, makes a campaign appearance in Detroit and says, "If you've seen one ghetto area, you've seen them all". . . . Soviet tanks rumble into Czechoslovakia. . . . Students revolt around the world. . . . U.S. astronauts orbit the moon. . . . On radios everywhere, pop artist Dion pays tribute to three fallen heroes in a mournful ballad, "Abraham, Martin and John."

FOR AMERICA, 1968 WAS AN EXCRUCIATING YEAR on many fronts. The fighting in Vietnam came into millions of living rooms in bleeding-color TV. So did the fighting in U.S. streets, ignited by anger in black ghettoes.

In Washington, Congress—with little enthusiasm—levied a 10% surtax on incomes, coupled with requirements for a heavy reduction in federal spending. The idea was to maintain a strong dollar abroad and slow down inflation.

In Chicago, the Democrats dug in for a convention that would resemble an armed fortress under siege. Money was no object when President Johnson and Mayor Daley agreed on Chicago as the convention site. Security was.

After all, a Democratic governor controlled the National Guard, and a Democratic mayor controlled the city police department. Would the planned picketing and rioting—by thousands of anti-war and social activists—have occurred in another city? No one knows.

One leading activist, Jerry Rubin, said, "The Democratic Convention would have been picketed in any city—the Democratic Party came to the convention with blood on its hands."

The first gavel would fall at a time when Americans cried out desperately for peace. They weren't sure how peace could be achieved, but that didn't stop many of them from demonstrating, marching, picketing, protesting and, in many cases, creating anything but peace at home.

*   *   *

Never, while preparing for a national convention, did I meet with so many law enforcement agencies as I did in 1968. From the early stages of planning, I knew we had to deal with professional agitators and sometimes easily led, enthusiastic amateurs. Many were well trained in everything from hand-to-hand combat to kicking police officers in the crotch.

David Dellinger, head of the National Mobilization Committee for Peace, stated that "regardless of the nominee, regardless of the platform adopted, we must stay in the streets to gain the peace and stop the riots in the ghettoes." Dellinger's forces were well-organized in Chicago. They prepared detailed plans for radio communication from everywhere, including strategically placed mobilization posts.

Tom Hayden of SDS (Students for a Democratic Society) was quoted as saying: "We should have people organized who can fight the police, people who are willing to get arrested. . . . My thinking is not to leave the initiative to the police."

Vietnam peace wasn't the only area of conflict in 1968. Black riots in urban centers had triggered violent reactions. In May of 1966, Stokely Carmichael, head of SNCC (Student Non-Violent Coordinating Committee) got national attention by shouting: "If a white man tries to walk over you, kill him. One match and you can retaliate—burn, baby, burn!"

In 1967, a new leader of blacks emerged. H. Rap Brown exhorted his fellow blacks to "wage guerrilla war on the honky white man."

Then, when Martin Luther King, Jr.'s, moderating voice was stilled by his assassination in Memphis, the fallout from Negro rioting and unrest carried over to the Democratic Convention in Chicago.

* * *

From a facilities standpoint, Chicago was a good choice. The political veterans knew the city. Hotels were ample. The International Amphitheatre provided excellent space for everyone. The two large hotels, the Hilton and the Palmer House, made it easy to make room assignments. Barron Hilton had a professional and cooperative staff. The Blackstone Hotel across the street from the Hilton was well-suited for VIPs.

We felt we could focus on external problems while the convention machinery would move smoothly. Little did we know otherwise. We didn't understand the bitterness that permeated the protests over Vietnam. We didn't understand in advance how determinedly vicious the extremists were. We didn't realize what would happen when professional agitators mixed with enthusiastic young idealists.

Nor did we understand the lack of control in some areas of the Chicago police department. We didn't anticipate a telephone strike that, justifiably, put media nerves on edge. We didn't anticipate taxicab and bus strikes.

In time, I became convinced that only a state of anarchy in Chicago would satisfy the extremists.

Even today, it's difficult to understand fully the emotional intensity of Vietnam, the ugliness of race riots, the divergence of protest groups, the compelling need to express a physical reaction to any symbol of law and order. Somehow, some were convinced that physical protests and demonstrations would bring about peace and equal opportunity.

As convention headquarters, the Hilton Hotel was a likely target for an attack. It also was the rallying point for supporters of Vice President Humphrey and Senator Eugene McCarthy. Professional protesters had diagrams of all floors of the Hilton Hotel, street maps showing dead-end streets and focal points where physical pressure could get reaction.

I had to take one protective measure: to make sure that the expressway to the International Amphitheatre was kept clear. One group of protesters planned to place junk cars at every entry and exit between downtown and the convention hall, thus blocking an easy access to the convention. We kept the expressway clear.

All the storm clouds hovered over the Democrats. By contrast, the Republicans had not been picketed. They were insulated from the riots that occurred during two nights across the bay in Miami's ghettoes. The Miami Beach Convention Center was protected by a newly constructed six-foot-high chain-link fence. Security was tight, and unless you had the right credentials, you couldn't get near the hall. For the most part, the Republicans basked in the sunshine with mounting hopes for a 1968 victory.

As convention time approached in Chicago, we felt we were sitting on a time bomb.

The convention week had been selected by the President to include his birthday. With an incumbent President running for re-election, a late convention is best. The campaign organization can be put in place during the spring and summer and fine-tuned for the campaign. But now, the unexpected withdrawal of President Johnson presented us with nothing but problems.

We had to provide campaign headquarters, tickets, floor badges, convention hall facilities, and large interview rooms for an unknown number of candidates.

Campaign plans were forgotten in the push for delegates. Several candidates, including Humphrey, seemed to feel that the President would find an excuse to re-enter the Democratic race.

I was told to plan for a script in which Johnson would grab worldwide headlines and massive amounts of prime-time television with a European summit meeting with Soviet Premier Kosygin. The President would return in triumph to a Chicago convention that would, by acclamation, nominate him to run as its candidate for President. I even designed contingency plans—just in case the script came true.

The Russian invasion of Czechoslovakia killed all hopes of a summit meeting. Even so, I still held onto my contingency plans.

John Meek, planning coordinator for the convention, was in charge of accommodations for 7,000 media personnel at a convention with 3,099 delegates, each matched by an alternate.

Then, too, we had to deal with problems caused by the telephone strike. On July 22, Illinois Bell said it would accept any plan the city and the union officials might work out so that installation of phone lines at the convention were separated from the contract-negotiation battle. But union officials stood their ground. "No work at the Amphitheatre before a settlement," they said. We continued to talk to all parties. We also faced a conflict between the IBEW and NABET, both unions being represented in television.

At the same time, we considered alternate sites. To move the convention at this late date would be a horrendous task, but television coverage was imperative.

Finally, it was agreed that union volunteers would install the necessary cables for radio and television in the Amphitheatre. Hotels were off limits for cable. Wages paid the volunteer installers would go into the strike fund.

With no hotel cables, the television and radio networks faced insurmountable difficulties in covering the fast-breaking news around town.

In an order I tried in vain to overturn, the police ordered all remote taping or film vans not to park on the public streets near the Conrad Hilton and Blackstone hotels. This was the hub of activity for candidates and delegates. The police contended, with some truth, that the mobile units only attracted demonstrators and made an already troublesome scene worse.

Remote trucks then were located in parking lots. Cable was strung to the sidewalks around the Hilton and Blackstone. A few cameras were installed inside the doors. We expected trouble—and got it. Some cable was cut and stench bombs were let loose in the street entrances of the hotels. Throughout the convention, the odor of stench bombs in some hotel lobbies never went away.

Still another problem centered on relay dishes for TV. Only in Chicago did the telephone company handle the installation and maintenance of relay dishes, by which pictures and voices could be sent through the air from point to point.

Without relay dishes, the networks couldn't switch scenes instantly for live reports, back and forth between the convention hall, the headquarters hotel, other hotels, and the networks' local originating studios.

The final blow to fast-picture service came with an order: No private helicopters will be permitted to fly over—or land—at the convention hall.

To say that media people were on edge was an understatement. I was caught in the middle and helpless. I was forced into a dozen roles a day, always mindful of our basic objective:

To present an orderly convention to attract support of the Democratic candidates; to convince viewers of the integrity of the Democratic Party's aims in Vietnam. In retrospect, it was "mission impossible."

* * *

On Monday, August 19, a week before the convention, the credentials hearings opened. Simultaneously, the platform hearings began in Washington, then moved two days later to Chicago. More coverage problems.

On Wednesday, August 21, the Republicans bought 30 minutes of network television time (8:30 to 9 P.M.) to present their candidate, Richard Nixon. At 8:35 P.M. the telecast was interrupted with coverage of the Russian invasion of Czechoslovakia. The Nixon program was rescheduled for Friday, August 23, replacing "Gomer Pyle." It should be noted that no political action can lose more voters faster than replacing a popular television series program with a political program.

Somehow, on Monday, August 26, John Bailey, chairman of the Democratic National Committee, called the convention to order—a word that would be loosely used all week.

The call to the convention was explicit with language mandated by the 1964 convention. The call language was designed to thwart Governor Wallace and his third-party followers, and other Southern defectors; to avoid fights about signing a loyalty oath.

The distribution of votes, as usual, reflected an increase in delegates and alternates.

Mayor Richard Daley of Chicago was applauded when introduced. He received more applause when he stated that as long as he was mayor there would be law and order in Chicago.

Housekeeping chores moved along with very few problems. We managed to win approval of the length of nominating speeches—15 minutes for each candidate for President; seconding speeches limited to two—each no more than five minutes. For Vice President, one nominating speech of ten minutes and one seconding speech of five minutes were permitted. Organized demonstrations for any candidate were prohibited. I wanted even more limitations, but was unsuccessful.

The rules committee report brought forth a minority report. The South was unhappy with the abolition of the unit rule. Tom Gordon, delegate from Abilene, Texas, stated in his minority report that the South had no objection to the elimination of the unit rule in 1972, but wanted to keep the unit rule in effect in 1968. The minority report was rejected by a voice vote.

Governor Richard Hughes of New Jersey presented the credentials report. His committee had to review 17 contests for seating of delegates in 15 states.

In Mississippi, the Loyal Democrats of Mississippi were recognized as the duly accredited delegates. The delegates certified by the Mississippi Democratic Party were seated as guests.

(Three Mississippi delegates were FBI informants who monitored the activities of other Mississippi delegates at the convention, according to a report by Jeff Prugh in the *Los Angeles Times* on July 2, 1978, based on FBI files obtained under the Freedom of Information/Privacy Acts. One delegate, the *Times* said, reported to the FBI under the code name "Mr. Magnolia." It is believed to be the first published report of infiltration by the bureau into either of America's major political parties.)

* * *

Early Tuesday morning, I met with Louisiana Congressman Hale Boggs, House majority whip and chairman of the Committee on Resolutions and Platform. I told him I was concerned about the President's safety in Chicago. I mentioned that while it was really none of my business, I felt the President should stay in Texas and not come to Chicago.

"Let me do some checking right now," Boggs said.

After a few calls, he said to me, "We'd better call the President." He engaged in a lengthy conversation, first with Tom Johnson, a key presidential aide, and later the President himself.

Hale Boggs hung up the phone. He told me, "I don't know what's going to happen—the President may come, or he may not come."

My heart grieved for the President. Four years earlier, he was in total command. Now, on his 57th birthday, it was suggested he not come to his own party's convention. It had been a rough four years—a rapid fall from the penthouse to the outhouse.

As I prepared for the Tuesday evening schedule, I kept one eye on the clock. In the meantime, a teletypewriter was clicking out a speech prepared for delivery by the President.

I had received a documentary film for distribution to the networks. I reviewed the film with the networks. It was all about Lyndon Johnson, designed to outdo the Kennedy film of 1964. The closing showed the President and Mrs. Johnson, walking hand-in-hand through a field of blackeyed susans toward the Perdenales River at sunset.

Soon it became apparent that the President would not come to Chicago, and Secret Service agents gathered all prints of the film. Why did the President stay away?

The biggest reason, in my opinion, was the Harris Poll, released the previous night. It showed Richard Nixon leading by six points over the President, Humphrey and McCarthy.

* * *

As Anita Bryant led the convention in singing "Happy Birthday" to the absent President, a security guard tapped me on the shoulder.

"What do we do with the cake?" he asked.

"What cake?" I said.

"The birthday cake we have downstairs."

It dawned on me that the President had intended to cut a huge birthday cake at the convention. The cake, the film, the speech—they all added up to a bigger planned celebration than the one four years earlier.

"Has anyone seen the cake?" I asked.

"No," the guard said. "It's in a panel truck, and it's a big one."

I made an impromptu judgment call: "Be sure no one sees the cake. Get rid of it as fast as possible."

That was the last I heard about the President's birthday cake.

* * *

In the meantime, the convention floor was bedlam. The Georgia regular Democrats' minority report on credentials set off waves of trouble that crippled every session.

When the credentials committee report, splitting Georgia's vote, was approved, delegation chairman James Gray stalked out of the convention, saying he would never support the convention's nominees. Some of Gray's supporters tried to take away the Georgia state standard. A security guard led one of the protesting regular Democrats off the floor, whereupon Dan Rather (CBS) tried to interview the Georgia delegate.

In an inexcusable use of force, the security officer wrestled Rather to the floor and kicked him in the stomach—all on national television.

Watching from the rostrum, I was furious, but helpless. Later, John Criswell and I delivered personal apologies to Rather.

Richard Salant, president of CBS News, promptly demanded that I have the chairman order all security forces on the floor to refrain from physical attacks on newsmen. But pleas by the presiding officer were lost in the turbulence.

Unfortunately, the Rather incident drew battle lines between media and security forces. It also worsened relations between the media and those of us who tried desperately to get the convention operating with some semblance of order. We simply had too many people on the convention floor to maintain any control. I resolved again to plead with the National Committee to cut down the number of delegates. To date, no one has been successful in this project.

* * *

President Johnson had selected House Majority Leader Carl Albert as permanent chairman. Before Albert finished his speech, the delegates were getting restless. As soon as Albert finished, a chant of "Peace! Peace!" erupted from the floor, followed by "We want Kennedy!" The convention was out of control.

It was long after midnight when Hale Boggs, chairman of the platform committee, reached the rostrum. He was in trouble before he opened his mouth. The delegates were tired, angry and confused.

Rumors, rampant on the floor, were being accepted as fact by repetition, to wit: Ted Kennedy was coming to Chicago to announce his plans as a candidate! (not true); All hell was breaking loose in Chicago with armed clashes between police, the National Guard, and anti-war demonstrators! (true or not true, depending on your interpretation of "all hell").

Congressman Boggs called on Congressman Phillip Burton (California) to present a minority report on Vietnam. No one would listen. The floor was again in chaos. Never have I seen a more turbulent convention.

I noticed somebody frantically waving the Wisconsin standard for recognition. I pointed this out to Carl Albert, the permanent chairman. Albert recognized Donald O. Peterson of Wisconsin. I glanced at my watch. It was shortly after 1 A.M. Wednesday. Peterson moved the convention be adjourned "because I think every delegate in this hall wants to go home and go to bed." Amen!

Even though he was an experienced parliamentarian, Albert didn't understand the angry mood of the convention and his own power with the gavel. Albert replied; "The Wisconsin delegate is out of order. Adjournment is not a recognizable motion."

The floor exploded in loud booing, clapping in unison and chants of "Let's go home!"

An irate Mayor Daley was recognized by the chairman. Daley threatened to throw everybody out of the balconies. His words were drowned out by the gallery and convention in a chorus of boos.

Albert had lost control of the convention. He didn't know what to do next. Daley rescued him with a motion to adjourn until noon. With great cheers, everyone in the hall, including guests in the galleries, approved. Parliamentary procedures weren't followed, but this was no time for propriety. In fact, there was no other choice but to adjourn.

Albert staggered back to his office at the rear of the platform. Stunned and bewildered, he turned to me and said, "These people are crazy. They don't pay any attention to my gavel. They don't understand the Rules of the House (under which the convention operated). They're the most ill-mannered group I have ever seen."

I didn't comment, but I realized then that I'd better find a strong backup for the permanent chairman. Luckily, I found one in Congressman Daniel D. Rostenkowski, who, in 1984, would serve capably as chairman of the House Ways and Means Committee, and in 1986 preside over a massive change in the tax bill. Rostenkowski was a pillar of strength and not at all intimidated by the fiery delegates. He worked well with Permanent Chairman Albert.

In the highly charged atmosphere in the convention hall and outside the Hilton and Blackstone hotels, I worried about the safety of the man responsible for the platform report, Hale Boggs. After his report to the convention, I hustled him out the back door of the Amphitheatre and into a limousine. I instructed the driver to make no stops and to leave Boggs at the steps in front of the Blackstone Hotel.

Much later, after I had dragged myself back to the hotel, I looked out a corner window. To my horror, I saw Hale Boggs standing in a group at the corner of Balboa and Michigan Avenue. All eyes watched Grant Park across the street, where the demonstrators were gathered. I rushed to the elevator and out to the corner. Out of breath, I managed to ask Boggs, "What are you doing?"

"Watching the action," he said.

I was tired and concerned. I minced no words: ". . . If you don't get back in the hotel, you'll be the center of action!"

Only then did I believe Boggs realized he might be in danger. I turned to a policeman and asked him to escort Boggs into the lobby of the Blackstone and into the elevator.

Boggs looked at me as if I had lost my mind, but he went back into the hotel. We already had enough trouble without the platform committee chairman triggering mob violence.

Later, I learned that Lincoln Park had been forcibly cleared, forcing protestors to move to Grant Park, where several thousand were congregated. There were no American flags, only black flags of anarchy, flags of the Viet Cong and red flags of revolution. I felt sick.

Before leaving for the convention hall early Wednesday morning, I learned that David Dellinger announced he and his activist followers would march on the convention hall, even though they had been denied a parade permit. More trouble.

As if that weren't enough, a bus strike was announced. I couldn't help but feel we were in the wrong city at the wrong time. Our troubles at the convention wouldn't quit. However, we soon forgot about the bus strike.

At noon on Wednesday, August 28, a surly group of delegates started debate on the platform's peace plank. Fervent speech followed fervent speech. The debate was thorough and emotional. At long last came the vote on the minority plank by anti-war "doves." The peace plank was defeated, 1,567¾ to 1,041½.

The entire Democratic platform, which had been printed and distributed to the delegates and media, was passed with a hearty voice vote. At 5 P.M., Governor Hulett C. Smith of West

Virginia moved for adjournment until 6:30. There was an enthusiastic "yes" vote.

* * *

Chairman Albert opened the evening session by reading two telegrams, one from President Johnson, the other from Senator Ted Kennedy—each saying he didn't wish to be nominated. A tribute to Adlai Stevenson was presented by Dore Shary, Ralph Bellamy and Paul Newman.

The convention floor was calmer than in any previous session. Little did we know that another area was about to rage completely out of control.

Rumors flew recklessly, all over the place. Many occurred because the telephone strike had stopped any use of the available instantaneous communications equipment. The real story in Chicago was bad enough; it didn't need exaggeration.

Fighting flared in the area of the Hilton Hotel when Colorado was recognized in the roll call at the convention. The Colorado chairman posed a question: Is there any rule under which Mayor Daley can be compelled to suspend the police state being perpetrated this minute?

Chairman Albert ruled that asking the question during a roll call was out of order.

Senator Abraham R. Ribicoff of Connecticut nominated Senator George McGovern of South Dakota. During his speech Ribicoff remarked, "With George McGovern as President of the United States, we wouldn't have gestapo tactics in the streets of Chicago." Mayor Daley jumped from his seat in a rage and shouted at Ribicoff.

New Hampshire moved the convention be recessed in protest against the Chicago police. Chairman Albert chose to ignore New Hampshire—a good tactical move. The convention floor was seething. It didn't need much to explode in open rebellion. Albert struggled on with the roll call.

Mayor Joseph Alioto of San Francisco was selected to nominate Hubert Humphrey. Carl Stokes, black mayor of Cleveland, was selected to give the seconding speech. It was a good showcase for Humphrey's nomination. Mayor Alioto was greeted with cheers and applause when he rose to make his nominating speech.

Then came another calamity. Not even five minutes into his

seconding speech, Mayor Stokes was wiped off the television screen. He was suddenly replaced by film and tape—some unedited—with all the gory details of the confrontation near the Hilton involving the police, National Guardsmen, demonstrators, bystanders and media personnel.

Actually, the disturbance had started about 6:30 P.M. and was over in less than two hours. Film had captured all the bloody skirmishing. The networks were blocked from instantaneous coverage because of the telephone strike, so they had to wait for the film and tape to be developed and edited.

It wasn't until shortly before 10 P.M. when the networks dropped coverage of the convention to insert videotape footage of the confrontation. First, small knots of spectators watched in disbelief. They attracted more unbelieving viewers inside the convention hall. The pool crew, of course, continued covering the convention.

We continued with the roll call. Rumors circulated so fast that one rumor tripped over another.

The distortions on TV didn't help. Most everyone in the convention hall thought the riots were taking place when the film or tape appeared on the television sets in the Amphitheatre. When the networks repeated some scenes, it was thought the riots had broken out all over again. Actually, after 8:30 P.M., the streets were relatively quiet.

The networks still labored under impossible conditions. They couldn't do a professional job of coordinating and editing. The upshot was comments and interviews that normally would be restrained.

Meanwhile, Frank Mankiewicz, formerly Robert Kennedy's press secretary and now backing George McGovern, stated the streets of Chicago "are flowing with blood." Repeated several times, this became a frighteningly inaccurate commentary.

The roll call pushed forward. In the end, Hubert Humphrey was nominated. The vote: Humphrey 1,761¾, McCarthy 601, McGovern 146½, Phillips 67½ and others 47¾.

* * *

As I wearily headed back to the hotel, I didn't know what to expect. All was comparatively quiet. My mind filled up with flashbacks of Humphrey's career. In 1948, Humphrey was the Eugene McCarthy of the era. He supported unpopular causes.

He had the political courage to preach an unpopular brand of liberalism 20 years ago.

I thought, too, of Humphrey's difficult life under Johnson—a no-win position. Humphrey was bound to an unpopular President, an administration in disrepute.

On this night, Humphrey was the nominee, yet still nervous about President Johnson's reaction—as well he should have been. President Johnson never endorsed his former Vice President as a presidential candidate.

Instead of feeling happy about Humphrey getting the nomination, I began to feel sorry for him. He had been thrown into the fight for the presidency with more handicaps than I could count. His convention victory had to be bittersweet—more bitter than sweet.

This would be an unusual election—two former Vice Presidents pitted against each other. The last Vice President who became a party's candidate for President immediately after his term as Vice President won the election in 1836. His name: Martin Van Buren.

* * *

I was told there would be a change in schedule for the Thursday evening session that would nominate a candidate for Vice President and hear acceptance speeches.

A film about Robert Kennedy would lead off the proceedings—obviously not at the suggestion of President Johnson. Hubert Humphrey must have approved the change. Although I was—and still am—a great admirer of Bobby Kennedy, I could see no reason to divert the convention away from Humphrey.

I telephoned Humphrey and said it would be better to close—not open—the convention's final session with the Kennedy film. I could tell from Humphrey's voice that I was talking to an exhausted, emotionally drained man.

As gently as possible, I explained in detail why the Kennedy film should not be shown before his acceptance speech.

Humphrey replied, "I promised the Kennedys. I approved the scheduling. I can't go back on my word."

"How about letting me take the blame for a mixup," I said, "and hold the film until later?"

"No, Leonard, I appreciate your suggestion," he said. "You may be right, but I have given my word."

I hung up the phone, knowing that we had a bigger problem than I had indicated to Humphrey.

The torturous process of picking a running mate for Humphrey had been finished. Edmund S. Muskie, senator from Maine, was approved by the Southern delegations. Because of bitter losses on the unit rule and in credentials fights, the South needed placating. It was fully consulted on the selection of a vice-presidential nominee.

The Robert Kennedy film was shown early in the program. True to my expectations, it set off an emotional reaction. "The Battle Hymn of the Republic" was sung again and again and again. Delegates swayed in the aisles, singing "Glory, glory hallelujah. . . ."

Once again, the chairman couldn't control the convention. While the singing seemed to go on forever, it lasted only 20 minutes. The emotional mood of the convention was set—and this was my fear.

Alderman Ralph Metcalf of Chicago presented a tribute to the late Martin Luther King, Jr. This quieted the singers, but didn't change the mood.

Time for the vice-presidential roll call. Senator Fred Harris of Oklahoma nominated Muskie. The subsequent roll call showed Muskie with 1,942½ votes. Several states that were passed over in the first roll call never did get an opportunity to vote, which didn't seem to bother anyone.

Meanwhile, the announcement that the telephone strike had ended fell on deaf ears. To paraphrase Rhett Butler in "Gone With the Wind," the convention seemed to be saying, "Frankly, we don't give a damn."

For the acceptance speeches, defeated candidate George McGovern was at the convention hall. Eugene McCarthy chose to stay at the hotel. In fact, McCarthy wouldn't endorse Humphrey until late in the campaign.

Muskie accepted first, followed by a worn-to-a-frazzle Humphrey. Humphrey's speech was not up to his high standards. The delivery, for the most part, reflected the effects of the candidate's strenuous week.

As Humphrey left the platform, he was hounded by reporters. I blocked them off—enough was enough.

So at 12:10 A.M., Friday, August 30, the 1968 Democratic Convention came to a close. So did the skirmishing by the three television networks, which fell all over themselves scrambling for the biggest slice of the ratings pie.

Because of tight finances, ABC slashed its coverage by introducing 90-minute, edited summaries, starting each night at 9 o'clock. Interestingly, ABC led the ratings war on Monday and Tuesday.

When the last gavel pounded, ABC had broadcast only 9½ hours of the convention, compared with 34 hours for CBS and 34½ hours for NBC. Even so, millions of viewers apparently liked ABC's idea of serving up the convention in capsules rather than huge gulps. According to a post-Republican Convention Trendex survey conducted by ABC, 87.7% of viewers polled wanted to see future conventions covered in summary fashion, compared with 12.3% who preferred start-to-finish coverage.

CHAPTER 22

Campaign 1968

IN THE WAKE OF ROBERT KENNEDY'S ASSASSINATION, the nomination of Hubert Humphrey was practically assured. Unfortunately, neither Humphrey nor his staff made any campaign plans. I always felt their sword of Damocles was the possibility the President would somehow get the nomination with a last-gasp grandstand play. Once again, Humphrey would have to be content with second place.

Humphrey had never lost a partisan election in 20 years. However, this time there was no Humphrey campaign plan, no campaign organization, no fund-raising strategy, no advertising agency. There was nothing but confusion. The late-August convention, originally keyed to President Johnson's birthday, left no time for planning or fund-raising.

Emotionally and physically exhausted, a battle-shocked Humphrey was in no condition to make the vital and urgent decisions to get the campaign rolling. There was no one to insist that candidate Humphrey pause and reflect while taking a few days for much-needed rest and recuperation.

With only one night's sleep at his farm in Waverly, Minnesota, Humphrey held one crisis meeting after another.

Before leaving Chicago, he persuaded Lawrence O'Brien, a Kennedy veteran, to become chairman of the Democratic National Committee (O'Brien had joined the Humphrey camp after the death of Robert Kennedy). Senator Fred Harris of Oklahoma and Senator Walter Mondale of Minnesota were named campaign co-chairmen.

Robert Short, a Minnesota businessman friend of Humphrey

(and erstwhile owner of the Minneapolis and Los Angeles Lakers pro basketball teams), was named financial chairman in charge of the deficit-ridden treasury. He faced the impossible task of raising campaign funds for a candidate of a party torn by dissension.

Lack of funds left Humphrey off the medium that could have helped him most—television. The President was no help, either; in fact, he had no comment about the candidate of his own party. The Democratic campaign was practically stalled during most of September when most of the money ran out.

Robert Short finally arranged two loans of $240,000 each from John (Jake the Barber) Factor and Lou Wasserman, head of MCA. Because of the $5,000 limitation on campaign gifts, the money came from 96 different committees organized at that time to receive political contributions for Humphrey. The Nixon forces, too, formed numerous committees to receive campaign funds and obey election laws. Need more money? Just organize a new committee.

In early September, the Humphrey campaign was in total disarray. Basic studies hadn't been completed. What were the key states in the election? Where were the key precincts in the key states (there are 3,130 counties in the United States, with 167,000 voting precincts, but no uniform voting laws)? The key issues? Where were the Democrats strongest? Where were they weakest? What would be the impact of George Wallace's third party candidacy?

Wallace certainly couldn't be ignored. What states, normally Democratic, do you concede to Wallace, thereby saving money, time and energy for states you know you might win? What to do about the blue-collar voter being wooed by Wallace? (Blue-collar voters would be salvaged for Humphrey by organized labor's intensive efforts.)

What do we say about the country's wrangling over peace in Vietnam? When and where do we schedule television time? Where do we get the money for television? And on and on it went. The calendar pressured every move with "must be done yesterday" decisions.

* * *

On Sunday, September 8, Humphrey spoke to the B'nai B'rith convention in Washington. The next day, he spoke to an unenthusiastic small crowd in Philadelphia, where professional hecklers constantly harassed him with bullhorns. The news media immediately contrasted the sparse turnout for Humphrey with a well-organized crowd of 400,000 who cheered Richard Nixon in Chicago.

Humphrey compounded his problem by saying that, with or without negotiations, we could start removing some American forces from Vietnam in late 1968 or early 1969. His statement immediately was repudiated by Secretary of State Dean Rusk.

President Johnson, in a speech the next day to the American Legion, stated that no one could safely predict when troops would return from Vietnam.

Humphrey, as a candidate for President, was put in the awkward position of appearing not to know what was going on. Even as Vice President, he apparently was not informed about the administration's positions.

Humphrey created another problem with his statement about the minority plank on Vietnam, which had been rejected by the Democratic Convention. "There isn't much difference in my feelings and the minority plank," Humphrey said. He didn't realize that the minority plank called for an unconditional halt in the bombing of Vietnam. Again, he had to backpedal. Not a very auspicious start for the Humphrey campaign.

Organized heckling at Humphrey appearances became vicious and disruptive. Even in Boston, Senator Ted Kennedy was stopped by hecklers. Language coming from the audiences became more vulgar. TV news programs showed the violence at the Humphrey rallies and his angry responses. Not very helpful, to put it mildly.

Then, too, Humphrey made things worse by constantly being late, even on his hastily improvised schedules. Bothered by hecklers, he overtalked and left his audience lukewarm and befuddled. Party leaders avoided Humphrey as if he had a contagious disease.

The Gallup Poll showed Nixon 43, Humphrey 28, and Wallace 21.

* * *

Knowing the looseness of Humphrey's schedule, I telephoned the campaign committee with a suggestion. Our company's Pittsburgh television station would hold its annual parade on a Saturday when the candidate would be in Pittsburgh. The parade usually attracted more than 250,000 spectators. I offered to make Humphrey the grand marshal. The campaign committee, still disorganized, turned down my offer, saying it was a commercial parade. As it turned out, an alert Humphrey voluntarily joined the festivities. The next day, the only picture on the front page of the Sunday *New York Times* showed Humphrey in the Pittsburgh parade.

When finally organized, late in October, I'm sure Humphrey's campaign committee would have jumped at the opportunity of the extra publicity in a key state.

September was filled with horrors for the Humphrey campaign—until September 30. Robert Short finally had squeezed out enough money to put Humphrey on national television from Salt Lake City.

Until then, most of Humphrey's speeches had sounded as if they were delivered to win approval from the President first and the voters second. Humphrey decided to state his own views on Vietnam and peace. If they were accepted, fine; if not, at least the country would know where he stood.

A one-minute plea for funds in the Salt Lake City telecast produced more than $200,000 in four days. Things started to look up.

Within a week, the heckling stopped. McCarthy's backers began to campaign for Humphrey, who now was recognized as a candidate in his own right. Inspired by pro-Humphrey chants, the candidate revved up his fighting spirit and went on the attack. He began to appear on television, for money now poured into the Democratic coffers. (Any increase in ratings usually brings an increase in contributions.) Party leaders began to ask for joint TV appearances with Humphrey. The campaign was whipped into shape. The uphill battle against Nixon began in earnest, and requests for a debate with Nixon became more frequent, more insistent.

For his part, Nixon had favored TV debates, even after he lost to John Kennedy. In *The Saturday Evening Post* of June 1964, Nixon wrote: "Television debates were not designed to serve a candidate for office; they were designed to serve the public. I believe that television debates contribute significantly to four major objectives which are in the public interest; a bigger vote, better informed voters, lower campaign costs and in the end a better President. . . ."

Nixon continued: "I believe the strongest argument for debates is that they make candidates put on a better campaign, with the result that the man who wins becomes a better President. . . ."

But in 1968, Nixon took a different tack: Play it safe—no

debates. The repeal of Section 315, necessary for staging the debates, was killed in the Senate by Everett Dirksen of Illinois. Dirksen, a Republican, frankly admitted that parliamentary maneuvering was designed to protect Richard Nixon from being forced into debates with Hubert Humphrey. Dirksen succeeded. There were no debates.

Returning to his own campaigning style, Humphrey stepped up his attack on Nixon: "Nixon's firm positions would make Jell-O look like concrete."

By October 20, the Democratic presidential campaign roared at full throttle, led by a confident Hubert Humphrey, who punched and counterpunched with all his consummate political skill. He emphasized a theme of trust. He was backed up by the effective campaign of his running mate, Muskie. During the last two weeks of the campaign, the Democrats would match the Republicans dollar for dollar in buying television time. The Nixon camp's confidence of September and early October began to waver with every new poll. The announcement of the peace conference in Paris showed that Nixon led in electoral votes with the bare minimum needed to win.

If the convention had been held four weeks earlier, would the Democratic campaign have achieved its momentum in late September, instead of late October?

I have always felt the timing of the 1968 Democratic Convention to coincide with the President's birthday made the difference in the election. An early convention could have insured victory for Humphrey, an experienced politician who had the potential of being a great President.

As it turned out, Humphrey rose from the ashes to make the race so close in those last few days that the election result wouldn't be determined until Wednesday morning, when the vote count was completed in California, Illinois and Ohio. (In 1964, the election of Johnson had been announced as early as 6:48 (EST) on Election Night.)

From the start, Richard Nixon's campaign was skillfully planned in every detail. The advertising agency was selected as early as April.

Nixon's campaign relied heavily on polls by Opinion Research Corporation of Princeton. Its communications system incorporated all the modern equipment available. It was speedy and efficient. Daily overnight poll results determined campaign strategy. The polls were accurate and carefully studied without any personal bias.

At the same time, hecklers were few and far between. Nixon's public appearances went smoothly, the result of painstaking preparation. He used regional television effectively. Everything went according to formula; a public gathering with a set speech on law and order; an appearance at a local TV studio with a carefully screened audience asking safe questions. Never was there an embarrassing question. Usually, Nixon's program was fed to the entire region. Nothing was left to chance. In Atlanta, WSB-TV, where I operated, was studiously avoided by Nixon. His interview session originated in another Atlanta station, WAGA-TV.

*   *   *

On October 11, President Johnson asked that Vietnam be dropped from all public debates.

Eight days earlier (October 3), George Wallace finally selected a running mate—General Curtis E. LeMay, a former Air Force Chief of Staff. The announcement made in Pittsburgh was a surprise and probably a mistake. Wallace appealed to the dissatisfied, the privates in life.

In 1964, only 35% of campaign television money was spent on spot announcements. But in 1968, that figure rose to 75% of the budget. It was felt the one-minute spots were more important in influencing the mass voters than thoughtful discussion of the issues. Some observers of political campaigns expressed their concern about the proliferation of the one-minute spots.

On Thursday evening, October 31, President Johnson announced cessation of all bombing in Vietnam. This came on the heels of the Sunday, October 27, peace meeting in Paris, where American negotiations finally achieved a clear-cut understanding with the Viet Cong. Future negotiations would include the South Vietnamese government and the National Liberation Front. Not long after the Sunday agreement, the buzz word "peace" rang out around the world.

Presidential politics now hung on that magic word "peace". At long last, the "doves" could sense victory.

After the President discussed the possibility of Vietnam peace on Thursday, he was followed by paid political telecasts by both Humphrey and Nixon. But both were ignored.

A presidential election hung in the balance. The President's peace announcement propelled Hubert Humphrey into a close race. In 11 days, he had closed the gap from an eight-point deficit. On Sunday, November 3, he trailed Nixon by only one point. Then, Election Eve, the Harris Poll showed Humphrey leading 43 to 40.

But in the meantime, the Saigon government announced on November 2 that it wouldn't meet with the Viet Cong at the peace table. All was confusion. What happened? Theodore White, in *The Making of the President—1968*, described how Anna Chan Chennault, the self-appointed representative of candidate Nixon, sabotaged the peace talks; how Hubert Humphrey might have won the presidency by blaming Nixon for Chennault's action; how helpless Nixon would have been with the accusation; how a decent, fair-minded Humphrey— feeling that Nixon had no part in the cruel sabotage act— refused to accuse Nixon of destroying the peace negotiations, an accusation that could have clinched the presidency for Humphrey.

Election Eve found Humphrey and Muskie in ABC's television studio in Hollywood. Nixon made a solo appearance at the NBC studio in Burbank. (Spiro Agnew, by then, was considered a liability for Nixon.) Humphrey and Nixon each went on national TV for two hours. The total cost for each party exceeded $500,000.

Both candidates answered questions from the voters. Because of prior careful screening by the Republicans, the Nixon telethon was a slick, smooth production.

An American electorate hoping for peace—confused by conflicting stories out of Washington and Saigon—wavered, then voted Richard Nixon into office as the nation's 36th President. The final count:

Richard M. Nixon:	31,770,237 (43.4%)
Hubert H. Humphrey:	31,270,533 (42.72%)
George Wallace:	9,897,141 (13.53%)
Others:	239,910 (.35%)

The electoral votes:

Nixon:	301
Humphrey:	191
Wallace:	46

One Republican elector in North Carolina voted for Wallace in the Electoral College. Wallace received the largest vote ever cast for an Independent candidate.

For a few hours on Election Night, America lived nervously with the specter of a possible constitutional crisis, of the vote being thrown into the House of Representatives, of a government in utter chaos, without a leader. No wonder so many voices raised in favor of abolishing the Electoral College.

It wasn't until mid-morning on Wednesday, November 6, that Nixon's victory became official. His presidency was assured by the results from Ohio, Illinois and California. Neither Nixon nor Agnew carried his home state of New York and Maryland.

In the House, the Republicans gained four seats, making the count 243 Democrats and 192 Republicans. A Republican gain of five seats in the Senate brought the totals to 58 Democrats, 42 Republicans. The Republicans won 13 of 21 races for governor.

In the end, the 1968 election was a repudiation of Lyndon Johnson, the President who in 1964 could do no wrong, but four years later could do no right.

CHAPTER 23

Campaigns and Elections
1972, 1976, 1980

POORLY ORGANIZED, the 1972 Democratic National Convention committed the unpardonable sin of washing the party's dirty linen on prime-time TV—and then in airing McGovern's acceptance speech at 3 A.M.

Adding to this confused picture on television was McGovern's handling of the selection of a running mate. He chose Senator Thomas Eagleton of Missouri. Then, ten days later, Eagleton disclosed that he had voluntarily hospitalized himself three times between 1960 and 1966 for nervous exhaustion and fatigue. More dirty linen filled air waves and headlines.

McGovern, who many thought should have "fought it out" and stuck with Eagleton, accepted Eagleton's withdrawal on July 31. Not since 1860 had a major party candidate withdrawn after he had been nominated. On August 5, McGovern announced R. Sargent Shriver of Maryland as Eagleton's replacement—and the newly enlarged Democratic National Committee approved.

* * *

George McGovern was a leading spokesman for a mixture of protest groups. He opposed the war in Vietnam. Television gave the impression that McGovern was supported by aggressive women, hippies, militant blacks and wise-cracking collegians. Homosexual rights and abortion were freely pushed, as was amnesty for draft evaders.

On television, the 1972 Democratic Convention turned the party into just another ugly face. At times, things seemed so disorganized and out of hand that several leading Democrats felt they had lost the election before the campaign began.

Six weeks later, the Republicans also convened in Miami Beach. Their convention went smoothly and showcased a party in unity and harmony. Governor Nelson A. Rockefeller of New York nominated President Nixon—to the delegates' chants of "Four more years! Four more years!" In 16 hours and 59 minutes, the Republicans completed their convention in about half the time it took the Democrats to finish theirs (32 hours and 18 minutes).

While television was accepted by both conventions, neither party used it to the advantage of their candidates. The ever-present cameras showed what the parties wanted to put on the air without any frills. To both parties, TV was just another medium.

Sensing a landslide victory, Nixon for the most part stayed at the White House—off the campaign trail. Naturally, there was no debate. Nixon wasn't about to risk participating in a rerun of 1960.

This time, Nixon's strategy worked. He received 60.7 percent of the vote, with more than 47 million votes. McGovern got only 37.5 percent, with fewer than 30 million votes. Only President Roosevelt in 1936 (with 60.8%) and President Johnson in 1964 (61.1%) exceeded Nixon's margin of victory. Younger voters had been enfranchised by the 26th Amendment, ratified in 1972. But fewer than half the 18-to-20-year-olds voted, their support about equally divided between both candidates.

Gleeful about their triumph, the Republicans didn't realize the troubles that lay ahead. In October of 1973, Spiro T. Agnew was forced to resign the vice presidency, charged with income tax evasion. Under the 25th Amendment, Nixon selected Congressman Gerald R. Ford of Michigan to replace Agnew.

George McGovern had tried to make the Watergate break-in at the Democratic National Committee headquarters an issue in the 1972 campaign, but hardly anybody paid much attention. Not until 1973 and 1974 did Watergate become a buzz word—in a scandal that reached all the way into the Oval Office. Eventually, 20 members of the Nixon Administration were convicted of various crimes related to Watergate. Then, facing impeachment, Nixon resigned as President on August 9, 1974. And Gerald Ford became the first chief executive who had not been elected either as President or Vice President.

CAMPAIGN AND ELECTION 1976

In July of 1976 in New York City, under the able leadership of Bob Strauss, the Democrats held their most harmonious convention in 12 years. This time no credentials fights were carried to the convention floor. Earlier, the Democratic National Committee had approved new delegate-selection and convention rules. The implicit quota system was eliminated; affirmative action of the states was approved *before* the first gavel.

In contrast to the 1972 convention, the burden of proof fell on the challenging individual or group, not on the state's party organization. Presenting a minority report required a 25% vote—not a 10% vote.

In 1976, the demographic makeup of delegates was changed—36% women, compared with 38% in 1972; 7% blacks, compared with 15% in 1972, and 14% young delegates, compared with 21% in 1972. The convention authorized the Judicial Council as an arbiter of party rules and eliminated the loophole primary.

A virtually unknown, former governor from Georgia, Jimmy Carter, took advantage of all the Democrats' rule changes to win enough primaries and secure the nomination. He entered 30 primaries, won more than half with about a 40% popular vote.

Significantly, Carter turned a sideshow—the Iowa caucus—into a main event. With the help of national television news, he created a media victory far out of proportion to its basic political importance. In fact, Carter ran second to "undecided" in Iowa. Since "undecided" could not be interviewed, Carter got all of the television attention.

Suddenly the media became captivated by this candidate they often referred to as a "soft-drawling peanut farmer from Plains, Georgia." And Carter himself embarked on a roller-coaster ride in the early primaries. He won in New Hampshire, but finished only fourth in Massachusetts—behind winner

Henry (Scoop) Jackson. One week later, however, Carter's stock soared when he won the Florida primary over fellow Southerner George Wallace. On June 8, Carter clinched the nomination by winning the Ohio primary. Coincidentally, the Ohio vote at the convention on July 14 would give Carter the nomination.

Carter had used television effectively when he interviewed prospective running mates in Plains. Then, after his nomination, he announced his choice: Senator Walter F. Mondale of Minnesota. Mindful of prime-time television, DNC Chairman Robert Strauss made sure that Carter's acceptance speech got on the air before 11 P.M.

* * *

When the Republicans held their convention on August 16–19 in Kansas City, they gathered—in contrast to the Democrats— to participate in a bitter battle for the nomination. Gerald Ford and a Westerner, Ronald Reagan, arrived three days early to shoot it out for delegates.

Reagan tried some oneupsmanship—to get the convention to adopt a rule requiring each candidate to name his running mate *before* the nominating process. Reagan had named his running mate, Senator Richard S. Schweiker of Pennsylvania, in an attempt to attract the liberal vote. But his ploy didn't work. All indicators showed that President Ford controlled the decisive votes.

In the six-hour nominating session on August 18, demonstrations on behalf of candidates took up 2½ hours—too much time for television. The final vote: Ford, 1,187, Reagan 1,070. Reagan promptly ruled out second place on the ticket. Ford picked Senator Robert Dole of Kansas as the party's vice-presidential nominee.

Ford cut away from his prepared acceptance speech to challenge Jimmy Carter to a debate—which turned out to be a major mistake. "The American people have the right to know where both of us stand," the President said.

* * *

The 1976 campaign matched "insider" Ford against "outsider" Carter, although both tugged at religious heartstrings; both were evangelical Protestants. Ford, however, hadn't exactly helped himself when he cleared Richard Nixon with a "full free and absolute pardon for any and all crimes." Although Ford insisted amid negative reaction that there had been no deal, the pardon aroused suspicion and cost him many votes.

When the first debate took place on September 23, Carter led in the polls by 18 points. He dropped 10 points in the days immediately thereafter. Ford appeared presidential, while Carter seemed ill-at-ease.

By their second debate on October 6, Carter had become more assured and confident, although Ford remained very presidential. In fact, Ford was in command until debate panelist Max Frankel of the *New York Times* asked him about the Soviet sphere of influence in Eastern Europe. Ford's answer was startling in its misconception of the real world: "There is no Soviet domination in Eastern Europe, and there never will be under a Ford administration."

Like everyone else, Frankel was bewildered and followed up: "Did I understand you to say, Sir, that the Russians are not using Eastern Europe as their own sphere of influence in occupying most of the countries there and making sure with their own troops that it's a Communist zone?"

Ford's followup answer also was unbelievable: "I don't believe, Mr. Frankel, that the Yugoslavians consider themselves dominated by the Soviet Union. I don't believe that the Rumanians consider themselves dominated by the Soviet Union. I don't believe the Poles consider themselves dominated by the Soviet Union. . . . Each of these countries is independent, autonomous; it has its own territorial integrity, and the United States does not concede that these countries are under the domination of the Soviet Union."

As Ford and his aides tried to rescue him from this *faux pas*, their attempted clarifying statements only made the damage worse. Ford was tagged as an inept bumbler and mistake-prone. After all, he had been appointed, not elected. In the third debate on October 22, Ford did fairly well and held his own. But it was too late. The mortal damage had been done.

Mostly, the 1976 campaign was yawningly inconsequential and, except for the debates, held no particular fascination among the voters. They saw little difference between the two men. Carter's 33-point summer lead faded away to almost nothing by Election Day.

In the end, Carter pulled 50.1% of the vote; Ford, 48%. The Electoral College score: 270 to 240. Carter's margin, while slim, was wider than John Kennedy's in 1960 and Richard Nixon's in

1968. Many professional politicians felt not so much that Carter won the election but that Ford lost on two counts—the Nixon pardon and the debate blunder on Eastern Europe.

CAMPAIGN AND ELECTION 1980

On July 14, 1980 the Republicans convened in Detroit—this time to nominate the 69-year-old former governor of California, Ronald Reagan, who had won 24 of 34 primaries. The last opponent to withdraw, George Bush, was picked by Reagan as his running mate.

Some Republicans had hoped that former President Ford would join Reagan on the ticket. Ford granted two network television interviews on the very evening that the nominating votes were being tallied. He said he would consider the vice presidency under certain conditions; in effect, he would be co-president.

Reagan, watching Ford's interviews on television, reportedly "blew his top" over Ford's presumptions. By 11:15 P.M., all talk of a Reagan-Ford ticket idea died. Meanwhile, the Republicans radiated at least the appearance of unity; all differences were deliberately blurred. The party platform was strictly a political document crafted to help Ronald Reagan to the White House.

*   *   *

Senator Edward M. (Ted) Kennedy had bitterly fought President Carter in the primaries. Carter won. Kennedy, however, decided to carry his fight to the convention floor when the Democrats gathered in August in New York City. Kennedy tried to persuade the convention to nullify a delegate rule adopted in 1978—delegates were bound to vote on the first ballot for the particular candidate under whose banner they had been elected in the primaries.

It was Kennedy's only chance to upset the President, who entered the convention with an expected 315-vote victory margin. Kennedy lost the test vote, 1,936 to 1,390, and then withdrew from contention. The animosity created by this fight lingers even today. Neither the former President nor his wife can conceal their bitter feelings about Kennedy.

Kennedy made one more flanking attempt. He addressed the convention Tuesday evening, August 12—and received a 40-

minute demonstration. Carter, however, was nominated with 2,123 votes to Kennedy's 1,150.

Strenuous efforts were then made by the Democrats to arrange a "unity" picture on television. Kennedy appeared on the platform late, with the media conjecturing about the strained relations between Kennedy and the President. Carter's backers sought a unity gesture from Kennedy. It never came.

* * *

A third party was introduced in the 1980 campaign. A losing primary candidate to Reagan, Republican Congressman John Anderson of Illinois ran for President on the National Unity ticket. He selected a former governor of Wisconsin, Patrick J. Lucey, as his running mate. The National Unity Party got on the ballot in all 50 states and was qualified to participate in the scheduled debates.

President Carter was adamant. He refused a three-cornered debate. Carter saw no reason to use his presidential presence to help Anderson as President Ford had helped Carter by appearing in the 1976 debates. However, Reagan readily agreed to include Anderson in a debate. The two debated on September 21 in Baltimore, without President Carter. Reagan did well, and his poll ratings continued to rise.

Finally, President Carter and challenger Reagan met in a debate on October 28 in Cleveland. Reagan outmaneuvered Carter at the beginning by striding across the platform to offer a handshake to the startled President. At the debate's end, Reagan repeated the gesture. On the firing line, meanwhile, Reagan exuded a self-assured calm. He appeared capable of handling the responsibilities of the presidency. Carter seemed on edge, projecting a pulpit style, but he came across as well informed. Now and then, however, Reagan didn't think Carter accurately represented Reagan's views. Shaking his head, Reagan looked at Carter and blurted out a memorable line: "There you go again."

As with all debates, everyone looked for gaffes. The President offered one: In a discussion of arms control, he said, "I had a discussion with my daughter, Amy, the other day before I came here to ask her what the most important issue was. She said she thought nuclear weapons and the control of nuclear arms." With these words, Carter left himself open to a deadly weapon ridicule.

Reagan's closing remarks upstaged Carter's well-prepared

summation. Reagan played to the emotions of a nation rocked by soaring interest rates and double-digit inflation: "Are you better off than you were four years ago?" It was a catchy line, easily savored by the masses out there in television and radio land, and calculated to swing undecided voters to his side.

Reagan's strategists constantly feared that their plans would be upended by an October "surprise"—say, Iran releasing the 52 Americans who had been held hostage for nearly one year (the hostages would be released on Inauguration Day). As in 1976, the 1980 election was a ho-hum chapter in history, save for the debates.

The Iranian crisis had helped Carter win the nomination against Kennedy. Democrats turned from Kennedy to rally behind Carter in a show of backing the President in a crisis. However, the bobbled rescue attempt in April—when eight American military men died—probably sounded the death knell to Carter's hope for reelection.

As Carter skidded downhill in all the polls, he became vehement in his attacks on Reagan, accusing him of being a racist and a war monger. Carter inferred that if he were re-elected, America would have peace; the election of Reagan, he asserted, would mean war.

Reagan's campaign style, however, was a natural for television news clips. Even so, his offhand remarks created problems for his staff, just as they would during his tenure in the White House. A sample of a Reagan quip is "I am told I can't use the word 'depression.' I'll tell you my definition: a recession is when a neighbor loses his job; a depression is when you lose your job; recovery is when Jimmy Carter loses his." Moreover, Reagan's skill at turning away hard questions earned him the nickname "The Great Deflector."

In the end, Reagan swamped the President with 51% of the vote to Carter's 41% and Anderson's 7%. Reagan amassed 489 electoral votes to Carter's 49—the biggest defeat of a President since Herbert Hoover lost to Franklin Delano Roosevelt in 1932. In addition, Carter became the first incumbent Democrat to fail in a re-election try since Grover Cleveland in 1888.

At the same time, the Republicans also wrested control of the Senate. But a lack of interest in the presidential candidates resulted in a turnout of only slightly more than 50% of the electorate.

President Carter further alienated Democratic candidates by conceding to Reagan one hour before the polls closed in the

West. As a result, the 1984 candidates—President Reagan and Walter Mondale—would agree before the election that they would issue no statement about the outcome until all of the polls had closed.

As usual, many Americans complained about the television networks projecting winners in geographic areas where voting was still in progress. Analyses of survey data done for the *Journal of Public Opinion* suggest that two-tenths of one percent of eligible voters stayed home because of early projections. Reagan's victory was called at 8:15 P.M. (EST).

Weeks after the election, someone alleged that Reagan's campaign manager had obtained Carter's briefing books in advance of the debates. The story was dubbed "Debategate." The briefing books were said to have assisted Reagan enormously. Nonsense! As Gerald Ford's one-time speechwriter, Robert Orben, wisecracked, "If those briefing books were so important, how come they didn't help Carter?" Indeed, there is nothing new in debate material. Image, appearance and impressions left by candidates count more than the material content.

If nothing else, the 1980 debates insured presidential debating a role in all future campaigns, even though incumbents had become the losers in 1976 and 1980. Future Presidents would have no choice but to face their challengers on national television.

CHAPTER 24

Primaries and Caucuses 1984

1984, the year immortalized by George Orwell's novel, begins with a court-ordered breakup of AT&T. . . . The Summer Olympic Games play in Los Angeles—without the Russians and without a hitch. . . . On a TV commercial for a hamburger chain, Clara Peller, a wisp of a woman with thunder in her voice, asks, "Where's the beef?" . . . That's what Walter Mondale, too, asks as he challenges his opponents during a televised primary debate in this, the watershed year for TV in American politics.

UNDER FRANKLIN DELANO ROOSEVELT'S LEADERSHIP, the Democrats had mastered the use of radio in politics. The Republicans, by contrast, never fully understood how to exploit radio in conventions and campaigns. In fact, they often shunned the microphone as if it were a live grenade.

In 1984, however, the Republicans took the world's most powerful medium—television—and molded it to fit their political strategy. This time, the Democrats lagged far behind in utilizing television properly. The 1984 Republican Convention and campaign changed forever the role of television in politics.

* * *

Walter Mondale fully expected to win the Democratic presidential nomination early in the primary season. To understand Mondale's confidence, it is necessary to look back.

The 1980 convention, like every convention since 1968, authorized the appointment of a commission to again study the rules on delegate selection. Headed by Governor James Hunt of North Carolina, the commission drafted new rules.

A compromise gave Iowa and New Hampshire a head start, but moved up primaries in the other states. Instead of five weeks between Iowa and other delegate selection dates, there would be only 15 days in 1984. This rule was designed to prevent a surprise Iowa winner from capitalizing on an early victory.

Maine crossed up everyone by holding a cosmetic presidential vote between the Iowa and New Hampshire elections. A "nothing" affair, politically, but television and other media gave the Maine vote coverage far beyond its significance.

Mondale apparently had a clear track with the new rules. He was protected by the high threshold rule: the rescheduling of primary and caucus dates, and complicated rules that governed the selection of 194 members of Congress as unpledged delegates. An additional 400 delegates were party and elected officials, also unpledged. In addition, labor—for the first time—endorsed a candidate before the primary-caucus season: Walter Mondale. Mondale managed to get eight states to switch from caucuses to primaries. Labor could help Mondale better in primaries than caucuses.

In 1976, the Iowa caucuses—relatively unimportant as political meetings—were overcovered by television. A political happening was created with the Iowa caucuses. Iowa became important since a winner in Iowa became the front runner going into New Hampshire.

Again in 1984, the Iowa caucuses were overwhelmed by excessive television coverage. Indicative of media overkill in the precinct caucuses was the attention focused on Democratic candidates not even in the running. When Reubin Askew of Florida campaigned in a church, his appearance was covered by six television camera crews. Flattering to Askew? Yes. Misleading to television viewers? Absolutely. Caucus canvassing produced headlines which also were misleading.

Eighty-five thousand voters, fewer than one-sixth of those who normally vote Democratic, participated in the caucus vote. Mondale polled 45% of the vote (38,250) and Colorado Senator Gary Hart 15% (12,750). Hardly anybody noticed, but George McGovern finished a close third with 11,361 votes.

Gary Hart's second-place finish with 15% of the vote (2.5% of the total eligible vote) resulted in television coverage that made Hart a leading contender for the nomination. TV had decided to focus on a two-man race. When Hart finished second in Iowa, commentators—ignoring McGovern's close third-place finish—agreed that Hart now had what he wanted—a two-man battle—even though he had received a mere 2.5% of the total eligible vote. With name recognition, Hart pulled in more campaign contributions.

Confident that the election script so carefully written in 1982 and 1983 was going to deliver an early victory, Mondale strategists chose to ignore Hart's second-place win in Iowa.

Hart won an upset victory in New Hampshire by 12,000 votes. Now network commentators speculated that Hart might get the nomination. With more television attention, Hart got more financial contributions and was able to buy more TV time. Hart raised almost $1 million in only two hours at Washington fund-raising meetings. Immediately after his New Hampshire win, Hart received added coverage of 11 TV news crews and 60 journalists.

By 40 days after the New Hampshire primary, half the Democratic delegates had been chosen. Hart was only 300 behind Mondale, the front runner.

The rapid expansion of Hart's campaign created staff problems which Hart chose to ignore. He rationalized in the age of television dominance that good media coverage is more important than good organization.

Meanwhile, Mondale lost his aura of invincibility in New Hampshire, but no one in his organization was concerned. The rules had been written to insure an early Mondale victory.

Mondale, instead of having smooth sledding, attracted more opponents: the Rev. Jesse Jackson (Illinois), Senator John Glenn (Ohio), Senator Ernest Hollings (South Carolina), Senator Alan Cranston (California), former Governor Askew of Florida and the 1972 presidential nominee, McGovern (South Dakota). What figured to be a victorious 100-yard dash turned into a marathon—with the rapid-fire pace of the dash.

* * *

Walter Mondale wasn't the only person who expected the primary season to be over early. Television networks front-loaded their plans for coverage. Large portions of their budgets were spent in Iowa, New Hampshire and the "Super Tuesday" states.

As the extended primary-caucus season dragged on, it became apparent that Hart was Mondale's only serious opponent.

Others, running out of money and in debt, dropped out. Jackson, out of contention, hung on tenaciously until the bitter end, hoping to use his delegate strength to influence the convention decisions and the successful candidate.

* * *

By early morning, June 6, the day scheduled for Mondale's victory announcement—it was evident Hart had won overwhelmingly in California. Fortunately for Mondale, Hart didn't fully capitalize on his stunning California victory. (In 1972, McGovern won California to beat out Humphrey for the nomination.)

By a careful count of delegates, Mondale still was 24 votes shy of the magic number on Wednesday morning, June 6. Mondale aides frantically telephoned unpledged delegates to stand by for a call from the candidate. By late morning, thanks to 50 phone calls, Mondale had collected 40 more pledged delegates.

At 11:59 A.M. Mondale announced at a news conference in Minneapolis' Radisson Plaza, "Today I am pleased to claim victory. I am the nominee. I've got the votes."

Hart's reply: "Welcome to overtime."

In all, Hart had won 12 primaries to Mondale's 11. Hart won 12 caucuses, Mondale 13.

So complicated and torturous was the road to primary and caucus elections that in some states some candidates did not have a complete slate of delegates on the ballot. In Illinois, Mondale had a full slate of 116, as did John Glenn. Cranston had 92, and Hart only 46. Under the new rules, none of the selected delegates was legally bound to support the candidate under whose banner they were elected.

With 1,967 delegates needed to win, Mondale now had 1,969 to Hart's 1,212 and Jackson's 367.

Across the nation, voters and politics watchers breathed a universal sigh of relief. The primary season had been too long and bland. Everywhere, the voting turnouts set record lows. Most voters, according to the CBS-*New York Times* poll, thought the candidates spent too much time fighting each other and too little time on issues.

Like Jackson, Hart wanted to carry his delegate strength to the convention to help shape the platform and work on a plan to overhaul the delegation selection rules.

At the finish line, all were in debt:

Mondale:	$3 million
Hart:	$4 million
Glenn:	$4 million
Cranston:	$1 million
Jackson:	$466,000

Hart and Glenn borrowed heavily from banks. It was speculated that they would be forced to default at least part of their loans. In case of default, a question is raised about the loopholes in the federal election laws.

What ran up the cost of television was the increasing use of spot announcements. One philosophy held that if you flooded the screen with 30-second spots for the candidate and saturated radio stations with more spots, you would win. Often this was true. In Ohio, Hart outspent Mondale 2 to 1; and Hart won.

Mondale didn't appear in his TV commercials. By contrast, Hart appeared in person in all of his. Mondale relied on three stock television announcements:

1. People praise Mondale.
2. Announcer says Hart switched his position on arms control no fewer than seven times.
3. A red telephone pictured with the announcer saying there is a need for a calm, mature President.

A still photo of Mondale appeared at the end of each announcement.

Hart countered with television ads that linked Mondale to a discredited past and said: "We can't afford to go back."

Networks accepted televised political spots for the first time in 1984. Their news shows even ran analyses of local political television spots. At a news conference, they publicized the major unveiling of the Republican spot announcements. The National Republican Congressional Committee showed ads in which portraits of George Washington and Thomas Jefferson appeared to weep over the high-handed tactics of the Democratic majority in the House of Representatives. The tag line: "Bring back the pride. Vote Republican." Another Republican television advertising line: "Now our country is turning around; why turn back?" Replied the Democrats, "This buy-and-lie campaign will not work."

In keeping with the old political axiom of always endorsing God, good roads and motherhood, Reagan took the high road, substituting the flag for good roads. Of course, he could afford to take this tack while the Democrats appeared on every TV news program in a self-destruct mode.

* * *

It was inevitable that "Let's have a debate!" became a universal battle cry in early 1984. By April 23, there had been eight debates. The tenth and last debate was on Sunday, June 3. It was difficult to apply the term "debate" to a televised presentation of eight candidates sitting awkwardly in chairs in a semicircle on a raised platform, fielding questions from a panel of reporters.

In November of 1983, the FCC finally ruled that the networks could conduct the debates. Apparently fearing loss of its control over presidential debates, the League of Women Voters went to court, seeking to have the FCC ruling invalidated. But the Court of Appeals upheld the FCC ruling. As a result, the sponsorship of debates in the 1984 Democratic primaries was as varied as the participants and the settings.

First to stage a "debate" was the Public Broadcasting System—from Dartmouth College in New Hampshire. The eight candidates, sitting in a tight semicircle on an elevated platform, faced a barrage of questions from two veteran TV talk show personalities—Phil Donahue of the widely syndicated "Donahue" program, and Ted Koppel, "Nightline" host on ABC. Each questioner's style was decidedly different—Donahue more showman, Koppel more newsman. The event, sponsored by House Democrats, was scheduled for three hours. Nine million television viewers saw the candidates frantically raise their hands to get attention and interrupt each other. They saw John Glenn attack Mondale's deficit-reduction plan as "gobbledy-gook," which drew a Mondale retort: "Baloney." It was more a free-for-all and more emotional than most subsequent television meetings among the candidates.

CBS was the first commercial network to present the Democratic candidates, on March 28, at Columbia University's Law Memorial Library. By now, the race had shriveled from eight candidates to three: Mondale, Hart and Jackson. The candidates and the moderator, Dan Rather of CBS, sat at a round table.

But even this debate finished third in the ratings—a 10.4 and a 16 share against ABC's "Fall Guy" at 20.0 and a 32 share, and NBC's repeat of "Real People" with 15.0 and a 25 share.

Did television contribute to the political process by presenting these ten Democratic debates? Did voters gain a better insight into the candidates and their views on vital issues? Did the candidates—based on the questions—get a better feel of the voters? And who won?

Moderators and panelists, for the most part, were the only winners of the "debates." Usually, the candidates played it close to the vest in their debate appearances, hoping to avert a serious mistake. If they performed well, the result was increased contributions. If they were ineffective, the money flow became a trickle.

Playing it cautious meant hopefuls soon became non-candidates. No one among the Democratic candidates in 1984 seemed to know what he wanted to accomplish in the debates. As a consequence, no decisive winners emerged. If nothing else, the only winner may have been style over substance.

CHAPTER 25

San Francisco Summer 1984

WALTER MONDALE HAD LIVED IN WASHINGTON for many years. Before officially announcing he was a presidential candidate, he bought a home in North Oaks, Minnesota, a suburb of St. Paul.

After he proclaimed himself as the winning Democratic candidate on June 6, Mondale turned his attention to the selection of a running mate. He invited prospective vice-presidential candidates to North Oaks to meet with him privately and, of course, on television.

Then came an announcement that turned heads: The National Organization of Women (NOW) threatened a floor revolt if a woman were not selected.

Whatever the reason, Mondale finally announced—in a carefully staged television news conference—that he had selected Congresswoman Geraldine Ferraro of New York as his running mate.

The choice had an electrifying effect on Democrats everywhere. The mood and morale before the convention changed from "listless" to "exciting." Mondale's bold step was seen as a portent of a unified convention, providing a shot in the arm to a campaign in which he trailed President Reagan by 19 points.

Picking Geraldine Ferraro was a bold, innovative step that no one could ignore. A no-news convention suddenly became a big-news convention.

But the euphoria of the moment was short-lived.

* * *

Before the first convention gavel fell, ABC News' political director Hal Bruno was leaving a San Francisco party when he unexpectedly ran into Charles Manatt, the Democratic National Committee chairman.

"How's it going?" Bruno asked Manatt.

"I'm leaving," Manatt said. "Bert Lance is taking my place."

Within minutes, Bruno telephoned ABC's bureau in Washington. The story that Manatt was being replaced by Mondale's friend, Bert Lance of Georgia, who had been Jimmy Carter's troubled Budget Director, was aired on "Nightline."

Mondale had forgotten the history lesson of 1956, when Adlai Stevenson tried to fire chairman Paul Butler—*after* the convention. Never had so much emotional support been aroused in the National Committee.

Manatt was not considered an effective chairman and not overly popular, but the proposed firing proved disastrous.

What a difference a few days made.

Gone were the glowing stories about Ferraro. Media pounced on the only hard news story available—the firing of Manatt and the appointment of Lance. Mondale's leadership qualities were questioned on every television news program, every radio news program, in every newspaper and in every newsmagazine.

Faced with a barrage of unfavorable stories, Mondale cut his losses by saying Manatt would stay as chairman and Lance would be a "campaign consultant."

As was pointed out, Mondale could have moved his own man into the control of the National Committee several days after the convention, away from the swarms of media at the convention. Manatt could have stayed as chairman with no authority and no responsibility. This had been done before. In 1960, Senator Henry Jackson was named national chairman after the convention. Robert Kennedy, as campaign chairman, called all the shots for John Kennedy.

The grumbling about the Manatt decision lingered throughout the convention. After the last gavel, Bert Lance sent a letter of resignation to Mondale, removing himself from the campaign.

Bad publicity was not the only problem. Valuable hours of campaign planning had been lost—forever.

On August 9, Bill Shipp wrote in a column in the *Atlanta Constitution*: "The Mondale-Ferraro office in Georgia has been shut down."

Experienced political observers noted that the professional politicians were surprisingly camera-shy. In the few interviews appearing on the air, Democratic professionals were guarded when asked about the possibility of a successful campaign.

* * *

Gavel-to-gavel coverage of the first nationally televised political convention in 1952 meant exactly that—gavel-to-gavel with the main focus on the podium. In 1952, the networks—dealing with the unknown—played it safe by aiming their cameras mostly on activity at the rostrum. Conventions were new to television viewers, who followed every detail with interest. In those days, the choice of TV programs was limited, and the conventions took up big blocks of time. There were few independent television stations that could offer alternate programming. As it turned out, both conventions had contested nominations. The year 1952, however, marked the end of multi-ballot conventions.

In 1984, network executives faced a thorny problem that forced them to make tough decisions. Sensitive to ratings and their impact on the balance sheet, and well aware TV audiences were increasingly tuning out conventions, the networks decided to cover the 1984 conventions as news events, not as the quadrennial political Super Bowl.

No longer would ABC, CBS, and NBC cover the conventions from gavel-to-gavel. Coverage would start at 9 P.M. (EDST) and last two hours, with a possibility of carry-over coverage.

With networks scaling down their convention coverage, station affiliates re-evaluated their roles. When the on-the-scene coverage ran beyond 11 P.M and overlapped into the affiliates' highly profitable late-evening news, most stations cut away from the convention and put on their regular news. As live television, the political convention was no longer sacrosanct.

Perhaps, in these days of fierce competition for audiences, a political party should schedule the convention window from

9–11 P.M and let the networks select what they want to cover. They will, anyway.

* * *

In 1984, the networks refused to carry the Democratic Convention's prepared films on Harry Truman, Walter Mondale, and Eleanor Roosevelt—each scheduled in prime time. After the convention, Democratic leaders sent letters of complaint to the three networks, arguing that since they didn't show the Democrats' films, they shouldn't show Republicans' films, either.

Actually, these prepared films are generally more meaningful than commentary by network newsmen. Most of the films should be available to network viewers. Of course, some argue that the films are propaganda. Well, isn't any political convention designed, for the most part, to be propaganda for the party and the candidates? It's simply good political business to prepare films and other footage for conventions, at convention expense—materials that can be inexpensively adapted to the campaign.

Because the candidates were known in advance, and Mondale's compromises with opponents assured no floor fights or controversy, the Democratic Convention planners had reasonable control over the schedule. But a planned, pre-programmed convention becomes too sterile and lacks audience appeal.

Television, the ultimate power of politics, was getting the political party to change its convention ways. Not that it was a one-way street. The Democratic Convention was eager to present the party at its unified best in prime time. The convention now was little more than a gigantic political rally and, not so incidentally, a huge fund-raising event.

* * *

The convention program turned out not as neat and tidy as planned. Consequently, the networks left themselves open to criticism. On Tuesday, July 17, the second night of the convention, ABC switched to the convention promptly at 9 P.M. Since the main events weren't on schedule, ABC switched back to New York for a rerun of a mystery drama, "Hart to Hart." As ABC News vice president David Burke observed,

"There is nothing that says you have to take to the air when there's no news to cover." As news, Burke said, the conventions were becoming "dinosaur events."

Television, meanwhile, was accused of distorting the reaction to Jesse Jackson's spell-binding speech on Tuesday. Virtually all the cutaways focused on black delegates (who made up only 18% of the 3,944 delegates), many of who responded tearfully to the speaker. Few, if any, cameras showed delegates who remained silent or walked out.

In their new abbreviated coverage, the networks missed the early platform fights: Mondale battling in caucuses to keep his delegates from switching to Hart; the unexpected booing of Atlanta Mayor Andrew Young when he spoke against a Jesse Jackson platform plank; speeches by up-and-coming leaders of the Democratic Party; the "rainbow coalition" speakers, and the nominating speech for Mondale by Los Angeles Mayor Tom Bradley.

By moving to prime time only, the three networks opened convention coverage to other television coverage. Two cable networks were quick to seize the opportunity, Ted Turner's CNN (Cable News Network) and Brian Lamb's C-SPAN (Cable Satellite Public Affairs Network). Both announced gavel-to-gavel coverage. Each approached the coverage in a different way.

CNN, recognized as the fourth network, promptly built an anchor booth in Moscone Center as large and prominent as ABC, CBS and NBC. CNN went all out in covering the convention, with 300 editorial and technical personnel on hand, many working in trailers outside the hall. During convention hours, CNN's regular audience more than doubled.

C-SPAN, with a limited budget, spent slightly more than $100,000. It deployed 35 staff members and a headquarters on the 24th floor of a skyscraper near Moscone Center. Viacom, the local cable system, provided additional personnel and equipment for C-SPAN. Another network, SIN (Spanish International Network), provided limited live coverage.

Cable TV, obviously, had come of age. Significantly, 36.1 million homes—or 42.9% of those with television—had access to cable.

To fill the gap, C-SPAN offered full coverage of the convention to all Public Broadcasting Stations. Unfortunately, very few PBS stations saw fit to accept the C-SPAN convention coverage. "A deplorable attitude" was the industry reaction.

While CNN moved around the convention hall like the networks of yore, C-SPAN was the favorite tune-in for all media working the convention. The *Wall Street Journal, Time* magazine, and other print-media representatives tuned to C-SPAN for the convention details.

It was fortunate for the print media that C-SPAN stayed glued to the rostrum. Almost half the media were in seats where they couldn't see the rostrum—an unpardonable sin in pre-TV days. As Robert Petersen, superintendent of the Senate Press gallery, commented unhappily, "It is an electronic media event."

From a minor subordinate role in 1948, television had become the dominating force in 1984. As network television was changing its approach to the Democratic Convention, satellite transmission was adding a new dimension to TV coverage. Two hundred of the 350 local television stations covering the convention used the satellite for live coverage of local stories. More than 300 radio stations also broadcast their own live coverage.

Cable television viewers, however, for the first time, were the only persons with TV sets to watch gavel-to-gavel coverage of the convention.

According to the Mondale plan, Monday was "Cuomo Night." As keynoter, Mario Cuomo, governor of New York, aroused the convention and the television audience with a low-key perfect television delivery. Many felt it was his first speech in the drive for the 1988 nomination. (He later withdrew as a presidential candidate.) Unlike keynoters of the past, Governor Cuomo didn't preside as temporary chairman. He made his stirring speech and immediately returned to New York. During the keynote address, Democratic convention planners dimmed the house lights, which made reaction shots from the floor practically impossible.

Tuesday was Jesse Jackson's night, and again spectacular oratory aroused the audience.

Wednesday was dubbed "Gary Hart Night" as the second-place candidate sought to set the stage for 1988—mindful, that he needed help to pay off his $4½-million debt. One Hart adviser expected a year would be required to clean up the 1984 debt—it was still not paid in 1987. Hart would also need $25 million more to run for the presidency in 1988—all from the same people. But, as the leading candidate for 1988, Hart withdrew in 1987 when his alleged extramarital activities became a major news story. His withdrawal came shortly after the announcement of a fund-raising dinner to help pay off his debt. The dinner was canceled.

Roll call was scheduled for Wednesday night, and Thursday was the big celebration—Mondale-Ferraro night with all the trimmings, balloons and indoor fireworks.

But were Americans watching at home? Both the TV ratings and share of audience were down from the 1980 convention tune-in. The tune-away from the 1984 Democratic Convention coverage was noticeable on each of the four nights. The three-network audience fell below 50% in 16 of the 17 hours in which convention activity was carried in prime time.

The combined network rating in 1980 was 27.1, but the 1984 figure dropped 14% to 23.2. By comparison, the Olympics on one network, ABC, averaged a 23.4 rating.

Where did the television audience go? Old movies, baseball games, and syndication programs took turns outranking the Democratic Convention. As the Democrats discovered, a planned convention becomes too sterile, with minimum appeal to viewers at home. A rerun of "Mork and Mindy" in Washington, D.C., attracted more television viewers than the three network stations combined.

In opting for a unified convention, the Democrats eliminated all the political drama of some bygone conventions. The networks know that a unity convention loses rating points and thus advertising dollars. The basic question for both major political parties is: Does a unity convention, achieved by pre-convention concessions and agreements, often behind closed doors, gain more votes than a convention that takes its natural course of reasonably controlled controversy settled by floor arguments, under the watchful eye of television? Or, does unity, achieved for the sake of party harmony on the television camera, turn off potential voters? And is lack of spontaneity apparent to TV viewers?

To guarantee a perfect television picture, spontaneity was sacrificed by the Democratic Convention planners. For the big Thursday evening celebration, the Mondale directions memo read: "JAM (Joan Mondale) and children step back and Ferraro to front stage. WFM remains on right side of podium and applauds Ferraro as she comes onstage from left; they shake hands at the rostrum and the two candidates wave together at rostrum with outside arms. *No joined hands held aloft—now or at anytime during the demonstration.* Flag drop and balloon drop. Zaccaro family comes onstage and Mondale family comes back to front of the stage. Candidates and families array themselves in semicircle at front of stage, each candidate has outside arm around spouse and waves with inside arm."

Mondale's backers hoped the organized excitement of the convention would give him a badly needed boost in opinion polls. They hoped a well-managed convention would radiate the take-charge image that Mondale hadn't yet conveyed. Despite a controlled convention, the hopes of Mondale's supporters didn't materialize.

There were 33 speeches at the Democratic Convention before Mondale made his acceptance speech. During the demonstration following Mondale's speech, small American flags replaced Mondale-Ferraro signs in an attempt to demonstrate that the Democrats were also the "flag party." It was a convention long on emotion, short on substance.

CHAPTER 26

Dallas
Summer 1984

BEFORE THE CONVENTION'S FIRST GAVEL, the Republican Party announced that it had registered 1.5 million new voters—all professed Republicans. Unlike the Democrats, who registered everyone in sight, the Republicans carefully screened those they signed up. Fifty-five thousand volunteers made 2.6 million telephone calls en route to a goal of 2 million new Republican voters. By August 15, the GOP registration drive had cost $1.1 million.

Joe M. Rogers, chairman of the Reagan-Bush Finance Committee, said he had 2.1 million names on his list. In only five months, the list had produced a record $26 million in contributions.

On Wednesday, August 22, reports filed with the Federal Election Commission showed Ronald Reagan with $5 million in his campaign treasury—and debts of $1,038,000. Walter Mondale's campaign showed a $2-million debt.

In keeping with their new campaign strategy, the Democrats spent $50,000 on television commercials in Dallas and Washington at the time of the Republican Convention.

Nothing was left to chance at the Republican Convention in Dallas. All principal speeches were edited by two campaign staffers; the exception was Barry Goldwater's. Clothes worn by those on the podium were checked for good taste and color. However, the color-coordinated curtain (which was to change colors) behind the speakers did not live up to its pre-convention billing.

As evidence of weak enthusiasm toward the Republican Convention, reservations for 12,000 hotel rooms were returned.

In 1984, the Republican Convention was presented in a meticulously planned setting. Unfortunately, for Republicans, the convention program again lacked audience appeal, except for the main attraction, President Reagan.

It was inevitable that discussion and analysis would focus on the party's 1988 prospects. Hopefuls such as George Bush, Robert Dole, Howard Baker and Jack Kemp were highly visible on television. They were willing to be interviewed anytime, anywhere.

No part of the convention was left to improvisation. Events that seemed spontaneous were carefully rehearsed and orchestrated. No signs were allowed, except those hand-printed in the convention shop in the convention-hall basement. If anything, the Republican Convention was *overproduced*. Example: President Reagan watched the nominating roll call from his hotel suite. When the Missouri vote put him over the top, TV cameras caught his "winning" smile. An aide called for more emotion from the people in the President's suite. Presto! More smiles and kisses on the television screen.

Republican Conventions have never gone money hungry. In 1984, life was made particularly easy, thanks to the federal government's $6.1 million, with $2 million more for additional security.

The law precludes the use of other contributions, except for those from corporations to the host cities, provided that such monies are used to help defray costs of all conventions and not costs of any single gathering. And politics borrowed a page from the Olympics and its incessant plugs of "official Olympic breakfast foods," et cetera. Several computer companies contributed more than $2 million in equipment and services, in exchange for being designated "official providers of convention computers."

The host committee, headed by Trammell Crow, provided $3.9 million from 878 contributors, plus donated entertainment and social events designed to dazzle even the most blase.

Security was so tight at the convention hall's entrance that unusual problems arose. Metal detectors sounded warning signals set off by women wearing underwire bras.

Expenses of political conventions have far outstripped inflation. I once advised Paul Butler, Democratic National Committee chairman, that the 1960 convention would cost more than
$1 million. He was horrified and deeply concerned since we
had no government subsidy. Not until 1976 did the government provide money to political parties for their conventions.
The FEC now receives a financial report on convention expenses 60 days after the closing gavel.

When I expected the 1960 convention costs to exceed $1
million, I was giving merely a best-judgment guess. You can't
run a convention like a business. Unanticipated expenses in-
evitably crop up all over the place.

At the 1984 GOP convention in Dallas, 12,000 media representatives registered to attend—about 2,000 fewer than the
turnout for the Democratic Convention.

Most of the newspeople grumbled about how hard it was to
find a story. As Daniel Schorr of CNN remarked, "Sometimes
you are reduced to spending a lot of time commenting that
there isn't much to comment on." And with little to comment
about on opening night, John Chancellor of NBC kept a count
on the number of times Republican speakers mentioned Mondale and Reagan. Score: Mondale 44, Reagan 40.

*   *   *

The longest Republican Convention occurred in 1880. It took
41 hours—stretched over six days and 36 ballots—to nominate
James A. Garfield. The shortest was in 1972 when the Nixon-
controlled convention at Miami Beach lasted only 17 hours.
The Dallas planners in 1984 hoped to have an even shorter
convention: 13 hours.

Frank Fahrenkopf, Jr., chairman of the Republican National
Committee, said he wanted a crisp television show. He even
dispensed with reading the traditional call to the convention.
He also ordered a lower rostrum, which offered more empathy
between speakers and delegates. This may be why Republicans
seemed more attentive to speakers in Dallas than the Democrats were in San Francisco. There, at the Moscone Convention
Center, many on the floor couldn't even see the speaker!

At the GOP convention, the gavel was tuned to give the right
resonance. Red seats and blue carpet were designed for color
television. The rostrum was decorated in earth tones, instead
of the customary red, white and blue. The overall layout eliminated television shots of empty seats in the press section.

What's more, each delegate was instructed on how to handle interviews, including taboo items. Another directive was issued with Democratic running mate Geraldine Ferraro in mind: Do *not* argue with a woman.

* * *

Hanging over the Dallas convention was the Geraldine Ferraro tax story developing in New York. Her scheduled news conference on Tuesday (the second day of the Republican Convention) became the day's biggest political story. Time and again, Republicans were reminded to refrain from making any comments about Ferraro and whatever problems she might have had with the IRS.

Mindful, too, of the increasing attention to women by the Democrats, the Republicans increased their female delegates from 29% in 1980 to 49% in 1984.

A pattern to be followed by other speakers was started by U.N. Ambassador Jeane Kirkpatrick. Immediately after her speech, she was interviewed by CBS.

Hispanics, in view of their increasing percentage of the U.S. population and hence voting importance, were showcased wherever possible. The Republican National Committee opened a "Hispanic hot line" aimed at making Hispanic delegates available to all working media.

Republicans even embraced winners of the just-concluded Olympic Games, introducing them in the convention program.

When U.S. Representative Phil Gramm of Texas, a candidate for the U.S. Senate, was introduced as a speaker Monday evening, the Texas delegation, on cue, held up signs: "Gramm for the U.S. Senate." And delegates and viewers were treated to a color card show—a takeoff on those famed California college football halftime stunts.

All of these touches went into millions of living rooms across America from well-positioned camera angles. Thanks to the convention hall's layout, TV cameramen in Dallas enjoyed better vantage points than they did in San Francisco.

* * *

The first speech Tuesday evening to be covered by all three major networks, as well as CNN and C-SPAN, touched off the only major demonstration on the floor. The whoopla began with the introduction of Jack Kemp, a favorite among conservatives as presidential timber for 1988. As the applause and cheering crescendoed throughout a demonstration that obviously was well-rehearsed, Kemp waved and nodded and grinned, looking properly surprised.

Immediately after his speech, Kemp rushed to the network television studios for interviews. NBC was interviewing Kemp when former President Ford was being introduced. As Ford began his speech, NBC cut from Kemp to the rostrum. NBC also managed to cover Texas multimillionaire Bunker Hunt's elaborate party, which was deliberately scheduled at the time of Ford's speech.

Also in interviews, Howard Baker, retiring as Senator from Tennessee in 1984, made no bones about his desire to run for the presidency in 1988. Mindful of his television audience, he remarked that a successful candidate for President should be unemployed. He became employed early in 1987 as chief of staff at the White House, replacing Donald Regan.

Meanwhile, the networks avoided showing films of introduction to congressional and senatorial candidates. Cable viewers, however, had an opportunity to see every film which was an integral part of the convention program, albeit political propaganda. The film on congressional candidates, prepared at convention expense, could easily and inexpensively be adapted to local races.

As soon as Senator Dole finished, shortly after 11 P.M., most local network affiliates abruptly switched to local news. Dole's wife, Secretary of Transportation Elizabeth Hanford Dole, fell victim to the convention schedule extending beyond 11 P.M. The proceedings were adjourned at 11:13 P.M., which most network affiliates learned the next day.

After the networks ignored the eight-minute filmed tribute to First Lady Nancy Reagan on Wednesday, she made a few extemporaneous remarks with no surprises. She was the only speaker whose remarks were not on the TelePrompter. The President, watching in his hotel suite, was shown on the massive screen over the rostrum. This screen represented a major technical achievement. Two Videophor projectors provided overlapping images that gave high-resolution pictures on that screen—even though the pictures were awash in 250-foot candlepower light.

At the end of her remarks, Nancy turned, looked up at the large screen and waved to her husband. The President returned her wave—to the delight of Republicans everywhere. This was the only ad-lib of the convention, but it was a human-interest touch with timing that even Hollywood couldn't have choreographed. For the first time, the convention broke out in spontaneous applause and cheers.

Senator Paul Laxalt of Nevada, the President's campaign chairman and close personal friend, placed Reagan's name in nomination. (He performed the same job in 1976 when Reagan ran against President Ford.) At the conclusion, on cue, inflated elephants and large American flags appeared everywhere while red-white-and-blue balloons tumbled from the ceiling. Laxalt, in the meantime, was being interviewed by Tom Brokaw on NBC. (Early the next morning, two men with air-gun rifles shot down all balloons that remained in the rafters.)

The Republicans' acute sense of timing continued. The start of the roll call was held off until 11:32 P.M. so local stations, having completed their 30-minute local news, could rejoin the network. An estimated three-fourths of the network affiliates had left the convention at 11 P.M. for local news. Most returned to the convention at 11:30 P.M.

Needed to win the nomination were 1,118 votes. Shortly after midnight, the Missouri vote made it official: Reagan and Bush again were nominated. At 12:32 A.M., the roll call concluded. Since both the presidential and vice-presidential candidates were nominated jointly, the roll call was carried out in its entirety. Keeping with custom, a committee was picked to notify the President of his nomination. Surprise, surprise!

Thursday evening was set aside for the acceptance speech by Vice President Bush, the filmed introduction of President Reagan, followed by his acceptance speech.

The big story was whether the networks would air the 18-minute, extravagantly produced film which introduced the President. The Democrats were on record opposing the film's showing on television; the Republicans countered that the film was nothing more than an introduction of the speaker, similar to Senator Edward Kennedy's introduction of presidential candidate Mondale.

NBC decided to show the film. A network official stated: "We are not showing the film because there is any news in it, but because of the popular interest that has been stirred up in the past week. It has become a *cause celebre*." ABC and CBS did not air the film and were roasted in the press.

A masterful production, properly cued with the right music, the film showed President Reagan on trips to Seoul, Korea, and to China, Ireland and Normandy. He was shown formally declaring the opening of the Olympics in Los Angeles, at Camp David, at his ranch and in the Oval Office.

The only flaws appeared not in the film itself but in television's coverage: The start of the film caught two networks doing floor interviews when the hall's lights were turned off. The film introduction to Vice President Bush was available only on C-SPAN.

Then came yet another new television touch: Live pictures of the President's motorcade to the convention were shown on those oversized screens inside the hall.

At the convention, the President was scheduled to speak for 40 minutes, but he talked for 55 minutes. He was interrupted by applause 79 to 91 times (depending on how you interpreted an applause interruption). Frequently, his remarks were interspersed with the chant "Four more years!"

Reagan delivered a rip-roaring, flag-waving speech—long on themes, short on specifics. As he would in the campaign, he portrayed the Democratic vision as one of government of pessimism, fear and limits. The Republican vision, he said, was one of hope, confidence and growth. When the President talked about foreign policy and defense issues, he drew his biggest applause. And as he would during the campaign, Reagan blamed Mondale for the past.

In the demonstration that followed the President's speech, 40,000 red-white-and-blue balloons were dropped from the ceiling, and 10,000 red-white-and-blue helium-filled balloons were released from the floor.

Ray Charles played and sang "America the Beautiful." The euphoric evening ended with the delegates singing "God Bless America."

On Friday, the pollsters agreed: After the "Ronnie Show," the race would be for Reagan—not Mondale—to win or lose. Reagan spent $20.2 million, the legal limit, to win his unopposed nomination. Mondale, on the other hand, spent $18.4 million to win his hotly contested nomination. And while the Democratic Convention launched 1988 presidential prospects galore, the Republican Convention did not project any outstanding candidate for 1988.

* * *

Despite, or perhaps because of, the precise planning of the Republican Convention program, television tune-in set records—all of them bad. Opening night marked the smallest audience tune-in of any convention in television history. This record held 24 hours until Tuesday evening, when an all-time low rating was established.

In New York City, the Marx Brothers' "A Night at the Opera" on an independent television station drew more viewers than any station showing the GOP convention. In Dallas, site of the convention, the combined network station rating was 20.2% compared with the normal 70%.

The network that dominated the 8–9 P.M. hour dominated the convention coverage. For instance, a patriotic dramatic series, "Call to Glory," gave ABC a 13-point lead which promptly dropped to 7.1. For the four nights, ABC averaged a 6.9 rating and a 13% share, CBS a 6.4 and a 12% share, and NBC a 6.2 and a 11% share.

The bottom line: The 1984 Republican Convention was one of the least watched conventions ever on television. (Ratings were first compiled in 1952.) For the first time in 24 years, the incumbent party did not attract an audience as large as that of the challenging party. It should be noted, however, that 1984 was the first year of extensive cable coverage of the conventions.

One footnote: NBC, the only network to carry the Reagan film on Thursday evening, won the ratings war that night by one full point. It should also be noted that rating comparisons with earlier conventions are distorted because the networks previously carried daytime sessions. Ironically, we live in an age when conventions tailored exclusively to prime-time viewing may no longer be so exclusive after all. Has the novelty worn off? Or have the primaries drained every last drop of drama and emotion previously saved for the conventions?

CHAPTER 27

Campaign 1984

BEFORE THE CONVENTIONS, The *Wall Street Journal* commented: "The Democrats go into the campaign on a wing and a prayer. The wing, new and untested, is Rep. Geraldine Ferraro; the prayer, old and familiar, asks Democrats to come home to the liberalism of their fathers."

Even months before the nominating conventions, President Reagan was demonstrating the awesome power of an incumbent in taking advantage of free television time. While Mondale laboriously fought for the Democratic nomination, Reagan was busy beaming a series of images and symbols, under controlled circumstances, to the voters.

Michael Deaver, the President's television guru, set a goal for each day: One story with one set of pictures, all carefully orchestrated and controlled. To avoid competing with himself and to maintain control of each released story, Deaver made sure that television got only one good picture story a day.

By contrast, Mondale's campaign staffers were slow in recognizing the advantage of staging one major picture story each day for the nightly television news. As a result, their lack of planning led to confusion on Mondale's part, which showed again and again on television for most of the presidential campaign. Instead of zooming in on Mondale's run for the presidency, television concentrated on Ferraro's finances and Bert Lance's cameo role. As late as August 31, news stories galore told of the vice-presidential candidate's husband and his troubles as a conservator for a widow's estate.

In a strategy meticulously crafted for television, the Republican-planned television news clips showed a smiling, confident President in the best of circumstances: He toasted the Chinese leaders in the Great Hall of the People; he mourned at the Tomb of the Unknown Soldier; he choked up at D-Day ceremonies on the beaches of Normandy.

The show went on and on: Reagan shown with a happy family picnicking in Alabama; with an assembly line worker in an automobile factory in Michigan; wearing a Smokey the Bear hat in Kentucky and proclaiming his love for the outdoors; at a wild life refuge on Chesapeake Bay; speaking to 15,000 campers at Bowling Green, Kentucky, affirming his desire to clean up toxic wastes.

On July 4, the President wooed blue-collar workers at the Daytona Beach 400 stock car race attended by 80,000 fans. There, 1,200 were invited to a private picnic with the President. Circling above the speedway in Air Force One, the President gave the traditional "Gentlemen, start your engines." Later, he was a guest commentator on the motor racing network.

As if that weren't enough, a worldwide television audience of 2 billion saw Reagan open the Olympics. The Republicans embraced the Olympic winners, first at the Republican Convention, later with lunch at the White House.

While in Dallas, President Reagan spoke before an ecumenical prayer breakfast to 17,000 Christian laymen and church leaders. He injected into the campaign a no-no issue, religion and the government. He delivered a blunt attack on opponents of a proposed constitutional amendment that would permit voluntary school prayer. The President said they were "intolerant of religion." He went on to say that "religion and politics are necessarily related" and "this has worked to the benefit of the nation."

When Mondale appeared later in Dallas, he succeeded in getting campaign funds and an opportunity to attack Reagan on his religious stand. But it all amounted to not even a "blip" in the presidential polls. First, Mondale wore his usual heavy dark-gray suit, instead of a seersucker suit. His weak speech, delivered listlessly, was one of the most unemotional in memory. He lacked a light touch, apparently not realizing that Southern Democrats revel in emotional tirades against the Republicans. Mondale raised money but no excitement for his campaign in one of his "must carry" states.

In August, voters were interested in everything but politics. The Democrats could have made better use of these summer "dog days" by fine-tuning their strategy on how to win 270 electoral votes. Mondale had made the grievous error of leaving the starting gate before he knew the location of the track.

More important, Mondale's campaign staff didn't seem to realize how drastically campaigning had been changed by television. No one understood the need for a professional media consultant and a professional polling staff. And it was too late to learn how to use the computer.

But then, neither the Democrats nor the Republicans fully realized how television viewing habits had changed. No longer did buying time on the three major television networks insure a captive audience. Cable TV added a new dimension of programs available to cable audiences. Pay-television movies, sports, continuous news, and syndicated reruns offered a ready haven for those who were weary of politics or simply not interested. More than ever, American TV viewers were fragmented.

* * *

Labor Day turned into disaster for the Democrats. They provided a shining example of what *not* to do in a presidential campaign. Mondale and Ferraro were to make joint appearances in New York, in Merrill, Wisconsin, and in California. Labor officials insisted on having the candidates at their Fifth Avenue parade. To keep the Wisconsin date, Mondale and Ferraro appeared in the New York parade at 9 A.M. to empty sidewalks and bleachers, all shown to millions on all network news programs.

One of my early political lessons was about staging political events: Always have an overflow crowd, even if you have to hold the event in a telephone booth. In this day of television and the tremendous impact of the evening news shows, it is imperative a presidential candidate appears before wildly cheering, overflow crowds. Every event should evoke the vital question: How will this look on the evening television news programs?

For the Democrats, Labor Day didn't look good on TV or in person. It rained in Wisconsin; and in California, a microphone malfunctioned. On the television news, the Democratic presidential candidate tapped the mike and asked, "Does this thing work?" Not a very inspiring start for the Mondale-Ferraro ticket. To win an election today, one must provide good, positive, upbeat pictures on network television from day one.

The dead-microphone incident showed poor organization planning. Apparently no Mondale engineer had checked the public-address system and microphones. Moreover, the sun's angle to the rostrum and the crowd should have been examined. In all outside events, the relationship of the sun and rostrum and crowd should be checked by the advance person. (The Republicans moved a Gulfport, Mississippi, rally back from the scheduled 6 P.M. start because of the angle of the sun.)

Inside events require careful placement of lights. At all times, the rostrum should be large enough to accommodate pages of the text, so that pages may be turned easily without bumping a microphone or light. There should never be shadows on the speech copy. Water, without ice, should be easily accessible. The rostrum, of course, should be the right height for the candidate and provide a good line of sight with the audience. To avoid a forest of microphones, an audio feed should be available.

In contrast to the puny Mondale-Ferraro crowds, the Republican rally that greeted President Reagan in Orange County, California, was large, colorful and enthusiastic. There was no doubt how these Californians would vote on November 6. A feeling of a Republican victory already filled the air.

* * *

The Labor Day flop of the Mondale-Ferraro campaign brought into focus two serious weaknesses of the Democrats:
1. Mondale was uncomfortable with television.
2. Mondale banked too heavily on a thorough discussion of issues. He seemed incapable of capturing the essence of modern-day presidential campaigning. He needed a central theme expressed in a few catchy words, easily projected in a 60-second clip on the nightly television news.

As a result, TV news coverage of the Mondale-Ferraro campaign merely confirmed the polls. Democratic Party professionals knew they had a struggling loser opposing, in the President, a supremely confident winner.

Make no mistake, the television camera shows all the warts. Nowhere was this more evident than in Mondale's statement on TV about the purported inequality in taxes: "I'm mad, I'm angry, I'm damned mad because I don't think it is right." In print, this statement radiated a strong emotional reaction to the tax issue. On television, the words came across almost without emotion, the words drained of all their sting and snap. As Senator Robert Dole (R-Kan.) wisecracked: "When Mondale gives a fireside chat, the fire goes out."

* * *

President Reagan's Air Force One stayed on schedule. His office not only released copies of his speeches in advance, but distributed details of Vice President Bush's more direct anti-Mondale attacks. They also circulated attacks on Mondale's tax and budget positions by Secretary of Treasury Donald Regan. The Secretary pressed for specifics in Mondale's tax increases and budget cuts. "Because he will increase rather than cut spending, Mondale will have to achieve all of his reduction through tax increases," Regan said.

The smooth-running, White House-directed campaign tended to dash hopes of Democrats across the country. Television portrayed a disorganized, stumbling Mondale; headlines played up the "puny" crowds at Mondale campaign events. Some discouraged Democrats sensed that the Mondale-Ferraro campaign not only started behind the goal line but wasn't even in the stadium. Compounding the problem, Mondale constantly had to answer reporters' questions about his poor standing in the polls.

In the meantime, Reagan was kept away from reporters. They had to use his prepared remarks for news about him. What a difference four years and an incumbency make.

* * *

As Walter Mondale's campaign deteriorated, cracks appeared in the Democratic Party's unity. House Speaker Thomas (Tip) O'Neill's unsolicited public criticism about the candidate's poor style made Mondale furious. Mondale conceded that he was not good on television, but in 1984 television represented the heartbeat of the campaign.

On TV, Mondale simply didn't appear fired up; he didn't seem to speak with conviction. Clearly, he was a not-ready-for-prime-time-player. As one observer commented, "He certainly is a nice person, but as a politician he seems wishy-washy and doesn't project well on television. He's too placid and too mundane in his discussion of issues."

Vice-presidential candidate Geraldine Ferraro, by contrast,

was more effective on television. She attracted large crowds who apparently came to see her as a celebrity rather than a candidate for office. Large crowds can give a misleading impression, as George McGovern discovered in 1972. In 1984, the Democrats were striving mightily to move the campaign into a battle over issues and not a personality contest—one that a Mondale aide ruefully admitted they were sure to lose.

Campaign strategy must be based on Electoral College arithmetic—270 votes needed to win. The 12 most populous states yield 279 votes. It is possible, therefore, to win even while losing as many as 38 states. Must-win states must remain on the front burner at all times—a fundamental that Mondale overlooked in September. Instead of concentrating on the Northeast and Middle West, where he had a fighting chance, Mondale opted to follow Ronald Reagan all over the map.

Walter Mondale's long-awaited television spots first appeared during the week of September 10: "Can you trust Reagan?" Another Mondale spot warned of worsening Soviet relations under President Reagan and stressed that Reagan had not met with Soviet leaders. (Whatever impact this ad might have had, however, disappeared when Reagan announced his meeting with Soviet Foreign Minister Andrei Gromyko in the White House.)

To outside professionals, the Democrats' television spots collectively looked like a mishmash of ideas. The hydra-headed authority on television advertising was apparent. Said one critic: "It's a classic example of building a horse by committee. What you end up with is a camel with five humps."

The new Republican 30- and 60-second television commercials focused on the economy, with President Reagan touting his accomplishments. The deficit was ignored.

* * *

Ronald Reagan's campaign committee bought time on the three major television networks and on a cable network, ESPN, as well as superstations WOR, WGN, WTBS. The television program attracted 50 million homes. In 1984, politicians had available 85 million television homes, compared with 51 million in 1964.

TV audiences, however, were more fragmented than ever. Even widespread purchases of television by the Republicans did not give them domination of TV viewers. Viewers could choose from a variety of alternative television programs on other independent television stations and on other cable networks, including pay movies. Those who watched the Republican campaign program saw an expanded version of Reagan's convention film—all upbeat, patriotic and crafted to play on emotions. It probably was the most effective television commercial ever aired—and it was difficult to counterattack. Once again, it was a triumph for the political cliche: You are always safe with "God, good roads and motherhood."

* * *

As Election Day approached, the Democrats bought five-minute periods on prime-time television. The Republicans, at the same time, purchased 25 and 30-minute chunks. Walter Mondale finally moved his campaign into sharper focus, stressing arms control, farmers, and the future. His five-minute television spot was one of the best in the campaign, but it was too late. His cry, "It's time for America to move on," was well done, but also too late.

Mike Royko wrote in the *Chicago Tribune*, "Reagan's greatest asset is his talent for striding briskly off his helicopter or his jet and snapping off those wonderful John Wayne-style salutes to the Marine guards or a half-salute, half-wave to the waiting crowds."

Mondale, by contrast, was constantly stigmatized by the legacy of Jimmy Carter. When asked why they preferred Ronald Reagan, a remarkable number of young voters simply replied, "Jimmy Carter."

* * *

In the closing weeks, the campaign consumed larger gulps of time on the networks. On the three nights each week that John Chancellor aired his commentary, NBC said it would devote as much as eight minutes to political news. CNN allocated eight minutes every hour to political news. On the CBS Evening News, Dan Rather doled out 25% of air time to the campaign. ABC also stepped up its political coverage.

Television clearly dictated strategy. Reagan continued to ignore the Washington press corps while catering to television. As James Reston pointed out in the *New York Times*, "In a switch from Jefferson's famous remark, the President said in effect: 'Were it left to me to decide whether to have a government without newspapers or newspapers without a government, I should not hesitate to choose TV every time.' "

Often you couldn't tell the difference between Reagan's television commercials and the evening news. A Reagan rally typically featured a bunting-bedecked stage with the rostrum properly angled with respect to the audience and the sun. Spectators faced the rostrum, their backs to the sun, and, hopefully, a blue sky and white clouds that would form a backdrop for the President. As Reagan delivered short, quotable, patriotic remarks that were as All-American as baseball and apple pie, his booster crowds radiated excitement. A few tears fell. Band music appealed to patriotism. Red-white-and-blue balloons floated skyward.

Technically, the producers of Reagan's TV footage left nothing to chance. They used 35-mm. film, whose quality is much superior to that of videotape. Elaborate lighting was purposely softened. Music never before heard in commercials added the right emotional touch. The best technology available was employed for cutting and dubbing—expensive, but worth the extra money.

All told, Mondale used 19 different TV spots, compared with Reagan's 39. (The Republicans filed away spots that were never used.) Mondale's spots were themeless; they wandered confusingly all over the landscape. His non-visual spots on the deficit were dry and uninteresting. Still another problem became obvious: Mondale's campaign was rarely in sync with what he said or did on the evening news.

On the other hand, Reagan's organization deftly controlled rallies for television exposure. A shining example occurred on November 1 in Boston. There, thousands of office workers provided a backdrop for a rally staged in a V-shaped area alongside City Hall. In front of Reagan's stage was a section accommodating about 7,000 persons—an area restricted to Reagan supporters who received blue or yellow tickets. To get inside, they passed through a metal detector.

A 7-foot-high fence guarded the rally site's most exposed side. Boston police officers reminded everyone that there was no admission to the general public, which was restricted to a small area just inside the high fence, but behind a high wire-mesh fence. Most important, this area was beyond the vantage point of television cameras—and thus the hundreds of protesters who hoisted anti-Reagan signs remained inconspicuous.

* * *

This would be the last election conducted on party alignments that had prevailed for 50 years. The Republicans had registered 32.6% more voters than in 1980, the Democrats only 7.3%. A 56% turnout at the polls was predicted, which meant 98 million votes.

CHAPTER 28

Debates 1984

EVER SINCE WE ARRANGED FOR THE KENNEDY-NIXON DEBATES in 1960, every "out" candidate—for even the most obscure office—clamors to debate on television. But his efforts usually go for naught. Incumbents have a way of stalling off challengers.

Before he knuckled down to serious campaigning, Walter Mondale demanded six debates with President Reagan, hoping to settle for four. Again, the word "debate" was used loosely since no one wanted a formal, structured debate. A "joint news conference" was a better designation; but, as in the past, everyone insisted on calling what was really a news conference a "debate." The usage of "debate" started in 1960 with historical references to the Lincoln-Douglas debate, and, by 1984 became firmly entrenched in our language.

Barely minutes after both conventions had nominated their candidates, the television networks went on record, offering free time for the 1984 presidential debates. Because of a new ruling by the FCC in November 1983, the networks had advised Democrats and Republicans that they would be happy to sponsor the debates. But the League of Women Voters, having lost their court appeal to strike down the new FCC rule, intervened and became the sponsors.

President Reagan agreed to debate Mondale on the premise that if he refused, he would appear afraid to meet the Democratic candidate. He chose James Baker, the White House chief of staff, as his negotiator. Mondale's negotiator was his campaign manager, James Johnson. Since three consecutive Presidents agreed to debate, it is unlikely that any future President will be able to refuse to debate his opponent, except in time of a national emergency such as war.

With both sides agreeing on two presidential debates, the Democrats demanded—and got—a single television debate between the vice-presidential candidates. The date was Thursday, October 11, with the same format as in the presidential debates and the same length, 90 minutes.

Of course, instead of debates, Americans watched, in effect, news conferences, with both candidates having to think fast on their feet for 90 minutes—a punishing endurance test.

An estimated 2,000 journalists poured into Louisville to cover the first presidential debate. A gallery of 2,000 invited guests watched in person in the Kentucky Center for the Arts. Despite pleas from the moderator for quiet, the audience interrupted the debates several times with applause.

* * *

For the first debate, the President wore a black suit, Mondale one of charcoal gray. Mondale won the toss, so Reagan was the first to be questioned. Mondale backers, seeing the debates as the last chance, were nervous as Reagan started his answer. Suddenly they realized the Great Communicator wasn't really communicating. He seemed ill-at-ease, fumbling for words. By contrast, Mondale answered his question with ease. And instead of taking an aggressive, strident approach, he was deferential to the President.

Throughout the first half of the debate, the President constantly groped for the right words. He appeared uncharacteristically unsteady, unsure of himself and hesitant in his responses, even though no one had given him any unexpected questions. Mondale, his confidence mounting, came across better than ever.

The President seemed to have forgotten a fundamental of debating on TV: Address the viewing audience, not the interrogator. This was a technique we stressed again and again with John Kennedy, who used it so effectively against Nixon. A rule-of-thumb in these events: Form always overshadows content.

Both candidates fell into a trap of talking like accountants—Mondale because it was second nature; Reagan because he had become sensitive to accusations that he didn't always grasp details.

Recalling that his question "Where's the beef?" had demolished Hart, Mondale looked for a similar opening against Reagan. The President reached back for his own "knockout" line that worked against Jimmy Carter: "There he goes again." Mondale was ready. He quickly turned those words to his own advantage. Not until the debate was about half over did the President hit his stride. Too late.

A quick consensus immediately after the debate gave Mondale a "victory," but no knockout—which he desperately needed to lift his hopes for a win at the polls in November.

A new issue had surfaced—Reagan's age. Reporters interviewed gerontologists. The *Wall Street Journal* headlined: "Fitness Issue—New Question in Race—Is Oldest President Showing His Age? Reagan Debate Performance Invites Open Speculation on His Ability to Serve."

Clearly, Reagan's air of invincibility was shaken. Before the debate, all polls had indicated that Mondale was headed for a catastrophic defeat. Even Democratic congressional candidates had shunned him. In one evening, the image of Reagan as "The Great Communicator" was destroyed. Suddenly the Republican bandwagon was stuck in the mud. Key Republicans bickered in public about Reagan's preparation for the debate. Many spoke of the President as if he were a computer—his floppy disk overloaded and down with minutiae and detail. Indeed, Reagan had spent more than 12 hours at Camp David and in the White House theater, in mock debates with Budget Director David A. Stockman cast as "Mondale." He had pored over a thick briefing book. Even the President sensed that these cram sessions hadn't worked. "I did too much studying and too little relaxing," he said.

Democrats gleefully felt that Mondale had gotten his second wind. "We have a new race," the candidate said. Soft-on-Mondale Democrats turned away from the Reagan camp. Mondale scheduled his first autumn trip to Florida. Contributions rolled in. Newspapers headlined: "Mondale Addresses an Unusually Large Crowd." Even congressional candidates jockeyed for appearances with their new television star.

Debate 1 had changed the tone and atmosphere of the campaign. Polls showed Mondale on the rise and Reagan losing points. The Harris Poll showed that Mondale had narrowed the "confidence gap" from 26 points to 6. Never in the stormy marriage between politics and television have 90 minutes meant so much to a presidential candidate as they did to Walter Mondale.

Yet for all the euphoria, many overlooked certain inalienable political facts: Reagan still held a solid electoral base in the South and West. And many who said Mondale "won" the debate also said that the President more closely reflected their own views. One poll result was especially dismaying to the Democrats: Only 4 to 5% of these questioned said they would change their vote from Reagan to Mondale—a margin within the error range of poll-taking. The debate had breathed new life into Walter Mondale's fortunes, but the prognosis for Election Day still showed a lightning-quick death.

* * *

The vice presidential debate took on a luster that no one had anticipated. Would Geraldine Ferraro pump more life into the Democratic upsurge? Or would Vice President Bush halt the Democrats' momentum? The pressure was very much on George Bush.

Bush led Ferraro by 28 points, 61 to 33, when voters were asked by the ABC-*Washington Post* poll before the debate to compare them as potential Presidents. Bush tried to take the edge off the vice-presidential debate. "The debate won't swing the election," he said. "The thing that is going to determine the election is the top of the ticket. I don't think it will change many votes. I hope it will, because I think I will do all right."

* * *

Inside the Philadelphia Convention Center the debate—shorter than expected, at 1 hour 25 minutes—ranged from emotional exchanges about Iran hostages and Beirut bombings to abortion and civil rights. Both candidates made factual errors, not unusual in a structured debate format. But there were no major gaffes.

Both Bush and Ferraro departed from their usual campaign styles. Mostly, that worked against them. Bush switched from his customarily mild approach to one with wild gestures and a gushing delivery. Ferraro took on the role of a stateswoman—her voice lower, her pace slower, very much unlike her normal feisty, rapid-fire self. She reverted to her courtroom manner and too frequently looked down at her notes. As a result, viewers often were watching the top of her head. She apparently forgot a fundamental of television: Always keep eye contact with the camera.

As with just about any debate, little is remembered of answers, except for an occasional catch phrase. Most important is how you look and how you field questions. Style over substance.

When it was over, comments varied, although Bush was given the edge. Tom Brokaw of NBC said that Ferraro sounded like a 45 RPM record played at 33⅓ RPM. Norma Quarles, a panelist, called it a draw. Mark Shields of CBS said Ferraro debated as if she were taking graduate oral exams. "Bush," he said "served the President well." One unidentified Democrat commented, "Our candidate was trying too hard not to be brassy and ended up just plain dull."

Poll results closely correlated with presidential preferences. Forty-nine percent said Bush won, while 29% said Ferraro won. Among men, Bush was a 59-to-18 winner; among women, Bush squeaked by, 39 to 38. As for any impact on voters, the vice-presidential debate could be summed up in six words: No hits, no runs, no errors.

* * *

For President Reagan, his second debate on October 21 in Kansas City would put his tailored-for-television image at stake. He needed desperately to appear in control—of himself and of the proceedings—although a draw could be considered a Reagan victory.

After the first debate, the Harris Poll showed Walter Mondale a 61% to 19% winner. But this time, 46% expected Reagan to dominate the confrontation, while 33% believed Mondale would win.

Reagan rehearsed by fielding questions from high school and college students in the South and Midwest. His strategists provided what they called "zingers"—sharp one-line attacks on Mondale and terse, pithy remarks crafted to enhance the President's standing. ("We believe in high tech, not high taxes.") In briefing sessions joined by administration officials, the only real concern was the age issue. The President had to show he was in charge, with a firm command of facts and not slowed down by being 73. Again, David Stockman assumed the role of Mondale; but now the President used a thinner briefing book (only 25 pages) with fewer facts—and he concentrated on broad themes.

At the same time, Reagan's staff planned to use a technique proven by advertisers of consumer products. Richard Wirthlin, the GOP's pollster, assembled a carefully drawn "focus" group of 40 in a Kansas City hotel room. Each clasped a hand-held trace computer, equipped with buttons signaling positive or negative responses to what they would watch in the televised debate.

* * *

For the final debate, negotiations were tense and sometimes bitter. Reagan's forces demanded, and got, a shorter distance between the candidates and the four panel members. They argued strenuously to prohibit camera shots showing one candidate's reaction to what the other one was saying. The most important concession gained by Reagan's staff was on lighting. Mondale's strategists agreed to dim some of the stage lights, providing softer illumination of the candidates. At the same time, lighting in the audience was brightened.

Apparently overlooked in the lighting discussion was a basic factor: The Music Hall, an old, high-ceilinged room, contained lighting whose extreme angle and lower candlepower worked in Reagan's favor. The President looked noticeably younger than he had during the Louisville debate. In the first debate, Mondale was smooth and youthful-looking. In Kansas City, he looked pouchy—the bags under his eyes accentuated by dark shadows. Obviously, his makeup man had not checked with the lighting director.

Both sides knew, too, that perspiration should not show up on television. It was too easy to recall the 1960 debates, when Richard Nixon paused several times to wipe sweat from his brow.

* * *

Thirty minutes before the debate, a Republican pep rally was aimed at sending Reagan into the Music Hall stirred up, yet loose and relaxed—his own natural self. (Incidentally, Kansas City was where Reagan fell heartbreakingly short of the nomination—and Gerald Ford won—in 1976.)

Carrying the debates live were ABC, CBS, NBC, C-SPAN, the Spanish International Network (SIN) and the radio networks. TV and radio each aired taped delays. Most important, and surely the key to each candidate's success, were the 30-, 60- and 90-second excerpts scheduled on all news programs across America.

The same structured format of the first debate held for the second debate; the subject, foreign affairs.

Some still clung to the old-style assumption that the candidates were sharply divided on major issues and their discussion of the issues would give the voters a clear voice. Instead, viewers had become theater critics, judging by style and not substance. An audience of 2,500 with 1,200 from the media, watched as the debate opened an hour earlier because of a previously scheduled National Football League game.

A sharp exchange over Central America got the debate underway. The key issue throughout was America's relationship with the Soviet Union. Most questions were unusually torturous and windy. Most answers were carefully rehearsed, designed to catch the opponent off guard—and often bore little relationship to the questions. More often than not, the answers actually were nothing more than political commercials.

It was easy to compare the debate to a heavyweight championship fight. Mondale swung hard, but his opponent, smiling and confident, let the punches slide by. On points, Mondale was ahead, but he had to unleash a knockout blow to win.

Reagan appeared relaxed, ready with one-liners, working the camera professionally as usual. Thanks to changes in lighting, he looked younger and vibrant. Mondale, by contrast, suffered from the lighting. He exuded all the vibrance of a figure from a wax museum. He gave a fine performance, but this time "fine" wasn't enough.

With one joke, Reagan demolished the age issue—the only one in which he was really vulnerable. To the question "Are you too old to handle a nuclear crisis?" came the well-rehearsed answer: "I am not going to exploit, for political purposes, my opponent's youth and inexperience." Laughter echoed across the room. His timing was perfect. As it turned out, this was the most remembered comment of the entire debate. What's more, the networks had their sound bite for TV news.

*   *   *

If this debate did anything, it gave a shot in the arm to Reagan's standing in the polls. An ABC poll of 695 viewers gave Reagan a 39% to 36% win, 25% a tie. On the candidate preference question, Reagan stayed ahead 56% to 43%, virtually unchanged. A *USA Today* poll gave Reagan a 44% to 27% win over Mondale.

The taped version of President Reagan's quip about age was the most repeated remark of the debate. He won the battle of clips by a wide margin. Ipso facto, Reagan won the debate.

To professional politicians in both parties, the campaign was over. The polls were correct, Reagan would win in a landslide.

Would the presidential debates influence the outcome of the 1984 election? Not at all. They added some excitement to an otherwise dull, listless campaign. It was all over but the voting.

CHAPTER 29

Election 1984

FOR WALTER MONDALE, the handwriting on the wall was supplied by his own pollster, Peter Hart, whose figures projected an inevitable Reagan landslide. Hart suggested that Mondale concentrate on states where he had a chance of cutting Reagan's expected margin of victory.

Mondale accused Ronald Reagan of being "the most detached, the most remote, the most uninformed" President in modern history. Mondale's harsh attack seemed to buoy the post-debate mood in his own inner circle. But most political pros thought it was probably a mistake for Mondale to come down so hard against a popular President.

One Democratic television ad showed Mondale standing on the deck of the aircraft carrier *Nimitz*. The objective was to convey an image of strength for Mondale. The Republicans retorted that there wouldn't have been a *Nimitz* aircraft carrier if Mondale had had his way.

As for results of polls on all three debates, they provided little solace to "Fightin' Fritz." Nearly 80% of those polled said the debates had no influence on their choice for President. The sample favored Reagan over Mondale by almost 2 to 1. Even Mondale's own poll showed Reagan dropping only six points.

With Mondale still given a chance in Oregon and Washington, and with California now acknowledged a "must" state, the Democrats unleashed a television blitz on the West Coast. Nine Mondale ads a day appeared on California television stations.

But the Republicans, too, accelerated their own aleady heavy television-spot schedule. Both parties intended to "win the West" by trying to outdo each other with TV spots. Significantly, more Democratic announcements appeared *without* Mondale, the voiceovers stressing fear and pessimism. As the Democrats began running out of money, the Republicans shifted into high gear on television. The Republicans were up to their campaign lapel buttons in money.

With television, money talks. Four years earlier, a 30-second political advertisement on ABC-TV's "Monday Night Football" cost about $50,000. In 1984, it cost $125,000. Political advertisers, who pay only the lowest possible rates, saw their costs skyrocket about 110%.

* * *

On October 26, only 240 hours remained until Election Day. On that same day, DNC Chairman Charles Manatt said that Mondale trailed Reagan in 46 states. The Associated Press reported, "It is difficult to find party professionals who believe Mondale can upset Reagan." At the last minute, Geraldine Ferraro decided to appear on the popular Phil Donahue television program. Donahue's audience of 7 million consisted primarily of women. Ferraro ducked issues, for the most part. She discussed, instead, the impact of the campaign on her family.

By week's end, with 216 hours until Election Day, every poll in the nation predicted a Reagan avalanche. Aides whispered to Mondale that it was all over. He couldn't win. He was told that 55% of the electorate seemed firmly committed to Reagan, while about 40% were equally committed to his own candidacy. But Mondale fended off the doomsayers in his camp with "I'm going to campaign with everything I've got through November 6."

With Walter Mondale, as with other lopsided losers, the reality of an enormous political defeat is rarely accepted until after the votes are counted. Even then, it takes days for the devastation to sink in fully.

ELECTION DAY

As Walter Mondale went through the ritual of voting, in the glare of full publicity, he could only hope for a miracle to temper the landslide defeat that everyone predicted. In this age of Big Television, it was difficult to believe that Mondale had flown more miles, stumped in more cities and spoken more words than any other political candidate in history.

As Ronald Reagan cast his ballot, the media stalking his every move, he envisioned a record victory for Republicans—and records, too, for a re-elected President. In this century, only Presidents Harding (1920), Roosevelt (1936), Johnson (1964) and Nixon(1972) received more than 60% of the vote. It was assured that Reagan would not join the list of elected incumbents who were defeated in this century—William Howard Taft, Herbert Hoover and Jimmy Carter. Long before radio and television had expanded the power and reach of a President's voice, Woodrow Wilson had observed that once a President had won the country's admiration and confidence, has rightly interpreted the national thought and boldly insisted upon it, he is irresistible.

Commented Russell Baker in the New York Times, "This election has gone from yawn to eternity."

While the election was anticlimactic, the networks plunged ahead with preparations for their razzle-dazzle Election Night telecasts. Cable was a new kid on the block; on cable the Financial News Network offered 12 hours of election coverage, and Cable News Network stayed with the story around the clock. PBS dropped out of election-coverage competition. Certain to increase the viewer count was the fact that almost 200 independent television stations existed in 1984—twice as many as in 1980. (And nine Latin American countries watched the returns via satellite.)

NBC spent two years designing a computer-controlled animation generator, which produced graphics. The network contended that this was the first major on-screen design change since the birth of TV news. ABC used hardware from its coverage of the 1984 Olympics to organize feeds simultaneously from 25 remote spots. CBS teamed 500 electrical workers with 200 computer operators and 9,600 observers around the country. Each network's gigantic control center cost $4 million.

But this was a decidedly more splintered audience than the one that watched on Election Night in 1980. Aggressive counter-programming on independent television stations provided major tune-away attractions.

One-hundred fifty million viewers caught some part of network election coverage in 1980. But, in 1984, there was a 10%

falloff due in part to another competitor—video-cassette recorders (VCRs). A. C. Nielsen Co. figures showed that 35% of the 84.9 million U.S. households with TV in 1984 watched the three major networks' coverage of election returns. That was a decline from four years earlier, when 45.5% of the 79.9 million television homes tuned in election results.

This was a night, too, for visual razzmatazz. The NBC map, once an innovation, seemed outdated compared with CBS' three-dimension presentation. With spinning, colorful charts, CBS won the battle of network graphics. Actually, there was too much technology for an event with results of minimal interest.

*   *   *

At 8 P.M., CBS announced Reagan an overwhelming winner. ABC followed at 8:13 P.M. and NBC at 8:31 P.M. (In 1980, NBC was first with the results at 8:15 P.M.) All networks constantly urged viewers to go to the polls. But California officials were predictably angry about the networks' early projection of a Reagan victory. Evidence on the effect of these early projections on voter turnout is still inconclusive.

It was apparent, however, that Reagan's mighty triumph had no coattail impact. In 1980, Reagan had carried 33 new Republicans into the House and 12 new GOP senators, enabling the party to gain control of the Senate for the first time since 1952. But in 1984, the Reagan administration failed to win back the 26 House seats lost in the 1982 election. The Republicans' margin in the Senate was reduced by two, but they increased their total of governors by one, to 16. Republicans, however, made inroads in every contested congressional race except in the Northeast, where there are more Jewish voters and fewer born-again Christians.

As it was, Reagan—by winning every state but Minnesota—became the first incumbent since Eisenhower to score back-to-back landslide victories. The final returns showed that Mondale had lost two elections by the largest margin of any candidate in history.

It was a victory the Republicans were quick to call a "mandate." Only blacks, Jewish voters and those earning $10,000 or less stayed with Mondale.

A demographic breakdown of voters gave rise to the conclusion that the election was dominated by males and whites. In the South, there was a pronounced white flight from the

Democrats. The Democrats had to be concerned about the huge vote for Reagan by young people. It's a truism in politics that 80 to 85% of voters stay with the party they first vote for in an election.

In the end, Walter Mondale delivered his concession speech. NBC News and CBS News left it up to their affiliates as to how they would cover it. In New York, the network stations switched to the weather report before Mondale finished. Ronald and Nancy Reagan weren't enthralled with Mondale's address, either. They felt it was too long and much too partisan.

In a *New York Times* interview on March 4, 1987, Walter Mondale said, "Except for a day or two after the convention, I never thought I'd win."

SCENE III

Looking Ahead

CHAPTER 30

Campaign 1988

WHEN DEMOCRATS GATHER to exchange post-mortems about Walter Mondale's debacle, they finger an unlikely culprit—television. Few recognize, however, the changes that took place in presidential campaigning.

Mondale's chief speech writer, Martin Kaplan, speculated that only two candidates could have defeated Ronald Reagan—Robert Redford or Walter Cronkite. Sheer nonsense!

As syndicated columnist Richard Reeves pointed out four months after the election, "If Mondale had said what Reagan did during the campaign, and vice versa, Walter Mondale would today be President and Reagan would be the one deluding himself. . . . Americans judged Reagan not as a performer but as President, and they decided he deserved another term. They didn't want Mondale and what he stood for."

George Will, on ABC's "This Week with David Brinkley," commented in 1985, "Laurence Olivier standing before the television cameras saying he would raise taxes would only get 40% of the vote. The negative vote against Reagan had always been figured at 40%."

Perhaps Walter Mondale himself summed it up best, 24 hours after the election. "I never warmed up to television," he said, "and television never warmed up to me."

In the real world of presidential campaigns, the proper use of television is vital. Equally imperative is the application of state-of-the-art computer technology, as well as full utilization of public opinion polls. In 1984, the Democrats lost in two of these three areas—TV and computers. In the last couple of years, they have leaped forward in computer technique.

The telegenic factor must be considered. The candidate doesn't necessarily have to be good-looking; he or she must be sincere-looking. He or she must possess the intuitive ability to maintain eye contact with the camera.

Today, the television editing room has replaced the "smoke-filled back room." The videocassette has become tantamount to a flyer passed door to door. Politics comes down to touches as simple as coiffures. Hair apparently has become a big attraction. Vocal quality, too, is crucial. Geraldine Ferraro talked too fast. Her Queens accent didn't play well, either, in the South or the West.

TV news dictates that answers to questions should be short and quotable—catchy, if you will, so they won't wind up on the editing room floor. Ronald Reagan, who had cut his professional teeth in radio, perfected the terse response. His quips made ideal clips for TV news. But Walter Mondale couldn't answer questions succinctly. He answered as if he were re-inventing the wheel or lecturing a class in Economics 101. His remarks contained too much detail; they weren't easily digestible for TV news clips.

Television also showed how the Democrats misread the nation's mood. Their TV ads were pessimistic and lacked a central theme. One rule-of-thumb for political ad-makers is to make the voter proud he supports a particular candidate. Until the final week, this thrust was entirely missing in Mondale's TV spots—a fact attributable to the lack of a centralized authority with television experience in Mondale's inner circle.

Ronald Reagan's television advertising, on the other hand, was professional, pure imagery—exactly the kind one might use to sell cars or clothes or cosmetics. In a sense, Reagan's TV ads were such that you could have taken some of the Reagan footage, substituted another voice-over on the sound track and turned out a fine commercial for a commercial product.

If anything contributed strongest to Reagan's victory, it was that most of his advertising people were accustomed to dealing with consumer products. They were experts in evoking emotion to make their messages more persuasive. They operated on the fundamental stated by Yale psychologist Robert Abelson, "Feelings are three or four times as important as issues or party identification." Some psychologists believe, too, that a candidate's facial expression is more important than issues. We held this belief when we planned for the 1960 Kennedy-Nixon debates.

What's more, Reagan's candidacy was constantly surrounded with pictures of America putting on her prettiest face. Every ad was upbeat and patriotic, which made the contrast with Mondale's pessimistic downbeat ads all the more glaring. Professionals in both parties praised Reagan's TV ads as the best ever in politics.

Even more important was an evolution in politicking, inspired by Reagan. His mastery of thematic politics shifted the emphasis from paid commercials to "freebie" news program spots. It was an open question, never resolved, as to who exerted the most control over the evening news—the White House or the networks.

By openly acknowledging that Mondale was very poor on television, his aides ignored the free time available on the network evening news. As Mondale insisted on sticking with the issues, his aides were stuck with such unappetizing television fare as the deficit. Then, too, Mondale was shackled by inept scheduling and a refusal to set up timely picture events glorifying Mondale.

It all added up to Mondale appearing again and again on the evening news as a drab, uninspiring loser. As Mondale himself commented, "Modern politics require television. . . . I don't believe it is possible anymore to run for President without the capacity to build confidence and communication every night. It's got to be done that way."

While Mondale's aides often disagreed, they generally kept Mondale off those Democratic presidential television spots. They handled Mondale as if he were a stump speaker and a coalition candidate. In the television age, stump speeches should be avoided because it's simply not possible to control the crowds. Ideally, a candidate should address TV cameras in settings designed only for those cameras conveying only what his or her campaign director wants on television.

Mondale's advisers should have taken a lesson from Gary Hart's campaign in the 1984 primaries. Hart flew in and out of airports, giving 15-minute news conferences, taking a few questions to appear responsive and then moving on, leaving television to provide him with his audience.

In other words, Hart whistle-stopped by airplane, instead of a train, in what now is known as a tarmac campaign. As always the candidate should have a carefully chosen 30-second bite every day, which will be featured on the evening news.

* * *

An incumbent President always has controlled the flow of news during an election campaign. With the advent of world-wide, instantaneous coverage by satellite, television offered the presidential incumbent an unparalleled advantage in the battle for air time on news shows.

Zoom in on Ronald Reagan stepping out of the presidential helicopter on the White House lawn and saluting the Marines. Cut to the President at the Great Wall of China. Dissolve to the President attending a religious service on the beach at Nor-mady, amid row after row of white crosses.The President can dominate the evening television news wherever and whenever he pleases.

The Democrats fought each other in primary after primary as if there were no other adversary.The President, for his part, enjoyed almost entirely favorable coverage on every television news program.

Example: On May 30, Jesse Jackson threatened a floor fight at the Democratic Convention. Angry words and accusations were being exchanged by all Democratic candidates for the nomination. That same day, President Reagan, with full news coverage, attended graduation ceremonies at the Air Force Academy.

As the Democrats fought each other for the nomination, the Republicans collected money and ideas while carefully plotting Reagan's campaign strategy. Later, as the fall campaign unfolded, the Republican's meticulous plans contrasted sharply with the fumbling start and regrouping by Mondale's forces.

By shrewdly planning "picture events" ideally suited for television news, Ronald Reagan warmed up for a lopsided campaign. Clearly, the score was "advantage incumbent."

* * *

While the Democrats ponder their election future, they must wrestle with the harsh reality of voter mathematics: 90% of the black community, 65% of the labor vote and 75% of the Jewish vote does not equal a majority of the American people.

Of the 174 million persons of voting age, 81% are white; 11% are black (proportionately higher in the District of Columbia, Mississippi, Louisiana and South Carolina); 6% are Hispanic (the main impact appears in the large, electoral-vote states of California, Texas and Florida, as well as New Mexico); 2% Asian, Indian and Pacific Island minorities.

The Joint Center of Political Studies in Washington has stated that to win the Democrats must put together a coalition that includes a substantial proportion of whites—40 to 45%—and maintain its nearly unanimous black support.

They must first select a candidate fully convinced he will be the next President.

The baby-boomer generation born between 1946–1964 represents one-third of America's population. Democrats must be concerned that in 1984 their presidential candidate *lost* votes in the vital 18–24 year-old group and those over 60. (The 18–24 year-old group represents 17% of the electorate.)

They should be concerned that Mondale got *fewer* labor votes than did George McGovern in 1972. Also worth noting: Women outnumber men in the electorate by 8 million and generally vote differently than men. White males comprise 45% of the electorate and usually lead the nation in voter turnout.

The District of Columbia usually has the lowest turnout of voters; the Midwest and Rocky Mountain states generally turn out in higher percentages than states in the rest of the country.

For now, Democrats are taking a hard look at the voter breakdown of 1984:

	Reagan	Mondale
Whites	63.5	36.5
Men	62.5	37.5
Catholics	56.0	44.0
Women	55.5	45.5
Union households	46.0	54.0
Hispanics	44.0	56.0
Blacks	9.8	89.0

In contested House races, the Republicans got more than half the total votes cast.Democrats, as expected, got the Jewish, black and inner-city votes; but, they lost votes among 18–24 year-olds and persons over 60. It is a political truism that, all things being equal, older persons are more likely to vote than younger persons.

Will the Democrats have learned the lessons of 1984? Will the Republicans remember the teachings of the Great Communicator? From these answers will come the future Presidents.

CHAPTER 31

Time for a Change

". . .all of the pent-up energy, exuberance, noise, signs, slogans, bands and balloons suddenly were released. It is partly political, partly emotional, partly propaganda, partly a social mechanism, partly a carnival, and partly mass hysteria. It can be described as nonsense, and often is—but somehow it works."

—David Brinkley, NBC News,
  explaining the scene at the 1964 Republican Convention
  to Europeans watching via satellite

OF COURSE IT WORKS. But does it work as well as it could? Answer: No. In a free society, a vigorous democracy needs a hands-on electorate. When too many voters are turned off, government can take too many wrong turns.

Far too many American voters feel they have too little stake in who represents them in government. So, on Election Day, they stay away from the polls in increasing numbers.

Numbers alone paint a disturbing picture. Sixty-three percent of America's registered voters cast ballots in the 1960 presidential election won by John Kennedy over Richard Nixon. By 1980, when Ronald Reagan defeated Jimmy Carter, that figure shrank to a dismal 53%—an all-time low turnout for a presidential election. In 1984, the voter turnout was 59.9%, according to the U.S. Census Bureau.

Politicians are beginning to express concern about television's impact on the entire political process. Over the years, I

talked to party leaders in both parties and to political observers about how to use television most effectively in politics.

The suggestions I make now are the result of these conversations, and more than 50 years of watching American
politics in "smoke-filled rooms," through wide-angle lenses; of
riding buses on "rubber chicken" circuits; of plotting political
strategy in the Oval Office. I have been fortunate to have been
part of the process—as a strategist, observer and voter—from
the New Deal to the Great Communicator.

HOW TO GET OUT THE VOTE

Everyone who has ever run for a political office has made "get-
out-the vote" a number one objective, usually with the same
result—little or no increase in the vote. In this television age,
we are eternally optimistic. Somehow, some way, a television
get-out-the-vote campaign will flood the polling places with
new voters. I have served with brilliant advertising people and
sincere candidates on many committees that had a dual goal—
register new voters and get a larger turnout of voters. The
result: Beautiful, appealing ads that everyone agreed should do
the job.

Did more voters go to the polls? The answer "no" becomes a
more emphatic "no" with each succeeding election.

Why this voter apathy? Could it be that we have the elections on the wrong day? Most European voters go to the polls
on Sunday. Voters in Australia and Belgium are fined if they
don't vote and they must account for their absence. The voter
turnout in Europe is generally much higher than in our country. Margaret Thatcher, in Britain, won her majority when the
voter turnout was 72.7%. France's presidential election had an
86% turnout; a general election in West Germany attracted
89% of the voters, while a like number, 89% of Italy's voters,
were represented in their last election.

Why, then, do we vote on a specified Tuesday in November?
In 1845, Congress, representing 26 states, designated the Tuesday after the first Monday in November as Election Day. Congress intended to avoid a disruption in business and book-
keeping the first day of the month. It didn't want to force
people to travel on Sunday to get to polling places.

The formula adopted in 1845 set Election Day no later than
November 8 or earlier than November 2. The first uniform

presidential Election Day came on Tuesday, November 7, 1848, when 30 states participated.

If we introduce a new Election Day, we can at the same time solve the problem of different closing times at the polls. This can be a serious problem because America has four time zones. A suggestion: Establish the second Sunday in November as Election Day. Establish concurrent, 12-hour voting periods across the country:

> 10 A.M. to 10 P.M. EST
> 9 A.M. to 9 P.M. CST
> 8 A.M. to 8 P.M. MST
> 7 A.M. to 7 P.M. PST

This brings into focus two new problems—exit polls and computer projections. For now, there is no statistical proof that either exit polls or computer projections have had any determining effect on voting results.

Before Americans were required to register to vote, it wasn't unusual for turnouts to exceed 80%, albeit some voted more than once. In 1984, well-planned drives increased registrations, which helped the final vote total. Still only 59.8% of the registered voters went to the polls.

Registration legislation proposed by President Carter was passed by the House of Representatives, but sidetracked in the Senate. The legislation called for a convenient, nationwide system of registration by post card. This idea, or an equally simple plan, should be adopted.

PRIMARIES AND CAUCUSES

While conventions continue to be an important part of the political calendar, it seems that candidate selection will come mainly from primaries and caucuses.

In the future, you will see well-planned television coverage of primaries and caucuses—and decreasing coverage of the conventions.

In this age of television, more states have instituted primaries and caucuses, primarily to attract TV coverage and all the economic benefits of income from the hordes of media personnel and campaign workers in their communities. Publicity value alone is important.

Local pressure groups thrive in the multi-method primary

and caucus systems. Political bedlam emerges from the need to cater to varied interests of voting groups, state by state. An organized minority is able to enforce its will on an indifferent majority.

Vice President Mondale and Senator Kennedy prodded the 1980 Democratic Convention to authorize the chairman of the Democratic National Committee to appoint a commission to review the presidential nominating process and draw up specific suggestions for change. Then-Governor James B. Hunt of North Carolina headed a 70-member commission. Never had the party undertaken a more exhaustive study of the rules.

The Hunt Commission reached a worrisome conclusion: Our system of primary elections threatens to eclipse the organized party and proliferate into even more primaries. It was suggested that the party rely less on primaries and more on caucuses.

Many political leaders feel that primaries cause candidates to take extreme positions on different issues in different states, which gives them the ability to mobilize dedicated workers who, generally, are zealots for a cause. Fewer moderates vote in primaries and caucuses as measured against extreme conservatives and extreme liberals. Moderates elect Presidents.

Many feel that caucuses have degenerated into media events. Example: Iowa in 1976.

In 1968, only 17 states had binding primaries, which represented 42% of delegate votes at the Democratic Convention. The number of delegates indicating a candidate preference selected in primaries and caucuses prior to April 15 showed a steady increase:

> 1972:   17%
> 1976:   33%
> 1980:   44%
> 1984:   64%

The Republicans were prepared to start their selection process late in January 1988. By the end of March, some 1,247 delegates out of 2,270 were expected to be chosen in 28 states.

As in 1984, the Democrats looked forward to starting their race in Iowa in February. By March 15, voters were expected to have selected 2,844 out of 4,158 delegates.

In late December of 1986, Ohio became the second largest Midwest state to move the presidential primary from May to March. Illinois and Minnesota had already made a similar move. On April 11, 1986, Michigan Democrats announced their caucuses would be held March 26, a date party officials hoped would increase the state's nominating clout. This placed Michigan between Illinois, March 15, and New York, April 5.

These moves were triggered by the South's Super Tuesday primary day, March 8, which includes Alabama, Florida, Georgia, Kentucky, Maryland, Mississippi, Missouri, Oklahoma, Tennessee, Texas and Virginia. On the same day, Massachusetts will hold a primary.

The main objective of Super Tuesday: to force concentration on the South and Southern issues so as to nominate a candidate acceptable to the South. It was felt Super Tuesday would be less vulnerable to single issue groups.

Will it work? Polls show little difference between Southern voters and voters elsewhere. It really depends on what happens in Iowa and New Hampshire. Should a surprise winner carry both states, he probably will be able to parlay the wins into the $5 million it will take to compete on Super Tuesday.

The importance of winning in Iowa and New Hampshire is reflected in the television network coverage. In 1984, there were 646 stories on the networks about the presidential primaries and caucuses. Iowa and New Hampshire garnered 250 stories; New York and California with June primaries had a combined total of only 25 stories. New York has moved to April 5 in 1988.

If the candidate has enough delegates to wrap up the nomination by mid-April, it obviously disenfranchises large segments of the population. Usually, Midwestern and Western states don't schedule primaries and caucuses until the spring and early June. How can these hundreds of thousands of voters get excited about an election already decided?

What's the solution? There is almost universal agreement that the United States should be divided into four regions. Then, designate a uniform primary and caucus date for each region. Allow at least one month's breathing room between each voting date. Thus, in one compact time period, all the primary and caucus voting is completed. Millions of dollars will be saved, to say nothing of energy conserved. The conventions should only recognize delegates and alternates selected on the designated voting dates.

Ideally, as the Hunt Commission report suggests, "Delegates in good conscience should reflect the sentiment of those who elect them, but they need to be flexible, too." Delegates usually vote for the candidate chosen in their state's primary or caucus, but they shouldn't be irrevocably bound to one candidate. Probably a good compromise: Have delegates bound for only one ballot.

COMMITTEE MEETINGS PRIOR TO THE CONVENTION

In 1956, the National Committee adopted my proposal to hold key committee hearings prior to the convention. This procedure has helped the convention process and should be continued.

DATE OF THE CONVENTION

The party out of power should schedule its convention in late June or early July. This gives the candidate time to build an organization, accumulate the necessary funds for the campaign, and enter the fray reasonably rested. The 1968 Democratic Convention is a tragic example of bad timing. The Democrats scheduled their 1988 convention in Atlanta, July 17 to July 20.

The party in power should schedule its convention late in August if the incumbent is running for re-election; otherwise, an earlier convention is advisable. In 1988, the Republicans scheduled their convention in New Orleans, August 15 to August 18.

CONVENTION PROBLEMS

With candidates chosen before the convention convenes, planners face an almost insurmountable task of presenting a convention that will attract and hold viewers (voters).

Television, for the most part, thrives on simplicity. Its bill-of-fare offers programs with problems and solutions neatly packaged in 30-minute or 60-minute segments. By contrast, politics is complex, even in a convention where the candidate is predetermined.

A political convention, organized to select a possible President, should operate more like a legislative body, deliberative and representative as possible. The vast increase in delegates makes an orderly convention impossible. Increasing the number of alternates (who in reality are an anachronism) only adds to the confusion.

Most everyone agrees that the size of delegations has gotten out of control. What is the ideal number? The Brookings Institute's study decided the number of voting delegates should be limited to 1,500. The National Committees should decide on how the 1,500 should be apportioned. Certainly all one-half and one-quarter votes should be eliminated.

The number of alternates should be limited to 750. Only the delegates should be given convention floor privileges.

Many of my friends in media have decried the floor confusion aided and abetted by the presence of media. No media should be allowed on the working convention floor at any time. Can you imagine what the House of Representatives would be like if media could roam the aisles at will?

To satisfy the political pressure, appoint several thousand honorary delegates with attractive badges. If possible, seat them on the floor of the convention but with no access to the working convention floor. It should be noted that professional burglars could take lessons from those who intend to get on the convention floor regardless of restraints.

National Committee members and elected officials should be included in the total of 1,500 delegates.

Appoint only ten professional working sergeants-at-arms with floor privileges. Appoint any number of honorary sergeants-at-arms with privileges to move anywhere except on the convention floor.

Arrange in advance the number of police, fire and medical personnel adjacent to and on the working convention floor.

* * *

I was responsible for many changes in Democratic Convention programming: Scrapping some time-honored elements, shortening others, changing the presentation time of still others— all because of television. As time went on, more changes were made.

Through it all, however, the four-day convention remained. Four days (or longer) stemmed from the host city's economic need for maximum spending by delegates and the media. Originally, host cities financed the conventions. Since the federal government now picks up most of the tab, we no longer need a four-day convention.

Members of each political party, however, having paid their own expenses to travel to the convention city, would not, in my opinion, be happy with fewer than four days. It is possible, of course, to schedule two days of political seminars and regional meetings preceding the convention. Good political speeches in seminars would get national television coverage.

Why not conventions lasting only *two* days? A two-day schedule would include presentation of the platform, approval of the national committee membership to serve until the next convention and the nomination of candidates. What's more, a two-day convention would appeal more strongly to television viewers. Most political speeches could be scheduled during pre-convention seminars. Political speeches during the convention would relate to the platform and nominating process.

What happens if the primary-caucus method doesn't produce a candidate, which is unlikely, thus forcing a contest at the convention? Simple solution: Have a three-day convention, preceded by a one-day seminar. In the age of television, it is unlikely the nominating process will take more than two or three ballots.

Actually, today's convention has evolved from a decision-making body to a ceremonial role, a large political rally, and a money-raiser. This radical change is the result of political reform and economics.

In the late 1960s, reformers decided that Democratic Conventions should represent the result of primaries and caucuses, not the decision of political leaders. State after state introduced primaries or caucuses, not always for political reasons but for the publicity, income and tax revenues accruing from candidates and media flooding their areas.

Costly primaries eliminated many candidates who couldn't raise the huge amounts of money necessary for television advertising. With predetermined candidates, conventions were preprogrammed to display party unity, regardless of the cost of such unity. Fights were confined to the primaries and caucuses, hopefully off-camera.

Issue-framing is still done at conventions, but no longer do we see bitter fights on television over a minority report. Gone is the emotional reaction to a platform plank that, in 1952, forced me to separate two prominent, quarreling Democrats.

They were arguing about language—actually an exercise in semantics. They finally decided to settle their argument with fisticuffs. Floor fights attract television audiences, but in today's controlled conventions, political leaders go to great lengths to avoid any over-the-air squabbles.

For the most part, too, the party platform today is greeted with yawns—and forgotten almost before the duplicating machine has cranked out the last revised copy. And the candidate generally ignores the platform as soon as he or she sets out on the national campaign trail.

Conventions, even with predetermined candidates, serve a much-needed political purpose, for at conventions—and only at conventions—Democrats and Republicans are national political parties. The two-party system, so essential to our form of government, is thus preserved by these quadrennial events. Conventions bring together the greatest concentration of politicians and media.

Television viewers—even as the networks' audience shrinks and the cable audience increases—are of vital importance to each political party. Here is an opportunity for each party's candidates to reach the largest audience of the campaign, except for the debates. Convention planners, therefore, should keep in mind they are in business, not to produce a Hollywood spectacular but the party's largest political rally—to sell the candidates and the party's philosophy to the largest number of viewers possible.

Accordingly, the convention planners should not try to make the conventions something they aren't—a high-rated entertainment program. A convention may be dull at times, and political speakers may put their listeners to sleep, but they all make up a vital part of our political process.

How to present an audience-appealing convention on television is a challenge—one of the most formidable yet faced by our major parties.

Roll Call for Voting

Under the present alphabetical sequence, states early on the roll call have an unfair advantage over states coming later in the alphabetical sequence. I believe a suggestion I first made in 1956 is worthy of consideration for every convention. On the morning of the first session, have the secretary draw the names of the states for the rotation in the roll call. This can be made a media event. The trades for yields can be made during the day before the first session convenes in the evening.

Presidential Acceptance

Only after the presidential nominee gave his acceptance speech in person in 1932 did acceptance at the convention become a norm. There are many reasons today for considering an acceptance speech several weeks after the nomination— first and foremost—more free television time. To build the audience, the delayed acceptance speech must have widespread promotion. Granted, there are circumstances that may make a convention acceptance advisable, but alternatives should be carefully considered.

Nomination of the Vice President

Usually, the naming of a vice-presidential candidate has been the least concern of delegates. The presidential candidate quite often names his running mate with a minimum of thought, under pressure. In this age of terrorists, we can no longer afford a haphazard choice of the vice-presidential candidate.

I suggest the convention empower the newly elected National Committee to meet two or three weeks after the convention and elect the vice-presidential nominee. The vice-presidential candidate may make his acceptance speech at that time or appear with the presidential candidate when he formally accepts the nomination.

Another approach would be to name, as the vice-presidential candidate, the runner-up in the primaries and caucuses. Actually, in 1960, Kennedy selected as his running mate the runner-up in the primaries and the caucuses, Lyndon Johnson, as did Reagan when he selected Bush in 1980.

Obligation to Host City

Since the host city contributes a large sum to the convention committee, it is suggested the National Committee meeting to select the vice-presidential nominee and the acceptance speeches be held in the host city. There is the added advantage of having built-in media facilities.

BEGIN CONGRESSIONAL TERMS SOONER

To avoid the embarrassment of do-nothing, lame-duck sessions, newly elected members of Congress should be sworn into office eight days after their election.

Democratic Senator Claiborne Pell of Rhode Island and Senator Charles Mathias of Maryland are backing legislation for a constitutional amendment. It would require senators and representatives to take office on November 15, following election, and for the President-elect to be inaugurated on November 20, instead of January 20.

Rather than November 20, a January date should be considered, possibly January 5 instead of January 20. After all, the newly elected President generally is exhausted after the campaign, yet he must select a Cabinet, organize a White House staff, make hundreds of federal appointments and handle other details before his inauguration.

POLITICAL ADVERTISING ON TELEVISION

Every political campaign sees another increase in the use of one-minute television commercial announcements. In 1984, the 30-second announcement was the predominant television vehicle in the political campaign. It could well be that 15-second political television announcements will constitute the main thrust of future campaigns. David Garth, a successful political practitioner of new politics, has said, "Political effort, outside the use of announcements, is a waste of time and money." John O'Toole, chairman of Foote, Cone & Belding, writing in Newsweek October 29, 1984, suggested the 30-second political spot be banned because there is no control over what is said or portrayed in the 30-second TV political commercial: "I simply believe that politics is giving advertising a bad name—and vice versa—and I would like it to stop."

Many political scientists feel that the paid political announcement does nothing to give the voter a better understanding of the candidate and the issues. There's enough concern about the paid political 30-second to justify a joint political-television industry study.

CHAPTER 32

Debates

IN A RELATIVELY SHORT SPAN, presidential debates have become very much a part of America's political landscape—even if they aren't really "debates" in the traditional sense.

In November of 1983, the FCC finally recognized the need for freedom from regulation in making possible a joint appearance of both candidates on network television. Still, the ideal was not achieved.

Presidential debates are hyped like the Super Bowl, with a definite winner and loser. Until 1984, many expected that whoever wins the debate would automatically win the election. Now presidential debates are dissected in every way possible. Just about every commentator and columnist publicly advises the candidates on how to win each debate. The masses are polled by countless organizations to determine who "won" each debate.

As one who developed the first presidential debate and helped set the formula for the first presidential debates in 1960, I have been greatly disturbed by what has happened in arranging subsequent debates. In 1976 and 1980, because of a myopic ruling by the FCC, outside sponsors were necessary to put the debates on national television. The 1983 ruling by the FCC made it possible for the networks to do their own negotiating for control over the debates. The League of Women Voters sued in court to invalidate the new ruling, fearing that its control of presidential debates would be lost. While the League lost its court case, it managed to "sponsor" the 1984 presidential and vice-presidential debates.

For the 1988 presidential debates, Chairman Paul Kirk, Jr., of the Democratic National Committee and Frank J. Fahrenkopf, Jr., chairman of the Republican National Committee, announced in February of 1987 the creation of a commission on presidential debates.

A ten-member bipartisan commission, nonprofit and tax-exempt, was formed to hold presidential debates between the parties' nominees in the 1988 and future general elections. The commission will not sponsor debates in the primaries. The commission is the result of a Twentieth Century Fund paper, "For the Great Debates," by former FCC Chairman Newton Minnow and Clifford M. Sloan. If there is a strong third party movement, there will, of course, be a provision made for a third participant in the debates.

League of Women Voters' President Nancy M. Neuman immediately held a press conference to make it clear the League would not bow out of debate sponsorship without a fight. The League had previously announced locations for debates.

What can be done to improve future presidential debates? My proposals are these:

Four debates should be scheduled in October, with the last debate at least one week before the election, to wit:

DEBATE ONE (first week of October) Presidential debate on domestic issues
DEBATE TWO (second week of October) Presidential debate on foreign issues
DEBATE THREE (third week of October) Vice-presidential debate on all issues
DEBATE FOUR (fourth week of October) Presidential debate on all issues with a new format

—Each of the first three debates would call for a panel of four questioners: one from television, one from radio, one from newspapers and one from periodicals. Panelists should be selected by their respective congressional news galleries.
—Each moderator should be picked by the galleries: one from television and radio, one from the print media, and one from the television network which provides facilities.
—The fourth debate should be held without panelists. A time-keeper could insure equal distribution of time. Both candidates question each other or give short talks about where they stand on issues.

—All debates should last one hour.

—A coin toss should determine which candidate speaks first in Debate One, his opponent to lead off in Debate Two. The candidate who speaks second would make the closing statement. Another coin toss would determine the rotation in Debates Three and Four.

—Panelists and the moderator would not be announced in advance of the debate.

—All debates should start at 9 P.M., Eastern time, and in a television studio with no live audience. Members of the news media should watch on television monitors in an adjoining studio.

—Since presidential debates are primarily television events, all arrangements should be consummated by representatives of all three major television networks plus the cable news networks and the new commission.

—Negotiations for the debates should start immediately after the second convention has selected the party's candidates.

The 1988 presidential campaign will go down in history as the most extensive debating campaign to date. Networks, newspapers and clubs vied for the opportunity to sponsor the presidential candidates in debates. Lesser known candidates even arranged their own debates; Babbitt met Du Pont; Gephart debated Kemp.

Seven Democratic candidates met in their first debate in Houston, Texas, July 1, 1987. The next debate for the Democrats was in Des Moines, Iowa, Sunday, August 23, 1987.

A Wednesday, September 2, Republican version of the Houston debates was postponed because Vice-President Bush refused to appear until a later date. The compromise date, Wednesday, October 28, 1987.

Did the proliferation of debates help voters? Probably not. Voters showed little interest in the early appearances of candidates.

Did the increased number of debates help the candidates? Probably yes. The extensive debate experience enabled the winning candidates to be at their best in the final round of presidential debates.

One final thought: Presidential debates have been made possible by FCC rule-making. Dependence on the FCC to allow debates is dangerous. The Congress should repeal Section 315 without further delay.

CHAPTER 33

Money

WHOEVER SAID MONEY IS THE MOTHER'S MILK of politics must have sensed that "feeding time" would last around the clock. With increasingly costly television ads taking bigger chunks of campaign budgets, TV and politics forever share the effects of a nagging problem: How to raise money for candidates.

And with this money comes a problem: In what ways are candidates obligated to those who contribute to their campaigns?

Out of the Watergate scandal of the 1970s came laws that restricted how much a candidate could collect: Up to $1,000 from any individual, and up to $5,000 from any group. In time, the courts ruled that limits on contributions to a candidate were, indeed, constitutional. But the courts also decreed *against* limits on spending by persons or groups on behalf of—but ostensibly independent from—a candidate.

On Monday, March 18, 1985, the Supreme Court struck down the $1,000 limit on spending by political action committees on behalf of presidential candidates in general elections. The high court ruled that the limit of $1,000 violated the First Amendment rights of free speech. The limit had not been enforced in the 1980 and 1984 campaigns because lower courts had held it unconstitutional.

Candidates for federal office must report to the Federal Election Commission (FEC) every penny they spend—and for what purpose.

As a result of the Supreme Court decision, the floodgates

opened for almost unlimited spending of private (or soft) money by key state and local organizations which endeavored to shore up their political parties. Money was poured into registration of new voters, get-out-the-vote drives, bumper stickers, campaign buttons, billboards, print media and, of course, radio and TV. Money was spent on virtually anything that could be rationalized as helping party and candidate.

And if that weren't enough, candidates in primaries and caucuses could tap another wellspring—federal funds. To qualify for this money, a candidate was required to receive 10% of the vote in two consecutive primaries, which was easy, considering the low voter turnouts. The law permits a campaign to spend $2 million above the operating costs on lawyers and accountants to keep everything within the letter of the law.

Out of those post-Watergate laws, too, came still another way to raise big money, the political action committee (PAC). PACs always seemed to be up to their billfolds in controversy. They were formed by labor unions, by businesses, by special-interest groups. Their influence is enormous because they are the principal source of political funds.

By the fall of 1984, 30 PACs had contributed $16,083,962 for congressional races, according to a report by Common Cause, the citizens' lobby. Besides labor, large PAC spenders included the American Medical Association, real estate groups, milk producers, the National Education Association, maritime workers and bankers, among many others. PAC gifts to congressional candidates were up 32% in 1986.

To a degree, the FEC was partially responsible for the spending problem: 1976 was the national campaign year when, for the first time, the Democrats were short of bumper stickers, buttons, balloons and other items considered essential in every campaign. Money had to be hoarded for television. In an attempt to spur grass-roots activity and ease the problem of 1976, the FEC suggested that voters form their own campaign committees. The FEC rules allow these committees to spend funds, without limit, for bumper stickers, buttons and all like paraphernalia.

Questions were raised, however, when separate committees filed reports in the same handwriting.

Week after week in the 1984 campaign, the primary and caucus results seesawed between Mondale and Hart. The vote totals also had an immediate, roller-coaster effect on contributions. Example: When Hart was defeated in Illinois on March

20, his contributions plummeted by $550,000, from $800,000 to $250,000. By May 13, Hart was $4 million in debt; Mondale was $1.5 million in the hole.

By now, it is clear that those post-Watergate reforms which limited personal donations to $1,000 had, in turn, forced candidates to rely on PACs for financial support. Of course, even the best-intentioned laws aimed at controlling political contributions are generally circumvented by determined donors. As Kenneth Guido, a Democratic lawyer, remarked, "Under the present law, it is possible to put $1 million into anybody's campaign legally."

In ten years, PACs increased from 600 to 3,600. Thus, while it's easier than ever to make unlimited political contributions, it's getting tougher to find out just *who* is financing federal campaigns.

Win or lose, however, presidential candidates usually wind up in debt. Not until 1982, for example, did the Democratic National Committee finally pay off the last of Hubert Humphrey's 1968 debts.

Even though the government now pumps $40.4 million into each party's national campaign, it's still not enough. Private funds are needed. Each party is permitted to spend $6.9 million in private money in direct support of its nominee. This money generally pays for TV ads.

* * *

How can the money-in-politics problem be solved?
1. First and foremost, the source of all political contributions should be readily known—publicly. On the day money or services are pledged, the recipient and the contributor should be required to announce all details of the contribution.
2. Adopt President Ford's idea: Enact a federal law which would make it illegal to give or receive a political contribution for a presidential campaign before January 1 of the election year.
3. Since television is the medium that drains most of a candidate's funds in expenses, Congress should limit funds spent for television. Those hoping for action by Congress should recognize that incumbents receive 77% more PAC money than do challengers.

One reason for the astronomical rise in campaign expenses is that campaigns start earlier than ever. Most public opinion polls show there is little interest in the issues until ten days before Election Day. Shortening the campaigns would help. Enormous savings could be effected, too, by limiting all advertising, whatever the source, to only four weeks before Election Day. "Advertising" means television, radio, print media, all printed material, buttons, billboards, bumper stickers and novelty items.

Any violator should be slapped with an immediate and heavy penalty. All money left over, after the campaign, should be returned to the donor or to the national party committee. This same rule could apply to all those expensive primary-caucus campaigns.

If the PACs are outlawed, new ways to raise campaign money must be found. Several bills before Congress provide for public financing. The Treasury Department's 1984 tax simplification plan, too, did away with the presidential campaign checkoff that appeared on tax returns. About 30% of all taxpayers marked the checkoff, contributing about $38 million a year into the Treasury's presidential campaign fund. The fund provided partial matching grants to presidential primary election candidates and full grants to general election candidates, according to a formula. It also financed both nominating conventions. In 1984, the fund distributed $133.3 million: $36.3 million to primary candidates, $80.8 million to President Reagan and Walter Mondale for the general election and $16.2 million for the Republican and Democratic conventions.

But then, even if public financing is legislated into reality, and if specific spending limits are imposed, will candidates who accept public money agree to abide by them? Stay tuned.

CHAPTER 34

Cable, the VCR and Satellite

AGAIN IN 1988, television will elect a President. But television has changed and political time-buying is changing. For the most part, political dollars go to local television advertising. There is nothing more local in television than cable.

Cable, with a multiple choice of programs, has changed television viewing patterns. The introduction of the VCR has also had an impact on the available viewing audience. The cable audience continues to grow. Cable became available for the first time in 1988 in Baltimore, Detroit, all of New York City, Philadelphia and Washington. Today, cable penetration varies from 30% in Baltimore, Maryland, to 88% in Santa Barbara, California.

As pointed out by veteran cable observer Paul Kagan, the arguments for using cable for political purposes are compelling. A Simmons Market Research Bureau study found cable subscribers were 19% more likely to have voted in federal, state, and local elections. Cable subscribers are also 42% more likely to have written to an elected officer, 54% more likely to have personally visited an elected official, 32% more likely to have engaged in fund-raising on behalf of a candidate.

"Cable is for the politician, video direct mail," says Robert Alter, president of the Cable Television Advertising Bureau. "Only cable can combine the power of television with the direct mail ability to zero in on a particular issue or voter block and do so on a cost efficient basis."

What's more, cable can segment the television audience on

the basis of age, sex, ethnic groups, religious status, financial status and location. "Radio with pictures is what cable will be," states long-time political consultant Robert Squier. "It is the battlefield of the future."

Gene De Witt, Executive Vice President of Media Inter-public, agrees: "You are paying one dollar cost per thousand for cable and five dollars per thousand for broadcasting at the same time you are getting more efficiency, prospect exposure, and leverage. To get more bang for your buck use cable like radio, high frequency with widely dispersed ads throughout the day."

If you use cable for fund-raising dollars the CPM becomes cents, according to Joe Ostrow, Executive Vice President, Foote Cone & Belding. John M. Florescu, a pioneer in cable political advertising, says, "Cable provides enormous flexibility. Candidates can expand on the issues, and raise money."

At the beginning of each televised session in the House of Representatives, a period is reserved for any member of the House to make a one-minute statement from the floor.

Conscious of the television coverage on C-SPAN, some House members have used the allowed minute to directly address their constituents. Carrying this a step further, they could increase their audience by advance announcements in the local paper. They could also ask the local television stations to tape the spot for the evening news program.

How, then, does a candidate use cable in his or her campaign? Answer: An enormous amount of skill is required because cable, while low in cost, is difficult to buy.

Let's look, for example, at presidential campaigns. First, there are certain givens. The largest audience of the Democratic and Republican campaigns will gather for the debates; the next largest audience will watch the national conventions. Until approximately ten days before the elections, voters generally will be more interested in most anything else but politics.

Cable is important in politics because it is not a mass medium but personalized communication. Even though cable is equipped to carry the 15- and 30-second spot, this advertising should go primarily to the mass media.

Cable presentations should be "programercials" which are longer than announcements. They give candidates an opportunity to explain their stands on issues and policies. Viewers can be encouraged to call an 800 number for additional information (cable viewers are conditioned to call 800 numbers). All the televiewer does, when calling the 800 number, is give his or her name and address. A pamphlet with a return card may be mailed promptly in reply to the inquiry. The mailing list, acquired in this fashion, is top notch for fund-raising. Just ask the television evangelists.

Once the candidate has established a list of must-win geopolitical areas, the cable time buyer goes to work. First, the time buyer must know about every cable system in the country, the availability and capability of each system. Some cable systems may be purchased in a group buy, others must be dealt with one-by-one. Most cable systems have local cut-in announcements on national cable programs; some have a local billboard which carries typed advertisements; some can originate live local programs with complete studio facilities.

The Cable Television Advertising Bureau publishes annually a rep/interconnect directory listing every cable interconnect and the name of the sales representative.

The NCTA has cable systems listed by congressional districts.

Some large cable organizations have advertising departments with excellent production facilities. The producers know how to communicate with their audiences (voters). Production costs are surprisingly low.

The satellite networks, ESPN, CNN, FNN, MTV, to name a few, offer local announcement opportunities. Purchase of announcements may be made locally on a selective basis.

Another approach to the cable viewer is through the superstations like WTBS, WGN, WOR.

To dominate a maximum television audience, the same time period may be purchased on all superstations, cable networks, and commercial networks. It costs less than you think, but it will require a super effort.

Whenever practical, back-up promotion for cable programs is advisable in newspapers, on radio and television stations.

A real sleeper in political strategy is access time. Many cable systems provide free time in access programs ususally scheduled on a separate channel. When using a free access time period, outside promotion is imperative.

As mentioned, a political time buyer must locate all of the cable systems in the areas the candidate needs to reach. There are several sources:

James P. Mooney, President

National Cable Television Association, Inc.
1724 Massachusetts Ave. NW
Washington, DC 20036
Telephone: 202-775-3550
For information on advertising possibilities:
Robert Alter, President
Cable Television Advertising Bureau
767 Third Avenue
New York City, NY 10017
Telephone: 212-751-7770
State cable associations are generally located in the state capitals.

With A. C. Nielsen's Cable on Line Data Exchange (CODE) service, candidates now have an opportunity to match their cable-buying activity with systems penetrating key election districts. Moreover, candidates can use that data in conjunction with cable's targeted programming, allowing them to match accurately their political message with likely voter prospects.

A study by Paley Communications, Inc., notes that ESPN (sports) provides access to 18 to 49 year-old males; MTV (music) provides access to the 13- to 32-year-old group. Other networks have equally specialized audiences: FNN (financial), CNN and CNN Headlines (news), Travel Channel, C-SPAN (coverage of the House and Senate, as well as other political events.)

It should be noted, too, that while politicians must learn about cable, cable executives must learn about the needs of politicans.

By buying well in advance, a candidate may, in some areas, monopolize the cable audience at a relatively low cost. To take full advantage of cable, a candidate must start early. If he or she enters a major campaign, a cable-wise staff must be put in place immediately.

THE VCR

Proper use of VCRs can be effective in reaching voters. A previously taped speech with a question-and-answer session may be taped for use at Rotary Clubs and other noon-time clubs; in fact, any local meeting. Each tape may have a local introduction spliced to the original tape. Airport appearances should be taped and widely distributed. Whenever possible the tapes should have a local introduction. Local groups may submit a list of questions which the candidate can answer on a video tape.

THE SATELLITE

To instantly reach a geographically widespread audience, satellite is the answer. Example: The night before the election, a satellite question-and-answer session can reach all crucial area television stations, cable systems, and radio stations.

CONCLUSION

The new technologies in television offer many new opportunities for the candidate to reach voters effectively. To be successful, however, the candidate must master these new television technologies and should have someone with cable experience on the staff.

Postscript

RONALD REAGAN BEGAN HIS CAREER on radio. As President, he makes absolutely marvelous use of it politically, which demonstrates that even today radio still carries enormous political clout.

Every Saturday, the President delivers a five-minute talk on national radio. He selects the topics for discussion, presents arguments on any desired issue, and isn't subject to any media questioning.

His radio address is quoted on TV news programs and makes headlines in the Sunday papers. The administration's controlled views are conveyed effectively on all media. In a sense, Reagan has resurrected the "fireside chats" of Franklin Roosevelt.

By contrast, the Democrats are hard-pressed to land any counter-punches. They don't have a recognized spokesperson. A different voice is heard each week, often lost in the crush of weekend sports results and other news.

Score one for the President. Score one for radio. In this day of Big TV with satellites, it's nice to see radio still hanging in there.

It's also personally reassuring that a contemporary—a President they call "The Great Communicator"—is still making his voice heard, half a century after he and I sat two press box booths away, each calling those Iowa-Northwestern football games, over that remarkable invention called radio.

Index